One must die so others may live

HANK
HANEGRAAFF

SIGMUND
BROUWER

THE
LAST
SACRIFICE

TYNDALE HOUSE PUBLISHERS, INC.
CAROL STREAM, ILLINOIS

Visit Tyndale online at www.tyndale.com.

TYNDALE and Tyndale's quill logo are registered trademarks of Tyndale House Publishers, Inc.

The Last Sacrifice

Designed by Daniel Farrell

Edited by James H. Cain III

Scripture taken from the Holy Bible, *New International Version,*® *NIV.*® Copyright © 1973, 1978, 1984 by Biblica, Inc.™ Used by permission of Zondervan. All rights reserved worldwide. www.zondervan.com.

The Library of Congress has cataloged the original edition as follows:

Hanegraaff, Hank.
  The last sacrifice / Hank Hanegraaff, Sigmund Brouwer.
      p. cm.
  ISBN 978-0-8423-8441-4 (hc)
  ISBN 978-0-8423-8442-1 (sc)
  1. Bible. N.T. Revelation XIII—History of Biblical events—Fiction.   2. Church history—Primitive and early church, ca. 30-600—Fiction.   3. Rome—History—Nero, 54-68—Fiction.   4. End of the world—Fiction.   I. Brouwer, Sigmund, date.   II. Title.
PS3608.A714L375 2005
813'.6—dc22   2005016381

Repackage first published in 2012 under ISBN 978-1-4143-6498-8

Printed in the United States of America

18   17   16   15   14   13   12
 7   6   5   4   3   2   1

To Christina.
Your encouragement for the Last Disciple series
is inspirational, your enthusiasm infectious.

CALENDAR NOTES

THE ROMANS DIVIDED the day into twelve hours. The first hour, *hora prima,* began at sunrise, approximately 6 a.m. The twelfth hour, *hora duodecima,* ended at sunset, approximately 6 p.m.

hora prima	first hour	6–7 a.m.
hora secunda	second hour	7–8 a.m.
hora tertiana	third hour	8–9 a.m.
hora quarta	fourth hour	9–10 a.m.
hora quinta	fifth hour	10–11 a.m.
hora sexta	sixth hour	11 a.m.–12 p.m.
hora septina	seventh hour	12–1 p.m.
hora octava	eighth hour	1–2 p.m.
hora nonana	ninth hour	2–3 p.m.
hora decima	tenth hour	3–4 p.m.
hora undecima	eleventh hour	4–5 p.m.
hora duodecima	twelfth hour	5–6 p.m.

The New Testament refers to hours in a similar way. Thus, when we read in Luke 23:44, "It was now about the sixth hour, and darkness came over the whole land until the ninth hour," we understand that this period of time was from the hour before noon to approximately 3 p.m.

The Romans divided the night into eight watches.

Watches before midnight: *Vespera, Prima fax, Concubia, Intempesta.*

Watches after midnight: *Inclinatio, Gallicinium, Conticinium, Diluculum.*

The Romans' days of the week were Sun, Moon, Mars, Mercury, Jupiter, Venus, and Saturn.

The months of the Hebrew calendar are Nisan, Iyar, Sivan, Tammuz, Av, Elul, Tishri, Heshvan, Kislev, Tevet, Shevat, Adar I, and Adar II. In AD 65, the date 13 Av was approximately August 1.

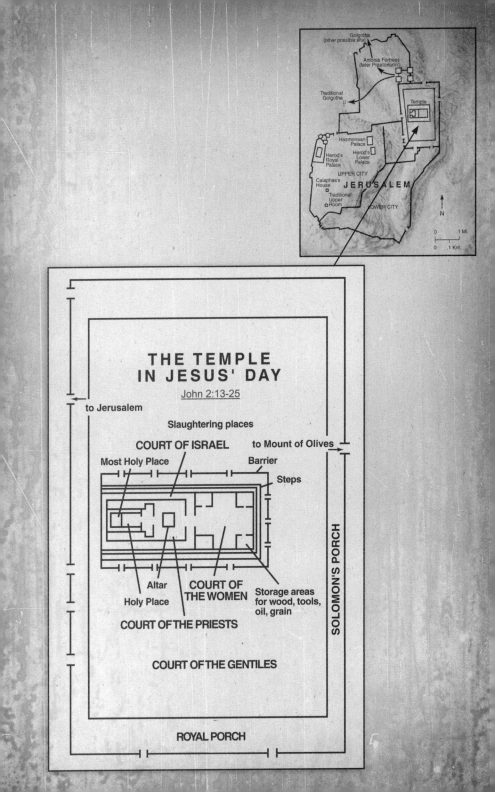

Golgotha
(other possible site)

Antonia Fortress
(later Praetorium)

Traditional
Golgotha

Temple

Hasmonean
Palace

Herod's
Royal
Palace

Herod's
Lower
Palace

UPPER CITY

Caiaphas's
House

JERUSALEM

Traditional
Upper
Room

LOWER CITY

N

0   .1 Mi.

0   .1 Km.

THE TEMPLE
IN JESUS' DAY
John 2:13-25

to Jerusalem

Slaughtering places

COURT OF ISRAEL

to Mount of Olives

Most Holy Place

Barrier

Steps

Altar

COURT OF
THE WOMEN

Holy Place

Storage areas
for wood, tools,
oil, grain

COURT OF THE PRIESTS

SOLOMON'S PORCH

COURT OF THE GENTILES

ROYAL PORCH

Dramatis Personae

Alypia: Wife of Lucius Bellator; former lover of Maglorius; stepmother of Valeria and Quintus

Amaris: Wife of Simeon Ben-Aryeh

Ananias: High priest; father of Eliazar

Annas the Younger: Former high priest

Atronius Pavo: Captain of the ship carrying John and Vitas to Alexandria

Bernice: Queen of the Jews; sister of Agrippa II

Boaz: A Pharisee of high standing

Caius Sennius Ruso: Wealthy senator; friend of John

Chara: Wife of Strabo

Chayim: Son of Simeon Ben-Aryeh; in Rome as a "hostage"

Cosconius Betto: Sailing master on the ship carrying John and Vitas; brother of Kaeso

Eleazar: Governor of the Temple; son of Ananias

Falco: Prominent Roman citizen

Gaius Calpurnius Piso: Plotted to kill Nero

Gaius Cestius Gallus: Governor of Syria

Gaius Ofonius Tigellinus: Prefect of the praetorian guard; member of Nero's inner circle

Gallus Sergius Damian: Slave hunter; brother of Vitas

Gallus Sergius Vitas: Famed general of the Roman army; former member of Nero's inner circle; husband of Sophia; brother of Damian

Gessius Florus: Roman procurator of Judea

Helius: Nero's secretary; member of Nero's inner circle

Hezron: Famed rabbi in Rome; father of Leah

Issachar, son of Benjamin: Silversmith in Alexandria

Jerome: Slave of Damian

John, son of Zebedee: Last disciple of Jesus of Nazareth

Joseph Ben-Matthias: Prominent citizen in upper city Jerusalem

Leah: Daughter of Hezron and a follower of the Christos

Lucullus: Roman commander on Patmos

Maglorius: Former gladiator; servant in the Bellator household

Malka: Old, blind woman Quintus lives with in Jerusalem

Nahum: Glassblower in Jerusalem; husband of Leeba; father
of Raanan

Nero Claudius Caesar Augustus Germanicus: Roman emperor;
persecutor of the followers of the Christos

Nigilius Strabo: Farmer on the island of Patmos; husband
of Chara

Quintus Valerius Messalina: Seven-year-old son of Lucius
Bellator; in hiding in Jerusalem

Simeon Ben-Aryeh: Member of the Sanhedrin; escaped
Jerusalem; fugitive of Rome with Sophia

Sophia: Wife of Vitas; fugitive of Rome with Ben-Aryeh;
a follower of the Christos

Sporus: Nero's young lover

Valeria Messalina: Daughter of Lucius Bellator; in hiding
in Jerusalem

ROME

Capital of the Empire

They overcame him by the blood of the Lamb and by the word of their testimony; they did not love their lives so much as to shrink from death.

—REVELATION 12:11

❧ SUN ❧

HORA OCTAVA

THE EARLY AFTERNOON sunshine blazed down on a large pen out of the sight of amphitheater spectators. The *bestiarius* began covering the eyes of the hobbled bull elephant he had selected to kill Gallus Sergius Vitas.

Perched on its neck, the beast master hummed as he did his work, patting the hide of the massive animal, trying to settle and soothe it. In his mind, he saw clearly how it would happen. He would remove the blinds only after he strapped Vitas to a tusk and led the beast to the center of the sand. Then, while two bears fought the elephant, another condemned man would be forced to dart between the elephant's legs to release the chains that kept it hobbled. After the bears had killed the condemned man, and after the elephant had killed the bears with Vitas still on its tusk, it would finally redirect its rage to shake and scrape Vitas loose, then stomp him into a red smear. The process would, with luck, entertain the crowd for half an hour.

It was routine, actually, except that the man who was to die today once had Nero's ear. So the bestiarius knew it needed to be done properly.

From below, a voice interrupted his thoughts: "Nero wants Vitas so close he can taste his blood."

The bestiarius, a small, dirty man with no teeth, secured the blinders and patted the animal's head before looking down to answer. At the side of the elephant, he saw the former slave most citizens in Rome recognized. Helius, Nero's most trusted adviser.

In his late twenties, Helius was a beautiful man, with smooth, almost bronze skin. His hair was luxuriously curly, his eyes a strange yellow, giving him a feral look that was rumored to hold great attraction for Nero. Helius wore a toga edged with purple, and his fingers and wrists and neck were layered with jewelry of gold and rubies.

"Did you hear me?" Helius said, impatient. He sniffed the air cautiously and wrinkled his nose at the smell of the elephant.

The bestiarius would have answered any other man with derogative curses. "No man alive," the bestiarius finally said, "can direct or predict the movements of a raging elephant."

"Nor can any man dead," Helius told him. "Make sure Nero is not disappointed."

The bestiarius cautioned himself that this was Helius, who had almost as much power over the lives and deaths of Nero's subjects as Nero himself. "I'll have two women chained in the sand below the emperor's place in the stands," he said after a few moments' thought. Once the bull was in a rage, he knew it would attack everything in sight, including those women. It would rear on hind legs and stomp with the full force of its weight, something that would surely excite Nero. The bestiarius would also strap Vitas on so tightly that the elephant would not be able to shake him loose too soon. That would bring Vitas in close enough to the emperor. "He will get the blood he wants."

"Ensure that the women are Christians and see it's done properly," Helius snapped. "You don't want me back here again."

✢ ✢ ✢

Nearby, but in a world removed from blue skies and fresh air, Gordio and Catus, the two soldiers assigned the task of finding and escorting Vitas, had already entered the labyrinth of prison cells below the stands of the amphitheater.

While both were large, Catus was the larger of the two. In the flickering light of the torch, they gave the appearance of brothers, each with dark, cropped hair, each with a wide face marked by battle scars. They were old for soldiers, sharing a common bond back to the days when they were both recruited from neighboring farms north of Rome, sharing survived battles in Britannia and Gaul and all the years of monotony between them.

As they traveled through the dark corridors by torchlight, the rumbling of the spectators above sounded like growls of distant thunder. Each soldier had drenched his face and shoulders with inexpensive perfume to mask the odor; each knew from experience that no other smell on earth matched the stench of fear exuded by hundreds of prisoners.

The torch Gordio carried was a beacon to all the prisoners, a flame serving notice that yet another among them would be plucked away for a horrible fate outside on the sunbaked sand. Halfway to the cell that held Vitas, a woman thrust her arms between iron bars in a useless effort to grasp at Gordio and Catus.

"Kill me!" the woman sobbed at them, her hands flailing. "I beg you!"

Neither of the soldiers broke stride.

"Have mercy!" she wailed at their broad backs. "Give me a sword or a knife. I'll do it myself!"

Behind them, the woman's pleading blended with the yells and groans and swearing of all the other men and women in the dozens of crowded, dank cells along their route. To Gordio and Catus, the men and women they were sent to retrieve for death were less than animals, troublesome debris, criminals deserving of their sentences.

"My fate is tied to yours," Catus growled to Gordio. "I want you to say it again. We are in this together."

"Yes, my friend," Gordio said. "We are in this together. How can you doubt me after all the years we have shared?"

The answer was unnecessary, for if ever there was a time for one to doubt the other, this was it. Nothing during their years as soldiers serving the empire had prepared them for what they had resolved to do next.

The unthinkable.

Treason.

✠ ✠ ✠

The chosen seat of the man who had been born Lucius Domitius Ahenobarbus placed him so close to the sand of the arena that on occasion blood would splatter his toga, spots of bright red soaking in and fading against the purple as they dried.

On this morning, slaves shaded and fanned him as he antici-pated the death of Gallus Sergius Vitas. A ferocious hangover diminished some of his anticipation, and despite the efforts of the slaves, the heat irritated him. But not enough to drive him away before the death of Vitas.

He waited with a degree of impatience and swallowed constantly, trying to work moisture into his mouth. His thin blond hair failed to cover the beads of sweat on his scalp. He'd once been handsome, but closing on his thirtieth birthday, his face was already swollen from years of decadent wine and food, showing a chin that had doubled and was on the verge of trebling. His eyes were the most telling of the horrors he had inflicted on others during the previous decade—they had a dulled mania and an emptiness that bordered on eerie. Few dared to look fully into those eyes, and most shivered under their attention. For this was the man now known and worshiped by his subjects as Nero Claudius Caesar Augustus Germanicus.

Nero did not sit alone in the spectators' box. To his right sat the boy Sporus, whose knee he touched casually; to his left, Helius, who had returned from the animal pens.

"How much longer until Vitas?" Nero said.

"Soon," Helius said. A pause. Nero's head throbbed as he con-centrated on listening. Helius then spoke quietly. "Have you told Sporus about your intentions?"

Nero shifted, turning to face Helius fully. "You seem anxious for him to know."

"The arrangements were your request," Helius said. "What you want done is what you want done. But the doctors say it must be done soon, that any day now he will reach puberty."

Nero frowned. "It seems you take pleasure in the procedure. Why should it matter to you when Sporus learns of it?"

"I'm only thinking of him," Helius said, looking down in deference. "Perhaps it would be best to give the boy time to prepare himself."

Nero turned away and, to disapproving murmurs from the crowd, kissed Sporus. He pulled back and stroked the boy's hair for a few moments, then leaned over and spoke again to Helius.

"Prepare himself?" Nero asked. "Are you suggesting Sporus won't be delighted to honor me in such a manner? that there will be anything of more magnitude in his life than my love for him?"

"He lives for you," Helius said. Another deferent look downward. "As does every subject in the empire."

"Of course they live for me," Nero said, feeling his irritation lessened by the obsequious reminder of his power. He allowed a smile, thinking again of Vitas suffering on the tusk of an elephant. "Unless I want them to die."

✦ ✦ ✦

"Gallus Sergius Vitas," the soldier with the torch said to the prisoner. The soldier spoke quietly, compassionately, respectfully.

The prisoner knew his moment was upon him. He hoped that all his preparations for death would be enough.

He had been deliberate in thinking it through. During the long night of waiting, this grim contemplation had prevented him from wondering about the pain of his final moments, from wondering about the method of execution that Nero had chosen for him. Meticulous planning helped him maintain an illusion of control in a situation where all power had been taken from him. And most importantly, focusing on how he would face death dispelled the doubts that pressed at the edge of his consciousness like snakes trying to push beneath a locked door, insidious questions about the faith he'd staked his life upon and whether that faith would lead him to the eternity he believed was beyond.

"If this is my time," the prisoner replied, his voice barely more than a croak, "let me prepare myself."

Without waiting for an answer, he moved against the wall and squatted to void his body wastes in the darkness. This was the first thing he'd decided was necessary. Aside from whatever bravery he could find as he faced the beasts in the amphitheater, no other dignity would remain when his naked body became an offering of entertainment to be shredded for the delighted scrutiny of a crowd of thousands; at the very least he did not want his body to betray his fear.

When he finished, sadness crushed him so badly he could barely breathe. The moment had arrived, and the emotion he had expected was far greater than he believed possible for a man to bear. Not fear but sadness. Sadness not for his death but that he would never see his wife or children again. It took all of his focus to push that sadness aside. It was not time to allow it to fill him. Not yet.

"I am ready," the prisoner said. He moved closer to the torch, its light hardly more than a blur to him.

Clanking told him the soldiers were opening the cell door.

The blur of the torchlight grew brighter, and he heard both soldiers gasp.

"His face," one said.

The day before he had been beaten so badly that his eyes were puffed shut to the point that he could barely see. His bruised face felt like an overripe fruit about to burst.

"Jupiter!" the other said.

The prisoner gave a weak wave and repeated himself. "I am ready."

"We are not," the second one said.

They stepped into the cell.

Had Nero given orders for him to be beaten further? the prisoner wondered. He took a deep breath and offered no resistance as he waited for the first blow.

"His face," the first again. "That will make it difficult for him."

"No. It will help. All he has to do is reach the streets. His face will make it impossible to guess his identity once he has escaped."

"Escape?" the prisoner said. Thirst made his throat dry, and he found it difficult to speak without a croak. "I . . . I don't understand."

"Nero has gone too far," the first said, his voice soft but firm. "All of Rome knows you are here. And the injustice behind it."

"The arena is where criminals die," the second said. "Not military heroes."

"We were not under your command in Britannia," the first soldier continued. "But your reputation is enough for us. You do not deserve this fate."

The prisoner felt something pressed into his hand. The handle of a sword?

"When the first line broke in the final battle against the Iceni," the second said, "any other commander would have served politics first. Thrown away the lives of soldiers by sending them to defend immediately, without support. You risked your reputation because you refused to have them slaughtered. They owe you their lives. I, too, owe you. My brother was among them."

"Some of them found a way for us to be here to repay you on their behalf," the first said. "You are a man soldiers would follow if ever you decided . . ."

The second spoke when the first faltered. "The complaints about Nero grow every day. If a general stood up to him and sought the support of the legions . . ."

"I am not that man," the prisoner said.

"No one will doubt that the legendary Gallus Sergius Vitas overpowered us," the first soldier answered. "Strike us hard. Make certain we are injured badly enough to be believed."

"I have my duty." The prisoner thought of his wife. How his death would spare her. "Take me to the arena."

"To die for the emperor who inflicted such an injustice upon you as this?" the first said. "Take my tunic. Leave here as a guard. When you are free, you can begin action against Nero. Or throw your support behind another general."

"You must live," the second urged. "His reign must end."

"I have my duty," the prisoner repeated. He lifted the sword. "Keep this."

"At the least then," the first soldier said, pushing the sword back at the prisoner, "spare yourself the horror and fall on this here. Or give us the honor of assisting you. We will end your life quickly and claim you attacked us."

"No," the prisoner said. He felt his legs grow weak. The sorrow again threatened to overwhelm him as images flashed into his mind. Of his younger boy as a toddler, rushing toward him to be comforted after stumbling on the bricks of the courtyard floor and scraping his knees. Of quiet summer evenings, intertwining his fingers with his wife's, sharing dreams with her beneath the starlight. Of comforting his daughter one morning as she knelt on grass still wet with dew and wept over the death of a tiny bird found among the flowers.

The prisoner used all his resolve to force these images from his head. *Not yet,* he told himself. There would be a time for the memories. Soon enough. But not yet.

"Take me to the arena," the prisoner said firmly. "I have my duty and you have yours."

✠ ✠ ✠

"I also need two women," the bestiarius snapped at Catus and Gordio. "Go back and get them from the cells of Christians. And send someone to help me strap this man to the tusk."

Neither soldier moved. The prisoner was behind them, head bowed, wrists shackled.

"Another thing." The bestiarius shook his head. "The women? Cut out their tongues. I'm tired of the hymns these cursed Christians sing as they die."

Still Catus and Gordio did not respond.

"Well?" the bestiarius demanded. Here he had near total authority. His skills with animals were seen as magical and very necessary to the success of the entertainment. "I need the women immediately. Nero waits."

Catus spoke. "You cannot strap such a man as Vitas to the elephant."

"You tell me what I cannot do?" Still angry at how he'd been humbled by Helius, the bestiarius vented his frustration on the soldiers. "Don't forget. You are expendable. I am not."

"This man fought for Rome," Catus said, pointing at the prisoner. "He helped defeat the Iceni. Led the triumph through the gates of the city. He deserves to die a soldier's death. Give him combat against gladiators."

The bestiarius spat, unswayed by the soldier's passion. "I follow the orders of Nero. If you choose otherwise, expect to be strapped to the other tusk."

"The crowd will know," Gordio said. "He's a hero. They will not tolerate it, no matter what Nero wants."

The bestiarius stepped between them and clutched the prisoner's hair, lifting his head and exposing his swollen, bruised face to the sun. "After a beating like this? No one will recognize him." He dropped the prisoner's head and yelled at the soldiers with surprising force for such a small man. "Now go! Get the women! And don't forget to cut out their tongues."

✝ ✝ ✝

With the soldiers gone, the prisoner stood near the elephant, drawing deep, hard breaths.

So this was how he would die.

He drew the deep breaths to calm himself. This, too, he had calculated for this moment. He'd anticipated the renewed fear. But after his time in the stench of the cells, he'd guessed the fresh outdoor air would be as joyful to his body as clear, cold water.

The calm he had hoped for did not arrive. This was beyond his power.

"Christos," he whispered. "Dear Christos. Let my death honor you."

He lost himself in silent worship. Then suddenly his body seemed to come truly alive with every heave of his lungs, every sense totally engaged. The portion of the sky he could see beneath his swollen eyelids had never seemed so blue; sounds had never seemed so clear. A fly landed on his arm; he thrilled with the sensation of the tiny movements across his skin. The nearby elephant swished its tail, a sound that seemed as loud as a shout.

"Thank you, Christos," he breathed. Yes! He was still alive; he wanted to drink in every sensation.

Doing so stretched each moment for him, and he was unaware of the passing of time. This amazing vibrancy lasted until rough hands grabbed and spun him, rough hands that belonged to men who were only a blur in his diminished vision. Until his body was lifted from the ground and held against the tusk of the elephant.

Men grunted as they strapped him in place. As his hands brushed against the tusk, he was startled to feel rough fissures in the ivory.

Strange, he thought. He'd always believed ivory was smooth. He puzzled about this, as if momentarily unaware of his body and the events happening to it. Ah, he realized, the only ivory he'd ever seen was carved and polished. Not still connected to a living beast. That explained it.

He became aware then of a different sort of movement. This new movement was the nervous swaying of the blinded elephant, unsure and nervous about the unfamiliar weight upon its tusk.

The prisoner was strapped in such a way that the sky filled his vision. It was interrupted by a flash of motion that he guessed at more than saw through the thin gap between his blood-crusted eyelids. A pigeon? He marveled that any creature could fly, as if he'd never seen a bird in the air before, and he regretted that he had never taken time or thoughts to observe the wonders of the commonplace that had surrounded him all his life.

The passing of the bird, however, reminded him of his daughter holding the tiny dead sparrow in the garden, and thoughts of his wife and young children flooded his mind again.

Not yet, he pleaded with himself. Even filled with the joy of faith, he could not totally leave behind all that had been important to him on earth. *Not yet. Save those memories for the approach of death.*

That had been his plan. To use those precious memories to find a calmer place as the madness of the arena began to sweep him away. But in the quiet moments beneath the blue sky, so intimately joined to the elephant that its swaying was the mockery of a lullaby, he could not find the willpower to push away the thoughts of those he loved most on earth.

This, he decided, was what he would say to every father or mother: *Time gives the illusion that it passes slowly, and only in looking back do you see how quickly it moved. So cherish each moment with your children, for you never know how and why you might be taken from them or them from you.*

He found himself weeping. With joy for what he was about to gain in death. Yet in sorrow for what he was about to lose in life.

✛ ✛ ✛

"The man you will see on the tusk of the elephant," Catus told a crowd of men in the upper stands, "is Gallus Sergius Vitas. Surely you've heard why Caesar has him in the arena."

Normally these members of the mob would have ignored a soldier, jeered at him. But Catus carried beer and was dispensing it to them as he spoke.

There were nods.

"Don't you think," Catus continued, "that such a man as Vitas deserves a chance to fight for his life? Especially if he is guilty of nothing more than defending his wife against Caesar?"

The men around him were half drunk already and bored because nothing had happened on the sand for a few minutes. Immediately a few shouted agreement.

Catus pressed coins into the hands of the nearest men. "Buy more beer," he said. "And pass word of this injustice to those around you."

✛ ✛ ✛

The two women chained to the sand below Nero and Helius were kneeling in silent prayer, blood flowing from their mouths.

Helius ignored them; he was lost in reverie. With his enemy Vitas about to die, he was on the verge of simultaneously enjoying another enemy's humiliation: Sporus. The boy whose knee Nero stroked with undisguised affection. Any moment now, Nero would deliver the news to the boy and . . . Helius shivered in delicious anticipation.

When the gates opened at the far side of the arena, however, Helius became instantly alert. Finally! Vitas, about to die! What joy!

The crowd noise abated briefly in anticipation of the drama to be provided next.

In this silence, the bestiarius prodded the bull elephant toward the center. It moved slowly, its front legs chained together. Well before it had reached the middle of the sand, a shout began in the upper stands, where the unruly mob always gathered.

"Let Vitas fight! Let Vitas fight!"

Spectators around Helius and Nero exchanged glances as they tried to decide what this meant. Exchanged glances became exchanged conversation as the news spread quickly around the amphitheater: This was Gallus Sergius Vitas! On the tusk! Where was honor in that? What an outrage!

The shouting was soon overwhelmed by boos, all of them directed at Nero.

Helius knew that if there was any one thing Nero could not control in the empire, it was the mob. He could influence it, bribe it, placate it, but never control it. Nero feared the mob; it was a beast as unpredictable and dangerous as himself.

Nero leaned into Helius. "Do I have a choice?"

Helius shook his head.

Nero stood, and all eyes of the thousands of spectators were upon him.

Bitterness filled Helius's stomach. How he wanted Vitas destroyed. He should have suggested to Nero that the man be poisoned. Or directed to empty his veins. But Helius had wanted to see Vitas humiliated in death. And this was the result. Yet another chance for Vitas to become a hero.

Nero raised his arms.

The crowd instantly quit chanting.

"Release that man!" Nero's voice echoed through the silence. "Let him fight!"

✤ ✤ ✤

Catus and Gordio found a spot among the mob and looked downward in satisfaction. They'd bribed the bestiarius into sending out one of his least skilled gladiators—a *retiarius*.

Considered the lowest of gladiators, the retiarius fought with a net and a trident, a spear tipped with three points. His only piece of armor was the *galerus*, a piece of metal that protected his left shoulder. The method of fighting employed by a retiarius was simple—dart in and out, looking for a single moment to throw the net and attack.

Catus and Gordio were confident that Vitas, weakened as he might be from the beating, would still be able to handle an inexperienced retiarius.

Below them, on the opposite side of the amphitheater, musicians began to play the long, straight trumpets they would use to accompany the rhythm of the battle, their music intended to rise and fall in waves that heightened the drama.

On cue to the beginning strains of music, the retiarius ran onto the sand and squinted upward, as if judging the interest of the crowd. If he was looking for support he received none, as most were chanting the name of Vitas.

Then the prisoner stepped into sight. In the animal pens, he'd been removed from the tusk and hurriedly equipped for the battle.

Both soldiers frowned. They turned to each other and exchanged perplexed glances.

Something was wrong.

✛ ✛ ✛

The will to live is an unreasoning creature.

The prisoner had spent hours in thought and prayer, finding the strength to face death. Now, with the chance to fight for his life, he could think of nothing except what it might be like to kneel again with his daughter and stroke her hair and hug her close. Or to run across open grass with his sons. Or fall asleep with his wife at his side.

He did not hear the roars of the crowd, feel the heat of the sun. He'd been given an honorable solution that might lead him back to his family. He would only face one opponent, and all it would take was a single fortunate blow for him to be declared victor. Yes, there were glory and joy in eternity with the Christos, but if it was the Father's will, perhaps he would be allowed more time on earth with his family.

So he gripped the handle of the sword and held out his shield as best he could.

His arms were weak, his legs sluggish. His eyes were swollen, and the weights of the sword and shield were unfamiliar to him. None of this mattered. At worst, he would die, but that was no worse than he'd expected, and his death would be merciful and quick, something he had not expected. At best, no matter how remote his chances of surviving, he would live. And see his family again. He was glad for the chance to fight for love.

He turned in slow circles, trying vainly to see his opponent through swollen eyelids. He held his sword in position, ready to swing at any flash of movement.

Then came the ragged breathing of his opponent closing in.

He staggered in one direction, then another, trying to get a glimpse of the retiarius.

His efforts were in vain. Far more quickly than he could dodge came the swoosh of net. It draped him completely, and he dropped his sword, clawing uselessly against the webbing. He felt the blow to his side, a body blow that knocked him onto his shield. The weight of a foot squeezed against the soft cartilage of his throat.

Dimly, he could see the outline of the man above him, a man with a trident poised to pierce his chest. A man waiting for the signal from Nero.

Hope of life on earth was gone. With its departure came the truest test of faith any man or woman could face—the specter of looming death.

He closed his eyes in prayer again. Joy returned to his soul. Yes, he would die but, in so doing, would give life to his wife and children, for their release from this same arena had been part of the bargain he'd made with a stranger the day before. He would die, but this close to the door to the other side, he fully sensed the presence of the Christos, even more than in his most joyful moments of worship. This was the truest and greatest hope, worth far more than death. And with prayer came peace, an outpouring of certainty that his faith was justified, and a full understanding that he would see his family again.

But not in this life.

✛ ✛ ✛

Helius was surrounded once again by boos and catcalls from the crowd.

This time the mob's anger was directed not at Nero, but at Vitas.

The fight was over before it had begun. Within seconds, the retiarius had trapped Vitas in netting and knocked him over, and he now stood with one foot on his throat, ready to deliver the death blow. There'd been no entertainment, no rising up of the hero against death. There'd barely even been time for the musicians to trumpet the macabre melody of battle.

The angry shouts grew louder as the retiarius gazed at Nero, waiting for a signal that would give him permission to dispatch his opponent.

This should have been a moment of joy for Helius. Vitas had been defeated, so humiliated that the crowd had turned against him.

Yet something was wrong.

What is it? What is it?

Then it hit Helius. *The shield!*

Vitas had been equipped with a visored helmet and a short sword. His thighs and torso were bare as was customary, and he wore a wide leather belt designed to protect the area below his waist. None of this was unusual, nor was the oval shield he'd been given.

What was unusual was how he held the shield.

For a moment, Helius wondered if he should alert Nero, but in that same moment, Helius understood the disastrous political implications if Nero realized the same thing. So Helius, too, remained silent and waited for Nero's decision, hoping Nero would suspect nothing.

With the eyes of all in the amphitheater upon him, Nero delayed his decision. He knew drama and when to prolong it.

Finally, Nero nodded.

The spear came down and the retiarius walked away, raising his arms in victory.

Helius could only close his eyes in stunned disbelief as the man on the sand bucked in his final moments of life, his blood soaking the sand below him.

What had gone wrong and how?

The matter with Sporus was suddenly utterly insignificant. Helius knew he should immediately rush from his seat and get to the penned area behind the spectators. He needed to examine the body of the dead man before it was thrown among all the other corpses.

Yet if he left now, Nero would certainly wonder why, and that, too, might raise dangerous questions. Helius had no choice but to pretend the same satisfaction that Nero showed in the death of Gallus Sergius Vitas.

Nero might believe it was over.

Yet Helius knew differently.

And again cursed the gods.

22 months after the beginning of the Tribulation

AD 66
ROME

Capital of the Empire

TYRRHENIAN
SEA

Off the coast of Sicily

I saw a beast coming out of the sea. He had ten horns and seven heads, with ten

crowns on his horns, and on each head a blasphemous name. The beast I saw

resembled a leopard, but had feet like those of a bear and a mouth like that of a

lion. The dragon gave the beast his power and his throne and great authority.

—REVELATION 13:1-2

❧ MOON ❧

HORA QUARTA

WHEN GALLUS SERGIUS VITAS WOKE, he was weak and parched, unsure of the swaying sensation that moved his body. He had no sense of the passage of time, only that he'd fought a long and restless fever. Flashes of the delirium still lingered, and he screwed his eyes shut to force them from his mind.

He shifted without rising to a sitting position, and a blanket fell from his chest. He didn't remember covering himself with the blanket.

Drawing a full breath, he looked upward and slowly found some focus. Though the sky was gray and featureless, the light still pained his bleary eyes. Above him was the foresail of a ship, full with wind. He heard the slap of waves against the hull, the dull murmur of voices farther down the deck.

A ship. It was the swaying of the ship that had taken him from Ostia, Rome's port. He dimly remembered that evening. A small riverboat had taken him in the darkness from Rome, down the Tiber to Ostia. There sailors had forcibly escorted him onto this seagoing ship, where the *magister*—the captain—had taken him below decks to a cabin. But he could not recall moving up to the ship's deck away from the stench of the stifling air below.

As Vitas tried to make sense of the fragments of memory, one thought exploded into his consciousness. *Sophia!*

The horror flooded back. His unsuccessful attempt to defend his wife against Nero. The blow from an emperor's guard that had knocked him out. Waking in a cell below the stands of the amphitheater. The beating in the cell from a stranger who had drugged him.

Vitas fought to a sitting position and touched his face, exploring it gingerly with his fingers. The pain was a brutal reminder that he could not deny the horror. Nor the overwhelming ache in his heart.

Sophia! Back in Rome!

Vitas groaned and fell back on the netting that had served as a bed. Another memory returned. He had been expecting guards to take him to his execution in the arena at any moment. Instead, that stranger had entered his cell and spoken cryptically before methodically beating Vitas across the face with a leather-wrapped dowel.

"I am going to leave you with a letter. You must decipher it to find the answers you need," the stranger had said, thrusting a scroll upon Vitas. *"Second, there is an obscure matter that Tiberius once brought to Senate vote. You will find it somewhere in the archives. It will be marked with a number. Remember this, for the life of your family may depend on it someday. It is the number of the Beast. Six hundred and sixty-six."*

Vitas swallowed hard, trying to work moisture into his mouth. He tried to find enough concentration to puzzle over this memory.

The answer to this mystery was in the scroll. He patted his body for it. His last memory of it was hiding it beneath his tunic.

No scroll!

When he'd boarded the ship, it had been night and far too dark to even glance at the contents. What was in the scroll? Would the answers inside lead him back to his wife? In his delirium, had he left it behind in the captain's quarters?

Vitas pushed up on his elbows. He had to find the scroll.

✦ ✦ ✦

Hundreds of miles away, on a hillside estate in Rome, the brother of Gallus Sergius Vitas sat beneath the shade of an olive tree with several oranges in his lap as his giant of a slave approached with a bound man.

Damian was several years younger than Vitas. His hair was a

mixture of blond and red. His nose had been broken several times and not once set properly before healing. The lower portion of his left ear had been bitten off in a drunken brawl years earlier, and the baby finger of his right hand was still crooked from a punch so poorly timed that he'd smashed a wall behind his opponent in that same brawl. Damian was a devout disciple of wine and parties, and it was more a factor of heredity than physical work that left him with a lean, trim body.

He frowned now, seething with frustrated rage, a mood hardly helped by a ferocious hangover. He was determined to leverage this mood into the resolve he would need to torture the man that his slave Jerome was about to deliver to him.

Jerome walked as effortlessly as if he carried a child. The captive was folded over Jerome's left shoulder, legs wrapped against Jerome's chest by one of the slave's monstrous arms, his head dangling down Jerome's back. Damian doubted the captive had struggled at all during the journey from a shed at the edge of the estate to the olive press; few men, unbound or even armed, would have dared to fight the monstrous slave.

When Jerome reached Damian, he squatted and rolled the captive off his shoulder onto the grass at Damian's feet.

Damian wrinkled his nose. The captive was a middle-aged man in rough clothing and smelled of body waste. This did not surprise Damian. The man had been in that shed with ankles and wrists bound since the afternoon of his capture, two days before. After refusing to speak a single word in answer to Damian's questions, Damian had allowed the man no more water. No more food. It had been Damian's intent to bring him to a horrible thirst and hunger and to humiliate him by making him soil his clothes like a baby.

"Too close," Damian told Jerome. Damian did not like treating a man like this, but the stakes were high. And, in a foul mood because of what had happened to Vitas, he was glad for a way to vent his anger.

Jerome grunted understanding and dragged the man a few steps farther away.

Damian looked at the captive, feigning disinterest. Although their glances met, the man, as expected, did not say a word.

Damian picked up an orange from his lap. The man's eyes followed it in silent desperation. He had been captured late afternoon of the day of Saturn. This meant he'd gone without water for a night, a day, and one more full night.

Damian bit through the skin of the orange, welcoming the oily, acrid taste of the small chunk of peel as a distraction from the hangover's foulness that clung to his tongue and the roof of his mouth. He spat the chunk of peel to the side, eased his head back, squeezed the orange with his right hand, and sucked the juice from inside. The relief of the fruit's juice was insignificant compared to the throbbing of his head and the queasiness of his stomach, but it was better than nothing. Thirsty as he was, he was not ready for water. He'd tried gulping some at dawn and had immediately heaved it out again, the effort leaving his body in trembling weakness.

This was a hangover Damian intended to conceal from the captive, but one that he welcomed as punishment. For yesterday, while the blood of his brother, Vitas, had soaked the sands of the amphitheater, Damian had been in the privacy of a rich woman's villa, enjoying in equal measures her wine and her lack of inhibition to fill the hours that he needed to wear down the captive.

In a way, Damian could not be blamed; he had not even known that Vitas had been sent to the arena. During the day that followed Vitas's arrest, Damian had been in pursuit of the man now bound in front of him. He'd spent the following morning at home, but had departed for the rest of the day to spend time with the lonely rich woman. Damian had been unreachable by any of his slaves who could bring the news; discretion had forced him to enter and leave the woman's villa unannounced. No one except Jerome had known where to find him, and Jerome had had his orders to guard the captive at the shed without straying from his post for a moment. For two days, then, Damian had been totally unaware of the efforts of Helius and Nero to arrange for the arrest and execution of Vitas and of the invitation sent to Sophia, Vitas's wife, to commit suicide.

Damian had only discovered all of this upon returning to his own estate last evening, and, in near shock, he had savagely consumed more wine until he passed out. While Damian doubted he could have done anything to prevent his brother's death, he loathed himself for entertaining a woman during the moments that Vitas had entertained Nero and Helius in the amphitheater.

Unconsciousness had provided far too short a period of oblivion for Damian. The discomfort of this day's early heat had woken him and spurred him out of his villa to pursue whatever revenge he could inflict upon Helius for his brother's death. Beginning with what he could learn from the captive in front of him.

"Well, Jew," Damian addressed him, "are you ready to speak?"

The captive blinked several times but did not answer.

"Lay this man across the olive press," Damian ordered Jerome, finally rising. "I'm tired of waiting for answers."

✦ ✦ ✦

"Father!"

Leah rushed across the courtyard to hug him. What an answer to prayer! When guards had taken her from the prison cell just after dawn, Leah had expected her destination would be the arena. And the death that came with it.

She had not expected to be escorted here, to the royal palace. Nor that female slaves would help ease her into a hot bath to wash away the stink of the prison, then dress and perfume her as if she were the emperor's wife.

But she was not an emperor's wife. She was a poor Jew, from an area of Rome crowded with *insulae,* apartments. She was young—at the age of marriage—and so modest that she'd unsuccessfully protested the attention of the slaves, taking no pleasure in their comments about her beauty.

She'd been arrested a day earlier and had spent the entire time in the prison, alternating between prayer and hymns with other Christians in her cell and silent worry about her elderly father, Hezron. He'd been arrested with her but taken to a different cell. She had expected never to see him again, and she agonized far more over how he might die than the prospect of the torture that awaited her.

After all, she'd been responsible for their arrest.

So as the female slaves had escorted her through the gardens, she had been too distracted by worry to enjoy the scent of the flowers and the gentle breeze and the ornate sculptures that filled the garden.

Then she saw her father through the arched entrance in the courtyard, and joy overwhelmed her. She did not even feel her feet touch the inlaid bricks as she flew toward him.

Now he was holding her in his strong arms, the arms that had always welcomed her all through her childhood, no matter how busy he might have been in his studies or how engrossed in conversation with the men who came to sit at his feet for teaching.

"Father," she said again, burying her head in his shoulder.

He stroked her hair.

Leah was aware that not all Jewish fathers were so affectionate to their daughters and that not all Jewish fathers treated their daughters with the same respect they accorded their sons. It made her treasure his respect and affection that much more.

"My child, my child," he murmured.

He did not push her away, but waited until she slowly withdrew from his arms.

And gradually became aware that they were not alone. She'd only had eyes for Hezron in her rush through the courtyard. Now she noticed two other men. One sat on a bench. The other stood beside the bench, arms crossed, staring at them with an expression difficult to read.

The first man she knew. Chayim, who had told her he was a Greek from the city of Agrigentum in Sicily and, like her, a Christian. Unlike her, though, he was wealthy. She knew all this because of what they had endured together just days earlier—a visit by soldiers to a secret meeting of Christians. This young man with handsome dark features drew her as if she were a shy doe seeking clear waters.

The other man, wearing a toga edged with purple, she also recognized. Helius—Nero's Helius. She knew his reputation well; he was a man capable of Nero's cruelty and who wielded almost as much power.

Her joy began to diminish. Who had betrayed them? What could this be about? Why was Chayim here? Had he been arrested too?

Perhaps Nero had special plans for them. Leah tried to push away the stories and rumors she had heard about the hideousness of Nero's perversions and how freely he indulged them. Surely she hadn't been bathed and perfumed for the enjoyment of the one man responsible for the Great Tribulation forced on those who chose allegiance to the Christos.

Dread weakened her legs. Nero had murdered his own mother, taking three very public attempts to succeed. He had divorced then murdered his first wife and kicked to death his second wife. He'd become a master of every sin known to man and openly reveled in it. As any ordinary man of ordinary means he still would have been a monster without compare, but as the most powerful man in the world ruling the most powerful empire in history, his unbridled absolute power allowed him to pursue evil as if evil were merely a whim. This was a man who believed he was a deity and killed Christians because they would not worship his image, the man who had killed the apostles Peter and Paul and seemed intent on ridding the earth of the first generation of Christians.

Without realizing it, Leah drew close to her father again.

As if sensing her fear, Hezron stepped in front of her, blocking her from Helius.

"You have nothing to fear," Helius said. "For reasons that are obvious now that I see your daughter, this man wishes to purchase your freedom."

Over Hezron's shoulder, Leah saw Chayim bow his head then raise it again to quickly explain to her father. "I have only honorable intentions, Rabbi. I had hoped to discuss this with you in far better circumstances. And only if Leah gave me encouragement to do so."

"You know this man?" Hezron said to her softly.

"I do," Leah said.

"How long?"

Implicit in the question was another: *Why have you kept it hidden from me?*

"Not long enough for her to understand my feelings for her," Chayim answered. "But after I heard of her arrest, I knew there was no other choice but to approach Helius and—"

"My question was not directed at you." In her father's quiet voice, Leah heard the steel that had made him legendary among the Jews of Rome. "My daughter can and will speak for herself."

Chayim bowed his head.

"How long?" Hezron asked her again.

"Only a few days," Leah said.

"Where did you meet?"

Part of her marveled. The royal palace was a place as foreign to him as it was to her. Helius, the second most powerful man in the world, was only two steps away. Yet Hezron ignored his circumstance, his surroundings, and the man with the power of life and death as if he were at the synagogue, where dozens gathered to glean wisdom from his interpretations of the Law.

Where did you meet?

Leah agonized. Chayim had been invited to a secret meeting of Christians. Soldiers had burst in to arrest all of them. Chayim had defied the soldiers, proving his trustworthiness to all the other Christians.

Yet to answer would be to let her father know that on that same evening, she had committed her heart and soul to the Christos.

That she—like her brother Nathan, who had already died in the arena for his faith—believed that the promised Messiah had arrived and fulfilled the laws and promises of God's covenant with Israel, thereby inaugurating the kingdom of God on earth.

Shortly after Nathan had died for his faith, Hezron had lost his eldest son, Caleb, because Caleb had tried to defend Nathan. Leah was Hezron's only remaining child, and despite all that he had lost and despite how fully she knew and understood his pain because of losing his two sons, she had still chosen the Christos. How could she explain that to him? That she'd made her choice, even knowing that she, too, might lose her life on account of her faith in the Christos, and worse, that the Christos Himself had warned faith would turn family members against each other?

"Where did you meet?" Hezron repeated. "Was it when the Sabbath ended, the evening you told me you needed to visit a sick widow?"

"Yes," Leah whispered, feeling great shame for the lie she'd told that night.

He turned and placed his hands on her shoulders. "Whatever happens here, know that I understand. I don't condone it. But I understand that love between a man and a woman is a powerful force. I would have done the same to be with your mother."

A tiny smile crossed his strong features, and she knew he was remembering her mother and their love. "In fact," Hezron said, still smiling, "your mother did the same for me before we married."

Again, he spoke as if they were alone. As if it were love for a man that had drawn her out of the house. He was unaware that she had betrayed him and his faith. Would he be this forgiving if he knew it had been a rejection of his teachings instead?

Hezron turned to Helius. "The Romans are men of law. While I am not a citizen, I have obeyed all your laws. We do not need our freedom purchased. I am formally requesting that you either release us or allow me to hire a lawyer to defend us against whatever charges have been laid against me."

"Christians get no such privilege," Helius said. "They are treasonous, and Caesar has made very plain the consequences for those who will not worship him."

Hezron snorted. "If that is your accusation, let me bring forth the witnesses who will attest otherwise. I am a rabbi, well-known for my teachings against the Christians."

"What about your daughter? Will witnesses clear her of the accusation too?"

Hezron drew an indignant breath, then released it slowly, as if finally understanding the sudden and unexplained arrest by soldiers.

He turned to Leah. "You? You too?" His voice was broken of the strength it had just contained.

Tears began to stream down Leah's face at his obvious pain. She ached for her father to reach out and touch her face, to wipe her tears as he had done all her life.

Hands at his sides, he spoke. "It is true, isn't it? You are a follower."

Before she could utter the words that she feared might kill him, Chayim interrupted, speaking to Helius. "The charges are irrelevant. I've arranged for you to receive the amount agreed for you to release them. You said nothing about bringing them here. Or bringing me here, for that matter."

"Things have changed," Helius said, still staring at Leah and Hezron. "This was before I found out who the old man was."

Hezron moved his gaze from Leah to Helius, who continued to speak.

"I began to wonder why anyone would pay such a large ransom to release you from the arena, so I made inquiries," Helius said. "I discovered you are a great rabbi. Which is very convenient. I need your help interpreting a letter written by a Jew. Once you have done that for me, I will release you and your daughter."

"Give me the letter now so that I can be done with it," Hezron answered. Strength seemed to return to him, as if he'd made a decision. "I will do anything to save my daughter, no matter what faith she follows."

Hezron lifted a hand and gently touched Leah's cheek. He brushed away a tear, and she knew that he was giving her a silent message of love and acceptance.

"You will be provided the letter and a place to work," Helius said. "See to it that you understand the letter well enough to explain everything in it to me."

"This was not what we agreed!" Chayim said.

"Silence," Helius said calmly. "Before I have your tongue removed."

Chayim looked across at Leah. Their eyes met briefly. Then she dropped her head, torn with emotion.

One man, a man she might be able to love, had taken great risk to rescue her by bribing Helius. The other man, her father, had been put at great risk because of her and was still willing to rescue her at any cost. She felt as if she'd been placed between them, and she could find no words.

The tension was broken by the appearance of a large man stepping through the archway of the courtyard. He had a well-scarred face and a savage smile. He carried a sack in one hand. Tigellinus, prefect of the emperor's soldiers.

Gaius Ofonius Tigellinus had become friends with Nero when Nero was still a teenager, and had always encouraged Nero's excesses. It was Tigellinus who had revived the hated treason courts, and Nero used this new power with ruthlessness, taking property and life with mere accusations.

Tigellinus caught Helius's eye and lifted the sack high, as if it were significant.

"Go now," Helius immediately told Leah, Hezron, and Chayim. He waved at the slaves standing at the far side of the courtyard. "These slaves will ensure each of you is placed under guard in separate quarters."

"Me!" Chayim said. "You have no right to do this to me. Not after what I've paid for this."

"Of course I do," Helius said. He turned his attention to

Tigellinus, who was nearing them. Red liquid seeped from the seams of the sack.

"If you want to make an issue of this," Helius told Chayim, "we could always have Tigellinus here add your head to the one he carries now."

✛ ✛ ✛

Vitas was tempted to let himself fall back into unconsciousness. The swaying of the ship would make it very easy. But he needed to find the scroll!

Before Vitas could rise, however, he sensed, rather than felt, a presence beside him.

"Drink," a soft voice said. "Your body needs it after your fever."

A hand cradled the back of his head and helped him sit completely upright. It hurt Vitas to turn his head sideways.

The man helping him was dressed in a simple tunic, a covering that left only his arms exposed, showing corded muscle. Vitas guessed him to be in his fifties, but he could have been older, for his face showed no softness that came with easy living. His hair matched his beard—gray hairs far outnumbering the remainder of black.

Vitas knew this man. He was a Jew. He'd been on the same riverboat from Rome to Ostia and had introduced himself as John, son of Zebedee.

Vitas groaned. Not from recognition but from renewed hopelessness. Both had been placed on this ship as prisoners; neither had known why or where the ship was headed.

Would the scroll have answers to these questions too?

John responded to the groan by lifting a ladle of water and helping Vitas drink.

"How long?" Vitas said after gulping the water.

"Your fever?"

Vitas nodded.

"The first night," John said. "All of yesterday. And last night."

Vitas blinked. A full day and a half on the water. A full day and a half of travel from Rome. From Sophia.

"Do you know why we are here?" Vitas asked.

The older man smiled. "The will of God."

"Our destination?" Vitas asked, impatient with the man's vague answer. Regardless of what the scroll might tell him, Vitas needed to get back to Rome. To find Sophia. "Did you find out from any of the crew?"

"Alexandria."

"Alexandria!"

Vitas was not a naval man, but he knew the route to grain ports of Alexandria. Depending on winds, the ship would reach the Straits of Messana on the third or fourth day. He could leave the ship when it stopped there.

Vitas lurched, trying to get to his feet. He was first and foremost a man of action. He'd find the magister and convince him that he needed to get off the ship at the first port.

The sudden effort was too taxing. A wave of nausea knocked Vitas to his knees. Then came the convulsions of his stomach. He'd eaten so little in the past hours that he was only capable of dry retching.

John had a damp cloth and gently wiped Vitas's face.

It was an odd sensation for Vitas, to be cared for as if he were a child. More fragments of memory returned. Vitas had not been alone during the fever. He'd woken occasionally, dimly aware of that same damp cloth during the worst of it.

"That was you," Vitas said. He struggled again to his feet. "The blanket. Lifting me onto the deck. With me all through the fever."

John nodded.

Vitas wanted to ask if John knew anything about the scroll, but caution tempered him. Perhaps what was inside the scroll was too valuable to let anyone know of it. Vitas, after all, had no reason to trust this Jew. The man was a stranger to him; all Vitas knew was that the Jew had defied Nero and had once been exiled for it.

Vitas tried a step and nearly fell.

John reached to steady him, but Vitas pushed away his hand. "Enough. I am well now."

The gray-haired man appeared to take no offense. "Of course."

Vitas moved a step past him. The search for the scroll could wait. First, he needed to find the captain.

Vitas glanced around the deck. The ship was a *corbita,* a common merchant ship. Over a hundred feet long, if the ship was going to Alexandria, it would be carrying exports from Rome. In Alexandria, it would pick up grain for its return. But perhaps not for months. Too soon the winter winds would stop all travel back across the Mediterranean.

Vitas could not wait months. He knew the commander of the legion stationed in Sicily. News of events in Rome would not have reached Sicily yet, and Vitas could plead his case to the commander. Sicily was far enough from Rome to be safe, yet close enough that he could return to Rome within days, not weeks or months.

Vitas surveyed the crew, searching unsuccessfully for the captain. There were a dozen crew members in sight, engaged in the various activities necessary for sailing a ship this size. Vitas had spent months on similar ships, transporting his soldiers to Britannia and back to Italy, so the activities were familiar to him.

There was the *gubernator*—the pilot—guiding the ship with the tiller bar that controlled the enormous steering bars on each quarter. A couple of crewmen were adjusting the lines of the huge square rig, the mainsail. Another couple worked the foresail. Several more were engaged in the tedious, unending task of bailing buckets of bilge water up from the hold. At the far end, the ship's carpenter and two assistants moved two heavy beams of lumber. Beside the carpenter, on the floor of the deck, was a large triangular frame of wood, with tools scattered beside it. It looked as if the carpenter had set aside that task to move the beams.

Vitas frowned.

No passengers.

Without fail, merchant ships carried passengers and their servants, men and women who would spend idle time in card games,
dice, or commenting on the crew around them. A ship this size
could be expected to have dozens of passengers.

None.

Vitas knew from experience that passengers would not be hidden below decks. The only quarters there belonged to the captain.
They'd be on the deck, in or near tents that their servants pitched
and maintained for them.

No passengers.

He frowned again, looking more closely at the carpenter and his
assistants. It appeared to Vitas that they were lashing together the
two beams, forming the shape of a cross.

This was confirmed moments later when all three men strained
to set the cross upright. They leaned it against the spar of the mainsail. All the rest of the crew stopped work. The exchanged glances
among them were obvious.

And chilling.

✛ ✛ ✛

"As a Jew, I'm sure you are aware of the Roman method of ruling
the provinces," Damian told his captive in the hillside olive grove.

Damian sat on the edge of the lower half of the olive press, his
feet dangling just above the ground. This half was a huge horizontal disk of stone, flat on the ground, like a wheel on its side. It was
fully three paces in diameter, and the top surface was the height of
a man's waist. A wide and shallow trough had been carved between
the center of the disk and its outer edge, going the entire circum-
ference of the disk. This wide groove was filled with freshly har-
vested olives.

"Caesar grants privileges and citizenship to those who cooperate,"
Damian continued, "and ruthlessly destroys those who do not."

The bound wrists of Damian's captive were tied to an upright
axle in the center of the olive press. His arms were stretched across

the trough of the press, just above the olives that filled it. The rest of his body hung down over the edge of the press, and he stood awkwardly, his belly pressing into the stone.

"You may recall my first words to you," Damian said. "I invited you to eat and drink. I promised to give you comfort in exchange for answers." Damian shrugged. "You should not be surprised, then, that when you refused to speak, your food and drink were removed. That, however, is only the beginning of what you face for refusing to cooperate."

Damian pushed himself off the edge of the olive press. He felt his hatred for Nero and Helius coiling in his belly, and he used it to lash out at this prisoner. Damian needed the hate—he was not capable of torture without it.

Damian spoke to the giant slave who had been standing silently to the side. "Let's show him what we have in mind."

A half hour earlier, Damian had instructed other slaves to deliver several wooden beams to be left near the press. These beams were the height of a man and the thickness of Damian's arm.

Damian picked up the end of one beam. Because of the fierceness of his hangover, his vision seemed to explode in small dots as blood rushed to his head. He fought the urge to vomit again and pretended nonchalance as he laid the beam across the olive press, several feet down from the captive's arms and parallel to them.

This beam now rested halfway between the captive's arms and the upper portion of the olive press, which was a second disk of stone that sat upright and fit snugly within the shallow walls of the trough of the lower disk. Like a wheel too, it had a wooden axle protruding horizontally, with a ring at the end that fit over the vertical axle in the center. This heavy wheel of stone was designed with the protruding horizontal axle to be pushed by three men walking around the outer edge of the olive press, so that the disk could be rolled continuously within the trough of the lower disk, its tremendous weight squeezing oil from olives that drained from the trough into a catch basin.

"Begin," Damian said, holding the outer end of the beam. He'd instructed Jerome on what to do next.

Jerome moved to the axle of the upper disk and grabbed it with both hands in front of his chest. He set his weight against the axle. His head was shaved, and the layers of muscle between the bottom of his skull and the top of his neck bulged as he leaned into the axle.

Although it normally took three men to move the stone disk, Jerome shoved it forward with little sign of strain. Olives in front of the round upright stone disappeared beneath it, becoming pulp as the disk passed over. Two steps later, moving around the outside of the lower disk, Jerome reached Damian and stopped with the upper disk resting against the beam across the trough.

Jerome paused.

Damian looked at the captive farther down, whose eyes were fixed on the beam. Damian nodded. "Jerome."

Jerome pushed the upper wheel forward another step as Damian held the beam in place so that it would not slip. The disk rolled over it, snapping it like kindling.

"I believe the sound of your arm breaking would not be much different than that. If we could hear it over your screams." Damian grabbed another beam and laid it across the olive press a few feet closer to the captive, allowing Jerome to roll the disk over it, too, with the same splintering results. "To refresh your memory, I am a slave hunter. A man of great power has hired me to capture you. But before I deliver you to him, I want to know more about your vision, the one that is in a letter circulating among followers of the Christos."

After all, if this was something Helius wanted badly, it would have value for Damian.

"Talk to me about your vision," Damian continued.

He watched the face of the captive closely. A muscle twitched along the man's jaw. But there was no other sign that the captive would respond.

"Jerome," Damian said, "this man needs more persuasion."

The giant slave began pushing again, until the massive wheel touched the captive's nearest arm. A quarter turn more and his arm would be pulverized.

Damian spoke to the captive in a conversational tone. "Perhaps now you'll answer my questions?"

✦ ✦ ✦

"Well?" Helius demanded of Tigellinus as soon as they were alone in the courtyard. "Whose head is it?"

"I don't like your tone," Tigellinus said casually and just as casually placed a hand on Helius's shoulder. "I searched among the bodies myself because I recognized the need for secrecy. But it doesn't mean you can speak to me like I'm one of your slaves."

Tigellinus smiled as he spoke but squeezed hard with his powerful fingers, digging into the meat of Helius's shoulder.

After all their years together in close service to Nero, Tigellinus had a rough affection for Helius. Tigellinus was brawn to Helius's elegance, crudeness to his effeminacy. As a devious man himself, Tigellinus admired Helius for the same quality. Yet Tigellinus knew that Helius would seize on the first sign of weakness, and he was ever vigilant to squash any signs of imperiousness.

Like now.

"You do want to apologize, don't you?" Tigellinus said, smile still in place.

"Of course," Helius said, his grimace plain. "I forgot myself simply because of my distress at this situation."

Tigellinus eased the pressure and stepped back.

"Was it Vitas?" Helius asked more respectfully.

"See for yourself." Tigellinus hid a grin as he lifted the sack and extended it to Helius.

Tigellinus was aware of Helius's squeamishness, aware that Helius had flicked a glance at his blood-crusted fingernails and swallowed back revulsion. But, because they were always involved in a subtle power struggle, Tigellinus enjoyed the chance to expose weakness in

Helius. A true Roman like Tigellinus had no compunctions about the blood that flowed when hacking apart another man's body.

"That's not necessary," Helius said. "I've done my part."

"By sending me at dawn into the pile of bodies outside the arena?"

"You agreed with me," Helius insisted. "Vitas was a soldier. He would not have strapped the shield on his right arm."

Tigellinus nodded at that. Soldiers—even left-handed soldiers—were trained to handle a sword with their right hand and strap the shield to the left arm. This way, an entire line of soldiers, each guarding the next, presented an unbroken row of shields to the enemy. It was inconceivable that Vitas would have fought the retiarius with a sword in his left hand. And that could only mean something else just as inconceivable: it had not been Vitas in the arena, but a left-handed man unfamiliar with military training.

"As you promised, the face was bruised badly, almost beyond recognition," Tigellinus said. "That's how I was able to identify the body."

"Does the head belong to Vitas?"

"Check the teeth first," Tigellinus said, holding the sack open and peering inside. "Vitas came from wealth. You'd expect the teeth to show that. And you'll also see that without blood to fill the bruises, the bone structure of the face gives a semblance of recognition."

"Please!" Helius stamped his foot, much to the enjoyment of Tigellinus. "You've already seen the head. Why do I need to do so?"

Tigellinus gave a wolflike smile. "For the same reason you asked me to bring it here."

Helius became still.

"After all," Tigellinus said, "you could have simply asked me to look closely at the body and report back to you."

Silence from Helius.

"Why then did you insist I bring the head here?"

"Enough games," Helius snapped. "Because I trust no one and you trust no one."

"You wanted the head here, in this courtyard, in case you did not like my answer. In case I told you it was Vitas. Because you are as suspicious in nature as I am. You are wondering who might have arranged for Vitas to escape, and it has occurred to you that I am one of the few with that power. You fear that Vitas and I might band together against you."

"Does the head belong to Vitas?"

"Yes," Tigellinus said.

Silence again from Helius.

Tigellinus waited, guessing the thoughts going through Helius's mind.

More silence.

Tigellinus shrugged, turned, and began to walk out of the courtyard.

"Where are you going?" Helius asked.

"To whatever business I had intended for the day before you begged me to scavenge carcasses. Since it was Vitas who died in the arena, you have nothing to fear."

Tigellinus made a bet with himself. That he wouldn't be able to reach the arch at the edge of the courtyard before . . .

"Stop," Helius said.

Tigellinus continued.

"I need to see that head!" Helius called to his back.

Tigellinus grinned in self-satisfaction. The arch was still three steps ahead.

"Certainly," Tigellinus said. He turned and waited.

Helius approached. "Yes, yes," he said, irritated. "You are proving yourself correct, and I'm forced to admit it. I have to see the head for myself."

"Because . . . " Tigellinus wanted this conversation to remind Helius that, brawny as Tigellinus might be, he was still as astute as Helius. It was a way to prevent Helius from ever attempting any betrayal of any kind against him. Such were the politics of those who served Nero.

"Because," Helius said after some hesitation, "if you helped Vitas escape, you would tell me it was his head in the bag and let me believe he was dead." He sighed. "Are you pleased with yourself?"

"Very." Tigellinus let his answer settle on Helius, emphasizing that he was still too smart for Helius to ever attempt to cross him.

With reluctance, Helius reached for the sack containing the head.

Tigellinus relented. "Don't bother. I can save you the effort of looking. It is not Vitas. That tells you two things. I was not—and am not—part of the plot to aid his escape."

"And?"

"The obvious. Vitas is still alive."

✠ ✠ ✠

Vitas turned to the Jew behind him.

John was already seated, his gaze on the horizon. Vitas sat beside him. The crew members had returned to their various tasks, but occasionally one would glance in their direction.

"What can you tell me about the cross?" Vitas said.

John slowly moved his eyes toward Vitas. His smile was sad, thoughtful. "I can't think of a better question for any man to ask."

This Jew, Vitas knew, was a Christian. Vitas also knew from his wife, Sophia, the significance that the cross played in the faith of the followers of the Christos. This, however, did not appear to be a time for any discussion about faith. The ship, for Vitas, was a floating prison, surrounded by hundreds of square miles of open water. If the crew had malevolent intentions, it was imperative to know.

"That cross there," Vitas said, again impatient, "against the mast. What did I miss during my fever?"

"The crew is near mutiny," John answered. "They believe this ship is doomed."

"There's no storm."

"The sky has been cloudy since departure."

Vitas knew the importance of that. Without stars at night or the sun during the day, navigation was difficult. "Still," he said, "the breeze at this time of year is steady. Any sailor can use it for rough navigation."

"You know as well as I do when this ship departed," John said. "At night. Without the customary sacrifices. Nor did the captain wait for the right omens. This crew is as superstitious as any."

Vitas needed no explanation. On occasion, captains waited days for the right omens. And they never departed without the appropriate sacrifices.

John looked away, paused in thought, and looked back. "And there is the matter of a dream the pilot had."

"This dream?"

Dreams were highly significant too—good or bad—enough to speed or delay a ship's departure.

"Both the first night at sea and the second night, he dreamed the sirens of the whirlpools at Messana drew the ship onto the rocks. He's reported this dream widely, and nearly all are afraid of drowning when we reach the straits. The men grumble that it will happen because the gods have not been properly appeased."

"The crew, then, blames us for the troubles they fear," Vitas said.

"I've been told," John replied, "that several dozen passengers had made a booking on this voyage, but were left behind because the ship left without warning. Without paying passengers, the crew expects to receive reduced wages."

"The crew blames us." Vitas grunted this repetition.

"They wonder who you are and why you are so valuable that the captain risks the wrath of the gods to speed you from Rome in the dead of night without the proper omens or sacrifices."

"They could be asking the same questions about you."

"They've seen me with you." John smiled and pointed at the damp cloth beside the netting, the cloth he'd used earlier to gently wipe the face of Vitas. "Most think I'm your slave."

"Then let me ask what they won't. Why are you on this ship?"

"Perhaps God intended for me to help spare your life."

"I don't understand."

"You understand," John, son of Zebedee said. "Why else did you ask about the cross?"

✦ ✦ ✦

"Your name is John, son of Zebedee," Damian told his prisoner. "You are a Jew. A fisherman in your youth, raised in Galilee. I know this much about you, but not much more, except that you, like all other followers of the Christos, defy Caesar by refusing to worship him or his image."

In the olive grove, Caius Sennius Ruso had not expected it to come to this—the rough edge of stone biting into his skin, a massive weight poised to crush the bones of his arm, the smell of fresh olive oil below his face a strange contrast to the horror of the impending torture.

"Speak to me," Damian said. "End your silence."

Ruso met Damian's eyes squarely but kept his silence. If he spoke, his accent would betray him, and this man would know he was not the Jew named John, son of Zebedee.

Damian gave a barely perceptible nod, and Jerome pushed the wheel forward slightly.

Ruso could not help the cry of pain that escaped him as the stone dug into his flesh.

Damian nodded again, and Jerome pulled the wheel back slightly.

"If I understand correctly," Damian continued, intently studying Ruso's face, "you were one of twelve disciples who spent a few years with this Christos before he was crucified by a Roman procurator. John the Beloved, I believe, is how many refer to you."

Ruso clamped his jaws. He could not deny to himself how afraid he was. Yes, Ruso had expected to be captured days earlier. Yet Ruso's careful plan had fallen apart in the moment of capture. Instead of delivering him to Helius, Damian and his monstrous slave, Jerome, had taken Ruso to a shed hidden in the olive grove and begun an interrogation.

Answering any of Damian's questions that evening had been
unthinkable. Doing so would have ruined what little of his careful
planning was still intact. So Ruso had chosen silence and been punished for it by over thirty-six hours of hungry, thirsty solitude. And
now this, a massive stone about to pulverize his arm.

"I'd prefer this to be a two-sided conversation," Damian said.
"I do have real curiosity about the Christians' claims. You, of all
people, would be in a position to answer, if indeed you were one
of the man's best friends. How can you maintain that this Christos
was risen from the dead and still expect me or any other man to
believe you are sane?"

Damian gave the slight nod again. Jerome pushed the wheel forward, and again the stone's weight brought a gasp of pain from Ruso.

Lord Jesus, he prayed to his Christos, *please give me strength
to endure.*

"If you are going to speak at all," Damian said, "I would much
rather know about your vision than a claim about resurrection,
which I cannot believe no matter how sincerely you might repeat
it to me."

This time, however, Damian did not nod for Jerome to release
the stone. It remained in place, squeezing on the muscles of Ruso's
forearm and biceps. An inch more, and he knew that it would snap
his elbow. Another few inches, and the bones would be mashed
into pulp.

"I've had a Jewish rabbi translate and interpret your letter for
me," Damian said. "The Lamb against the Beast, your Christos
against the Roman emperor and the Roman Empire. Am I correct?"

Ruso was so thirsty that it felt like he verged on madness.
Moments earlier, watching Damian suck juice from the orange had
forced him to use all his willpower not to beg for a single drop for
himself. Dizziness disoriented Ruso further; he could not think
beyond a single act of resolve.

Remain silent!

Ruso was intensely focused on Damian. Dreading the next

slight nod that would release the giant slave to push the stone forward that next inch.

Remain silent! Speaking would immediately reveal to Damian that Ruso did not have the Galilean accent that Damian expected to hear.

"Your letter predicts the death of Nero and suggests the possibility of civil war," Damian said. "That, truly, is what I want to discuss with you."

Remain silent! At first, in the shed, Ruso's silence had been simply to ensure that the man Damian did seek would have time to escape by ship.

"Do you have any evidence of a conspiracy that allows you to promise Nero's death to the followers of the Christos?" Damian's voice had lost its conversational tone, and he leaned in, stopping inches away from Ruso's face.

Remain silent! If Damian discovered he'd captured the wrong man, he'd realize he needed to kill Ruso or face a trial and probably execution. It would be much easier for Damian to bury his mistake than allow Ruso to go free and tell the world about it.

"This is all I need from you," Damian said. "Tell me and you have your freedom. Speak or the second arm will be crushed after the first. Then your legs. And finally, your skull."

Seconds passed like hours to Ruso. He fought the urge to vomit, such was his fear. Yet even now, was John the Beloved safe from this slave hunter?

Then came the slight nod that Ruso dreaded. Jerome eased the wheel forward again, and Ruso felt the joint of his elbow begin to separate. He did not have the courage to remain silent. Eyes closed in shame, he screamed in primal fear and pain.

The pain suddenly ended.

Ruso opened his eyes. Had shock mercifully ended it?

He saw instead that Jerome had pulled the wheel away from him, while Damian shook his head in disgust.

Had the slave hunter somehow understood Ruso's shame?

"I'm a weak man," Damian said to Jerome. "I cannot do this. Not even to avenge my brother."

Damian leaned against the lower half of the olive press, still speaking to Jerome. "Put this man back in chains. Give him food and water, but make sure he remains under guard."

✠ ✠ ✠

"Shall we wager on who will kill us?" Tigellinus asked, grinning. "Nero or Vitas?"

Helius was in no mood to make light of their situation, much as the proposed wager accurately summed up their situation. It had taken great resolve to go ahead with the previously arranged appointment with Chayim and Leah and Hezron. He'd barely been able to focus on the conversation as he worried about Tigellinus and whose head he would bring back to the palace.

Well-justified worries.

If Vitas was still alive, Helius and Tigellinus faced a double threat. The first would come from Nero, who would lose all confidence in both of them if he discovered that they had allowed Vitas to escape Nero's wrath and punishment.

The second, just as dangerous, would come from the revenge that Vitas might seek. Aside from the fact that Vitas most certainly knew Helius and Tigellinus had encouraged Nero to provoke the physical attack that had resulted in Vitas's arrest, Vitas would discover that they had also engineered his wife's suicide and the confiscation of his estate.

Helius had no doubt that if Vitas so chose, the man had the ability and patience to find the time and place to hunt and murder each of them, no matter what precautions Helius and Tigellinus arranged. Vitas was a former soldier and war hero renowned for coolness under pressure. Who knew when he would strike with his legendary fighting abilities?

Worse, what if Vitas decided instead to marshal a circle of military allies in an attempt to overthrow Nero? The possibility was all too real. All it would take was the support of enough generals united in opposition to Nero. Their emperor, after all, had no son as successor. And, as Julius Caesar had proven decades earlier, the real power was in the loyalty of soldiers.

"We kill Vitas first," Helius said. "It is that simple. Then we have no need to worry about our own deaths."

"*Parturiunt montes, nascetur ridiculus mus,*" Tigellinus said, lapsing into the formal grammar of a common adage. *The mountain groaned loudly in great labor, then bore a tiny mouse.*

"What are you implying?" Helius snapped.

"That your solution is no better than a mouse. Yes, Vitas's death is necessary, but it's hardly enough."

Although Helius was tempted to protest the insult, he was curious enough to remain silent.

"Listen," Tigellinus said. "His escape was plotted by men with power, agreed? Men who had a way to find or force someone to die instead of Vitas. Men who were able to smuggle him out of the cell. Men who were intelligent enough—"

"Your point is made."

"Even if Vitas was killed tomorrow, we still face those unseen enemies. And their malevolent motives."

"Piso . . ." Helius said softly. Piso, the man behind a massive conspiracy that had nearly succeeded in the assassination of Nero. Piso and dozens of conspirators had been executed, but the discontent behind their effort had spread.

"With each passing month," Tigellinus said, "Nero orders more suicides, confiscates more estates, creates more enemies. The empire is nearly bankrupt, yet he is determined to tour Greece, and you know better than I do how ruinously expensive that will be. If he is killed or dethroned before we have a say in picking a successor, we, too, are dead."

"By the gods," Helius swore, "do you have any idea how difficult it will be to find those who set Vitas free while keeping the hunt for them secret from Nero?"

"No," Tigellinus said. "I'm a stupid man, capable only of holding a sword."

"Too stupid to recognize a rhetorical question."

"Sarcasm for sarcasm. That is certainly helpful at this point."

Helius couldn't understand how Tigellinus could appear to take all of this so lightly. "What if Vitas suddenly appears? How will we explain that to Nero?"

"We make sure Vitas is captured first," Tigellinus said, "then tortured until we find out who conspired with him against us."

Helius paced several steps. "Since you called my solution a mouse, let me point out that your solution is like mice deciding to bell the cat. Easier said than done."

Tigellinus shrugged. "Start with his brother, Damian. Perhaps he was among those who arranged Vitas's escape."

"No," Helius said with enough certainty that Tigellinus raised his eyebrows. Helius realized he'd made a tactical error, but in comparison to their shared trouble, it was minor. "I have a spy in Damian's household."

"Interesting that you've kept that knowledge from me."

"And you don't have your own private spies scattered across the city?"

Tigellinus gave that a broad grin. "If I do, I'm not stupid enough to let it slip out in your presence."

"Hopefully your spies are as useful as mine."

"In other words," Tigellinus said, "you are confident that Damian had nothing to do with it."

"And that Vitas did not visit him or seek refuge at his estate," Helius added.

"Good. Is Damian someone we should have killed as a precaution? He, too, may have plans of revenge."

"Probably," Helius answered. "I've been informed that he's captured John and is holding him prisoner. But as he hasn't brought me John yet, I can only conclude he is plotting in some way against us."

"John?"

"The Jew. You agreed with me that we would give Damian a bounty to capture him for us."

"Ah yes. The Jew from Patmos. Responsible for that cursed letter circulating among the Christians. One that you fear may pose a threat to Nero."

"We need to understand it to know for certain. You *do* recall that conversation."

Tigellinus shrugged. "Barely important enough to remember. Especially under these circumstances."

"'Barely important enough to remember'? Let me remind you of just one rumor I've heard about it. It predicts the death of Nero. If that gets to him, we'll have another bloodbath. He sees conspiracies everywhere. If Nero hears about it—and he will—we need to be prepared."

"We won't be around for that bloodbath unless Vitas is taken care of. Which means we must have Damian killed and then take his prisoner. I assume you're going to put me in charge of the torture of both to find out all that has, shall we say, conspired?"

It was Helius's turn to smile. "As a favor to you, of course."

"Of course," Tigellinus said, seemingly unaware that Helius was playing ironic. "I'll make the arrangements today for Damian's capture. It won't be easy. He doesn't go anywhere without guards. And there's that giant of his."

"Jerome," Helius said. "He's not a problem."

"No? It would take ten men to kill him."

"Leverage, my friend. You can manipulate anyone as long as you have the right leverage."

"Leverage."

"His family. My spy tells me that Jerome's family lives on Damian's estate. Why attack Jerome if you can get him to betray Damian by threatening his family?"

Tigellinus slapped Helius on the back with affection. "Sometimes you are a good man to work with."

In his thoughts, Helius had already moved past the logistics

of killing Damian. He was thinking about John's letter. Once
Hezron interpreted the strange Jewish code, he'd get John
of Patmos and interrogate him to see if his answers matched
Hezron's. Once satisfied that he understood the letter completely, he'd have Hezron and John tied in sacks and dumped
in the Tiber. As for the Jew girl, Helius supposed he could give
her to Chayim as reward for arranging the capture of Hezron. It
seemed that Chayim had somehow convinced the girl that he,
too, was a follower of the Christos. Chayim was turning out to
be very capable and would undoubtedly prove to be of good use
in the future.

But that didn't solve the far graver problem of Vitas. Without
that solved, everything else was meaningless. Helius was all too
aware that Nero's increasing lust for power was becoming more
of a danger. Time and again, as Nero's secretary and confidant,
Helius had rushed from one situation to another, using a mixture
of diplomacy and threats to find ways to satisfy Nero while limit-
ing the outrage among highly placed citizens. Until now, he'd been
able to juggle the dangers, fearful each time of failure and the possibility that Nero might desire to literally have his head to hold at
arm's length.

Until now . . .

"Back to my question," Helius said. "How are the mice going to
bell the cat?"

"Leverage, my friend." Tigellinus spoke with irony, mocking the
earlier words of Helius. "You can manipulate anyone as long as you
have the right leverage."

"Leverage."

Tigellinus nodded. "If we can't find Vitas, we find his wife.
Once we have her, we have leverage against Vitas. Leverage to stop
him from taking revenge. Leverage to find out from him who is
behind this."

"What good does her corpse do? In hindsight, it's a pity we
invited her to suicide, but we certainly can't bring her back to life."

"Are you sure she's dead?" Tigellinus asked. "After all, you were once certain that Vitas was a prisoner of Nero."

Helius blinked several times, suddenly understanding his companion's line of thought.

"Find her body," Tigellinus said, "and confirm she is dead. Or torture all of her slaves until you get the truth."

HORA QUINTA

WHEN FOUR OF THE crewmen came for John, Vitas neither stepped aside nor tried to stop them.

John neither protested nor tried to fight. He allowed the men to lead him to the cross. Allowed them to lift him and spread his arms along the crossbeam. Closed his eyes as they lashed his wrists, then his ankles to the wood.

Vitas watched John's stoic acceptance of his fate with a degree of admiration. And guilt. Yet, Vitas argued with himself, what could he do? Stepping forward to prevent John's death would be an act of suicide. He was a man weakened by a prison beating, weakened by fever. Alone on a ship, surrounded by hostile men who had all been toughened by a hazardous life on the seas. Not only would he give futile resistance, but if Vitas died, he would be unable to return to find and help Sophia and the child she carried in her womb. His own death, then, would harm the one person he loved most and the child he desperately wanted to raise.

Yet when the crew members moved the cross and the captive bound to it over to the side of the ship, Vitas moved toward them, trying to project a confidence and strength he did not feel. He passed over the tools and triangular wood frame left by the carpenter, who had interrupted his work to assist in binding John to the cross.

A few of the men looked over at Vitas. He stopped just past the carpenter's tools.

"Take that man off the cross," Vitas commanded the sailors. "Immediately."

✠ ✠ ✠

Damian was aware that he had his share of enemies in Rome and
equally aware that he deserved them.

A few years before, he had gambled recklessly and continuously
on the races, nearly always with poor judgment. To escape his creditors, he'd become a gladiator; only through the intervention of his
brother, Vitas, had he survived and begun life again outside the
arena. In the year since, he'd become a slave hunter, substituting
for his urge to gamble the excitement of the pursuit of escaped or
criminal slaves. His success in this area, like his failure in gambling,
had led to the accumulation of more enemies.

Because of those enemies, Damian prudently spent his public
life in the company of a retinue of large slaves and was discreet with
his private life. To continue his success as a slave hunter, however,
he needed to be accessible.

Damian had learned that one of the keys to pursuing other
humans was to rely on those who would betray them. He paid well
for information and often paid for tidbits that served no good in
the short term. Long term, however, that reputation among Rome's
lower strata of citizens meant that he had a surprisingly large web of
informants and spies. Slaves themselves proved to be of great value,
for they were often ignored by those they served and knew far
more about the happenings of the city than their masters generally
understood.

Since few informers could or would approach him as he walked
down the street with his slaves, Damian needed a place that guaran-
teed him safety yet allowed adequate privacy for those who did not
wish to be seen speaking with him.

For this reason he visited a public steam bath every day at the
same hour. Those who had information knew when and where to
give him that information.

More importantly, it was impossible for anyone to approach
Damian with a hidden weapon; his group of bodyguards waited

in an outer chamber, serving as a protective perimeter, and anyone who wanted to speak to Damian undressed in front of those slaves before entering the steam bath.

Inside the steam bath, Damian only needed the help of a single slave: Jerome. In bare-handed combat, Jerome was capable of crushing a man's skull by squeezing it between his massive hands. Damian literally trusted Jerome with his life every morning, during the regular hour he spent in the steam bath. It was a good system, and it contributed a great deal to Damian's success in finding slaves for bounty.

On this morning, then, Damian was not surprised when a man emerged from the fog of the steam to ask for a private conversation.

"Certainly," Damian said.

Jerome loomed over the slight man, who glanced upward nervously.

Damian was accustomed to this fearful reaction, even from men nearly as large as Jerome. "Unless you attack me," Damian said, "you are safe." He wiped sweat from his forehead. His hangover was receding, but far too slowly.

"And what you say will go no further than me," Damian continued, anticipating, from experience, the man's other objection. "Jerome had his tongue ripped out when he was a boy. And he can't write. Even if he wanted to tell anyone else about our conversation, it is impossible for him to communicate."

The slight man relaxed, but he kept his distance from Jerome. Not that distance would have done any good if Damian had unleashed the slave; the giant was far quicker than his bulk suggested.

"What is it you have for me?" Damian never asked for names. People preferred to remain anonymous in the steam room. The fog, too, made them feel safer. If Damian wanted more information about an informer, he would give a secret signal to Jerome that would be passed on to his guards outside, and someone would follow the informer to learn his identity.

"Quickly," Damian said because the man had hesitated. "If you have something worth telling, tell it. Or leave."

Damian dipped a ladle into a pail of water beside the bath and sipped from it, pretending indifference. But it was only pretense. He never knew when he'd learn something of value. Damian loved this game more than he had loved to gamble, which was the only reason he'd been able to conquer the self-destruction of that habit.

"I understand you pay immediately," the unknown man said.

"In the outer chamber, from one of my other slaves. But only if what you tell me is worth anything."

"I wouldn't be here otherwise." The man was uncomfortable, with only a towel draped across his midsection, but he seemed to gain confidence as they began the bartering process.

"I can decide that only after you've told me."

"After?"

"After." Damian's tone was firm. He sipped more water. Sweating, he had discovered, seemed to take the poisons out of his body, but the thirst of a hangover intensified in the steam bath.

"What's to prevent you from deciding not to pay?"

Damian was very familiar with this protest. "Nothing. Except then you would leave the steam bath telling everyone you know that I cheated you, and soon enough no one would trust me." Damian grinned. "And frankly, this is all about trust. Wouldn't you agree, Jerome?"

The large slave grunted.

"Tell me," Damian said, "what do you have of value for me?"

"When I tell you the name of my owner, you will recognize it."

"That's not of much value."

The little man gave Damian the name of a prominent senator.

"Wonderful," Damian said. "I have a name I know already."

"He's in massive debt."

"Always wagers on blue in the races," Damian said, maintaining a bored air. "Misplaced, expensive loyalty to a worthless color. Tell me something I don't know."

"He was at a party two nights ago," the informer said, naming the party's host—another prominent senator. "A party where some jewelry disappeared. Not only was the jewelry of great value, but the senator's wife was hysterical because of its sentimental value."

This *was* interesting. Damian had heard rumors about the theft. "And?"

"I can tell you where my owner hid it," the little man said.

"Indeed." In a flash, Damian saw how he would work it. A reward from one senator for returning the stolen jewelry, without, of course, telling where he had found it or how; this only enhanced Damian's reputation. And an additional payment from the other senator for not revealing to all of Rome that he had stooped to something as low as common theft. Damian would make a hundred times what he paid this nervous little slave for the information.

"Ten thousand sesterces," Damian said. "Half when you leave, and half if the jewelry is where you say it is."

"How will I collect? I can't let my owner know that—"

"Return here next week."

"If you decide not to pay then—"

"Listen." Damian lost his patience. "If I break my word, even once, then no one will ever trust me with information again. Do you think that's worth five thousand sesterces to me?"

"In a cistern," the little man said after a pause. "You'll find the jewels in the cistern near the place where his wife has set up her household gods."

This, Damian thought, was what made his business so worthwhile. Almost enough to make up for his hangover.

✦ ✦ ✦

"Did the suicide go as I ordered?"

A spasm twisted Helius's bowels. Had Nero already heard from another source that Vitas was alive? that perhaps Sophia, the wife of Vitas, had not killed herself according to the letter of invitation sent a few days earlier by Nero? Had Tigellinus been indiscreet in his search for the head of the man who had died in Vitas's place in the arena? Or had Tigellinus betrayed Helius in the short time since their meeting?

"Which suicide?" Helius asked, stalling.

Nero giggled. "It *is* difficult to keep them all straight, isn't it?"

"Our bookkeepers ensure that you get all proceeds, so it doesn't matter."

Nero nodded. "Did that suicide go as ordered?"

"I'll—" Helius hated himself for his fear of Nero— "I'll go to the estate today to ensure that your will was done."

The two of them sat at the edge of the lake within the royal garden, shaded by umbrellas held by slaves.

"Why travel so far?" Nero snorted. "Send a slave. I want you here with Sporus this morning."

Nero stared at the lake, watching a small boy fishing from a small boat. A boy Helius thought looked familiar in some way. Surely this boy was too young for Nero's tastes.

Helius knew better than to ask.

Nero turned his head and burned Helius with a frown. "Unless you expect trouble securing the estate." Nero's frown deepened. "Is that why you are going?"

Another spasm. Nero was so unpredictable that Helius was beginning to loathe audiences with him. How was that for irony? Helius had spent years maneuvering to be in this very position.

"The estate is yours," Helius said. This, too, was true. "I expect no trouble."

"Trouble?" Nero was still frowning. "Surely everyone believes the accusation against Antonia. You're the one who assured me that the charge of attempted rebellion would be sufficient cause."

Sudden relief made Helius light-headed. It *was* difficult to keep all the suicides straight. Nero had been speaking not of Sophia but of Claudia Antonia, daughter of the previous emperor, Claudius, who had adopted Nero and made it possible for Nero to inherit the empire.

"Your public adores you," Helius said. "The mobs were out-
raged that she would betray you."

This was a lie. The mob knew the truth and was gossiping
already. Because Nero had kicked his previous wife, Poppaea, to
death, Antonia had sensibly refused to take her place as Nero's
wife. While Antonia might have expected Nero to want her dead
for spurning him, she'd believed her position as daughter of the
previous emperor would protect her. She'd been wrong, of course.
A slave had sent her an invitation to suicide on the same afternoon
that Sophia had received hers.

"Just as well Antonia didn't want to marry," Nero said, smiling again and resuming his gaze on the boy fishing from the boat.
"I would have had to divorce her for Sporus."

Were Nero not beside him, Helius would have found the scene
idyllic. The gardens were spectacular with beauty; the sun was
bright but not too hot; the sky was clear and the lake placid. But
beside Nero, Helius could not relax. Ever.

"And the arrangements for Sporus?" Nero asked.

"Exactly as you requested. The doctors will wait for us to arrive."

"Tell me again," Nero said. "Tell me that it will not endanger
the boy's life. I do adore him."

"He's a strong boy," Helius said. "The doctors have assured me
there will be no complications."

"Excellent," Nero said. "Now, tell me the news I don't want
to hear."

✝ ✝ ✝

Five of the ship's crew faced Vitas. Three others held the cross, balancing it on the edge of the ship's railing. One quick shove, and it
would fall into the water.

"Back to your sickbed," snarled the largest of the crew members.
He was built like a bear, with dark, greasy hair and yellowed teeth.

Vitas glanced at the cross, where John was lashed securely. John's
eyes were closed, his face serene. Who was this man?

"What you are doing is murder," Vitas said. The swaying of the ship made it difficult to keep his balance in his weakened state. "If you drown him, I'll see you are all sent to the arena."

The leader of the crew grinned widely when Vitas staggered, suggesting he knew how little strength Vitas had. "So you've brought an army aboard and not a miserable old slave?"

"Rome enforces its laws," Vitas answered. "There is no place in the world for this ship to land that doesn't have Roman law and the army to back it."

"Shut your mouth," another said. "If we don't make a sacrifice, this ship will never make it to land."

There were nods and grunts of agreement. Although this was a small group of men, it was rapidly forming the mentality of a mob.

"The captain is aware of this?" Vitas asked.

"We gave the captain a choice," the first said. He picked up a short piece of lumber and slapped it against his opposite palm. "We told him one of you would pay the price for making us set sail without a sacrifice or omen. He gave us your slave."

The large man advanced on Vitas. His grin became a snarl as he raised the improvised club. "We can always put you on the cross instead."

Vitas was a former soldier, a former general, a man who had faced his share of street fights in his younger days. His mouth was dry, his body vibrant with adrenaline. He took a step backward, remembering that there was a knife among the tools on the deck.

He squatted without removing his eyes from the man with the stick. A quick glance down showed him the knife. He grabbed it, stood, and marched forward, knowing that offensive tactics were the most effective move against bullies who expected their opponents to show fear.

The large man stopped, uncertainty flickering across his face.

"Set the cross down," Vitas commanded. If he could bluff their leader into delaying an attack, perhaps the others would listen. "I'll talk with the captain myself."

"Go ahead," came a voice from behind him.

Vitas half turned. He wanted to keep the crew leader in the corner of his vision.

"I'm the captain," the voice continued. "Drop the knife. Speak to me now."

The captain, a large man too, spoke with an accent that clearly placed him from Sicily. Beneath sparse dark hair, he had a narrow face with the surprising juxtaposition of a flattened nose, obviously broken more than once, obviously healed badly.

"You will let your men commit murder?" Vitas said. He lowered the knife to his side but did not drop it. "Knowing the Roman court holds a captain responsible for the actions of his crew?"

The captain smiled, his arms crossed, posing for his crewmen. "Tell me, my friend. Who arranged for you to be on this ship?"

Vitas did not answer because he could not answer. He did not know who had arranged for his escape from the amphitheater. Or why. The answer was in the scroll, which perhaps lay somewhere in the captain's own quarters.

"Who arranged for you to be on this ship?" the captain repeated.

This was a question Vitas wanted answered far more badly than the captain did. He glanced to his left at the crew member with the stick. The large man had dropped the stick to his side, seemingly no longer a threat.

"You should know," Vitas said. He wished he could think more clearly. He felt dizzy, and his thirst made it difficult to concentrate, but it seemed too dangerous to reveal that he could not answer who had placed him on the ship to escape Rome. He continued his attempt at a bluff. "And you'll have to answer for the actions of your crew."

"I'll have to answer for your safety," the captain said. "If my crew is happy, you'll reach Alexandria. That's far more important than the life of a Christian whose presence aboard my ship puts me at the risk of Nero's wrath."

The captain nodded at the man with the stick. "Hit this Roman.

Not hard enough to seriously hurt him. But enough to keep him
from stopping you."

The movement from Vitas's left was a blur. The blow across his
left thigh, just above his knee, was a crack of agony that sent him
sprawling across the deck.

Vitas rolled twice, losing the knife and tumbling to the side
of the ship. He bit back a groan and tried to struggle to his feet.
He made it upright, balancing on one leg. The other was numb.
The bone felt shattered, but Vitas knew better. He'd broken
bones before.

"No," Vitas said as the men moved the cross closer to the side
of the ship.

The captain merely shrugged at Vitas and winked.

Before Vitas could take a step, the captain nodded at the men
holding the cross balanced across the railing. They lifted the end
up and over.

An instant later, the cross splashed into the water.

Vitas clutched the rail and looked downward.

The cross had landed with John beneath it, and it bobbed in the
ship's wake. It receded from the ship with the man bound, trapped
facedown in the water.

✝ ✝ ✝

"I am Crito," a disembodied voice said from the steam. "I am here
about the Jew from Patmos."

This was barely moments after the little man from the senator
with gambling debts had stepped outside.

"The one named John, son of Zebedee."

Damian, who had hunched forward for an Ethiopian slave
to scrape his back with a bronze strigil, eased upright again. The
Ethiopian immediately stepped away and disappeared. Over the
previous months, this slave had learned quickly to read Damian's
body language for signals that indicated he wanted privacy. Jerome,
of course, stayed.

"Why should I care about your name?" Damian put boredom into his voice. "And why should I care about a Jew from Patmos?"

Jerome stood and loomed over a man who in other circumstances would have appeared large.

Jerome's bulk, however, did not appear to deter the visitor. Although it was difficult to make out his features in the steam, his appearance suggested a young street thug. Dark, well-groomed hair. Solid muscles. The posed stance of a man who believed himself invincible and wanted the world to know it.

"This Jew," Crito continued. "You'll pay to know where he's gone."

It was posed as a statement. Damian wasn't surprised. Senators and lawyers and other notable citizens walked down the streets surrounded by clients and did business in courtyards and near public fountains, relying on receiving and giving favors. Damian did the same, except in this public bathhouse, receiving information as favors and giving money in return. It would be strange if the man in front of him didn't expect money.

"Perhaps a few days ago," Damian agreed. He'd put word out many days earlier, and by now it was common knowledge in the circles that he traveled among the lower-class residents of Rome. "But no longer."

"He was kidnapped. Don't you find that of interest?"

Damian shifted to speak to Jerome and contemptuously snapped off a common quip, emphasizing it with the use of formal grammar. *"Malleum sapientiorem vidi excusso manubrio." I've seen hammers with the handles off more clever than him.*

As Damian expected, Crito's posture immediately changed to a stiffened stance of threat.

"Go away," Damian said in a tired voice. "Whatever you might tell me is old and secondhand and utterly wrong."

A rumor had reached this man already. Someone had seen Damian and Jerome force a man into the litter they had used to take him from the market. Others had known Damian was looking for John. Whispers had spread and distorted the matter more, until

now the thug didn't even know that it had been Damian doing
the kidnapping.

"Old information?" Crito's fingers were still clenched because
of Damian's insult. "This happened only two days ago. Just before
sunset."

"Old," Damian repeated. "Secondhand. Wrong. Go away."

"Secondhand? Wrong? I was there."

"Liar," Damian said. If the man had been there, he would have
seen Damian. That fact alone would have kept him from approaching Damian with obviously false information. "Go away."

"I am not a liar!" Crito took a step toward Damian.

It did not appear that Jerome had moved, but suddenly Crito
was off his feet and gurgling for air. Jerome had spun him and
wrapped a forearm around his throat. The man kicked but it was
futile. Jerome didn't even grunt with effort as he held the man off
the tiles of the steam room.

"*Verbera eum,*" Damian told Jerome. *Thrash him.*

Damian was within his rights to order a different fate for the
informer: "*Neca eum*"—*kill him.* This man had tried to attack a citizen. No jury would find fault if Damian's bodyguard was overzealous.

Yet a dead man would not be able to return to the streets and
let it be known that Damian would not tolerate those who tried
to play him for a fool. Damian would take no joy in the beating; neither would Jerome. But this was the Roman way: lavishly
reward loyalty, and punish disobedience with extreme severity.
Nothing between.

"*Verbera eum,*" Damian repeated.

Without releasing his forearm from the man's throat, Jerome
used his other fist to smash the sides of the man's ribs.

Damian winced at the sound of those dull thuds, glad that the
steam hid his reaction. Romans were not supposed to be queasy
about violence. But Damian's lifestyle had led him to his share of
beatings at the hands of angry gamblers, and he knew too well the
pain that Jerome was inflicting on this man.

"He's on a ship!" Crito managed to gasp.

Damian wasn't sure if he heard correctly. "Jerome!" he barked.

Jerome stopped the beating.

"Let the man speak." Damian addressed the street thug. "What did you say?"

"He's on a ship," Crito groaned. "I kidnapped him and put him on a ship."

"*You* kidnapped him?" This was so unexpected that Damian thought there would be no harm in listening. He could order Jerome to resume the beating at any time.

"Not alone. Four of us kidnapped the Jew."

"Tell me more," Damian said. Cautiously. If this was true, then who had Damian captured?

"Four of us," the man repeated, his words hardly more than painful gasps. "Hired to kidnap a man and take him to a ship. No questions asked."

The man gestured at the bench beside Damian, a silent request for permission.

Damian nodded absently, trying to make sense of the man's statement. "You say you kidnapped John."

Crito sat, slowly and gingerly. "I didn't know then that he was the Jew you are looking for. But as we threw a hood over his head, he called out to the man beside him."

"Where were you?"

"In an alley."

"Where?"

"Via Sacra. Just outside the center of Rome."

Exactly where Damian had kidnapped the man who refused to speak. Damian began to tingle with anticipation, feeling the sense of the hunt. If the man Damian had captured truly was not John, it might explain his determined silence.

"And what did the Jew say to his companion?" Damian asked, not hinting that he was prepared to believe this man to be telling a true story.

"'Ruso, are you there? Have they hurt you?' Those were the Jew's exact words."

Damian snorted. "Based on that, you come to me asking for money?"

Some of the young man's cockiness returned. "Four of us were hired. I had a—"

"Who hired you?"

"A slave."

"You agreed to kidnap a man at the request of a slave."

"No, I agreed because of the money."

"How did you know he was a slave?"

"The brand on his forehead."

"Did he give you his name?"

"No."

"Unlikely, then, that you know the name of his owner."

"I do know it," Crito said. "I followed him back to his owner because I thought there might be more money in it later. That's what you will pay me for. And the rest of what I know."

"Don't guess at my intentions," Damian snapped.

"The slave belongs to a senator. The same man with the Jew when he was kidnapped." Crito paused, as if sensing victory. "In other words, the senator named Ruso paid us to kidnap his companion. How much will you pay me for the rest of my story?"

✠ ✠ ✠

"Now tell me the news I don't want to hear."

Helius fought another stab of internal pain. With that statement, had Nero been referring to the fact that Vitas had escaped? This was the difficulty with a guilty conscience. Every moment with Nero was like walking a knife's edge.

Fortunately, Nero continued speaking, taking any ambiguity out of his remark. "But don't bother me with tedious details. Just give me the report about Judea, and then we can attend to Crispinus."

Crispinus. That's why the boy in the boat had seemed familiar.

Rufrius Crispinus was Poppaea's stepson, perhaps the closest to an heir that Nero had. He was eight years old, and named after his father, a famous knight who had helped avert an assassination plot against Claudius, the previous emperor.

"Judea," Helius repeated, gathering his thoughts. Helius stared out at the boy fishing and pretended a degree of composure. The knowledge that Vitas was still alive had made him too jumpy. He'd forgotten a simple thing like Nero's earlier request for news about the trouble the Jews were causing in the province.

"What I have was sent by courier from Cestius," Helius said, wondering if he needed to remind Nero that Cestius was procurator of Syria. The emperor rarely showed interest in the matters of the provinces, and when revolts began, he took it as a personal insult that he had to be bothered with the particulars.

"Where the report comes from is a tedious detail." Nero was focused on Crispinus. "Is there danger of war? That's all I want to know."

"For a few weeks, it appeared to have been averted." While Helius knew he'd have to give Nero the bad news, he dreaded doing so. Nero was in a good mood now, and if he lost his temper, there was no telling what might happen in the next hours.

"*Appeared?* That's tedious. I don't want what it appears to be. Is there danger of war against Rome?"

"In May, as you know, Florus was forced out of Jerusalem after a few days of riots." Gessius Florus was the Roman procurator in Judea. His cruelty was well-known, and the riots had been justi-fied, Helius knew. Vitas had returned from Jerusalem with strong accusations against Florus, but Helius and Tigellinus had buried the report and arranged for Vitas to be executed before it could reach Nero.

"How can I make this clear?" Nero's voice became higher pitched with the beginning of irritation. "I don't want details. Is there danger of war?"

Helius knew he could not procrastinate longer. "It has worsened.

There is danger of war. Agrippa and Bernice are appealing to the people to maintain peace."

Helius paused to gauge Nero's reaction. To see if he needed to tell Nero more, and to guess at the least offensive way to present the bad news.

The report from Gaius Cestius Gallus, procurator of Syria, had been thorough. In June, Cestius had investigated the riots of May, and the Jews had insisted on the removal of Florus as procurator of Judea. When Cestius delayed and Florus sent reports accusing the Jews of instigating the trouble, riots began again. Agrippa, king of the Jews, and his sister, Bernice, refused to send ambassadors to Nero, and the threat of riots returned.

"The Jews are nothing but trouble," Nero said with a sigh. "Poppaea was a fool to support their cause. Even so, if she were alive, I suppose I would grant her wishes."

Helius marveled at this man. Poppaea was dead because Nero had lost his temper and kicked her to death, then spent months in mourning and remorse and was now on the verge of marrying a boy simply because he looked like her. It was this unpredictability, combined with his absolute power and the delusion that he was a god, that made Nero so dangerous.

"And now?" Helius asked, still thinking about Judea.

"Now I hear rumors that her stepson plays war games, pretending to be a general." Nero spoke to himself, making it obvious his thoughts were still on Poppaea. "And also pretending to be an emperor. Imagine that. Only eight years old and posing as emperor."

Helius looked again at Rufrius Crispinus. He was only a little boy in a boat, innocently delighting in a sunny day on the water. A boy who could never have understood why he, of all eight-year-olds in the world, should have never played the types of games that any other child that age could play without danger.

"My father died when I was three," Nero said softly.

Helius knew that. Nero mentioned it often.

"I inherited one-third of his estate," Nero continued, still staring at the boy in the boat. "I should have had a wonderful childhood, even with the loss of my father. But Caligula took everything and banished my mother. Do you have any idea what my childhood was like? Poverty. No real family."

Helius did, of course. Because Nero told him often enough. And because Helius had had a similar childhood.

"The world is not fair," Nero told Helius. "Not fair at all. That is the greatest lesson I learned. Why then should children born after me enjoy what I could not? Why shouldn't they learn that lesson too?"

"The Jewish war," Helius prompted. He had more than a suspicion of why Nero had arranged for Crispinus to be invited to fish on the lake. Helius wanted to deliver his report and get as far away from the lake as possible.

"I expect Cestius will handle Judea," Nero said. "So don't inconvenience me with anything about the Jews unless matters get out of hand. I don't want my trip to Greece spoiled."

"Of course," Helius said. "Is there anything else?"

"When I give the order, the boy's slaves will drown him," Nero said, speaking with dreamy satisfaction. "It should be amusing, as I've been told they love him like a son and he in turn loves them."

Unspoken was the fact that the boy had never shown enough affection for Nero. *But then,* Helius thought, *children have good instincts. Just not the power to do anything about them.*

"Do you want to watch him die?" Nero asked. His eyes gleamed with an excitement that Helius recognized all too well.

Helius had to ask himself if it would seem like a betrayal if he declined the offer. Or a moral judgement against Nero, something the emperor detested. The gods, he often said, were above morals.

"Of course you do," Nero told Helius, still watching the little boy.

Yes, Helius told himself, this was a test of loyalty. Nero knew that Helius had a softness for children. Nero wanted to show he had as much power over Helius as he did over the boy he was about to have drowned.

"Look at that," Nero said. "He's caught something."

The boy had turned to shout to his slaves with glee, holding a tiny fish aloft as if it were a monster.

"I think now is the perfect time," Nero said. "Don't you?"

"Of course," Helius said. What choice did he have? "The perfect time."

Nero snapped his fingers.

The boy's slaves, two of them, began to wade out toward the boat.

✛ ✛ ✛

The cross receded from the ship.

With John trapped beneath it.

On the deck, Vitas took the step necessary to scoop up the knife he had dropped.

"Now you intend to punish us yourself?" The captain laughed. He spoke to his crew as Vitas remained in a crouch. "Unless he's stupid enough to try something with that weapon, ignore him, men. He can sulk all the way to Alexandria."

At Vitas's feet was the half-finished framework of some spare masting, a triangle of wood barely taller than a man.

He hoped it was enough.

Vitas ignored the stabbing pain in his left leg and grunted as he hoisted the frame upright.

"What now, fool?" the captain asked. "A dancing partner?"

The question, in a way, was appropriate. Vitas was indeed forced to struggle with the framework as if it were a clumsy dancer. He hoped none of the crew could guess his intentions.

He thrust his left arm into the frame and bent the arm to cradle it, leaving his right hand still free with the knife.

Vitas lurched backward, dragging the frame. "Insanity," he muttered to himself. "Utter insanity."

He knew better, however. It wasn't insanity but calculated anger. And a calculated gamble.

One more lurch and he felt the railing in the small of his back. With a quick, hard heave of his left arm and upper body, the wood frame was in the air. He let the momentum of it fall backward and pushed off with his feet.

There was a startled shout from the captain. But it was too late. Vitas was already in the air, falling toward the water, still clutching the frame with his left arm.

The impact against the water nearly knocked him loose from the frame. That would have been his death. Vitas, no different from most sailors, could not swim. He needed the frame to keep him afloat. Because his left arm was curled around one side of the frame's lumber, the momentum of his fall seemed to pull that arm loose from its socket. His arm slipped, and he clawed with his other arm to pull his head up and out of the water.

For a few seconds that seemed to drag on like minutes of terror, it seemed he would lose the frame. Or the knife in his right hand. But finally, he brought his upper body to the surface. The frame was nearly submerged by his weight, but it was enough to keep him afloat.

Vitas ignored the shouts of the crew at the ship's railing. He blinked against the sting of salt water in his eyes and got his bearings.

The floating cross was maybe a half-length of the ship away from him.

Too far?

Vitas kicked, knowing each passing heartbeat took the man trapped beneath the cross that much closer to death by drowning.

The frame was unwieldy, but Vitas fought it with desperation. The smoothness of the water inside the ship's wake made his struggle easier. He kicked and splashed, his lungs heaving, fueled by the imagination of the horror that John faced beneath the cross.

When he finally reached the cross, he knew that only half the battle was finished. Vitas frantically cut at the top of the rope binding one of John's arms. It seemed to take far too long to slice through each strand. He shouted with savage satisfaction when the last of the rope finally snapped.

Still, death remained too much of a possibility for both of them.

Vitas would have to briefly push away from the frame that kept him afloat.

He snapped his teeth on the blade of the knife, freeing his right hand. He released the frame, pulled himself onto the massive beams of the cross, then reached under.

There!

The man's free arm! The man's wrist! Vitas grabbed John's hand. Movement!

Fingers clutched him.

John was still alive!

Vitas pulled, uncaring of how much pressure he placed on the arm that was still bound to the other side of the cross.

He reeled upward on John's arm until the man's head emerged from the water. John was bent and crooked, barely able to find the angle that allowed him to keep his nose and mouth above the surface. He gasped and sputtered, his fingers an iron grip on the hand of Vitas.

It would still be tricky.

Vitas sprawled belly down on the cross, maintaining precarious balance. If he slid off the slippery wood now, both would drown.

Vitas used his feet and knees to cling to the cross, as if it were a horse, not a thick beam of wood. As John clutched Vitas's left arm and fought to keep his face above the water, Vitas reached for the knife in his mouth and grabbed the handle with his right hand.

The bobbing of the cross made it even more difficult.

Vitas managed to grab the handle of the knife. He began sawing at the rope that held John's other arm to the beam.

Again, that satisfying snap when the final strands released.

Except suddenly, John no longer had a grip on Vitas's left hand. The man had disappeared.

Vitas, exhausted, let his own head fall onto the beam.

Then John resurfaced. His feet were still bound to the bottom of the cross, but he had found a way to twist and jackknife his body so that now his head and shoulders were above the water again.

John used both arms to clutch the beam. His upper body swelled each time he drew in a great lungful of air.

Vitas relaxed, knowing he could take his time to work downward to the last of the ropes that held John's legs in place. Totally exhausted, he closed his eyes and rested his head against the wet beam.

"Insanity," Vitas muttered again. "Utter insanity."

HORA SEXTA

THE WOMAN IN FRONT of Damian pushed aside the shoulder of her tunic, exposing pale white skin until she stopped tantalizingly short of indecency.

"The rest is yours to reveal," she whispered, leaning toward him. "After all, what's the harm in combining pleasure with business?"

The time in the steam room had invigorated Damian. Barely a minute earlier, he and his entourage of slaves had stepped outside the building into the cacophony of the marketplace.

The woman in front of him now had been waiting inside an expensive litter carried on the shoulders of four slaves, with curtains open. He had accepted the invitation to join her inside, on the condition that the litter remain in place. Now, with the extended poles still resting on the shoulders of the slaves, they were both suspended in the particular hush and dimness that came with the thick drapes closed.

She had an open amphora on the cushion beside her—the pottery vessel was a slim cylinder with handles at the top and a rounded rim—and he could smell the wine inside it. Mixed with her perfume and the sight of her beauty, it was indeed a seductive setting.

Instead of responding to her invitation, Damian pulled the tunic back over her shoulder to cover her skin. The litter was large by most standards, but the cushions had been arranged in such a manner that their knees touched.

She pouted. "Damian, your reputation with the women led me

to expect something a little bolder." She exposed her shoulder again. "Certainly you like what you see."

What he saw was a woman named Alypia, the recent widow of Lucius Bellator. A wealthy old man who administrated taxes in Jerusalem, Lucius had been her third husband, just as elderly as the two before. He'd been butchered in the riots of that city in May, and she'd immediately returned to Rome.

Alypia was a young woman. She wore a blonde wig made from the hair of slaves from Gaul, and it was woven elaborately on a wire frame and secured on top of her head with her natural hair, a style matching the latest fashion rage in Rome. Her eyes appeared large and innocently wide, an illusion that Damian was experienced enough with women to know was simply an effect of artfully applied makeup. Yet she did not need the help of her richly colored silk tunic or the expensive perfume or the delicate makeup to seem beautiful. The lines of her face and body were a mold of natural sensuousness that she used like a beacon to draw men.

Damian carefully kept his eyes on hers. "I will not betray the man who saved my life. The same man for whom you declared your undying love." Alypia's affair with the ex-gladiator Maglorius was well-known.

"Maglorius murdered my husband and forced me to flee Jerusalem."

"So you say. I'd prefer to hear it from him. When I do, I will believe it."

"Who would have thought that you actually *do* have principles?" Alypia said, smiling, lowering her tunic farther. "Or do you?"

"You might be the only person in Rome to accuse me of having principles," Damian said. It took great effort to focus on her face. Damian knew well his weaknesses and was already tempted to his breaking point. She was a siren, and any glance below her face would be like unplugging his ears. "I appreciate your efforts, however."

"Efforts."

"I will not be hired to travel to Jerusalem for you." Damian gestured at her and the rich interior of the litter. "While I appreciate the offer of a different currency, I'm still not interested in leaving Rome."

"A different currency?"

"One much older than money."

"Not interested, yet you stepped inside this litter," she said, pulling up her tunic and covering herself. "I think you were curious to see what I would offer."

Damian grunted.

"Did you get your cheap satisfaction?" she asked.

"Cheap satisfaction?"

"I've made no secret that I find you attractive. You stepped inside this private litter because you wondered if I would attempt to seduce you and how far I would go to do it. To me, that is a man interested in cheap satisfaction."

Damian thought about it, realized she was right. Then grinned. "More like cheap virtue. It's not often I get to feel as if I actually have any principles."

"Then I'll take satisfaction that you've used me for something."

"And I'll take satisfaction in leaving you satisfied."

"Like all your other women."

"Of course," he said. He reached for the curtain to leave.

"I had more in mind than pleasure with you," Alypia quickly said. "I also came here to tell you that I've booked passage for you on a ship leaving for Caesarea tomorrow afternoon."

"I admire your persistence. But you can find someone else to search Jerusalem for you."

"I'll double what I've offered you." She smiled. "Money. Not the other currency."

"Remarkable that you would love your stepchildren so much."

"If that means no, I'll double it again. And you don't have to escort them all the way back to Rome. Deliver them to Florus. He'll look after them for me."

"Double? For that price, you could hire ten men to find them for you."

"But you're the best. You would succeed where those ten men might fail." Her voice became pleading. "Don't think of me. Think of the children. Jerusalem has been torn apart by riots. If they're still alive, they need help."

"You brought Maglorius into your household as a bodyguard," Damian said. "He'll protect them."

"The way he protected Lucius? I was there. I saw him kill my husband."

"As *you* said."

"You don't trust me."

Damian laughed. "Don't be insulted. I trust no one."

"Except Maglorius."

Except Maglorius. And my brother, Vitas, Damian thought. Only to feel the next thought hit him like one of Jerome's fists. *My brother is dead.*

The moments in the litter had been enjoyable, but not for any of the reasons Alypia might take pride in. In this small, private world, Damian had temporarily been away from the reality of the death of his brother. Until this reminder.

He still couldn't reconcile himself to that fact. In his mind, Vitas was alive and laughing, sitting in the courtyard only a few mornings ago, introducing him to his wife, Sophia, telling him that they were expecting a child. *How can Vitas and Sophia now both be dead?*

Alypia must have caught the change in his mood. Her voice lost its teasing quality. "Consider my offer, at least. You have until tomorrow afternoon before the ship leaves."

"I have no reason to go to Judea," Damian said. He flung open the curtains, almost savagely.

Directly in front of the opening to the litter was one of his slaves named Castinus. The movement of the curtains appeared to startle him.

"Didn't I tell you to immediately go back to the estate?" Damian's voice was sharp. His dark mood had returned.

"To release the captive." Castinus nodded and smiled obsequiously. His greasy hair was cropped as if someone had placed a bowl over his head and clipped any hair that stuck out. Castinus had an irritating habit of blinking both eyes when he smiled. "But I wanted to be clear on the rest of your instructions. It was . . . complicated."

"Have him released, then follow him yourself. Discreetly. Find out where he goes and immediately return to my estate. How can that be complicated?"

Castinus bowed his head.

"Run!" Damian barked.

Castinus trotted away through the market.

At least, Damian told himself, he could use the hunt for John, son of Zebedee as a distraction. And so much the better if it led him to anything he could use against Helius.

✦ ✦ ✦

"Who are these people?" Sporus whispered to Nero. They walked side by side through an arch into one of the inner courtyards of the palace.

Helius followed behind them. His mind was still filled with images of young Rufrius Crispinus flailing at his slaves as they forced him beneath the water, the slaves themselves in obvious anguish. The boy had been innocent, no threat to Helius. Sporus, on the other hand, was adored by Nero, and Helius would have no compunction about watching Sporus drown.

"Are they senators?" Sporus said when Nero didn't answer.

Two middle-aged men turned from their conversation with each other and straightened to attention in the presence of Nero.

Helius seized on the chance to take his mind off the death of Crispinus and smiled at the stupidity of Sporus. *Senators!*

This would be too good in the retelling. The poor boy child actually thought he was important enough that Nero was taking

him to an audience with senators. So important that he didn't
even notice that neither man wore a senatorial toga, something
that every senator would do for a private meeting with Nero.

Senators indeed! No, they were far lower than senators in social
status, and their dress reflected it. Poor Sporus was too unobservant
to judge people by appearance.

"Doctors," Nero answered Sporus. Nero wobbled slightly.
He'd already indulged in wine since watching the drowning of
the stepson of the wife he had murdered. Now, for Nero, this was
just another event in the day. Nero patted Sporus on the shoulder.
"They are the best in all the world. There's nothing to fear."

Helius knew well the tone of Nero's voice. It was exuberant
anticipation, dulled by wine. He was always like this before any
event that would indulge an outrageous whim.

"Doctors?" Sporus said. "You mean there *is* something to fear?
You wouldn't say that unless—" He gasped. "Are you ill?"

Helius choked back a laugh. This was wonderful! Almost worth
all the worries he faced. The boy child might be pretty, but he
wasn't that intelligent.

"These doctors are here for you," Nero said, patting Sporus again.
"But *I'm* not ill."

Helius coughed to hide a snort. Too good! Simply too good!
When would the child finally comprehend what was happening?

Nero held the elbow of Sporus. Helius could not tell if Nero did
it to guide the boy or because Nero needed support as he walked.
The result, however, was the same. Nero and Sporus neared the
doctors, with Helius a few discreet paces behind.

Nero curled his arm around Sporus's waist and stopped in front
of them.

"Isn't Sporus beautiful?" Nero asked the doctors.

Each nodded. If they felt distaste at the sight of a man sweating
from alcohol pawing at a beautiful boy, they did a good job of hiding it. Of course, their lives depended on keeping Nero happy.

Nero patted Sporus on the cheek. "Remember," he said, "you are doing this for me."

"You haven't told me what it is. You told me this was a surprise. What is it?"

"We're getting married," Nero said. "You will be a goddess."

"Goddess?" Sporus echoed.

Helius was in near ecstasy. He'd told Nero he would supervise the doctors, but that was only an excuse. The moment he'd been waiting for was so near, the delicious moment of comprehension and horror as Sporus realized the price he would pay to be Nero's pet.

"I am a god," Nero explained. "When you marry me, you will be a goddess. Worshiped by all of the empire, just as Poppaea was until . . ." Nero frowned, obviously realizing he should not complete the sentence.

But Helius would remember and whisper it later to Sporus. *Just as Poppaea was . . . until Nero kicked her to death. Yes, Sporus, Nero kicked her to death. In the last stages of her pregnancy, kicked her to death in a drunken rage after losing too much money at the races.*

Too delicious!

"I can't become a goddess," Sporus said. "I'm not a woman and—"

"Shhh," Nero told him, placing a finger against the boy's lips. "That's why we have the best doctors in Rome."

Sporus still didn't understand.

Helius took the boy's elbow and guided him away from Nero. "I'll see that it is done properly," he promised Nero.

Nero waved at them both and then retraced his steps out of the courtyard.

"Do you have rope?" Helius asked the doctors.

"Rope?" the first one, a gray-haired man with a stoop in his shoulders, said.

"He's young and strong and will undoubtedly resist," Helius said. "I expect it will be best if we tie his arms and legs to immovable posts."

"Helius?" There was obvious fear in the boy's voice. "What did Nero mean? Why did he leave?"

Helius stroked the boy's face and watched his eyes closely, knowing his words would land like a blow. "He left because he loves you too much to watch. And he means that you are about to be castrated."

✛ ✛ ✛

"I'm going to tell you my name," the ship's captain told Vitas. "But I don't want to know yours. You're enough danger to me as it is."

Vitas had no intention of giving his identity anyway. If Nero knew he was alive, Sophia would die.

"I'm Atronius Pavo," the ship's captain continued. "And you should know that on this ship's previous voyage, I drowned a Jew in pig's blood."

Each of the two sat on a short, three-legged stool in the captain's quarters. It was a square room centered beneath the deck, a location that gave it the best stability on the ship. There was a straw bed raised above the floor at the back; beneath this bed was a chamber pot. On the side, a table had been built out from the wall, and sea charts were unrolled across it, held down by lead weights on each side.

Vitas had been scrutinizing the small room carefully, hoping for a glimpse of the scroll that he'd lost during his fever. The only light, however, came from an oil lamp. It threw the captain's shadow against one wall, casting an odd gleam on the oily skin of the man's face.

"I only tell you this story," Pavo continued, "because I want you to truly understand what kind of man I am."

A rat rustled in the straw of the bed. The captain ignored it. He pointed to his once-broken nose and touched it lightly with the tip of his forefinger.

"The Jew was a brute," Pavo said. "We'd been in a storm for

two days, and he believed I'd made the wrong decision by pulling anchor to run ahead of it. I had the charts that told me we had open seas. He thought we would run aground."

The captain pushed his nose sideways. He grinned at the sound of a crack. "I can't stop a sailor from having opinions that differ from mine. But when he's gathered the crew on the deck to share those opinions, that's another matter."

A push of the nose in the opposite direction. Another crack of cartilage. Another near-demented grin. "That Jew was responsible for this. You see, the crew ignored my orders to punish him. That left me two choices. Either fight him myself, or lose command of the ship. It wasn't even a gamble. Losing to him would have been no worse than not fighting at all."

The grin ceased. Pavo spoke grimly. "The gods favored me. He'd busted my face with a stave and was ready to finish me off when a wave almost capsized us. He slipped on the deck. I found my feet first. There wasn't much left of his face when I finished working him over with the same stave he'd used on mine. But I left him alive." The captain held up his hand, making it obvious he was pausing his story. "You don't find this interesting?"

Vitas snapped his eyes away from his search of the cabin and back to the captain. "I've seen men fight other men."

"I had him bound," Pavo said. "Still alive, but bound. I waited until the storm had passed and all of the crew knew I'd made the right decision by pulling anchor. Then I slit a pig's throat and filled a bucket with its blood. You do know that Jews are defiled by pigs, don't you?"

Vitas said nothing. After years in Nero's inner circle, there was nothing about any other man's savagery that could impress or intimidate him.

"I sat on that Jew and held his head in the blood until he drowned," the captain said, grinning. "And let me tell you, until he died, his body kicked and bucked so hard I could barely keep my balance. A wild mule would have been an easier ride."

If he expected Vitas to grin in return at what was obviously a well-worn punch line to an often-told story, he was disappointed.

"As a Roman citizen," Pavo continued, "I fully understand our ways of ruling the provinces. Reward those who obey. Destroy without mercy those who defy. The crew saw me drown that Jew, and I knew it taught them something they would not forget."

The captain studied Vitas, looking for any reaction. Again he was disappointed. "Tell me why you dove overboard for the Jew with you," Pavo said.

"It was wrong to sacrifice him."

"And you would sacrifice yourself, too?" Pavo stared hard at Vitas. Vitas stared back.

"No, you knew I could not let you die," Pavo said. "That's why you present a problem for me. The crew won't forget that it looks like I serve you."

"Set ashore at Messana," Vitas said. "I'll leave the ship."

"You defied me in front of my crew. Forced me to turn the ship around to pull you and that Jew from the waters. How can they not wonder who has the greatest authority on my own ship?"

"Set ashore at Messana."

"There is the truth, of course. That I fear not you or your authority, but that of some of the most powerful men in Rome. Yet I have my warning from them. To even hint at their involvement in your presence aboard my ship would mean my death and the death of my family."

Vitas tried to maintain an appearance of disinterest. He had no idea of who had arranged to pluck him from the prison cell and put him on this ship. Nor why. It seemed, however, foolhardy to admit this to the captain until he knew more. The scroll. He needed the scroll that he'd been given in the prison by the stranger. Surely the scroll held the answers.

"Set ashore at Messana," Vitas said. "I won't be a problem for you off the ship."

"So that not only do I fail to deliver you to Alexandria, but my crew thinks I'm too afraid of you to keep you on board?" Pavo snorted. "Why not ask me to tie lead weights to my ankles and jump into the sea?"

Pavo stood. Indeed, he was a large man.

Vitas stood too. Not quite as tall. Muscled, but without nearly the body weight.

"There's another reason I told you about the Jew I drowned in pig's blood," Pavo said. "I now face a similar dilemma."

Vitas stared back, barely inches away from Pavo's face. He did not fear the silence that Pavo let fall upon them. He also did not break the silence like a rabbit bolting from cover in the presence of a hawk.

Long moments passed. Vitas did not expect Pavo to throw a punch or pull a knife. Though the tension between them was building, it was clear that Pavo needed to protect Vitas. Otherwise Vitas would still be floating in open seas. Yes, that had been the gamble Vitas took in his moment of calculated anger, leaping from the ship to rescue John. That if the captain had left Rome as he did, then Vitas was very valuable to him. Too valuable to let drown.

It was Pavo who broke the silence he had imposed. "If my crew now believes your authority is greater than mine or that I fear you, I lose my crew, my ship, and most certainly my life. Yet I must protect your life at all costs, or I lose my crew, my ship, and my life to those in Rome who put you aboard." Pavo shrugged. "Either way, I lose everything."

Vitas wanted badly to ask which men of Rome had put him on the ship. Where was that scroll?

"There will be a day," Pavo said, "when you speak again with those who arranged for your escape. That is why I brought you down here to explain in privacy what must be done. Tell them that if I lost my ship to my crew, I would have been unable to deliver you to Alexandria. Tell them that there was only one way I could keep my crew and ensure you made it there."

Pavo sighed. "I respect you. Even admire you. Your gamble

that I would turn the ship around to pluck you from the sea was remarkable. But I must do what I must do. And you must allow it, because if I lose my authority on this ship, you, too, will die."

Another sigh. "I promise, however, that if you don't fight what must be done and make it appear like I am in full command, I will protect the Jew. I presume he is a valuable slave; otherwise you would not have risked your life to save him."

"What is it that I must allow?"

"The whip," Pavo said. "A minimum of ten lashes. From me. With all the crew gathered to watch."

HORA OCTAVA

DAMIAN STOOD ON the deck of a small riverboat, uncomfortable on water, as always, even if it was only the current of the Tiber taking him away from Rome. He and Jerome were the only passengers.

"Do you travel this river at night?" These were the first words Damian had spoken since boarding the boat, a question he addressed to the captain, a man named Volusius, who was a middle-aged, barrel-chested man with an obvious limp. Despite the limp, however, he moved efficiently, something Damian had silently observed as the man had made all preparations to cast from shore nearly an hour earlier.

"Perhaps you'll want to take a nap," Volusius answered. He held a steering oar in both hands and looked past Damian, downstream, where the current carried them. "Go down to my cabin. It's cramped, but the best you could expect on a craft like this."

"I came back here to talk." Until this point, Damian had been content to stand in the front of the boat and stare at passing scenery. Behind them, the seven hills of Rome. Ahead, the twists and turns of the Tiber. On both sides, the buildings that had crowded the shore were thinning out as they moved downstream from Rome. The wind was in their faces, and Damian found that to be good news. The current would take them to Ostia. A wind would bring them back to Rome. He'd be at his villa by dark and would get a report from his slave Castinus about the captive he'd ordered released.

"You'll find it cooler down there," Volusius grunted. "Out of the sun."

"I want to talk."

"You bought passage. Nothing more. I'm not interested in idle chitchat with tourists."

Volusius leaned on the oar, and the ship grudgingly shifted to miss an unseen sandbar.

Damian cleared his throat.

Jerome, sitting midway down the deck and apparently asleep, opened one eye.

"We have a problem here," Damian told Jerome. "Our captain has no interest in conversation."

With an impassive face, Jerome rose. He stripped his tunic off down to a band of cloth wrapped around his loins, showing a broad chest that rippled with muscle like the front quarters of a stallion.

"He blocks a lot of sun, doesn't he?" Damian said to Volusius. "Once I saw him punch an ox between the eyes. Buckled it to its knees. A slave like Jerome is very useful, as you might guess."

Volusius gave that some thought. "River like this holds a lot of water, doesn't it?" he said moments later. "Once I saw a boat like this hit another coming upstream. Both boats tore apart, drowning ten men. An experienced pilot like me is very useful, as you might guess."

Jerome ambled closer.

"Looks like he's going to keep me busy," Volusius said to Damian. "Take the steering oar. Someone has to keep this boat from sinking. You do know what parts of the river are safe and what parts aren't, don't you? If not, I hope you can swim. Drowning, as I've seen, is a horrible way to die."

Damian held up his hand and Jerome stopped. "You know the river as well as any pilot, I've been told," Damian said.

Volusius ignored him and made another adjustment with the steering oar.

"If anyone can move on the water at night, it's you."

No answer.

Damian sighed. "Jerome," he said. "Start with the mast."

Volusius gave Damian a startled glance.

"His strength is impressive," Damian said. "Persistent, too. If he's unable to push the mast over, I'm sure he'll tie a rope halfway up and pull it down."

"Not the mast."

"Not bad," Damian said.

"Huh?"

"Not bad as a start to a pleasant conversation. Let's continue it. Tell me more about the mast. Expensive? Hard to replace?"

"I can move on the water at night," Volusius said, his teeth clenched. "What of it?"

"Think back. Not too far. Today's Moon. Not last night then, but the night before. Did you make a trip from Rome to Ostia in the dark? With, say, a passenger delivered to you in a large tapestry?"

The startled look on the face of Volusius told Damian enough.

"Four men delivered him to you," Damian continued. "Brought him aboard and bound him securely. To continue our pleasant conversation, all I need is a simple yes."

"Break the mast," Volusius said. "It can be replaced."

"I like your efficiency in conversation. While you left a lot unsaid, what I heard was that someone paid you to make the trip, and you fear betraying that person far more than you fear a broken mast."

"What I left unsaid was your questionable parentage. So let me say it now." In language suitable for a port town's inn, Volusius then went into great detail and speculation.

"Tut-tut," Damian said. "Distracting me with insults won't work either. Especially as we still have a few miles left together on the river."

Volusius worked up a great gob, but before he could spit at Damian's feet, Damian shook his head.

"Don't push me." Damian said it in such a tone that once again he was rewarded with a startled glance from Volusius. "I'm not going to ask you who paid you to take that night journey. All I want to know is where the passenger went once you arrived in Ostia. It's something I could find out myself by asking around anyway, but you'll save me several hours. Fair enough?"

Damian stepped back and, with a gesture, invited Volusius to spit out the contents of his mouth.

With some relief, Volusius did so, then spoke. Quietly. "Fair enough."

"Thank you," Damian said. "I always prefer my conversations to remain this civilized."

✦ ✦ ✦

"You've spoiled my appetite," Helius said. He was meeting with Tigellinus for the second time in a day, and although the Vitas issue weighed heavily on his mind, he disliked being reminded of it.

"We should pretend this problem doesn't exist? And if Nero finds out and sends us into the arena, pretend the lions don't exist either?"

"Who do you suggest is the one person in Rome to help us?" Helius asked. Nothing on the table appealed to him anymore.

Tigellinus picked up a slice of cake and, with little elegance, shoved it into his mouth. He cocked his head sideways as he chewed. "Acceptable."

"Who do you suggest?" Helius said, as usual irritated by Tigellinus's lack of manners and entirely forgetful that he'd just spit food to the side.

"He's already in your employ."

"Good. You've narrowed it down to thousands."

"He has two unique qualifications," Tigellinus said, moving on to a dish of snails. He paused to wolf down a couple of mouthfuls. Only after wiping the grease from his mouth with the back of his hand did Tigellinus continue. "Few are better at hunting humans, no matter how far they travel across the world. And no other person in the world knows Vitas as well as he does."

Helius thought about it, then snorted. "If you're actually suggesting—"

"Damian. His brother."

"When the day began, you agreed we should have him killed."

"Only to remove him as a threat," Tigellinus said. "If he is actively searching for Vitas for us, then he's not a threat."

"Unprincipled as Damian might be, I doubt even he would take any amount of bounty for the capture of Vitas."

"Helius," Tigellinus said softly, "don't underestimate Damian."

"You believe he would betray his brother?"

"The opposite. Damian is far more principled than you believe." Helius snorted again. "He's a gambler. Womanizer."

"A gambler who enrolled in gladiator school to pay off his debtors. A womanizer who does not spend time in affairs with married women. He has his own moral code and does not break it."

"You defend his character in one breath and in another expect me to hire him to search for his brother on our behalf?"

"For a man of intelligence, there are times you can be exceptionally obtuse," Tigellinus said.

"I'm not the one speaking nonsense here. Explain to me what could convince Damian to find Vitas for us."

"What's the name of the spy you have in Damian's household?"

"Castinus," Helius said after a careful pause.

"I'll need to ask him some questions this afternoon."

"Why?"

"Leverage," Tigellinus said. "Isn't that what you told me? With the right leverage you can manipulate anyone."

"What kind of leverage do you have in mind?"

"The same leverage you mentioned earlier today." Tigellinus grinned. "But not in the way anyone would expect."

"You're still making no sense."

"It might be difficult to capture Vitas. So I say we just have him killed. Whatever plan the conspirators have will certainly fail with Vitas dead."

"And you have a way not only to find Vitas but have him killed?"

"Listen carefully," Tigellinus said. "I'll speak slowly as I explain, and with luck, I won't have to tell you twice."

✢ ✢ ✢

The first lash of the whip came down like a forceful blow of wood across his shoulders and drove all the air out of Vitas's lungs. It was a shock of pain that sent his near-naked body into a spasm, and the grunt of agony that he managed to expel sounded to him like it came from another person.

He was unable to jerk away from the next blow.

His hands were tied to the mast of the ship so he faced the deck. A sailor on each side firmly held a rope knotted to each ankle, so his body was pulled its full length and his legs spread apart.

The next two lashes wrapped the cutting strips of leather around the back and front of his exposed thighs. Vitas clenched his teeth but could not prevent the scream of rage that escaped through them.

Another blow across the lower waist. The end of the whip snapped around his belly. He lost the willpower to hold back his scream and cried out his anguish.

The sixth blow cut across his shoulders. The seventh, his thighs again.

Then nothing.

Vitas found air. Heaved. Became aware of a warmth that he realized was blood.

He turned his head sideways to see why Pavo had stopped.

The captain was grinning, slapping the handle of the whip against his palm, as if he'd been waiting for Vitas to look. Behind him, two other men held John, restraining him from any action.

Pavo drew back the whip.

Vitas turned his head away, unable to bear another blow.

The whip cracked in the air above him, and the crew laughed

at his instinctive reaction, an unsuccessful pulling at the ropes that held him.

Another crack of the whip.

Vitas looked over at Pavo, knowing the captain was toying with him.

There was a salty taste in his mouth; Vitas had bitten through his lip and blood flowed freely. Vitas forced himself to stare at Pavo. He would not show his fear again by flinching or pulling at the ropes. Then he remembered: he'd made the agreement with the captain to allow him full authority. Defiance meant John would not be protected from the crew.

Vitas dropped his head and stared at the deck . . . and waited.

The next blow cut his back again. And again.

Finally, mercifully, Vitas lost consciousness.

HORA NONANA

"MY SISTER'S GOT what you're looking for."

This offer to Damian came from a boy whose head barely reached Jerome's waist. Despite the rags the boy wore for clothing, he seemed healthy and well fed.

Damian squatted to look the boy full in the face. "How does your sister know what we want?"

"Livia's not deaf or blind; that's how." The boy grinned. "Everybody around the harbor knows what you want. She sent me to find you."

"News travels fast." Damian remained level with the boy. "Or was it the fat reward I offered?"

"Bring your coins," the boy said. "Even if there wasn't a reward, she doesn't talk to men unless they pay her afterward."

Damian nodded. "Your sister Livia is in the talking business, is she?"

"Especially with sailors," the little boy said with straightforward innocence. "She must be good at sea stories, because they want her all the time to visit and talk."

"Of course," Damian said with equal seriousness. He straightened and winked at Jerome. "A good storyteller." Damian gestured with his hand. "Lead the way."

The boy trotted ahead of them.

Damian and Jerome had walked the perimeter of Portus Traiani, the inner harbor of Ostia, for only fifteen minutes after they had landed. This harbor, and Portus Augusti, the outer harbor with its lighthouse, were connected to the Tiber by a canal. Ostia itself was a mile farther down the river. One road led northwest from the inner harbor to Rome, another through the short stretch of coast that separated it from Ostia.

The harbor, despite its distance from the town, was a swarm of activity. It had relatively few apartments compared to Ostia but, for obvious reasons, had an abundance of hotels, brothels, bars, and market shops.

Both harbors together held upward of two hundred ships. Although Volusius had supplied them the name of the captain of the seafaring ship to which he had delivered John, it would have taken Damian days to go from ship to ship. He hoped it had not yet sailed, but feared that if he didn't find it quickly, it might depart during his search.

The easy solution had been to wander into a couple of bars and spread the word that he would give a reward to whoever might lead him to the ship he wanted. And minutes later, the small boy had appeared from an alleyway.

Damian and Jerome now followed the ragged boy through the alley.

Damian wasn't worried about a trap set for him by sailors looking to rob him of easy money. Not with Jerome beside him. He followed the boy with confidence, remaining aware of the twisting passages to be able to find his way back.

The alley was barely wide enough for Jerome's shoulders. In perpetual shade, it was too narrow to be baked dry by sunshine and smelled of salt tang and fish and urine. Cats scurried beneath their feet. At least Damian hoped they were cats, because he'd never liked rats and would not like to find out they grew that big.

Abruptly the boy turned and scampered through a narrow archway that led to a courtyard behind an old apartment building. He pointed at a woman standing in shadow along the courtyard wall.

"Hello," Damian said to her. He grinned broadly. "Livia. I'm told you have a wonderful way of telling stories."

He believed it. While she did not smile, and there was nothing inviting or sensuous about her posture, she was a beautiful woman in a plain tunic. She had her arms wrapped around herself as if trying to hide that beauty.

"Don't get any ideas," Livia said, glancing at the boy. "I never tell stories here. Only on ships." To the boy, she said sharply, "Now go upstairs and wait for me."

The boy dragged a foot.

"Go!"

When he was out of earshot, Damian moved closer to the woman. "Your son seems like a capable young man. You must be proud of him."

"My brother."

"As you say."

She pushed strands of dark hair off her face. "Is it that obvious?"

"It's the way you look at him."

"That's why I never bring sailors here to—" she caught herself—"to tell stories."

Livia straightened her hair again. Nervous. "I want triple what you've offered to learn about Atronius Pavo. I risk too much already in sending for you."

Damian felt sympathy for her. The Roman world was not easy for a woman without a man. "If it's worth it. Where is the ship?"

"Gone. But you could learn that from anyone."

"And what can I learn from you that's different?"

"Everyone in the harbor believes his brother drowned before the ship set sail. But he's in Rome somewhere, waiting for ransom money. That alone should be worth what you have to pay."

Her words were directed at Damian, but she had shifted her gaze to stare at Jerome in admiration.

"A magnificent man, isn't he? And totally devoted to his wife and three young children. The only . . . um . . . stories he listens to are the ones told at home. But he can't tell you that because pirates cut out his tongue."

Livia continued to stare at Jerome, who kept his face, as always, devoid of emotion.

"When you say 'his' brother," Damian said, "you mean Pavo's brother."

She shook her head, finally looking at Damian again. "Pavo is the magister navis. He, too, believes the brother is dead."

"Whose brother then? And what ransom money does he expect?"

"They."

"They?" Damian felt no impatience. Often it was like this as he gathered pieces of information.

"Cosconius Betto and his brother, Kaeso. It was part of their plan."

"Brothers," Damian repeated.

"Betto is the ship's gubernator. He's gone now, of course. To Alexandria with the ship."

Gubernator. Sailing master. As captain, Pavo was essentially the man with authority. But without a navigator, the ship would never depart harbor.

"Betto and Kaeso," Damian mused aloud to help himself remember the names.

"I'm a favorite of theirs," Livia said. "Each, however, is jealous of my attentions to the other. In the afternoon before the ship left harbor, I—"

"When did it leave?"

"Saturn."

Nearly two days at sea already, Damian thought with regret. "Continue. Please."

"Kaeso had a room in a hotel. I was there with him." She actually blushed. "Telling stories."

"Of course."

"Betto was at the door. I was forced to hide. I overheard Betto give Kaeso instructions. Kaeso couldn't tell him to stop talking; otherwise he'd have to explain why."

"Yes." Damian had learned it didn't hurt to be a pleasant listener.

"Betto expected that a man of great importance would be arriving to sail with them. Because—" Livia bit her lower lip, glancing upward as if searching her mind to recall the reasons—"because Pavo had insisted they would leave that night."

"Night." Ships never departed at night.

"When Betto told Pavo that the omens weren't right and the sacrifices had not been made, Pavo said it didn't matter. Betto told him that none of the paying passengers expected the ship to leave for days. Pavo said he didn't want or need the paying passengers. That the Roman they were to take to Alexandria would make everything worthwhile. All of this Betto explained to his brother while I was hiding."

"And their plan?" Damian wasn't looking for a Roman but a Jew. Still, it was part of his nature to ask questions and part of his job to gather as much information as possible.

"That if this Roman was so important, it would be worthwhile to kidnap him at sea. And send for ransom. Enough to pay off their gambling debts. Betto said he could arrange it in such a way that he and Kaeso would never be suspected. And that if it looked like Kaeso had drowned, he would be able to escape the creditors demanding payment of his gambling debts."

"How?"

"That's when Kaeso suggested to Betto that they go to a bar for some beer. I'm sure he didn't want me to hear the rest."

"They left you alone."

Livia nodded. "He didn't come back. That evening, I heard that Kaeso had drowned. But already this morning I've received messages from Kaeso inviting me to see him in Rome."

Men and their follies, Damian thought without any degree of righteousness, because he knew he was just as vulnerable to his own desires. Whatever careful plans Betto had made were subject to the whims of fate simply because Kaeso wanted the same woman his brother wanted.

What puzzled Damian, however, was trying to decide if it had been John placed on the ship and that somehow Livia—and Betto and Kaeso—believed John to be a Roman important enough to kidnap at sea for a ransom demand, or if it truly had been a Roman on the ship and Damian was wasting his time looking here for John.

"Is there anything else you can tell me?" Damian asked.

"Not until I'm paid for all of this."

"I'm not sure you're telling the truth. After all, you make your living as a storyteller."

"Don't mock me," she said. "I have a son. Should I want him to know who and what his mother truly is?"

"No," Damian answered almost meekly. "But I'm not sure if what you're telling me is worth that much. The man I'm looking for is not a Roman."

"Oh." She was casual. "It's the Jew you want."

"What!"

That was a mistake.

She easily understood his excitement. She held out her hand until he counted out all the coins she demanded.

"Tell me about the Jew," he said.

"I went to the ship that night and waited nearby to watch. Thinking it might be worth money to know about a rich Roman stealing away." She hefted the coins. "See, I was right."

"The Jew."

"Two men were brought aboard the ship. The first was wearing a hood. He said nothing and could barely walk. The other tried to help him. But they went too slowly, and Pavo kicked at both of them. Called the second one—the one without the hood—a stupid Jew."

Two men, Damian thought with a degree of admiration for Volusius. When interrogated, the fox had left out the fact that he'd transported two men that night.

John, the Jew.

And a rich Roman worth kidnapping for ransom. Very interesting.

"Where can I find Kaeso?" Damian asked. That was the next logical step. With the ship long gone, Kaeso could answer questions. With, perhaps, Jerome's persuasion.

Livia's eyes shifted to the ground, then back to Damian. "How much is it worth to you?"

✝ ✝ ✝

"I can't tell you anything about Sophia," said the teenage boy. "But just before noon of Saturn a man called at the gates to see Ben-Aryeh, the old Jew."

In the orchard on the estate of Gallus Sergius Vitas, the boy, a slave, had difficulty focusing on Tigellinus and Helius. His eyes kept darting to his father, a few paces away. One rope had been tied to each of the man's ankles. The other ends had been tied to the halters of two opposing oxen. Tigellinus stood between the oxen, holding a whip.

"Saturn," Helius repeated. Vitas had attacked Nero at a dinner party the night before. Saturn, in the afternoon, Sophia had been sent an invitation to commit suicide. "What did this man look like?"

The boy gave a description that could have fit thousands, if not tens of thousands. He was unclear on what the man had been wearing and couldn't recall anything unusual about his appearance.

"Why then," Helius asked the boy, "do you remember this man?"

"I wondered if he had been sent by Caesar." The boy swallowed. "Word about Vitas had spread among the slaves already. We didn't know what would happen to us."

Tigellinus nodded encouragement to the boy, holding the whip casually, as if he'd totally forgotten that the oxen were poised to pull apart the boy's father.

"And?" Helius asked.

"The man held a scroll. I led him to the old Jew. Later, when the man left, he had no scroll."

"The Jew kept it?"

The boy nodded again. He was trembling, on the verge of break-down. This was exactly what Helius wanted. Fear would make it impossible for the boy to think clearly enough to lie.

"What else do you know about the scroll?" Helius asked.

This was far more important than Helius showed. Sophia's grave, as Tigellinus had suspected, had been found empty. There had been a conspiracy then, people working in concerted effort to make sure both Vitas and Sophia escaped Nero. People with power. It was absolutely crucial that Helius discover who these people were, without Nero learning about any of it.

With all the slaves witnessing it, they'd already ripped apart one slave with the oxen. It had been enough for the teenage slave to burst forward from among the remaining slaves with the promise that he knew something about Sophia's escape. After Tigellinus had tied the boy's father to the oxen, only a few paces from the torn body of the first dead slave, Helius had been ready to begin his questions.

"If I tell you, you will untie my father, right?"

"I've assured you of that a dozen times," Helius said. "Just tell me what you know about the scroll."

"The old man read it in front of the messenger and said a few words."

"Which were . . . ?" Helius felt it was like pulling the boy's tongue to get him to speak. Maybe a pair of red-hot tongs would do.

"'Not another ship. I hate ships.'"

Helius frowned. "'Not another ship. I hate ships.' Nothing more?"

"That's all. Right after that, the messenger pointed at me and told the old man to be discreet."

That was interesting, Helius thought. The messenger was more than a messenger, for he had known enough about the situation to give a warning.

"But I heard more." The boy continued to stare at Tigellinus

and his father. "Our master, Vitas, had been arrested by Nero," the
boy said. "All of us were afraid of what might happen next."

That needed no explanation. The fates of slaves were tied to the
fates of their owners.

"I climbed on the roof and got as close as I could," the boy said.
"In case there was something I could learn that would help all of
us slaves."

"And?"

"The visitor was telling the old Jew if he hated ships he could go
to Corinth by road and then gave him instructions to find the road
from here. But that was the end of their conversation."

"You didn't hear why the old Jew needed to go to Corinth."

"Nothing else. It took me too long to get on the roof. The
visitor left right after that."

"Nothing else?" Helius said.

"Nothing else." The boy seemed to relax now that he'd given
up all he knew.

Helius had been looking for that—the relaxing of the boy's body.
He was, after all, an expert on interrogating people.

"You've done well." Helius turned to Tigellinus. "Let's see if we
can find another slave to corroborate this information. We have no
more use for the boy's father."

Tigellinus raised the whip.

"No!" the boy screamed.

✛ ✛ ✛

"Go away," Vitas groaned in his first moments of consciousness.
The sun, hidden behind clouds, gave no hint at the time of day.
But it was hot. Vitas guessed it to be the early part of the afternoon.

The person applying salve to his back ignored him. "While you
were unconscious, I bathed your wounds in salt water."

It was the Jew, John.

Vitas was flat on his chest and stomach, on a blanket on the deck
of the ship. He flinched as a hand again softly touched his lower back.

"The captain has provided some wine mixed with myrrh," John said. "It's in the wineskin beside you."

"Go away," Vitas repeated. "I don't want your help."

"How can I stand by as you suffer?" John asked.

"You can't understand my pain." Vitas had woken from a dream-like vision of Sophia. It had begun pleasantly, a memory of standing beside her on a ship much like this, returning to Rome from Caesarea. Only a few months after that journey, their life together had ended in a nightmare, at a dinner party with the emperor, when Nero reached for her hand with a leer. "I want to be left alone."

"As you wish. But not until all your wounds are covered."

Vitas groaned again. He reached for the wineskin, a movement that sent searing pain across his back.

John reached the wineskin for him and tilted it to Vitas's mouth. Vitas gulped it like water. Anything to dull the intensity of the pain that filled his consciousness.

"Only enough to ease the pain," John cautioned as he applied more salve.

Vitas did not want to admit that it soothed him.

"What is your name?" John asked.

"Go away." Vitas wanted to owe this man nothing. Wanted to share nothing of his anguish. All he cared about was returning to Rome to search for his wife.

"It is against the law for a Roman citizen to be scourged," John said. "And given that the crew believes I'm your slave, all would have understood if you had ordered me to take your place."

"Go away."

"What are you afraid of, Roman? What makes you so determined to contain yourself against the world? to be the one so arrogant that you help others and refuse to be helped yourself?"

"Go away."

"You are your own man," John said. "You make your own destiny. Is that it? You need nobody?"

"Go away."

"You think I am helping you because I owe you my life twice?"

"I think you are deaf. How many times need I ask you to leave?"

John's laugh was gentle and good-natured. "Roman of the unknown name, I can guess you come from wealth and power. Months ago you defied Nero to save my life and the prisoners with me. Now someone has gone to great lengths to put you on this ship. This is not something to expect from a common man. Yet let me ask you something: how much is all your power and wealth worth when your life ends?"

"No philosophy," Vitas said. He sighed as the warmth of his first gulps began to ease his pain. "I'll take wine instead."

"What's your burden?" John said. "No matter how heavy, I can show you the way to ease it."

"You'll take my burden away. And you call me arrogant?"

"I can't take your burdens. Of course, neither can your wine. But I know someone who can. He came from God and—"

"Go away," Vitas groaned. "Leave the wine but go away."

There was a final soothing touch on his upper back.

"Certainly," John said. "I will pray for your quick healing." The man stood.

Then Vitas was left alone.

He struggled to drink from the wineskin by himself. Yet more wine could not help him escape the Jew's questions.

What are you afraid of, Roman? What makes you so determined to contain yourself against the world? to be the one so arrogant that you help others and refuse to be helped yourself?

The wine and myrrh began to take effect, a mercy that took away more and more of his pain.

"My name is Vitas," Vitas mumbled just before he fell into an exhausted sleep. He had not shed tears since boyhood and hardly realized he was weeping now, "Gallus Sergius Vitas. And I want forgiveness for killing my son."

HORA DUODECIMA

JEROME STEPPED through the archway into a strangely silent household.

Usually, even when he arrived home after sunset, like he had on this evening, his two little boys and the daughter who was still a toddler were waiting to squeal and giggle as they jumped on his massive body. He would walk around with them clinging to him, his heart filled with gratitude and joy that in his domestic refuge he was not a mute freak to be feared or marveled at, that nothing within these walls would require him to use his strength to hurt other humans.

Not on this night.

The light of a lamp glowed in the room beyond.

Jerome frowned. *Where are they?*

The too-short hours spent with his wife and children were all in this life that sustained his soul. Damian permitted Jerome the late afternoon and early evening with his wife and three young children. Damian did expect, however, that Jerome would return from the slaves' quarters to Damian's bedroom by the second watch of the night, when Jerome and two dogs would sleep in the doorway as Damian's protectors.

Jerome called out as best as he could, a low-pitched mewling sound. It was a noise he hated. Too soon his children would grow up and realize what it meant about their father. That he was a man

incapable of expressing his thoughts, which for all practical pur-
poses made him less than human.

No children came running from the darkness of the other room.

He thought, however, that he heard the sound of sobbing.

Marcia! His wife.

Marcia had been given to Jerome years before by the Roman
who owned him before Damian. She was Parthian, taken in a battle
as booty, and at the first sight of Jerome, she'd fainted in fear.

But Jerome had proven unwilling to use her in the way that his
previous owner had intended—as a gift for the giant—and for the
first month, they had lived in Jerome's slave's quarters, shyly aware
of the other but sleeping separately. Because Jerome could not speak
or read or write, Marcia had been forced to take the first steps,
speaking short monologues at first, then longer and longer, trying
to judge his reaction by watching the muscles of his face.

Now, all these years later, it gave Marcia great pride that he only
smiled for her and for the children; outside of their quarters his
expression had a perpetual impassiveness that hid his feelings from
the world.

In the kitchen area, he found her on the floor, sitting against
the wall.

Yes, sobbing. Her face was buried almost in her chest, the glow
of the lamplight bouncing off her dark hair.

Jerome lurched forward and knelt beside her. He put a massive
arm around her delicate shoulders.

She refused to look up at him.

Where were the children? He despised himself for being unable
to do something as simple as ask.

Again, he forced himself to mewl, hoping she would respond,
knowing that he made noise only under great duress.

She continued to sob.

Jerome saw that the fingers of each hand were clenched.

He lifted her hands in the lamplight.

She did not resist.

In her left hand, he recognized a wooden doll that he had carved for their daughter.

On the fingers of her right hand were dark, wet smudges. When he opened those fingers, something fell at his feet. Lightly. It landed with no noise.

He couldn't make sense of it immediately.

When he picked it up and placed it in his palm to see better in the light, a great fear and horror washed through him.

It was a tiny ear.

✛ ✛ ✛

"You look ridiculous," Helius said. "Take that wig off."

Castinus gave Helius a craven smile, blinking both eyes. "I decided today it would be safer to come in disguise," Castinus said. "If Damian ever suspected—"

"Of course it's a disguise." Helius found both habits irritating. The frequent smile. The blinking that made it appear as if Castinus flinched with each smile. "Are you suggesting I'm not capable of realizing that myself?"

"N-no, no," Castinus stammered. Another smile. More blinking.

"Well then?" Helius demanded. "Get on with it."

"Today, there was a woman at the steam bath—"

"I meant, well then, why haven't you removed that ridiculous wig?"

"Oh." Castinus did as ordered.

He stood before Helius in a woman's tunic. Skinny hunched shoulders. Chicken neck with prominent Adam's apple. Rouged cheeks. Darkened eyebrows. Wig tucked under arm.

Helius snapped, "Now you look even more ridiculous."

Castinus began to stammer an apology.

"Enough," Helius said. "I'll endure what I have to. Tell me why I should care about a woman at the steam bath. From what I hear, women visitors are common for Damian. I'm not interested in sordid details."

Indeed, he was not. With Nero as emperor, a man or woman's improprieties had no leverage. Nero, as he often exclaimed, was convinced that nobody could remain chaste or pure in any part of the body; if anybody confessed to obscene practices, Nero would forgive that person of any crime except treason.

Castinus wiped at his greasy hair, and Helius grimaced openly. The slave was a hideous man, but to see him as a parody of a woman made it even worse. Castinus explained the appearance of the private litter outside the steam bath and how he had stood close enough to the curtains to hear all that had been spoken.

"Let me understand this," Helius said. "The widow of Lucius Bellator is on a determined quest to find her stepson and stepdaughter."

"She is willing to pay any amount for Damian to find them in Judea and return them to Rome."

Helius knew Alypia and knew her reputation. It was odd, this sudden maternal devotion. He had a good guess as to her real intentions. It would bear watching; if he was correct, it would prove a good opportunity to bleed her estate. Without Nero's knowledge.

"Excellent," Helius said. And regretted it immediately. The hideous man's face lit as if Helius had patted him on the head.

"What of the slave Jerome? Were Tigellinus's men able to find his wife?" Helius said.

"Yes. His men found the woman as I directed."

"Her children?" Helius asked.

"Gone. She was nearly hysterical, waiting for Jerome to return."

"Excellent," Helius repeated, not caring this time that the slave beamed again. At least one thing was going well. He knew where Tigellinus had intended to keep the children and would deal with it later. "Most excellent."

"There's more," Castinus said. "It's about the captive that Damian has held hidden since the evening of Saturn."

"Then continue," Helius said. "This is what I pay you for."

✠ ✠ ✠

A steady drumming woke Vitas. He was still facedown on blankets on the deck, and afternoon light was fading.

It took him a moment to realize that a portion of the growing darkness resulted from a tentlike shelter that had been built above him. And that the drumming resulted from a steady rain.

His ears told him that the wind, too, had lessened. The sails snapped with less frequency; the mast did not creak as loudly from the strain of ropes holding the sails.

He was shivering. Perhaps his muscles trembled in a delayed reaction to the whipping. Or perhaps because the air temperature had dropped—the pleasant afternoon warmth was giving way to the bite of the evening.

Vitas moved his arms and legs cautiously, intending to stop if the scabs on his back and thighs began to crack. But the salve that the Jew had applied allowed an unexpected suppleness.

The wine he'd taken earlier to ease his pain, however, had left him with a terrible thirst, made more excruciating by the sound of the fresh, clean water falling from the skies onto the sheeting that had been rigged to protect him.

Vitas doubted he had the strength to rise to his feet and look for a wineskin of water. Not yet.

He wanted to call for the Jew but had too much pride. He'd sent the man away in anger. To call out now would be a sign of weakness. That thought brought a snort to Vitas. A sign of weakness.

Had he ever been more broken in his life than this? A month earlier, he'd had all he ever believed a man could want. Enough wealth. Enough power. And a completion of his life through the marriage to a woman he loved and adored and cherished.

Now? She'd been taken from him. He was a fugitive from the emperor. He was powerless to stop the ship that carried him away from Rome, too powerless even to look for water, a substance so inexpensive and plentiful that even the poorest of poor in the slums of Rome never lacked for it.

What in his life could he truly control?

It was a terrifying thought. He tried to push it out of his mind. But could not.

The Jew had called him arrogant. Vitas wanted to believe he'd made a decision to jump off the ship and rescue the man from drowning because he hated injustice. Because the man had needed help. Because in his lifetime, Vitas had seen far too much of the abuse of power.

But had he really done it to prove to the captain that he, Vitas, still controlled the situation? Was John right? Had he done it because he was arrogant enough to believe that he controlled not only his destiny but the destiny of others?

Or worse, had he done it because of the horror he could never escape, memories of his final battle against the Iceni in Britannia? Had he done it to try to repay the gods for the unpunished wrong he had committed there?

Vitas growled.

He was a man. A Roman whose family had been founded almost as far back as Rome itself. A Roman who had fought savage battles and lived to receive the spoils of triumph because of it.

He was a man of action. Why was he wasting his energy on these thoughts?

Despite his pain, Vitas felt his resolve grow. And that gave him strength. A man did what a man must do. It was that simple. His situation looked bleak now, but he was alive.

He would heal. He would find a way back to Rome. He would rescue his wife, find a place in the provinces where Nero would not know of his existence, and use his brains and talent to recover what he had lost.

A man did what a man must do.

With that settled in his mind, his desperate sense of thirst returned. *Water!*

He decided it would be strength, not weakness, that allowed him to call out for John. He needed the water to begin his healing process. A man of will knew that, and a man of will would do what a man must do.

Even with this argument in his mind, he could not force himself to call out for the Jew.

Soon enough, he told himself, he would find the strength to leave the shelter and find his own water. But his thirst overwhelmed him. Could he not even control the desires of his body?

As he fought his pride, the Jew appeared unbidden. Silently, John handed him a wineskin, this one filled with cool water.

Vitas drank with savage greed. "Thank you." It was enough of a concession, was it not?

John nodded. There was still enough light for Vitas to see the man's features. There was gentleness in his face. And strength.

"This is yours," John said. "It fell from your tunic earlier. When I brought you up on the deck during your fever. I intended to give it to you much sooner, but circumstances, of course, did not allow it."

John placed a scroll in the hands of Vitas.

"You've read it?" Vitas said.

"It is not mine," John answered.

The man departed, leaving Vitas with a vague shame for questioning his honor.

Vitas pushed himself up on his elbows to examine the scroll.

That the scroll had not been read was easily confirmed, for the wax seal was unbroken. Vitas hoped the seal would give him a clue to identify the person who had sent it through the stranger in the cell. He examined it closely, but it gave nothing away.

Then, with only minutes of light remaining until it would be too dark to read further, Vitas broke the seal and unrolled the parchment.

✛ ✛ ✛

Jerome was standing, and Marcia was cradled in his arms, holding his neck, sobbing noiselessly.

He heard footsteps outside the kitchen area, the slap of leather sandals on brick. He turned, still cradling Marcia.

It was only one man stepping into the lamplight. He was medium height, wearing a dark tunic with a hood. He carried a stylus and a wax tablet.

"It gave me no pleasure to disturb your woman." The man's voice was muffled. "And a child's ear is a barbaric way to get your attention. But I am only a messenger."

Marcia snapped her head toward the sound. Clutched Jerome fiercely. "He . . . he . . . gave it to me. Just before you got here. . . ." She was unable to finish as her body convulsed with the effort of holding back hysterics.

Jerome set her down. Slowly, purposely, he took a step toward the hooded man.

"I know you can snap my neck," the man said. "But if you do, you'll never see your children again."

Jerome turned his eyes to Marcia.

"In the market," she said, understanding the question he could not speak. "This afternoon. Two men started pushing me, arguing that I'd stolen vegetables. When I turned back for our children, they were gone."

"You'll get the children back." The hooded man extended the wax tablet and stylus to Jerome. "Write down their names and the time and place tomorrow where you would like to meet them, and they will be waiting for you."

Jerome bowed his head.

"He can't read or write," Marcia said. "Let me speak for him. Whatever it takes to get our children."

"I'm only a messenger. I was told that he must write it down."

Jerome strained to talk, a vestige of the days before he'd been captured by pirates. But he swallowed the sounds before they left his throat. Stared at the hooded man, wishing he could reach forward and shake the life from him.

The hooded man then spoke to the woman. "I'm not afraid

that he'll ask for help. He can't. But if you breathe a word of this to anyone, I'll return with much more than an ear."

He turned back to Jerome.

"I was told if you couldn't write anything down for me, to pass on some instructions." He dropped the wax tablet and the stylus from his hand. "Damian is going to learn that his brother, Vitas, is still alive and needs his help. Once Damian finds his brother, you are to kill Vitas. Bring back his hand with his signet ring on it as proof of his death. Then you will see your children again."

"But a slave who kills a Roman citizen faces execution!" Marcia said. "As does his entire family! Either way, our children will be killed."

"Damian trusts your Jerome," the hooded man said. "I'm sure your husband will find a way to kill Vitas and not be suspected. And since Vitas is officially believed dead, there will be no investigation. Your children will be safe. As long as Jerome does what is required."

✛ ✛ ✛

"At the steam room," Castinus told Helius, "Damian gave me orders to return to the estate and have the captive released."

"Why?"

"I don't know. But he did tell me to follow him."

"And?"

"The captive went to the estate of Caius Sennius Ruso."

"Ruso."

"A senator," Castinus explained.

"Did I ask you a question?"

"No."

"Then keep your mouth shut. You get paid to tell me what I don't know. Not what I know."

Helius took several paces. They were in his private apartment. The floor was inlaid with gleaming mosaics. The plaster of the wall was painted with elaborate designs. Statues of varying sizes and materials—from ivory to gold—had been arranged in an array of obvious luxury, with ostentation winning over taste.

Helius returned to Castinus. What did Senator Ruso have to do with all of this? "What else can you tell me about this Jew?" Helius asked. "Did Damian learn anything from him before releasing him?"

"In answer to your second question, I heard no rumors among the other slaves. And in answer to your first question, the man wasn't a Jew."

Helius frowned. "You told me he was. Explain yourself."

"I told you he was because Damian believed he was. But Damian was wrong. The man I followed to Senator Ruso's estate was Ruso himself."

"Damian had captured the wrong man?" Helius asked.

Castinus nodded.

Helius could think of no reason that Ruso would have endured over two days' captivity without declaring his identity and immediately demanding freedom. Why had Damian captured the wrong man? How had he discovered the mistaken identity? This, like the matter with Alypia, would bear further investigation, simply because it was so unusual.

"And the rest of Damian's day?"

"He took all his bodyguards to the Tiber, then boarded a river ship to Ostia. With only Jerome as protection. This is what I heard when his bodyguards returned."

"Is Damian still in Ostia?"

"He and Jerome arrived back at the villa just as I was sneaking out."

"So you have no idea what he was searching for in Ostia."

"You made it clear that I was not to be late for this meeting."

Helius paced again. Ostia. What would Damian want in Ostia? "All right then," he told the slave. "Find out everything you can about the matter. I want you here again tomorrow evening." Helius shook his head. "Without the dress and wig."

Castinus took a step to leave.

"I'm not finished with you," Helius said. He had plans for the children of Jerome. "Sometime during the night, unlock the gates of Damian's villa."

"Damian is well guarded. Unless you send at least two dozen—"

"If you continue to presume my intentions," Helius snapped, "it will be very bad for your health. Just make sure the gate is unlocked."

Helius pointed to a sack in the corner of the room. "There's one last thing. Leave this where Damian will find it."

Castinus frowned. "That's all?"

"That's all," Helius said.

What was in it would be enough to put Damian in pursuit of Vitas. With Jerome nearby and ready to kill.

✦ ✦ ✦

"Iniuriam facilius facias quam feras."

This was the beginning of the letter addressed to Vitas within the scroll. *It's easier to do a wrong than to endure one.*

The writing continued, like the first sentence, in Latin:

> *Yes, dear friend. This injustice inflicted upon you by Nero is an injustice you must endure for a greater cause.*
>
> *Many of us in Rome need you to survive. Yet we dare not identify ourselves. Remember Piso! The emperor has not declared a successor, and if he dies, a strong man will be needed to hold the empire together and prevent civil war.*
>
> *As there was no surety that you would survive to read this letter and a great danger that it would fall into the wrong hands had you not escaped to reach the ship with the scroll, precautions have been taken to protect us. These you will discover in time.*
>
> *In time, too, you will discover a messenger you can trust by remembering this: eleven hundred and eighty-one.*
>
> *Arrangements are in place. If it is you reading these words, Vitas, the promise is simple. The pieces are scattered in such a*

*way that only you will be able to put them together. That will
keep us safe.*

*Destroy this portion as soon as you've read it. The remainder
of this letter is locked, but you will find the key nearby.*

Darkness had nearly descended, but there was still enough light,
just barely, for Vitas to see that the writing on the scroll continued.
Yet it was not in the familiar form of Latin. The etchings were symbols that became a blur to his eyes as he struggled to make sense of
them. Then the light was gone.

The effort to stay on his elbows had already taxed him too
greatly, and he allowed his body to collapse.

Getting the letter back had seemed to promise hope, but it had
not delivered.

For Vitas fell into a troubled, painful sleep with none.

⊰ MARS ⊱

HORA TERTIANA

LYING IN THE DOORWAY of Damian's bedchamber, a guard dog on each side, Jerome heard a sound he dared not believe.

Throughout the night, the dogs on the tile at his feet had shifted and turned in sleep. Damian had grunted and snored from the nearby bed, occasionally yelping and muttering during his dreams.

Jerome, however, had remained sitting and awake all through the night.

Each minute had been agony. He knew he was a man of limited imagination, yet he'd been haunted by vivid pictures of the horrors that his children might be facing.

Those images left him too afraid and heartsick to be angry or vengeful toward whoever had taken his children. Had he been an analytical man, he would have realized that any anger at this point would have been self-centered, a focus on his incapability to take action against the unknown foe. Instead, the fear that dominated his every waking moment resulted from wondering what his children faced.

Both dogs instantly became alert as the approaching sounds woke them. Jerome was on his feet before the dogs moved, and when the animals smelled a familiar scent, they relaxed and dropped their heads on their paws.

For it was Marcia, with their daughter Helvia's arms wrapped around her neck. Helvia was singing a familiar lullaby in the little-girl voice that always brought joy to Jerome.

He ran to them both and hugged them hard, wrapping them completely in his large grasp.

A moment later, he pushed back and gently lifted the hair from Helvia's ears. Both were intact.

"She's fine," Marcia whispered. "So are both of the other children. The ear must have belonged to someone else."

Jerome made a sound in his throat, ending it on a higher pitch. An unspoken question.

"Just as dawn broke," she explained, "Attius and Arrius came running into our quarters. Without Helvia. They pulled me outside and led me to the gate. A man was standing there, holding her. He wouldn't give me Helvia until I agreed to deliver a message to you."

Jerome took his little girl from Marcia's arms and held her to his chest. Relief brought tears. He felt weak and suddenly very tired.

"It was the same message as before," Marcia said. "You must do as instructed."

Jerome grunted another questioning sound.

"He said our children can be taken from us again at any time," Marcia said. "He said the body parts we receive next time will belong to them, not someone else."

She was ramrod straight now and very determined in tone and expression. "I don't care what it takes," she told Jerome. "You do what you must to protect our children."

✛ ✛ ✛

"I'm told you came for the children last night," Tigellinus said.

Helius nodded.

"Where are they?" Tigellinus looked around Helius's private suite as if Helius had actually hidden them somewhere.

"Delivered back to Jerome."

"What!"

Helius flinched. He had expected this reaction, but Tigellinus was such a physical presence that his anger was capable of filling a room.

"Because," Helius said quickly, "keeping them would alert Damian that something unusual had happened."

"We did not discuss this previously. Our plan was—"

"—to keep them hostage until Jerome did what was needed." Helius shook his head, half expecting Tigellinus to step forward and grab him by the throat. "But how long might that be?"

"Until we killed them," Tigellinus growled. "Which is what I'd like to do to you at this point."

Helius knew he was safe again. If Tigellinus really wanted him dead, Helius would get no warning.

"If Nero heard about us keeping three children hostage," Helius countered, "he'd have questions we don't want to answer. But if we kill the children too soon, we have no leverage over Jerome."

Tigellinus grudgingly agreed.

"We've already made our point with Jerome," Helius said. "An entire night wondering about his children has given him a taste of what he has to lose and how easily he can lose it again."

"I already said you were correct. Stop beating a dead horse."

Helius smiled. "When that dead horse is you, I never tire of it."

✛ ✛ ✛

"Who are you, Jew?"

Vitas sat on a crate at the front of the deck. He'd been here since dawn, thinking about the scroll, staring at the southern horizon and the band of distant low mountains that marked the eastern tip of Sicily and the whirlpool at the Straits of Messana between Sicily and the mainland. The clouds had broken during the night, and the sun was already warm, casting a clear light that bounced off waves that seemed to run ahead of the ship.

John was carrying bread and cheese. He ignored the question and offered the food to Vitas.

Vitas broke the bread and gave half of it back to John. It hurt, holding himself upright, but he was determined not to show the extent of the effort it cost to pretend the whipping the day before had not happened. Just rising and placing the tunic over his body had taken ten agonizing minutes. Walking to the crate, another ten minutes of similar pain.

"Who bound you in rope and made you a prisoner before this ship's departure?" Vitas continued. He was famished—a good sign that his body was healing. Yet he made no move to eat his food, instead holding it with his hands resting on his lap. "What had you done to deserve it?"

"May I examine your wounds?"

"The captain said you are a Christian," Vitas said. "I knew this, of course, because of that night in Nero's garden. But how did he know?"

Members of the crew were busy farther down the deck, but they all ignored John and Vitas. Undoubtedly captain's orders.

John had lifted the back of Vitas's tunic. "It could be worse," John said. "Much worse."

He dropped the tunic and stood beside Vitas, staring, too, at the southern horizon. Seagulls circled the ship, another indication that they were nearing a landmass.

Then came the unexpected.

John lowered himself to his knees beside Vitas. He placed one hand on the back of Vitas and raised his other hand high.

"Our Father in heaven," John said softly, so softly that Vitas had to strain to hear, "ease the pain of the stripes this man withstood on my behalf, and heal him now that he might experience Your mercy, and open his heart that he might glorify the holy name of Your Son, Jesus Christ."

John stood again.

Vitas had an impulse to mock the man for asking an invisible God for something that could not be delivered, but he knew enough about the followers of the Christos to understand they did not worship as the rest of the empire did.

Besides, Vitas wanted answers. There was no sense in antagonizing the man. "Why are you on this ship?" Vitas asked.

"As I told you the night we departed," John said, "a friend wanted me away from Rome."

Vitas remembered his own first moments on the ship. Seeing John bound and captive, on the deck of the riverboat. Remembered John's ambiguous statements. *All of us marked by the Lamb are hated by those marked by the Beast. . . . If you are on this ship, perhaps you, too, are fleeing the Beast."*

"Friend? What kind of friend has you taken captive and forced on a ship?"

"One who knew I did not want to leave Rome."

"If you didn't want to leave Rome, then you did not believe as he did. That your life was in danger."

"He was not mistaken," John said. He still stared at the horizon. "A slave hunter had begun pursuit of me."

Vitas lifted his arms slowly to take a bite of bread, grateful that at least this small movement did not send knives of pain through his body. He used the pause in conversation to think through the answers John had given. Each seemed to lead to more questions. If John knew his life was in danger, why had it taken force to remove him from that danger?

"You are an escaped slave then," Vitas said, coming up with a logical answer.

"No," John answered. "A free man. But like many in Rome, my faith makes me a fugitive."

Vitas wondered if John was being deliberately obtuse. Despite the open answers, so much remained unsaid. "Slave hunters, however, are not hired to pursue the other Christians."

"I cannot speak for them," John said. "Only myself."

"Then speak for yourself. Why was the slave hunter in pursuit of you?"

"I don't know."

"Guess then."

"It would be fruitless."

"And equally fruitless that you won't," Vitas said with a touch of irritation. "You've answered questions, but I haven't really learned anything about you."

John turned to him and grinned. It showed a flash of handsomeness on the elderly face. "And you have been forthcoming about yourself? Tell me, Roman, why have you dyed your hair so recently?"

Vitas reached up and rubbed his hair, wincing in preparation for the knives of pain that would come with the movement. He looked at his hand. Smears of a light color were obvious on his palm.

A thought began to run through his mind. *What happened to—?*

"Who beat your face but left your body untouched?" John asked. "Why didn't you know where this ship was headed? Who placed you on this ship? Why won't you even tell me your name?" John grinned again. "I prefer straightforward talk, but if needed, I can play the game too."

Vitas found the grin disarming. "My situation has forced me to trust no one."

"Then let me be straightforward first," John said. "Your questions tell me you hope to learn enough about me to know how far you can trust me."

Instead of answering, Vitas took a bite of cheese. The Jew was not a stupid man.

"What does the scroll say about me?" John asked.

This startled Vitas. He flinched slightly, expecting spasms of pain across his back.

"Roman," John said, "you're not the only one to spend time wondering about our situation. I doubt it is coincidence that you and I are on the same ship. You arrived on board with a sealed scroll. Now you show your first real interest in me only after reading the scroll."

"Are you able to read and write?"

John nodded. "Greek, Hebrew, and Aramaic."

"Not just Latin?"

John nodded again. "Jews live at the crossroads of the world. Necessity makes for a broad education."

Had the writer of the scroll known this? Vitas wondered. There was only one way to find out.

✛ ✛ ✛

Damian was still stretching and rubbing his eyes to find some degree of wakefulness when Castinus approached his bedroom, holding a sack in his right hand.

"I found this inside your property, near the wall," Castinus told Damian. He had to lean around Jerome to speak, because the giant slave stood guard directly in the center of the doorway. "It looks like someone threw it there from the street during the night."

"I'm not interested in garbage," Damian grunted. He made a waving motion for Castinus to leave. Damian didn't like mornings. Food didn't appeal to him until noon. He didn't like early conversation either. That was another reason he kept Jerome nearby this early. Along with Jerome's eternal vigilance, the slave's silence was a balm.

"It's not garbage," Castinus said. "I think you need to see it."

Castinus blinked and smiled and blinked again. It was an irritating habit.

"What I *need* to see is you walking away to gather at least a dozen slaves. We're going to a part of Rome where even Jerome might need reinforcements."

"There's a head inside," Castinus said. "A human head."

Damian stopped halfway through the beginning of a yawn. He snapped his mouth shut with an audible click of teeth.

"There was a message with it," Castinus said.

"A human head," Damian repeated, almost stupefied at the unexpectedness of it.

Castinus made a motion to pull it out.

"I'll believe you," Damian said sharply. Why would Castinus think he'd want to see a human head at this hour—or *any* hour? There was a reason Damian had avoided military service. Unlike most Romans, Damian saw nothing agreeable about severed body parts—especially the possibility of his own.

"This message," Damian said. "Dare I hope the head was intended for someone else?"

Castinus shook his head.

Damian took a deep breath. In his business, any number of people could have been responsible for sending a head with a message.

"Tell me then," Damian said without enthusiasm.

Castinus smiled and blinked. "The message says that the head belongs to the man executed in the arena in place of your brother, Vitas."

Damian became very still and attentive. *In place of Vitas.*

"It says Helius has discovered that Vitas is still alive," Castinus continued, "and that Helius has started pursuit of Vitas and intends to have him captured or killed."

Vitas? Still alive? Damian put up a hand to silence Castinus. He needed to think.

Who had delivered the head during the night? And why? Was the message true? Who was close enough to Helius to betray this information? What was the motive?

"Anything else?" Damian finally asked.

"Just the head and the note," Castinus said. "Could it be true? That Vitas escaped the arena and is still alive?"

Damian saw that Jerome's impassiveness had disappeared. That Jerome was staring hard at Damian, as if wondering too about Vitas.

"It's true or it isn't," Damian said. He was thinking aloud, speaking more to himself than to Castinus. "If Vitas is dead, this is just a cruel hoax and something I should ignore. If Vitas is alive and hasn't sent word to me for help, obviously he doesn't need it. In that case too, I should just ignore the note."

"What about Helius?" Castinus said. "If Vitas is alive and Helius has begun pursuit . . ."

"Whatever Vitas did to escape proves he can outsmart Helius at any time. I'm not worried about that." Damian smiled. "What about that? Vitas, still alive. If that's the case, I'll bet Helius is ready to do anything to keep Nero from finding out."

✚ ✚ ✚

It was time for Vitas to place some trust in the Jew. He took a
deep breath.

"My name is Gallus Sergius Vitas. I once served Nero as one of
his trusted advisers. On Venus—only four days ago, yet it feels like
a lifetime—in defense of my wife, I tried to strangle Nero. I was
unsuccessful. In the prison, after I was beaten across the face, a man
visited me and helped me escape. The dye in my hair was to ensure
I would not be recognized."

Vitas did not want to tell John the purpose of that beating. Or
what price the man had paid to help him escape.

"I am truly sorry for your troubles," John said.

Vitas sensed the truth in this man's compassion and appreciated
it, but did not show it. This would be weakness.

"Your wife," John said. "Did you prevent Nero from—?"

"Yes," Vitas said quickly. Then realized how quickly he'd said
it and how much the intensity of his anger reflected the fear and
worry he didn't want to face.

Vitas rubbed his eyes with one hand, took a deep breath. "I was
told that Nero did nothing to her."

And, Vitas thought, *I'm clinging to that belief as if it were driftwood and I were drowning.*

"She's still in Rome?"

"Yes." Another deep breath. He thought of how Helius had visited him in the jail cell and made a bargain with him. Could Helius
be trusted? Vitas had no choice but to believe it. "I need to go back.
To take her away from there. I had just learned she carries our first
child and—" Vitas started to lose control over his emotions and
stopped.

John smiled, as if sensing he needed to help Vitas. "This does not
sound like a typical Roman marriage of convenience and politics."

"No." Vitas smiled in return. "She's a Jew. A former slave. And
she made me move worlds until she agreed to marry me."

"She's a Jew," John said.

"You're making a generalization that your own people are bull-headed?"

John snorted. "Perhaps. What I meant, however, was that it is very difficult for a Jew to marry a Gentile."

"Ah," Vitas said. "Believe me, that came up. But as a follower of the Christos, she tells me that through the Christos, Jew and Gentile are the same, as are free men and slaves. That even from the beginning, God's people have been defined by faith, not ancestry."

"You, then, follow the Christos?"

"I've agreed to keep my heart open."

"Perhaps on this voyage," John said, "you'll let me tell you what I know of the Christos."

"I've read the letters circulating about him," Vitas answered. "More truthfully, listened to them as Sophia read them to me."

Vitas thought of all the hours that he had been content just to be near Sophia, listening to her voice. He'd known each moment how fortunate he was and now, away from her, knew even more how much he loved her.

"And?"

"And I will have many questions for you," Vitas answered. "But frankly, my other questions are more compelling for me."

"The scroll," John said with a nod.

"I don't even know the author of it, because I don't know who arranged my escape and the voyage on this ship." Vitas took another experimental breath, deeper than the one before, stretching the skin and muscles across his back. "The person or persons behind it are naturally cautious, as Nero would kill them and their families for their treason."

Remember Piso! That had been a clear-enough warning in the ambiguous scroll. Less than two years earlier, as Vitas well knew, a well-known and popular senator named Gaius Calpurnius Piso had led a conspiracy against Nero with many other Romans of prestige.

Eighteen of the forty-one prominent Romans implicated in the plot were killed by Nero, including Nero's former adviser, Seneca.

But beyond the warning was the implication: to mention Piso was to obliquely suggest a new conspiracy to assassinate Nero.

This injustice inflicted upon you by Nero is an injustice you must endure for a greater cause.

With his escape, Vitas had become part of that conspiracy. But Vitas would not know friend from enemy unless he found all the answers in the scroll.

"You ask me what the scroll says about you?" Vitas said. *The pieces are scattered in such a way that only you will be able to put them together. . . . The remainder of this letter is locked, but you will find the key nearby.* "In one way, nothing. It does not mention your name, or that you and I would be on this ship together."

"In another way?"

"I think I know why the writer of the scroll arranged our journey together," Vitas said.

Slowly, Vitas reached inside his tunic for the scroll. He'd been fighting the realization over the last few minutes but could no longer deny it.

His pain was gone! The agonizing pain that he'd quickly learned would accompany each of his movements no longer afflicted him. He'd moved his arms to eat, reached up to touch his hair, taken deep breaths. All without pain.

Vitas stood, scroll in his right hand.

Still no pain!

"Who are you?" he asked John again, wondering if he'd managed to keep the awe out of his voice. The cessation of pain had to be a coincidence. Or somehow John had suggested something in such a way that Vitas believed it possible and thus made it so.

"What answer does the scroll give to that question?" John asked in return, showing he either did not understand why Vitas had asked in such a manner or did not want to acknowledge the awe.

Vitas wasn't prepared yet to believe the pain was totally gone.

Instead of telling John about it, Vitas took the scroll and tore away the section in Latin. There was no need for John to see the suggestion of treason in it. Since Vitas had memorized the words, he crumbled the Latin portion and threw it into the sea.

"This," Vitas said, handing John the remainder of the scroll. "Can you read that?"

John unrolled more.

"Hebrew." John lifted his eyes to Vitas. "But you guessed that, didn't you? That's why you need to trust me."

Vitas nodded. He would ponder his lack of pain later and test his body more. For now, it was enough that two of his hunches about the scroll had been right: The symbols were Hebrew.

And John was the key to the lock.

HORA QUARTA

THE PROSTITUTE named Livia stood in front of a door on the top floor of a squalid apartment building. Rooms like these were the cheapest of the cheap. No water. No toilet facilities. Cooking was not allowed. Sometimes, apartments like this simply collapsed.

"Kaeso!" she said. She knocked on the door. "Kaeso!"

Moments later, a male voice inside answered. "Go away."

"It's Livia."

The door swung open. Kaeso grinned broadly and opened his arms. "Livia!"

Kaeso wore a tunic that had obviously been thrown on in a hurry. He was short and broad, with a face to match. It looked like he'd once taken a sword to the face. A thin scar ran diagonally across his forehead and continued below his eye, down his cheek. His grin showed broken teeth, and the smell of beer on his breath managed to assail Livia despite the competition of all the other stenches.

She stepped backward, away from the doorway. "I only see you. Not a fat purse like you promised."

"Livia," he scolded like an indulgent husband. "Live with me. You'll be taken care of."

"I see no money."

"Believe me, in a month or two, I'll have all the money you can spend."

"I believe no one." Livia tossed her hair. "I'd rather go back to Ostia."

"Livia!" Now Kaeso pleaded, stepping farther away from the door to follow her. "You've come all this way. Don't go."

Yet she did.

Kaeso took a step, and his tunic tangled around his legs. "Livia!" He hopped a few times, trying to adjust his clothing. "Livia!"

Livia reached the top of the steps and looked down.

She nodded to both of the men waiting partway up the steps. Damian and Jerome.

Abruptly, she turned back to Kaeso, moving several paces back toward his apartment. She allowed him to clutch her, then spun sideways, so that she was facing the steps again and Kaeso could not see Jerome approach.

Kaeso buried his face in her hair. "Livia!"

His moan of joy lasted only until Jerome grabbed his shoulder and smashed a fist into his face.

✠ ✠ ✠

"Let me say that you were very convincing yesterday," Helius told Chayim.

"I've brought you what you need," Chayim answered, holding a scroll. He never felt comfortable around Helius. This time was no different. "You can let both of them go now."

"Not so fast." Helius stroked his chin. He was standing in the shade of a tree, in the same courtyard where Chayim and Leah and Hezron had faced him the morning before. "Let's talk about your performance. I'm intrigued."

"Hezron says the letter has dozens of references to the writings of our prophets. That unless you think like a Jew and thoroughly know the language used in the writings of our prophets, it's difficult to make sense of it. A casual reading by a Roman or anyone else without that knowledge may well lead to a grotesque interpretation."

"The girl is certainly attractive," Helius said. He reached into the tree and pulled down a pomegranate. "I'd like to know how you so completely convinced her you are a believer. After all, it was what, two days ago that you joined their cult?"

Chayim held up the scroll. "You'll read, for example, references to a thousand-year reign in the letter from the Jew on Patmos. Hezron makes it clear that . . ."

Chayim paused and unfurled the scroll. It was difficult to concentrate with the general unease he felt in the presence of Helius and the added foreboding that came with the apparently casual questions about Leah. Helius never asked anything without purpose.

"Here," Chayim said, and read from the scroll. *"The thousand years is prophetic hyperbole and contrasts sharply with the three-and-a-half-year reign given to the Beast. It is emblematic of the enduring vindication of the martyrs who die on account of the Lamb."*

Chayim looked up. "Hezron references nearly a dozen times that our prophets used this number as a symbol of limitless or inexhaustible measure."

Chayim returned his gaze to the scroll. *"The Lord God revealed through his prophet Moses that he would show love to a thousand generations of those who love him and keep his commandments. Obviously this does not mean that God will stop showing love to the one thousand and first generation."*

Noting Helius's impatience, Chayim nervously skipped ahead. *"Hebrew prophets also use hyperbolic language to reveal the eternal significance of earthly events. An example of this form of prophetic hyperbole can be seen in the writing of the prophet Ezekiel concerning the siege of Jerusalem by the ancient Babylonian empire. Ezekiel prophesied that the destruction would be so great as to never be equaled again. The point was not that more Jews would die in this siege than in any other time in history or in the future. Rather, only hyperbolic language could fully capture the eternal significance of God's wrathful judgment on his people for their idolatry.*

"Here is how all of this relates to the Patmos letter. Just days before he was crucified, the false prophet Jesus of Nazareth used the same language

*of ultimate destruction to prophesy a coming judgment on Jerusalem. This
Revelation of John is merely an elaboration on Jesus' prophecy.'"*

"Enough! Set aside the interpretation and answer my question
about the girl!" Helius's voice became sharp. He stepped out of
the shade of the tree, the pomegranate almost hidden in his hand.
"I want to know how you fooled the girl so completely. In these
times, Christians are often afraid to trust anyone, even others who
claim the same faith. How did you do it?"

Why was this so important to Helius?

With trepidation, Chayim explained. Soldiers bursting into
the meeting. How he had accepted arrest along with the other
Christians. How he had engineered their freedom.

"Ingenious," Helius said. "But why should I be surprised? The
way you arranged to look like her rescuer again shows the same
deviousness. What woman wouldn't fall in love with a man who
released her from the arena prison? Especially a handsome young
man like you."

"You gave me a task," Chayim said. "Infiltrate the Christians
and find out the meaning of the letter. I did this to serve you."

Helius snorted. He ripped open the pomegranate. "You made
one mistake, my friend."

Chayim's heart rate increased. Mistake? In the courts of Nero,
survivors did not make mistakes.

"You needed her trust to succeed," Helius said. "But it's obvious
to me that you want more than an interpretation of the letter. You
want the girl. You weren't acting when you told her father you had
feelings for her. Am I right?"

"She's a Jew," Chayim said, trying to keep his answer light as he
lied. "You know I have more . . . exotic tastes."

"I know you Jews stick together. And no matter how you might
try to live differently here in Rome, your own blood is still Jewish.
So it forces me to wonder what you truly have in mind for her."

This was not something that Chayim dared to reveal to Helius.

"No answer?" Helius asked, the sharpness in his tone gone.

He picked at the seeds of the pomegranate. "You wouldn't care if I ripped her apart as I did this tender fruit?"

"You wanted the letter interpreted," Chayim said. "I have the document here for you."

"Ah, so you do care. That's valuable for me to know." Helius paused. "If I went to her now and explained that you were working for me all along, that would matter to you?"

"No," Chayim said. "What would it matter what she thinks? I've got the translation as you requested."

Helius shrugged. "Wait here. I'll send for a slave to escort her here to the courtyard. With you right here to watch her face as I tell her the truth. That you had arranged for her arrest so that we could use her as a means to bargain with her father, the famous but reclusive rabbi who hates the Romans so much he would never help us for any other reason."

Helius waved for a slave to join them.

Chayim thought of Leah's face as she learned of his betrayal. Knew Helius was not bluffing. Knew that Helius, in fact, would enjoy watching her pain. And enjoy watching him squirm.

"All right," Chayim said. "You are correct. It does matter to me what she thinks."

"It's more than that, isn't it?"

It was. Chayim slowly nodded.

"Good," Helius said. "I just wanted to be clear on this." Helius discarded the pomegranate. "Now, tell me more about the letter that the Christians call the Revelation."

✝ ✝ ✝

Eleven hundred and eighty-one.

Vitas was in deep thought, standing at the railing, not far from where John had given him the bread and cheese earlier. John was sitting cross-legged nearby, dipping a stylus into a pot of ink and writing on parchment.

Occasionally, whenever his mind returned to the present, Vitas marveled at how little pain movement brought him. But each time, he would return to the puzzle that he could not solve.

Eleven hundred and eighty-one.

How could this represent whoever had committed a dangerous act of treason to make the arrangements to place him on the ship?

Eleven hundred and eighty-one.

Vitas frowned at a sudden lurching of the ship. The wind had been at his back, and now the ship had turned, placing the breeze across his face.

At the ship's unexpected movement, low shouts came from among the crew at the rear of the deck.

"Unusual to tack with such favorable winds," John said.

Vitas turned. He'd been so deep in thought that he had not noticed the Jew's approach.

"I'm not a sailor," Vitas answered, "but even I find this strange."

He glanced at the outline of the island looming only miles away now. Buildings dotted across the hillsides were visible as tiny white spots.

His attention was diverted when John offered him a rolled-up papyrus. "My translation of the Hebrew into Greek."

"Thank you," Vitas said.

"I'm sorry it took so long." John handed Vitas the scroll and with a smile held up his hands to show ink on his palms. "My fingers are not as nimble as they were in my youth. The movement of the ship was an added difficulty."

Vitas nodded, but his mind was on the scroll he held, not on John's apology.

"I'm glad you are able to read Greek," John said. "I often write in Greek, although I tend to think in Hebrew, especially regarding spiritual matters. My habit of thinking in Hebrew made it easier to translate the scroll for you."

"Thank you."

John gave Vitas another of his gentle smiles. It occurred to Vitas that a subtle shift of authority had taken place. Vitas was treating

John as a father or elder statesman. Something about the man made such respect natural.

John said, "The words, I think, are clear. You may not find their meaning quite as transparent."

Without ceremony, Vitas unfurled the scroll and began to read John's translation:

You know the beast you must escape; the one with under-
standing will solve the number of this beast, for it is the
number of a man. His number is 666. You have fled the
city of this beast, from the sea it came and on the sea you go.
North and west of the city of the second beast, find the first
of five kings who have fallen. (The sixth now reigns, and
the seventh is yet to come.)

"That's it?" Vitas said. "Nothing more?"

"The beginning should be simple for you to understand," John said. Behind them, the crew still shouted back and forth. "You know the name of the Beast."

"I know, of course, gematria," Vitas said. "Who in the world does not, except those who cannot read?"

Gematria. Vitas thought of the graffiti he'd seen during a walk in the markets a few days earlier, which had made him smile because he, too, was a man in love.

It had been a Greek inscription on a wall:

$$\varphi\iota\lambda\hat{\omega}\ \hat{\eta}\varsigma\ \dot{\alpha}\rho\iota\theta\mu\acute{o}\varsigma\ \varphi\mu\epsilon$$

During that walk Vitas had immediately made a mental translation: *I love her whose number is 545.*

The man in love had found it necessary to conceal her name. He knew, however, that when she saw the graffiti, she would recognize her identity, for all she'd have to do is add up the numerical values of the letters in her name. Others, unaware of the relationship, would not be able to easily identify the beloved, for many names might have the same numerical value.

Vitas was aware too of a popular Greek graffiti that lampooned and infuriated Nero:

Νεόψηφον· Νέρων ἰδίαν
μητέρα ἀπέκτεινε

A new calculation: Nero murdered his own mother. Every reader of this, from children up, understood the slyness of it. Count the numerical values of the letters in Nero's name and in *murdered his own mother*, and you would find their sums to be the same.

Gematria. Every letter in the Greek alphabet corresponded to a specific number. In Greek, all the numbers in Nero's name added up to the same numbers found in *murdered his own mother*. It was a clever verse and clever piece of gematria, showing the widespread knowledge that Nero had indeed murdered his mother, Agrippina.

Despite his thorough knowledge of something as common as gematria, Vitas could not agree with John, especially after several moments of calculation.

"I know that I flee Nero," Vitas said, his mental addition complete. "But his number is 1,005."

"Yes," John said. "In Greek. You should know that what I've transcribed for you are indirect references from a letter circulating among the followers of the Christos. It describes a vision and is known as the Revelation."

"I presume you're familiar with this Revelation."

"Very familiar. Given the chance, there is a lot I can tell you about it."

Vitas waved his hand, as if impatient to stay on subject. "I'm less interested in your reaction to it and more interested in the content. But just a summary."

"Of course." John stared at the horizon briefly, then turned his eyes back to Vitas. "It contains further revelation from Jesus the Christos regarding the coming destruction of Jerusalem he prophesied on the Mount of Olives just days before his death. It describes how God's eternal plan of redemption for the righteous and judgment for the wicked and unrepentant is being fulfilled in this generation. It foretells the ultimate destruction of the evil one and the vindication of the crucified and resurrected Lord, Jesus. It is a message of hope and a call to perseverance through persecution for those who have placed their faith for eternal salvation in Jesus, receiving his righteousness on their behalf. And it is a desperate call to repentance for those of the spirit of antichrist who continue to live in rebellion against God, denying that Jesus is the Christos."

Vitas snorted. "How accurate can this vision be if something as simple as the gematria of Nero's name is miscalculated?"

"It is helpful to think like a Hebrew. To us Jews, he is known as *Neron Kesar*. You're aware that written Hebrew does not use vowels?"

"No."

"That's why," John said, "you would not identify Nero as 666, when insightful Jewish readers familiar with the Hebrew spelling of his name would do so, especially given the other clues in the Revelation that identify Nero as the Beast."

Vitas read over the beginning of the scroll again. *"You know the beast you must escape; the one with understanding will solve the number of this beast, for it is the number of a man. His number is 666."*

Vitas spoke his thoughts. "I know that I must escape Nero, and the writer of the message knows that I must escape Nero. Why go to the effort, then, of telling me the obvious?"

"You called me the key to the lock," John said. "Perhaps it's the first test or confirmation that I can help you."

Vitas thought of something else. *Eleven hundred and eighty-one.*

"It's telling me something else," Vitas said. "I'm to use gematria to solve something in the first part of the scroll." He explained it to John, realizing that doing so was a further extension of trust.

Eleven hundred and eighty-one.

"Greek, Hebrew, or Latin?" John asked. "Which language should you use to add up the numbers of the name?"

"That's what makes it so difficult to solve the name from just knowing the numbers. But within the proper context, once I have the name, I can test it against the gematria and have near absolute certainty that I was correct."

Vitas paced a few steps, ignoring the growing shouts coming from the crew behind them.

"There is also no doubt that I need you to understand the letter," Vitas told John. A part of his mind was still astounded that his wounds gave no pain. "Without you, none of this made sense."

John was given no time to comment.

One shout came clearly from the rear of the deck. "Call the captain!" It was the voice of Betto, the sailing master. "The steering oar has broken!"

✦ ✦ ✦

"Amazing how much you bleed for a man reported dead," Damian told Kaeso. "You weren't trying to escape gambling debts by spreading the story you had drowned, were you?"

Jerome had lifted Kaeso off his feet and shoved him back into the cramped, filthy apartment. Kaeso was sitting on the floor, holding his nose, trying to stem the blood that flowed from it.

Kaeso groaned.

"Just so you know, I don't like it when people get hurt," Damian told Kaeso. "You may not believe me, because I'm sure your nose has had finer moments. But if I really wanted you hurt, my slave here could bring you so close to death you'd beg for him to make it happen."

Jerome stood behind Damian, arms crossed. As always, no expression on his face.

Damian squatted and grabbed at Kaeso's tunic. He ripped off

a large piece and pressed it against Kaeso's face. "See how much I care for you?"

Kaeso grunted. He appeared to be too stunned to think. Which was exactly what Damian wanted. It was far better to break resistance immediately than to give a man the chance to find some courage.

"Tell me when we can expect money for the people who sent us," Damian said. "That's all. Then we'll leave you alone and in no further pain."

"You'll get the money soon," Kaeso said, his voice muffled by the wad of cloth against his nose. "I promise."

Poor man, Damian thought. Damian knew too well a gambler's desperation. "I want to believe you," Damian said in a soothing voice. "But I've heard too many like you make up too many stories."

For that matter, there had been a time in Damian's life when he'd become very skilled at making up those same kinds of stories for the same reason: to stall repayment of a gambling debt, convinced he would win big on the next race.

"It's not a story," Kaeso mumbled. Tears from his eyes ran into the wadded cloth.

"Convince me and perhaps we'll leave you alone."

"My brother's on a ship," Kaeso said.

"That's very nice for your brother. Is he trying to escape gambling debts too?"

"No! He's the sailing master."

"He's going to send you his wages?" Damian said. "I doubt that's enough."

"Just listen to me," Kaeso said, exasperated despite his obvious pain.

Damian was proud of himself. If Kaeso actually knew how desperately Damian wanted to hear the story, all of this would be more difficult.

"I'm listening," Damian said. "It had better be good."

"There's a man on the ship," Kaeso said. "A wealthy Roman citizen. Fleeing Nero. Along with a Jew who's probably his slave."

"That doesn't make this man special. Any wealthy Roman citizen should be doing the same, given Nero's habits of late."

"You don't understand. This man had been sent to the arena to be executed."

"Of course, of course. And the soldiers released him and encouraged him to find a convenient ship for escape." Damian hardened his voice as he spoke to Jerome. "Perhaps this man needs your attention again. He seems to be wandering from the truth."

"No!" Kaeso yelped. "My brother heard it all. Someone was speaking to the captain, and Betto—"

"Who is Betto?" Damian sounded bored.

"My brother. Just listen, will you?"

"Time is short."

"Listen," Kaeso pleaded. "The captain was paid a great deal of money to leave immediately with this man. At night. You can go to Ostia and ask anyone who knows about the ship. It left just a few nights ago. Stranding dozens of passengers who had expected voyage on it."

"Even if the story is true, it doesn't explain how you expect money from it."

"My brother is the navigator. He's going to make sure the ship has troubles."

"Not much money in that."

"Yes, there is." Kaeso grimaced. "Once I tell you the rest of it, you'll understand how I'll have enough money never to be in debt again."

"Make it good and make sure I believe it," Damian said. "Or you'll find yourself tossed into the street below."

✚ ✚ ✚

"Revelation?" Chayim said to Helius. "This entire scroll from Hezron has a thorough—"

"You did read it." Helius was curt.

"Yes."

"Then give me something I can understand immediately. Without spending an hour on laborious markings by an old Jew."

Chayim knew this was another challenge. He focused. And began. "It says that the Christos, a certain Jesus from Nazareth who claimed to be Messiah and the Son of God, is the true Lord, not Caesar."

Helius, who had been pacing casually, froze.

"It is a story about a war between the Beast and the Lamb, and it claims that the Lamb will be triumphant. It says that the God of Israel is coming in judgment—very soon—on Israel and on Rome. On Israel because they rejected and crucified Jesus. And on Rome because of the persecution of the followers of this man they call the Christos."

"War?"

"It promises resurrection and eternal life to followers of the Christos, and says that at the end of time, there will be a new earth and a new heaven established, with a final judgment on those who reject the Lamb."

"Leave me the scroll," Helius said. He would definitely have to read more and understand exactly what the Revelation entailed. It was nonsense, of course. There was no power in this world capable of defeating Rome. But, given Nero's superstitions, it was still dangerous.

Chayim reached to hand it across. "Leah and her father . . ."

"Under house arrest until you return. This is, I'm sure, a concept you find familiar." Helius was referring to Chayim's presence in the royal palace. Chayim himself was a hostage of sorts, sent to Rome from Jerusalem because it ensured that his father, a highly placed temple priest, would influence those around him to cooperate with the Roman authorities.

"House arrest. You said that—"

"Don't make me weary," Helius said. "Politics are about

promises. Not promises kept. Certainly by now you've realized that about Rome. If you haven't, then you should thank me for providing you with a valuable education."

Chayim stared at Helius.

Helius coughed discreetly. "I believe I just made a suggestion."

Chayim swallowed. "Thank you, Helius. It's kind of you to teach me such a valuable lesson."

"Think nothing of it." No matter how often he exercised his power—in small ways or large—Helius never found that it lost any allure. "As for this travel, I am going to provide you with a letter from the emperor. And a substantial retinue of soldiers. Spare yourself no luxury. Just remember that the sooner you return, the sooner Leah and her father will be released."

Helius left unspoken what they both knew. If Chayim did not return, the only way Leah or Hezron would leave the palace was as a corpse.

"I want you to find someone for me," Helius said. "And no one must know about your task. If Nero finds out, I'll have you tortured and executed."

This was why Helius had chosen Chayim. The young Jew's obvious lust for power had ensured compliance and trustworthiness so far. And with Leah and Hezron prisoners at the palace, Chayim now had extra motivation to do as directed.

"Certainly," Chayim said after a pause so brief it might have been imagined.

"You are to find a woman named Sophia," Helius said. "She is Vitas's wife. You might recall that certain episode a few evenings ago when Vitas attacked the emperor?"

The dinner party. Chayim was sure he had been invited specifically to see how Helius and Tigellinus dealt with their enemies.

"The man was arrested and killed a few days ago in the arena," Chayim said. "His wife, I believe, was invited to commit suicide."

"She fled Rome," Helius said. "With only an old man as companion. Their destination is Corinth. Find them both. Either on the way to Corinth or in Corinth. The sooner the better. Wherever you find them, your letter will give you authority to allow your soldiers to arrest Sophia."

"And the old man?" Chayim asked.

"He'll need to be killed, of course. That way there will be one less person able to talk about it."

Chayim nodded.

"One last thing," Helius said. "The soldiers will not know why you are looking for the woman and the old man. But they will know enough to let them decide if it looks like you are going to betray me. And if that happens, they have orders to supervise your crucifixion."

✢ ✢ ✢

"I know the beast I must escape," Vitas said to John. "I've fled the city of this beast—Rome. But *from the sea it came*?"

The crew around them was working with urgency but not panic. Because Vitas could do nothing to help anyway, he remained focused on the questions that were compelling to him.

"But *from the sea it came*?" John repeated the question Vitas had posed. "Answering that is impossible for any Roman who demands a literal interpretation of symbolic language."

"I'm trying to understand this Hebrew message, which is telling me either that Nero rose from the sea or Rome rose from the sea. Which is it?"

"Does a province of Rome serve the emperor or the empire?" John asked.

"Why does it seem that you enjoy tormenting me by answering questions with questions?"

John laughed softly. "I'm a Jew. We don't think of it as torment. We think of it as a learning method. You now understand how I was taught in my youth by rabbis in the synagogues."

"So I should suffer as you did."

"If you must consider it suffering. But answer me. Does a province serve the emperor or the empire?"

"Both."

"Then you have your answer. The Beast is both Nero *and* Rome. Even when Nero no longer rules, the Beast will exist."

"You dance around like a fox pouncing on mice in tall grass. I feel like one of the mice. All of this, and I still don't understand how Nero and Rome rise from the sea."

"Rome is west of Judea. Across the Mediterranean. To us Jews, when you came to conquer, it was as if you rose from the sea and descended upon our land. But the language is even richer than that and speaks on a different level too, if you understand our culture. The sea is also sin, its dark depths an abode of evil and chaos."

"To understand this, then, I need to understand how you Jews think."

"You must understand our culture and history to understand many of the references in the message written for you and, of course, the vision of Revelation that the message draws from. This vision was written and passed on to others," John continued. "It circulates now among the followers of the Christos. To understand its richly symbolic language, you need to have familiarity with the sacred writings of the Jews."

"Why?"

"Our prophets often allude to earlier prophecies and symbolic language within those prophecies. To Jews, the blood of the lamb, for example, is not only the literal blood of animals slain in sacrifice, but is an allusion to the way that God allows redemption for—"

"You understand the meaning of these symbols."

"I know the allusions, yes. And hope to have time to explain over the days of this voyage."

"Please," Vitas said, "just explain the symbols in the letter that was delivered to me. Without taking days to educate me."

John shrugged. He had the scroll with his Greek translation of the letter to Vitas in front of him. *"From the sea it came and on the sea you go. North and west of the city of the second beast—'"* John paused—"you want me to identify the second beast for you."

"Yes!" Vitas said. "Then sentence by sentence, continue doing the same with the rest of this message."

"Jerusalem," John said. "That is your second beast. Does that satisfy you?"

Vitas was about to agree, but gave it some thought. He sighed. "It does not."

"Because even if you trust me," John said, "this letter is so important to you that you must know you can trust the answers I give."

Vitas sighed again. "Yes. It makes no sense to me that the city of the second Beast is Jerusalem. If Rome is the first Beast that has devoured your people, how can it be that Jerusalem, the very center of Judea, would be considered a Beast of danger to your people?"

"As I said, we have a long journey," John said. "I look forward to speaking at length about all of this. I would guess whoever put us on the ship together knew that."

"How about satisfying me with shorter answers first." Vitas stared at the writing on the scroll: *North and west of the city of the second beast, find the first of five kings who have fallen. (The sixth now reigns, and the seventh is yet to come.)*

"I know where it is telling me to go next," Vitas announced after some thought.

"As a Roman," John said, "you should."

"Julius Caesar, Augustus, Tiberius, Caligula, Claudius, and Nero," Vitas said. "*Find the first of the five kings who have fallen. The sixth now reigns and the seventh is yet to come.*' Nero now reigns, but the first . . ."

Vitas grinned with satisfaction. "North and west of Jerusalem is the city of Caesarea, named for Julius Caesar." Then he frowned. "Flee Rome; go to Caesarea. Those are vague instructions. Surely there is more."

"Not on the scroll you gave me," John said.

Comprehension came to Vitas. "*'The promise is simple,*'" Vitas quoted aloud from the letter that had accompanied the scroll: "*'The pieces are scattered in such a way that only you will be able to put them together.'"*

"There are more parts to the scroll," John said.

"Where?" Vitas answered, thinking aloud.

"I can't answer that," John said. "But at this moment, we face a more immediate concern."

Vitas looked where John was pointing.

Ahead, at the approaching whirlpools of Messana.

HORA QUINTA

IN HER PRIVATE COURTYARD, Alypia sat in the sun, knees raised, face upward, eyes closed. She'd allowed her tunic to slide across her thighs in a way that showed far more than allowed by modesty. She also pretended not to be aware that Damian had arrived. That she was giving him a voyeur's moment.

Damian enjoyed it and disliked himself for it.

"I've changed my mind." He was brusque. A way to combat the desire she stirred.

Alypia opened her eyes and slowly swung her face toward him. Her wide cheekbones were beautifully framed by her long, dark hair, unencumbered by the blonde wig she'd worn during their previous meeting in the litter.

"Come closer, then. We have as much privacy as we need here."

"I've decided to look for your stepchildren." Damian knew the balance of power had shifted because he'd returned to her. There was, however, a simple way to tilt it back toward him again. "But I'm going to need double what you've offered."

"Double?" She sat forward and tucked her legs beneath her, careless of how the tunic fell across her legs.

"Otherwise I'd prefer to stay in Rome."

She examined him. "You're bluffing. And it's a pitiful bluff at that."

"If what you say about Maglorius is true, he'll be a dangerous enemy in Jerusalem."

"You're not afraid of him. Have you incurred more gambling debts?"

Damian looked away, hoping she'd see it as a sign of weakness.

She laughed. "You are far too easy to read. Too bad you aren't that easy to seduce."

"Do we have an agreement?"

"Of course. I'm not worried about money."

"Then let's make the arrangements," Damian said.

"I'd love to," Alypia said. She smiled and patted a place beside her. "Why don't we take the rest of the day to make sure we've covered all the details?"

"I'll be sending one of my slaves," Damian said, very tempted but doing his best to hide it. "Arrange to have half of the amount available. I'll collect the other half when I return."

He forced himself to walk away without looking back.

✦ ✦ ✦

"We could have met at the forum," Helius said, "but I don't want people wondering what matter I have to discuss with you."

"I see," Caius Sennius Ruso replied, gesturing at the opulence of the private chambers of Helius. "So we are here because you are concerned strictly about my reputation?"

"You'd better be," Helius said.

"I have nothing to hide."

"Then tell me where you were the last three days," Helius said, expecting Ruso to tell a lie. That would give Helius an immediate edge, including a sharp response to Ruso's sarcastic insolence.

"Yesterday I was at home," Ruso said evenly.

Evasion like this was no surprise to Helius. "And the day before that?"

"With Gallus Sergius Damian," Ruso said. "You're familiar, of course, with his brother, Vitas, as you just had him executed in the arena."

Ruso was a senator, with his share of influence and power. But that power paled in comparison to the whims of Nero. Most senators, upon an invitation to a private audience with Helius, would show some degree of apprehension. Was Ruso responding with this arrogance because he truly had nothing to hide?

"Did Damian treat you well?" Helius asked.

"No," Ruso said. "He had me bound and kept me in a shed without food or water."

Helius tilted his head slightly. This candor was startling.

"Not the answer you expected?" Ruso asked, amused. When Helius remained silent, Ruso continued. "Let's stop playing games, shall we? I'm sure you already know what happened. Either a spy in Damian's household or mine told you. Otherwise, why invite me here?"

Helius leaned forward. "You, a senator, captured and bound in broad daylight. Yet I haven't heard any complaints or calls for the arrest of Damian. Something is strange about this."

"He was looking for a Jew named John," Ruso said, "who has written some kind of treasonous letter."

"Damian told you this?"

"No. He interrogated me as if I were that Jew. I presume you hired Damian."

Since Ruso had made that accurate presumption, Helius saw no harm in acknowledging it, especially if he could learn more about Damian's intentions. "Did Damian tell you why he didn't hand you over to me immediately?"

"No," Ruso said, still amused.

"Why didn't you tell him who you were?"

"And risk my death?"

"I don't understand."

"Put yourself in my position. You are walking through a market when, without warning, you are gagged and kidnapped and thrown into a private litter. When you are finally taken out of the litter, you discover that the man who has captured you is a famous slave hunter who believes you to be a Jew sought by Nero. You are now isolated in this man's complete power. What might he do if he discovers he has captured the wrong man? Perhaps kill you to make sure you don't have a chance to let the world know of his mistake. So I remained silent, hoping that my own clients would somehow come to my rescue."

"That sounds rehearsed," Helius said.

"Of course it is," Ruso snapped. "You call me for a private audience the day after I'm released. I would be an idiot not to expect your questions."

"Why were you released?"

"Somehow, it didn't seem like a question to ask. I was happy for my freedom."

"And now that you are free, why haven't you had Damian—" Helius stopped as a small slave entered the courtyard, bowed, and waited to be acknowledged or given permission to speak.

Helius sighed. "What is it?"

"The emperor wishes to see you," the slave said. "Immediately." Without waiting for Helius to respond, the slave bowed again and trotted from the courtyard.

Helius felt the familiar spasm of his bowels, and it took all his effort to remain composed. Nero? What had the emperor discovered? Was this it? Would he be sent to the arena?

"You were asking why I haven't had Damian arrested," Ruso said. "What good would it do? He won't make that mistake again. And I know that he knows my identity. That alone should keep him away from me in the future."

Helius blinked, forcing himself to remain in the present. "You know that he knows . . ."

"The slave who released me followed me to my estate. It was pitiful, actually, his efforts to remain hidden."

"I see." Helius had hoped to find some leverage on Ruso and at the same time learn more about Damian. He'd failed in both and succeeded in letting Ruso know that he was indeed in pursuit of the Jew who had written the troublesome letter.

"I'm finished with you," Helius said. He gave Ruso a tiny wave of the hand, suggesting that his brief audience with him was finished and barely of consequence anyway. With legs that hardly wanted to obey him, he escorted Ruso to the hallway and immediately turned the opposite direction.

Nero hated to be kept waiting.

✤ ✤ ✤

Earlier Pavo had made a decision not to lower the sails, hoping the steering oar would be fixed so soon that it would be more efficient to tack westward than to waste the time it would take to raise the sails again.

He'd lost his gamble.

Even with the wind pushing the sails at an angle instead of from behind, the ship's speed had been enough to send it dangerously close to the eastern edge of the large island looming ahead.

He and the pilot had also misjudged the tidal currents between the Tyrrhenian Sea to the north of Sicily and the Ionian Sea to the south. At the beginning of the straits, the distance between Sicily and the mainland was under two miles, with a sea bottom so deep it had never been charted. As water rushed between the rising hills on each side, it created a series of whirlpools, the largest of which formed a dangerous vortex beneath the mainland cliff of Scylla.

Charybdis.

This was the giant whirlpool that Ulysses had faced in his great odyssey, with the opposing cliff of Scylla like a monster ready to destroy any vessel that escaped Charybdis.

"Drop the sails!" roared Pavo. "Drop the sails!"

Men scurried to follow his orders.

Although still a half mile away, the sucking and gurgling of the tidal currents at Scylla were easily heard above the screaming of seagulls and the shouting of the crew.

Vitas was mesmerized by the sight of large pieces of jetsam bobbing into the vortex and disappearing. Intellectually, he knew the whirlpool wasn't as strong as legend suggested; it could not pull down a ship like this. But without a steering oar or sails, he had no doubt it could spin the ship and dash it into the cliffs of Scylla, where the white splash of waves against sharp rocks was easily visible at this distance.

"May the gods be with us," he breathed.

"May God be with us," he heard John say.

Vitas turned to John and marveled at the serenity on the older man's face. His eyes were closed. Vitas didn't want to intrude on John's private moment.

He moved closer to Pavo and overheard Betto say, "You should have let us sacrifice the Jew."

"We'll deal with that later," Pavo snapped. "Right now I have a ship to save."

"Without sails, we're at the mercy of the current. And you can feel it gaining speed."

"We'll drop the sea anchors," Pavo said. "We won't drag bottom, of course, but perhaps it will slow us."

"No," Betto answered. "We're going to lose all maneuverability with the sails down. If we get sucked into Charybdis, the last thing we want is something that would prevent us from being spat out again."

"What do we do?"

"Send me down to the steering oar," Betto said.

"What!"

"Lower me by rope. Let me see if I can do anything to fix it."

"We don't have time."

"We don't have a choice."

Vitas watched Pavo's face and saw the flickering of a decision.

"Go," Pavo said.

✠ ✠ ✠

Three palace guards escorted Helius down a corridor toward Nero's inner chambers. Helius racked his brain, struggling to find a reason for this summons other than a death sentence. But he of all people knew that when Nero wanted to see someone "immediately," the prospects for a long life were dim indeed. So Helius contemplated his death, and he discovered something he had suspected all along: he had no courage.

A man can wonder, he realized, but not until the test arrives can he actually know. On occasion, he'd been with soldiers when Christians were arrested and found himself astounded as the mousiest of women became lions of resolve. More often, however, he witnessed this same courage in the arenas as those Christians endured the savagery of the beasts, and he would force himself to ignore traces of jealousy.

As for himself, immediately after the summons, he'd retreated to a lavatory. After vomiting, he lost control of his bowels, too.

His terror was the arena. If he believed in the gods, he would have prayed for the mercy of an invitation from Nero to empty his veins instead.

The arenas. How ironic, Helius thought, that after all he'd helped Nero inflict upon Christians, he'd now learn for himself the horrors of their tribulation.

In the lavatory, preparing to meet with Nero, an image had flashed through Helius's mind. Of a lawyer found guilty of embezzling from a client and sent to the arena. Rather than face the lions, the lawyer had used a sponge on a stick—the same sponge used for personal hygiene in the lavatory—and shoved the sponge so far down his throat that he successfully committed suicide by asphyxiation.

In his own lavatory, Helius had contemplated immediate suicide, but with the guard outside and no way of getting to a knife to slit his wrists, he found he didn't have enough courage to force a sponge down his throat.

This contrast, too, seemed ironic. He was one of the most powerful men in the empire, yet he did not possess the courage and defiance in the face of gruesome death owned by the most penniless of Christians in the arena.

After washing, he'd meekly gone toward his audience with Nero, telling himself he would talk his way out of trouble, rehearsing his plea.

Yes, I deserve execution. But with me dead, Vitas will surely escape. And what will serve you better? Punishment, just as it is, meted out to me? Or the capture of Vitas to end any threats of a plot against you?

Helius knew this was Nero's biggest terror. A plot to assassinate him. He would carefully capitalize on Nero's fear and hope for the best.

Helius continued to rehearse his arguments as he passed the expensive tapestries hanging on the walls, the sculptures and busts. To think he would no longer enjoy these beautiful luxuries as if they were his.

It was a consolation of sorts that if he was killed, he'd still have his revenge on Vitas. For if the escape of Vitas had led to this—a death sentence from Nero—then at least Helius had started a chain of events that would kill Vitas. Vitas would pay for what happened today.

When Helius reached Nero, his legs were trembling. He was glad that his toga draped most of his body.

Worse, Sporus sat on a nearby cushion to witness whatever nightmare Nero would decree on him. Helius took no satisfaction in the boy's pallor and obvious pain. If Nero could castrate someone as an act of love, it was unimaginable what he might unleash in rage; except Helius knew too well by now what to imagine.

"Helius," Nero said in a hearty voice.

Faked camaraderie?

Helius remembered how he himself had stroked the face of Sporus before pronouncing the boy's fate, knowing that pretended affection would accentuate the horror about to be inflicted. Was Nero playing the same game?

"I sent the guards because I wanted you here immediately," Nero said. He frowned as he examined Helius. "Are you feeling well?"

"Indigestion," Helius lied.

"Find the cook responsible and feed him to the lions." Nero laughed at his own joke. "Let him spoil their digestion in place of those unpalatable Christians."

Was Nero setting up a terrible punch line?

"Excellent plan, as always," Helius managed to say.

"That's why you're here," Nero said.

It was like Nero had reached out to squeeze Helius's heart.

"Excellent planning?" Helius uttered in a choked voice.

"Indeed. It's about my trip to Greece."

Greece. This was the first ray of hope for Helius. Greece?

"I may be gone for months," Nero said. "As you know, I am their favorite god."

What Helius knew was that Nero lavished money on Greek cities willing to put up temples for the purpose of worshiping him.

"You are their only god," Helius said. "As is just and fair and right."

Nero nodded. "While I cannot leave Sporus behind," he said, "I'm afraid I won't be able to take you with me. I hope you'll understand."

"Of course," Helius said. His mood had gone from terrified self-preservation to rage at the unfairness of it. He'd been totally replaced by Sporus. A boy with no manhood!

"After all," Nero continued, "you are the one person I trust to handle all the affairs of Rome in my absence."

Rage died. Had Helius heard right?

"You will accept this responsibility, won't you?"

All of the affairs of Rome? Helius would become de facto emperor!

"Helius?"

He realized he'd been so stunned by this unexpected offer that he had not replied to Nero.

"You are pleased, aren't you?" Nero sounded anxious.

Helius smiled broadly at his emperor.

"Pleased?" Helius answered. "Beyond anything you could imagine."

✛ ✛ ✛

The ship was now five hundred yards away from Charybdis. Between the landmasses, the wind had funneled and blew hard.

Three crewmen were holding a rope that had been used to lower Betto at the stern of the boat.

Finally, Vitas heard the words that gave him relief.

"Sails up!" Betto shouted. "Put a man on the steering oar!"

As the three crew members pulled Betto back onto the ship, the other crewmen began hoisting rope to pull up the square rig and topsail.

Four hundred yards to Charybdis. It seemed the ship was still gaining speed in the tidal current.

A gust of wind caught the square rig and tilted the ship dangerously. A cacophony of curses burst from the crew as they tried to trim the sails.

Three hundred yards.

Vitas saw more debris pulled into the vortex and sucked out of sight. The dashing of waves on the rocks of the cliff behind the whirlpool threw spray at least thirty feet into the air. If the ship spun into Charybdis, it would certainly spin out again into the sharp rocks.

Two hundred yards.

Betto was on deck again. He dashed to the steering oar and leaned into it. The ship seemed to groan. The mainmast creaked. Again the ship tilted, throwing Vitas off balance.

Then slowly, surely, the ship began to turn away from the giant whirlpool.

A hundred yards.

Would the steering oar hold under the tremendous pressure against wind and current?

Fifty yards.

Vitas ran across the pitching deck toward John. "Rope," Vitas said tersely. He was angry at himself for not thinking of it earlier. "We've got time to rope ourselves to the railing."

But Vitas was wrong.

What seemed like seconds later, the hull of the ship touched the edge of the vortex.

Vitas prepared himself for the violence of a plunging, swirling ship.

But the weight of the ship was too great, and the wind in the sail too strong. The ship continued through the edge, untouched by the whirlpool. The cliffs of Scylla began to recede.

Pavo approached. "Ahead is Messana," he growled at Vitas. "It's obvious we're going to have to stop in the harbor to repair the steering oar."

Messana. With a nearby legion. Surely among the soldiers was someone who knew of Vitas. He could stay here, send for Sophia, find a way to—

"I'm going to have to place you in chains until we leave harbor again," Pavo said. "So don't entertain any thoughts of escape."

Before Vitas could protest, Pavo pointed at John. "You'll be in chains as well. I don't like the two of you together. It makes me wonder what you're plotting, and it makes the crew nervous. So you'll each stay in those chains, kept well apart until just before we arrive in Alexandria."

AD 66
JERUSALEM

Province of Judea

✠

Now learn this lesson from the fig tree: As soon as its twigs get tender and its leaves come out, you know that summer is near. Even so, when you see all these things, you know that it is near, right at the door.

—MATTHEW 24:32-33

❦ 13 AV ❧

THE TENTH HOUR

QUINTUS BEGAN TO stalk the soldiers just after they crossed the moat that protected the vulnerable north and east walls of Antonia Fortress.

He had waited on the flat roof of a nearby wool shop for three hours for this opportunity, rising and dashing down the steps on the outside of the building on sturdy little legs as soon as the massive fortress gates had begun to swing open. His patience in the late-summer heat was all the more remarkable because he was only seven years old. He was small for his age but intelligent and quick—two qualities that, along with his newly learned patience, had served him well during weeks of foraging the crowded market streets of Jerusalem.

Quintus had known there would be time to find a hiding spot in an alley near the moat before the soldiers passed by. The troops would assume a protective formation on the bridge until the gate closed behind them again, a military procedure that Quintus had observed previously and understood and appreciated without needing anyone to explain.

The smell of dye permeated the hot, calm air of the alley, along with faint traces of the stench of curing hides from the tanning factories past the clothes market and blacksmith shops that lined the street farther down. There had been a time when Quintus would have curled his nostrils at the slightest of smells, but he was past that now. The expensive laced boots of leather that he'd been

so proud of in the days of servants and hot baths were cut open at
the toes to allow room for his growing feet, and by necessity he'd
long since discarded the blue tunic that would have marked him
as a spoiled Roman boy. Now he wore rags he'd found in a garbage heap.

As the soldiers marched past him, heading west into the afternoon sun, Quintus counted. A dozen soldiers were mounted on
horses, wearing the colors of the royal troops sent by King Agrippa.
Another dozen were on foot, obviously part of the Roman garrison
stationed in Antonia Fortress.

This was good, he thought. Not too many to discourage an
attack by the rebels but enough troops to defend themselves well.
With luck, there would be serious casualties on both sides and
sufficient chaos to take advantage of it.

Yes, Quintus told himself, *definitely worth the risk.*

He waited until their long shadows disappeared from the cobblestones in front of him and then scurried out of the alley to follow.

It didn't matter to him why they'd left the safety of the fortress.
Only that there was a good chance the rebels would learn of it soon
enough to attack.

✦ ✦ ✦

"Why the delay?" Falco asked the centurion. In the shade at the
base of a small cliff, he was tired of travel and still far too hot. Ahead
would be rest and food and a place to bathe himself of the wretched
Judean dust.

The cliff was just off the road that came from Caesarea, near the
crest of a broken hill that gave travelers their first view of Jerusalem.

"If you'd been to Jerusalem before, you would understand."
The centurion normally would not bother to explain himself, but
if Falco was important enough to command this escort from the
procurator, there was no sense in offending the man.

"What's to understand?" Falco said. "We've stopped when I'd
rather finish this hellish journey."

"This." The centurion, a hulking man who limped heavily, led Falco away from the twenty soldiers under his command, along the last few paces of the road to the crest.

Falco sucked in a breath of surprise at the vista ahead. In contrast to the reds and browns of the other hills, the Temple Mount seemed to blaze as the gold-plated marble bounced sunlight in all directions. Other blocks of marble, brilliant white, formed the mansions of the upper city. Rooftop gardens made jewels of emerald green.

"It's a shame, isn't it?" the centurion said. "Such a quarrelsome people and such a beautiful city."

"This doesn't explain our delay." Although Falco was balding and pudgy and wheezed continuously like a sweating peasant, he was a sophisticated man who lived in Rome. He refused to echo the centurion's grudging admiration for Jerusalem.

"I've been commanded to take you there," the centurion said, pointing at the western wall of the city. "Herod's palace. It's in the upper city and safe from rebels, but if we go through the city itself, we expose ourselves to attack."

The centurion pointed at hills west of the city. "If we detour to come in from the west, we may not make it before sunset, and besides that, I'm sure you don't want an extra couple hours of travel."

Falco grunted. "I trust, then, you are suggesting a safer alternative." He mopped his forehead with a square piece of silk.

"Along the top of the second wall of the city," the centurion explained. "It leads to the palace. There may be trouble from catapults, but it's unlikely. The rebels are poorly armed and poorly trained. To this point, their limited success has been the result of enthusiasm rather than skill."

"The second wall?"

"The outer wall in front of us," the centurion explained, "is one of three. It protects the new portion of the city that's expanded beyond the second wall. The only danger we face is along the market street from the gates of the third wall to the tower at the Damascus Gate at the second wall inside."

"Danger? I was promised a secure trip."

"Which is why we're waiting. With luck, the runner I sent ahead has already delivered my request for reinforcements from Antonia to meet us at a gate of the third wall. If we form a large enough group, the rebels won't dare to attack as we travel from there through the city to the second wall."

✦ ✦ ✦

So this, Boaz thought with a sense of triumph as he stepped through the doorway into opulence, *is the mansion that I've legally stolen for one month of a tradesman's wages.* Boaz allowed his gaze to move leisurely from one object of luxury to another. Tapestries. Bowls of colored glass. Ornate tile flooring. All of it so very, very beautiful. But not as beautiful as the one object in front of him that had filled him with lust for years.

Amaris. The wife of Simeon Ben-Aryeh. Wearing a simple tunic and a shawl.

"Greetings," he said to her. They were not alone. A woman servant had escorted him here to the center of her upper-city residence and stepped to the side of the room.

Amaris nodded. Not suspicious. Not friendly. But neutral.

This was a woman worthy of glory, the kind Solomon praised with his songs of love. A woman who carried herself with a grace that promised much to the man who could conquer her. Dark thick hair that would brush a man's face as he held her close on hot summer nights. Lips with a hint of pout, and eyes that seemed to look into a man's heart. Sensual, but not brazen.

How Boaz wanted her. His mouth was dry with this desire, but at the same time he resented her. Because he knew how he appeared to her and all other women. Short. Clumsy. A bulbous nose and little hair, except for a straggly beard. He knew it was more than his appearance, however. It was as if women sensed his hungry appraisal of them.

Yet they could never show revulsion, because of his wealth and high standing. Even now, he wore phylacteries fastened by long leather strips to his forehead and around his left arm, near his heart. These were small scrolls of parchment in square capsules, covered with leather, containing sections of the Law of Scripture. They constantly rustled against the expensive fabric of his robe. Wherever he walked in the city, people knew he was a Pharisee of great stature.

"This visit is unexpected," Amaris said, "but certainly not unwelcome."

The female servant hovered nearby, but Amaris did not dismiss her. Decorum. Without a husband in the household, it would not be proper to be alone with another man.

Boaz didn't mind that their conversation would not be private. The servant would stay with the household and would have soon enough learned the reason for his visit anyway. He didn't waste time with chitchat. No amount of charm would win Amaris, so why embarrass himself with something he did badly anyway?

"It's unfortunate," he said. "Not only has your husband deserted you, but he also made no arrangements to honor his debts in his absence from Jerusalem. I'm here as an unsatisfied creditor."

Aside from a widening of the eyes, Amaris gave him no response. It was far less satisfying than he'd expected.

"Your husband has defaulted on several contracts that I own." This close to her—this close to possessing her—Boaz ran a dry tongue against the equally dry roof of his mouth. "As a result, I am here to claim this house."

"My husband never borrowed money from you." Amaris actually stepped forward.

"I doubt you're familiar with all his financial affairs."

"Of course not. Neither are you."

Despite his discomfort, Boaz found it fascinating that she refused to be intimidated. It added to his desire to possess her. How much sweeter, then, to make her beg to stay with him.

"But I'm sure you know my reputation as a businessman," Boaz said. "And I know far more about finances than nearly any man in the city. There are complicated matters beyond your understanding."

"I understand that wealth does not make a man happy."

If she meant that as a taunt, it was masterful. Boaz was not a happy man. Not yet. But did she know she was the solution?

"In the archives," Boaz said, "the record keepers have several contracts that your husband set up with various merchants. These merchants, in turn, have secured loans from me by using those contracts as assets. The terms are due."

"Then I shall reimburse you."

Boaz smiled. "It is too late. According to the terms of the contracts, the debts were not paid in a timely fashion."

"How could I pay those debts if I was unaware of them? Surely—"

"A judge has already decided in my favor. This house is the settlement. See how little understanding you have of the matters of men?"

"What I understand," she snapped, "is that you are a puppet for Annas the Younger."

Boaz shrugged. Puppet or not, a close business relationship with Annas the Younger had proven lucrative over the years. Like this situation, for example. Because of the turmoil in the city, Annas had suggested it was the opportune time for Boaz to take advantage of a lenient judge. Whatever outrage the friends of Ben-Aryeh might raise about this would be lost in the greater troubles inflicted on the upper city by the rebels.

Amaris continued, her eyes blazing. "We all know how pleased Annas was to threaten my husband with execution. Let me guess: Annas arranged for you to purchase these contracts and then sent you here."

"Your husband," Boaz countered, upper lip curled in a sneer, "raped a woman. Then fled before he could be put on trial for the capital punishment he deserved. He chose to abandon you, leaving behind these debts."

Let her consider that, Boaz thought. Perhaps then a short man with a lot of money might seem very attractive in comparison.

"Leave," she said. "I will not allow my husband's character to be slandered in his own house."

"It is no longer his house," he said, not moving, "but mine."

"Leave." Her arms were crossed. The bare flesh of her forearms against her shawl was very attractive.

"It doesn't have to be like this." Boaz licked his upper lip. "We could make an arrangement. You are not a young woman by any stretch. And neither are you a virgin. But I am willing to overlook that to allow you to stay in my house."

"You poor man," she said. "You poor, poor man."

"It's simple," Boaz said, pretending her opinion did not matter. "You stay in the house. Or you leave. Ask yourself how long it will be until you are selling your body in the streets. And you certainly won't get what women twenty years younger than you command for a price."

"I've seen you on public corners," she said. "Your prayers are long and extravagant." She moved closer and reached for him.

He flinched, but she was only pointing to the phylacteries hanging from his forehead.

"You have adorned yourself with God's words, but you do not bear the mark of God. Your actions reveal the true condition of your heart. You neither believe God's Word nor obey it." She stepped back. "Is this what you really want to do?"

"This means you agree to my terms?"

"This means it's not too late for you to walk out of here and ask God for forgiveness."

They stared at each other.

She was such a force that for a moment—a very brief moment—a faint echo of conscience touched his heart. But the roar of greed and lust drowned it out immediately.

"I will let you pack personal belongings," Boaz finally said. "This house is mine and I command you to leave."

"No."

"No?" He smirked. "Then *I* will leave. And in the morning I will return with men authorized to remove you from this house."

✦ ✦ ✦

"How long can we sustain the standoff?"

Eleazar's question caught Gilad by surprise. As governor of the Temple, Eleazar was a man of such piety and faith that despite his youth and the politics that had given Eleazar his position, he'd earned the respect of all the priests. *Surely,* Gilad hoped, *of all men, Eleazar does not wrestle with doubts about the course of action that he began.*

A month earlier, Zealots had attacked Masada, one of Herod's fortresses to the south, and had killed all the Romans there. Eleazar had proclaimed this victory a sign from God and persuaded the priests who officiated in divine service to unite in refusing to accept sacrifices from foreigners. Eleazar's zeal and reputation were such that not one of those priests had broken rank since, despite all the pressures that followed.

"We have food," Gilad said. "We have water. We have the entire lower city. And most importantly, we have the Temple. Nothing can get through the walls or over them."

They stood in Eleazar's apartment in the inner court of the Temple. It was sparsely decorated; on his first day as governor, Eleazar had removed all the luxuries installed by the previous governor. Whether it had been a calculated political move or a reflection of his true desire to serve God did not matter. The bold symbolic gesture had immediately alerted the temple priests that this governor was different. Every action Eleazar had taken since confirmed it, especially his leadership over the last weeks.

"We don't have swords, shields, or military training," Eleazar said.

Gilad stared at him as if seeing Eleazar for the first time. A young, bold man, Eleazar was slim and muscular, with oddly angled cheekbones and eyebrows that added to his charisma. Was this doubtful man the same Eleazar who had decided to defy the Roman procurator Florus, Herod the Great's direct descendant King Agrippa, and the entire ruling establishment of Jerusalem?

Gilad protested. "We have hundreds of priests inside the Temple. And we have Zealots in the lower city. All are ready to die for God."

"And the Roman soldiers garrisoned in Antonia are ready to kill them. As are the three thousand cavalry sent by Agrippa."

"Florus refuses to send reinforcements."

"Only because he wants civil war and chaos to hide his atrocities from Rome," Eleazar said. "We are playing right into his hand. Serving the most evil procurator that Rome has ever inflicted on our people."

"I . . . I . . . don't understand." Gilad could not help but waver. "Are you suggesting that we give up?"

"I'm suggesting you're the man I trust most. Tell me why we should continue."

Gilad straightened. He was a decade older than Eleazar and one of the chief priests. He was widowed and childless. Temple service and its importance were all he had.

"We continue," Gilad said, echoing what Eleazar had repeated again and again in different speeches, "because despite all the odds against us, God has promised a Messiah and will not desert His people. His covenant with His people will not be broken."

"What if God's people desert Him?" Eleazar asked. "What if *they* break the covenant?" Eleazar shifted and began to pace, throwing his arms out to gesture. "Who in Jerusalem have been most oppressed by the Jews who serve Rome?"

"The lower city."

"Yet they are the very people indifferent to our fight."

"At least they don't help the troops," Gilad said.

"Don't try to fool me. I've heard the complaints. They are losing husbands, fathers, brothers, and sons. Each night we force them to remove the bodies of their loved ones to keep from defiling the Temple. So many have died that we cannot give them funerals. They know we have no training or weapons. They no longer see

182 THE LAST SACRIFICE

any chance of victory. So why take our side to be punished later when the upper city triumphs?"

To this, Gilad had no answer.

Unexpectedly, Eleazar smiled. "See? My argument is correct."

"You take satisfaction in this?"

."Iron sharpens iron, as you well know," Eleazar said. "I wanted to see if I had assessed the situation correctly."

"You think we will be defeated?"

"How many times in the past," Eleazar said, "has it looked so bleak for our people that, indeed, many lost hope? And how many times has God triumphed?"

"At Jericho," Gilad said, catching Eleazar's fervor, "the walls came crashing down. Again and again, King David defeated far greater armies. Angels struck dead the Assyrians."

"As long as we honor the covenant with God, He will honor us." Eleazar paused. "That's why I'm worried that the temple fire might stop burning."

For centuries, the fire had remained constantly lit. Eleazar was not going to be remembered with shame as the one who let it die.

Gilad understood instantly. "The Festival of Xylophory."

Eleazar nodded. "How much wood is left in the Temple? A month's worth? Two months' worth?"

"Not enough."

"I worry about this. I may have a solution to earn the support of the people, but if the festival does not proceed . . ." Eleazar stared directly at Gilad. "Do you agree? The festival is of paramount importance?"

Gilad didn't hesitate. "We agree."

"Good," Eleazar said. "Because I need help that I trust only you to give."

"Whatever it is, you have my oath."

"Deliver a message to my father to meet with me tomorrow."

"Your father? Surely you are testing me again."

"I wish I were." A faint smile. "Ironic, isn't it? The one man who desperately needs my defeat is the one man who can prevent it."

✛ ✛ ✛

Young as he was, Quintus had enough street sense to recognize the signs of danger.

The shops and markets grew unnaturally quiet; someone had seen the rebels begin to set up an ambush and had spread the word throughout the shops.

While the soldiers realized that conversations and bartering would cease at their approach and resume as they moved on, this silence was more than that, and the horses responded to it by whipping their heads in agitation, as if they were sensing the first tremors of an earthquake.

The soldiers knew just as well as the people around them that attack was imminent. From his safe distance behind them, Quintus saw this by the way the soldiers bunched closer together and cast wary eyes toward alleys and rooftops. Yet no amount of vigilance could ever give them much warning of an attack. Unlike the new city beyond the second wall, the lower city was a maze of alleyways and crowded buildings.

Then it happened.

Rocks and clay pots cascaded down on the soldiers. At the same time, men flooded the streets from the narrow alleys, screaming. Some were armed with hoes, others with sticks. Only a few actually carried swords and spears and shields.

Quintus sprinted toward the fighting, then stopped abruptly only steps away from the nearest soldier, who was slashing his sword at three men trying to beat him. Quintus dodged beneath a cart filled with the blankets of a shop owner, narrowly escaping more rocks that cascaded down.

He peered upward from the street as a pot slammed against the soldier's head. He staggered, and one of the men landed a solid blow across his forehead. The skin split, and the injured man fell to his knees, putting a hand on his eyebrows to keep the blood from blinding him.

Before the other two men could attack, however, another soldier moved forward and stabbed the midsection of one of the attackers with his sword. The soldier pulled the sword loose without hesitation and began swinging at the other two, who stepped away.

By the shrieks and groans and grunts, Quintus knew the battle was frenzied. But he didn't expect it to last long. The rebels rarely pressed once they'd lost the advantage of surprise.

He was not disappointed.

One of the rebels screamed an order to retreat, and all of them fled, temporarily leaving behind their dead. They'd learned the soldiers would move on quickly, giving them time to remove the bodies later.

It was this small gap of time that Quintus relied upon.

The soldiers regrouped and hurried down the street.

On the ground, beside the cart that protected Quintus, was the rebel who'd been stabbed by the soldier's sword. He gripped the center of his abdomen in agony, futilely trying to stem the flow of blood.

Quintus crawled toward him. The man's eyes widened, and he groaned as he tried to speak to Quintus.

Quintus lifted the bottom edge of the man's tunic. The man was too stunned and too close to dying to react. Quintus felt for a money belt.

Nothing.

But on the man's neck was a glint of gold.

A chain!

Quintus flashed his hand upward and grasped it in his fingers. With a quick yank, he snapped it loose.

And ran.

❧ I4 AV ❧

THE FOURTH HOUR

"WHERE WERE YOU yesterday afternoon?" Valeria asked her younger brother Quintus.

Quintus had come to visit her on the roof of the glassblower's house. As an apprentice, she'd been given a room on the roof as part of her wages. It was a simple square of mud walls with a sheet as a doorway flap. Inside, all it had was a mattress and a chamber pot. She was expected to take meals with the family below.

Quintus walked to the edge of the roof and looked down at the street. He spoke without looking back at her. "Where you tell me to spend all my days. With Malka."

"Really?" Valeria was unable to keep an edge out of her voice. "Strange. I was there and couldn't find you."

"Maybe I was at the market for her." He kept watching the street. "That's right. Now that I've thought about it, she sent me for bread."

"Don't lie to me!"

Valeria moved to the edge of the roof and pulled Quintus back with a roughness that surprised even her. "Malka told me that you left more than an hour before I arrived."

"Don't believe her," Quintus said, wrenching away from her grip. "She's blind. She can't see when I come and go."

"That's what worries me," Valeria said, much more softly.

"What worries you?" Quintus immediately lost his boyish indignation.

"She's old and blind. If you're going to disappear into the lower city for hours at a time, maybe I need to find someplace else for you to stay."

"No." Quintus stepped forward and pulled at Valeria's tunic with both hands. "Please, no. She needs me."

Valeria cocked her head. This was nothing that she would have expected from her younger brother. "She needs you?"

Quintus dropped his hands. "I help her cook and clean. I listen to her stories. She's so happy when I'm around. I never leave unless I know she's going to be fine until I get back."

"Quintus . . ." *Cooking and cleaning for an old woman? Sad and serious?* He'd been a selfish, happy-go-lucky boy until the May riots. Commanding slaves around as if he owned them. "Don't you remember the first day with her and how you cried when I left you there?"

The riots in late spring had left them homeless and on the run. Valeria had decided that if she and Quintus found a place to stay together, it might be too easy for the enemies of their family to find them.

With this in mind, they had roamed the markets until they saw a blind woman totter slowly, tapping the street with a cane to guide her steps. They'd followed her to a shack in the most crowded part of the lower city. When Valeria had offered her a pittance to take in a small boy, Malka had gladly accepted.

Quintus, however, had not been so happy. Before the riots, he'd lived in a mansion in the upper city; Malka's shack was dark and cramped and had strange smells.

"I remember the first day," Quintus said, his little-boy face very serious. "But that's changed. She sings to me. She tells me stories. She holds me when I cry in my sleep because of nightmares."

Quintus left unspoken what Valeria understood. Their own mother had never been like that to either of them.

"You're going to have to say good-bye someday soon," Valeria said. "Someone from Rome will come for us."

He puffed his chest. "Then we'll take her with us." Thinking about it, he began to smile. "Can you imagine what that would be like for her? Slaves to pour her hot baths. Feasts every day. New clothes. Perfumes. She could live like a queen."

Quintus became more excited. "Yes! Yes! In Rome, we have money, more than we could ever spend. You tell me that all the time. We'll take Malka with us and make sure she never has to worry about anything ever again in her life!"

"We'll talk about this later," Valeria said, with no intention of ever discussing the subject again. Malka was no more than an employee, paid to keep and hide Quintus. "I want to know where you went yesterday afternoon and where you've gone all the other times you leave her alone."

Quintus frowned.

"Yes," Valeria said, "Malka told me. She also said that you've been bringing food home from the market. Where do you get the money for that?"

"You're not my mother," Quintus said. "So stop acting like it."

"I'm the only person you can depend on in the entire world. Where do you go and how do you get money for food?"

Quintus spun away and marched back to the edge of the roof. He crossed his arms as he resolutely stared away from Valeria.

"I can't help us if you don't help me," Valeria said. "This is a dangerous city, especially now."

"I can take care of myself."

"Tell me how you get the money. That's all I want to know."

"I can take care of myself." He stamped his heel, betraying his boyishness.

"I order you not to leave her house." Valeria took a step toward him and then froze as a high-pitched wail of anguish reached the rooftop.

It came from directly below.

The wail grew louder.

✠ ✠ ✠

"I have a question for our high priest," said Annas the Younger.

In the upper city, in the palace of the high priest, fifty-two men were assembled in two semicircles for a council of the Great Sanhedrin, the highest authority among the Jews. Of the seventy-one members, only twenty-three were needed for a quorum. This was important to Annas the Younger, who had finally been granted the floor to address the high priest, Ananias.

Annas the Younger had been given the name to distinguish him from his father, Annas the Elder, whose legendary political maneuverings as a high priest had ensured that a son-in-law and each of his five sons—including Annas the Younger—had had turns occupying that position over the last four decades.

Annas the Younger had never made a secret of how badly he wanted to regain his position as high priest. He had lost his appointment in disgrace two years earlier because of a man named Simeon Ben-Aryeh. Three months ago, Annas had inflicted partial revenge on Ben-Aryeh, and today, with luck, that revenge would be complete with the help of a Pharisee named Boaz. What a message that would send to anyone who dared defy him politically!

Given this reputation and the situation against the rebels, Annas the Younger knew many of his peers had wondered when he might issue a challenge to the authority of the high priest.

He also knew he wasn't going to disappoint them, for he had spent days pondering and planning his attack.

"Ask your question." The high priest, Ananias, leaned on a cane as he faced Annas, his flowing gray beard almost touching the top of his hand on that cane. Sad weariness had etched deep lines into a face already well wrinkled, and that weariness leached his voice of any power.

"Eleazar, the temple governor, has brought civil war to our city with his refusal to allow foreigners to make sacrifices at the Temple," Annas the Younger said. "For bringing unrest to

Jerusalem and to the Jewish people, he must die. Yet Eleazar is also your son."

Annas was a handsome man in his forties. He ran his fingers through his thick, dark hair as he waited for the tension to build.

Then Annas struck, as if he were trying to inflict a blow on the older man. "My question is this: is our high priest prepared to throw the first stone at the execution of his son?"

✢ ✢ ✢

As Maglorius sat in the shade of the inner courtyard and waited for the arrival of Boaz and the men he'd promised would evict Amaris, he stared at his wrists. He could not escape the sensation that both were bound together.

The rope, of course, was imaginary. He didn't know what was more troubling—the predicament he faced, the sensation of an imaginary rope, or the fact that he was actually engaged in thought about the situation.

In the shade, Maglorius actually growled at himself for these thoughts. Men who spent too much time in analysis, he'd always believed, were weak men. Now he was one of them. And yes, felt weak for it. Maglorius had spent his adult life killing other humans and, in his prime, had been among the best in the world at this task. Half a dozen men, no doubt poorly armed, would be far easier opponents than the desperate and fully armed criminals he'd executed in the arenas as a gladiator.

He was a man of action. Not philosophy. Amaris was his friend Simeon Ben-Aryeh's wife, and every instinct urged Maglorius to protect her—by whatever means necessary. Yet now he was bound. By a struggle with his newfound faith. For Maglorius now followed the Christos.

The man whose teachings had brought him peace and hope, the man he'd committed his heart and soul to follow, this man had accepted crucifixion for a crime He did not commit rather than fight back against injustice.

So should Maglorius do the same here? allow Amaris to be forced from her house by the same type of religiously hypocritical man as those who had pierced Jesus of Nazareth?

Yet, Maglorius thought, had his Jesus not also given a directive to clothe the poor, feed the hungry, and defend widows and orphans? What was Maglorius to do while remaining faithful to the Nazarene who had given His life on behalf of humanity?

It was one thing, he told himself, to fight in the heat of defense, doing what was necessary to preserve his life; reacting without thinking; unleashing the strength, agility, and killer instinct that had made him feel so alive in the pursuit of the death of other men.

If thieves were to attack him and Amaris in an alley without warning, he would destroy first and deal with his conscience later. But here, waiting to face down a different kind of thief was an entirely different situation.

Too much thinking.

To complicate his decision, he'd made a vow to protect this woman in the absence of her husband. Walking away, permitting the travesty for the sake of peace, breaking the vow— wouldn't this, too, be a moral wrong?

Maglorius growled at himself again.

Too much thinking.

Maglorius stood. Beside the chair, where he'd leaned it against the wall, was an iron bar the thickness of a cane and roughly twice as long. He grabbed it, held it with both hands across his waist, and paced back and forth in front of the closed door that led into the house.

This, he thought, feeling the coldness of the iron in his fingers, was what he wanted to use. Not thinking, but action.

Would his faith allow him that?

✠ ✠ ✠

Annas wasn't surprised as murmurs went through the assembly at his question to the high priest. Politically, the question was as masterful as it was vicious, for Annas was forcing Ananias to choose between his office and his son.

The murmurs faded as all eyes turned to Ananias. The old man's hand on the cane shook. The ephod, breastplate, robe, embroidered coat, girdle, and miter of the high priest's garments gave him an appearance of dignity and power, but his frailty in the moment betrayed him.

"Let me repeat my question," Annas said when Ananias delayed his answer. "Is the high priest prepared to throw the first stone at the execution of his son?"

When Ananias spoke, it was with little energy. "For the record, my relationship with the governor of the Temple is irrelevant to this discussion."

Ananias nodded at both of the scribes who were, as customary, taking note of the proceedings. "In the written record, you should not use the word *son* in that question. The man we speak of must be referred to as Eleazar, or, as I've just pointed out, governor of the Temple. Let us move on to the reports and discussion of strategy against the rebels."

Victory, Annas thought. He'd rehearsed all possible answers and had decided there was only one way for Ananias to escape the difficulties the question raised—by immediately agreeing he would throw the first stone and, in so doing, ending the debate before it could start.

But Annas had also decided the real weakness that Ananias faced was the love of an elderly man for his firstborn son and that the high priest would choose that love over power. *The fool.*

"I would respectfully ask our high priest to explain why his relationship to the governor of the Temple has no relevance," Annas said, speaking to the assembly. "This is a time of extreme crisis. A time that demands decisive leadership. Yet the man who asks that we continue to grant him authority appears unable to exercise authority over his own son."

This statement, too, Annas the Younger had planned. He wanted the debate to be a personal attack on both father and son.

"Eleazar is the governor of the Temple," Ananias said. "He did not start the rebellion as a son acting against his father, but as a man in high position acting upon his conscience and the abuses of Rome."

"Ah," Annas the Younger said. "So you approve of his action? Is the kind of high priest we need leading us in our crisis?"

"My feelings here are irrelevant." Ananias clutched his cane. "You will note that I have done everything in my power as high priest to press the battle against the temple governor, the temple priests who support him, and the Zealot rebels who fight for him. That is what matters."

"So make it public record, then, that you will set your feelings aside and throw the first stone at the execution of your son Eleazar. Tell all of us assembled here that your loyalty is to your duty, not the governor of the Temple."

Ananias lifted a shaking hand and covered his eyes.

"Make it public record," Annas repeated. "Unless your loyalty—"

"This is my son!" Ananias dropped his hand. Tears were obvious on his wrinkled face.

Annas relished the old man's pain and seized the advantage. "During Passover just over thirty years ago, there was a man some claimed to be our Messiah. A man stirring trouble in the Temple to the point that it seemed rebellion might start against Rome. Weren't you among those in the Great Sanhedrin during his trial? Didn't you agree then that it would be better for one man to die than an entire nation? Didn't you agree to the execution of that man?"

No reply.

"Once again," Annas said, "we face the same danger of rebellion against Rome. Your son does not claim to be the Messiah, but by refusing permission for any foreigners to make temple sacrifices, he has, in effect, declared war against Rome. We all know why, don't we?"

Still no reply.

"Your son Eleazar believes that the Messiah is imminent. He

believes that God will lead us to victory against Rome, because God has promised a Messiah to deliver us. And I say you must once more agree with the Great Sanhedrin that it would be better for one man to die than an entire nation. We who rule Jerusalem must show Rome that we will punish the rebel leaders."

"We are the chosen people," Ananias said. "God will spare us as He has done again and again throughout our history. The Messiah will come. That is the foundation of our faith."

Annas the Younger pounced. "So you support your son."

"I do not support rebellion against Rome."

"Then promise to throw the first stone at his execution." Annas paused. "Agree that once again it is better that one man die than an entire nation and do your duty. Or step down from your office."

Ananias drew himself upright. "The rebels have no weapons. We are armed with royal troops. Soon enough we will have the Temple back and soon enough we will accept sacrifices from foreigners."

"We have royal troops. But not Roman troops. Your other son, Simon, could not convince Florus to send help."

"Florus is determined that a war start among us. You know that."

"I know that both of your sons have failed the Jewish people," Annas told the elderly man. "And it appears that you are willing to do nothing about it. As a father or a high priest."

"The rebels have no weapons. They will lose sooner or later. Let us decide then what to do with their leaders."

"So you are telling the Sanhedrin that you will not punish the leaders, among them your son."

"I am telling the Sanhedrin that we are all Jews. We must reduce the division among us to remain strong against Rome. Jews killing Jews is not the solution."

"Is that the advice of Ananias the high priest? Or Ananias the father?"

"It is the advice of a man who knows it is futile to fight Rome and who agonizes over the suffering of the Jewish people under the tyranny of Rome."

Annas the Younger had not been prepared for the old man's simple eloquence in that answer. He needed to get his answer immediately.

"Tell us," Annas said, "for the scribes to record: are you prepared to throw the first stone at the execution of your son?"

Bound by duty, Ananias gave the only answer he could. "Yes." He began to weep openly.

Annas sensed sympathy for the old man stirring among the Sanhedrin. He decided there was no sense in pushing any harder, nor in asking for a further vote to remove Ananias from office. Yet Annas was far from dissatisfied. He had gotten the answer he needed on the transcript of the proceedings.

And perhaps the old man's weeping would work in Annas's favor. For Ananias was right about one thing. The rebels would lose, probably sooner than later. That's when Annas would be ready to help the members of the Great Sanhedrin remember the old man's weakness, long after they'd forgotten the old man's tears.

✝ ✝ ✝

At the loud moans of anguish, Valeria hurried down the steps and inside the small house. She found Nahum, the glassblower she served, seated on a cushion, cradling his son, Raanan, in his arms.

Leeba, moaning in anguish, knelt in front of them, holding Raanan's limp arms. A broken spear protruded from the blood-soaked tunic at Raanan's abdomen, and his eyes were shut tight as his body shuddered in pain.

A trail of blood from the doorway told Valeria part of the story. Nahum had carried Raanan in from the street. It would have taken him great effort; Nahum was middle-aged and Raanan was almost into manhood, a large, strapping teenager known for practical jokes and an intensely competitive spirit.

"Royal troops," Nahum explained to his wife, Leeba, in a broken voice. "Yet another street fight."

"Run for a doctor!" Leeba said.

"A doctor can't do anything more than we can." Nahum caught Valeria looking down at them. "Valerius, find a blanket."

She stood numbly for a moment longer, not responding to her assumed name. To both of them, she was Valerius, a boy slave who had watched the wealthy Greek family he served die to Roman soldiers among the thousands who had been slaughtered during the May riots.

"A doctor!" Leeba said again.

"We will remain with him to the end." Nahum's voice held a mixture of calm and rage and pain. "We make him as comfortable as we can."

Nahum was the family's patriarch, the man responsible for all family matters. Valeria wondered what effort it was taking him to remain in control.

"No!" Leeba wailed. "Our only son! Don't let him die!"

Valeria was paralyzed by the scene.

Nahum looked at her again. "Please, a blanket."

When Valeria returned, Raanan was still shuddering. There was a small wooden rod between his teeth, and he was clamping it hard against the obvious pain. His eyes were open wide. With one hand, he clenched his mother's hand. When new spasms hit him, he would clutch his father's neck with the other arm.

The agony left him briefly.

"I'm cold," he said in a small voice. He looked down and saw the blood soaking his tunic and the cushion. "Mama, I'm cold and I'm afraid."

She smothered his forehead with kisses. "My son, my son, my darling son."

Raanan's life left him as she was speaking.

THE SIXTH HOUR

"UNLESS HE'S KILLED by sentries on either side, the boy will arrive," Joseph Ben-Matthias told his Roman visitor. They were on the rooftop of Joseph's house in the upper city, shaded by the awning of an open tent set up for the daily purpose of enjoying the breeze that swept across Jerusalem.

Joseph Ben-Matthias had been surprised—no, astounded—when the man named Falco arrived at his mansion. While Falco's escort of soldiers provided by the procurator, Florus, had certainly contributed to Joseph's sense of surprise—what man received this kind of support when Florus wouldn't send a single soldier to protect Jerusalem?—it was the man's mission that had been most astonishing.

Falco, as he had pompously announced, had been sent to Jerusalem in response to a letter that Joseph had been hired to send to a senator in Rome a few months earlier, hired by a boy from the slums of the city. "How can you say he'll be here with such certainty?" His visitor wheezed slightly after speaking and kept mopping his face with a piece of folded silk. "It's been, what, nearly three months, since you dispatched the letter to my *patronus* in Rome? By your own admission, you still don't even know the boy's name."

Joseph, in contrast to his visitor, was a tall, muscular man with a craggy but handsome face. He was not yet thirty years old. He was married, as any respectable Jew would be at his age, and had

199

a young son and two younger daughters. Joseph was comfortable
and content with his life and his status and, just as importantly,
knew he was comfortable and content. While his marriage was
more a marriage of convenience than love, he adored his children.
He knew he was respected in the community, partly because of his
royal descent, partly because of his business acumen and connections, and partly because he was known as a great thinker.

"I don't need to know the boy's name to see his determination,"
Joseph answered. "Every day for the last month he's arrived to inquire
about his letter and every day refused to leave unless I gave him an
answer myself."

"*Every* day?" Falco raised an arm and gestured below at the
buildings crowded along narrow, crooked streets. "It's nearly civil
war down there. I can't believe Florus has not decided to intervene
on your behalf."

Joseph grunted but said nothing. An act of discretion.

When Joseph did not speak, Falco gave him an exasperated look.
"Florus gave me soldiers because of the senator I represent," he said.
"I'm no friend of the procurator's, so feel welcome to speak freely."

"I will say this," Joseph said, still wary. Who really knew Falco's
allegiances? "Many in Jerusalem speculate that Florus wants a civil
war to hide his abuses of the province from Rome."

"Are you one of the many? I'm told you are a respected man
with considerable influence."

"My opinion," Joseph said, "matters little. But here are the facts.
A few months ago, in response to a mild insult as a result of stealing treasury money, Florus visited the city and ordered his soldiers
into the marketplace to slaughter as many civilians as possible. Even
with the pleas of mercy by Queen Bernice, a supporter of Roman
policy, Florus ordered more slaughter on the second day. It was
only because our people did not revolt—as begged by our leaders—
that Florus had no excuse to mount a serious war against us. Civil
war was narrowly averted, and for reasons known only to Queen
Bernice, Florus withdrew from the city."

Falco smiled wryly. "Bernice. Yes, I've heard stories about her. She's not in the city, is she?"

"I understand many of the stories are exaggerations," Joseph said. "I also understand she's become a changed person of late, taking her royal responsibilities much more seriously than before. And no, she's not in the city. She's in Syria, I believe, trying to influence Cestius to remove Florus as procurator before civil war does start."

"*Does* start?" Falco snorted again, waving his hand to take in the city. "What's this?"

"Jews against Jews," Joseph said. "Not Jews against Romans."

"But I heard something about foreigners barred from the temple sacrifices. Isn't that going to lead to—"

"When the wealthy upper city wins, temple sacrifices will be open again to Caesar, long before news of the transgression can reach Rome."

Falco nodded with a smile of understanding. "Now I see. Florus is not sending you any help. He wants the lower city to gain and hold power until Caesar is provoked."

Falco laughed lightly, shaking his head at the tactics of Florus. "Politics."

Joseph spoke softly but intensely. "Friends of mine lost wives, children to the soldiers in the market. Holding a five-year-old daughter and having her bleed to death in your arms is not mere politics."

"I'm sorry," Falco said, meaning it.

"Florus is hated beyond anything you can understand, and by extension, so is Rome. It is all the ruling establishment can do to prevent rebellion. And rebellion will cost us more of our wives and children." Joseph paused. "Do you have a boy or girl?"

"No."

"When you do, you will understand what the loss or threat of loss means. And you will not treat this as politics."

"I said I was sorry."

Joseph reined in his flare of anger. "You did. Let me apologize in turn."

The silence was awkward until Falco broke it. "You say the boy will come to see if there has been a response to his letter."

Thinking about the difficulty of the boy's journey, Joseph turned his gaze away from the visitor. He thought he heard a faint scream, but realized it could have been his imagination. Fighting between the royal troops and the rebels had become sporadic over the last few days and had settled into an uneasy standoff, the line of demarcation essentially an aqueduct that entered the city on the south side near the Gate of the Essenes and traversed the hillside of the upper city all the way to the Temple.

"Every day," Joseph told Falco again. "The standoff has not stopped him from getting here, even though he lives in the lower city."

"I'm astounded he takes those risks. I would not have entered the city myself without the armed escort Florus provided. As it was, soldiers sent out from the city to meet us had to fight through a rebel attack to get to the outer gates."

An escort provided by Florus, Joseph thought. *Very mysterious.*

Florus was the Roman procurator of all Judea, fat and happy in Caesarea, safely away from the conflict in Jerusalem. This was the same man who had refused to send any Roman soldiers into Jerusalem to battle the rebels who held the Temple and lower city. Yet because of an unnamed boy from the poorest part of the lower city, Florus had arranged to secretly aid this man Falco during the height of the tensions. Why?

And Joseph had more questions.

Aside from Florus's involvement, there was the determination of the boy. Every day he showed up to ask a simple question: was there any reply to the letter? Every day Joseph had replied there was not. Every day the boy had silently walked away, saying nothing else. What, Joseph constantly wondered, was driving the boy?

Then there was the fact that the boy's letter—sent weeks earlier—had actually been answered by the arrival of Falco.

Falco was, as he had introduced himself, the representative of the senator addressed in the letter, a senator who was a friend of someone in Rome who owed Joseph a favor. Something, then, in the letter from the boy in Jerusalem had compelled the senator to send Falco across the world. Not only that, the senator had enough influence that Florus had been willing to intervene. How did the boy know someone in Rome with this kind of power? And why would that senator exercise his power on the boy's behalf?

Joseph hoped that patience with this Roman would lead him to the answers.

✛ ✛ ✛

Since the day his father, Ananias the high priest, had appointed him governor of the Temple, Eleazar could not recall a single moment when daily familiarity with the Temple Mount had led to the slightest loss of any of the sense of awe at the dwelling place of the one true God, the God of Abraham, Isaac, and Jacob.

Anytime he walked through the immense Court of the Gentiles, Eleazar had a new appreciation for the workmanship. Under Herod the Great, the slopes of Mount Moriah had been flattened and extended as a foundation for colonnades that enclosed the inner Temple, paving it with the finest marble possible.

In the Court of the Gentiles, any direction he looked, he was filled with joy at the sights and sounds of thousands of worshipers and hundreds of attendant priests. The blowing of the shofars, the psalms of praise from the choirs of Levites, the smoke from the altar, the low murmurings of reverence, even the bleating of terrified lambs facing slaughter, and the smell of the blood that ran down from the altar—all of this enforced for him the greatness of the Temple, a physical reality that pointed to the greater spiritual reality of God's glory and holiness.

As Eleazar stepped out of the shade of Solomon's Porch, the

portion of the colonnade opposite the Holy of Holies, he noted again with pleasure the burnished gold that plated the marble blocks of the sanctuary. There was profound truth in the saying of the rabbis: "The world is like an eye. The ocean surrounding the world is to the white of the eye; its black is the world itself; the pupil is Jerusalem, but the image within the pupil is the sanctuary."

The holy dwelling place of the Lord God Almighty!

It was so sacred that no dead body was allowed to remain anywhere in the entire city overnight. No accident had ever interrupted the services of the sanctuary. Rain had not once extinguished the fire on the altar; no wind had ever blown the smoke back into the sacrifices; never had worshipers failed to bow at the massive altar.

Yet on this morning, the usual hum of activities was muted. The markets for the selling of animals for sacrifices had been closed. The temple police were standing guard along the tops of the walls and at all the entrances.

It wasn't the muted activity that filled Eleazar with concern. Weeks earlier, he'd been deliberate in the act of rebellion that had led to this—prohibiting foreigners to make sacrifices in the Temple—and had no regrets at his course of action, nor at the consequences that, for the most part, he'd easily foreseen.

Indeed, he'd known well that by preventing foreigners from making sacrifices, he had in essence barred Caesar from the Temple, and that the last sacrifice on behalf of Caesar meant war had been declared on Rome.

He'd expected, too, that the establishment of Jerusalem would beg and plead against this sedition. And, of course, he'd planned for the militant action against them: the taking of the Temple and the lower city.

Yet one thing concerned Eleazar.

Tomorrow, the fifteenth of the month of Av, was the Festival of Xylophory, the wood-burning festival. It was the last of nine occasions during the year when offerings of wood were brought to the Temple to keep the altar fire going. The first eight occasions were

BROUWER + HANEGRAAFF 205

granted to certain families and all descendants with the family
name, but in this, the month of Av, all the people were allowed
to bring wood—even slaves, proselytes, and men and women
born out of wedlock.

The altar fire had never been quenched since the rebuilding of
the Temple. Eleazar had not expected a stalemate to go on this long,
and if the Festival of Xylophory was disrupted, the fuel supply for
the altar for the rest of the year would be threatened.

He could not let this happen.

✝ ✝ ✝

Because of the standoff with the rebels, Boaz had not been able to
secure robust men in their prime as an armed escort to the house
of Ben-Aryeh. They were too valuable along the front lines of the
standoff in the city.

Instead, Boaz entered the outer courtyard with two elderly men,
two barely more than teenagers, and one with an obvious limp. The
important thing, however, was the fact that Annas the Younger had
used his connections to ensure they'd been loaned spears and shields
for this.

Yet Boaz was not overly concerned that the escorts were not the
finest of soldiers. What more could it take to evict Amaris and a
couple of women servants?

Boaz was surprised, however, upon reaching the inner courtyard.
Who is this? he wondered as a large man stood and blocked the door
of the house. *And what does the fool expect to accomplish?*

Despite the looseness of the man's tunic, he was obviously well-
muscled. And he was holding an iron bar horizontally across his
waist. He seemed relaxed. Too relaxed.

Boaz hesitated for a moment, and one of the elderly men
behind him reacted too slowly, bumping his back and knocking
him forward slightly. Boaz was forced to stagger to keep his balance, and that sign of weakness, along with his instinctive fear,
made him angry.

Yet he still hesitated as he evaluated the man. There was something familiar about him. He was obviously not Jewish. His hair was sandy gray, so he probably wasn't Roman either. He was not a young man, but still he radiated strength and power. His face bore the scars of an assortment of slashes.

Then it hit Boaz.

The famous gladiator! Maglorius.

Yes. Boaz had a good memory, especially for gossip, since gossip used wisely could make a man rich. In a flash, he recalled what he knew and had heard about Maglorius.

The ex-gladiator had not fought since reaching Jerusalem, less than a year ago. After earning his freedom, Maglorius had moved to Jerusalem to serve as the personal bodyguard to Lucius Bellator's family. It was rumored that he'd taken the position simply to continue an affair with Bellator's wife, for the old man had no vigor. Then came the riots of May, when Roman soldiers slaughtered citizens of Jerusalem without discrimination, pursuing them through the markets and up the streets. The elderly Bellator had been killed in his own household, here in the upper city. His wife had sold the house in less than a day and fled back to Rome, and Bellator's children had disappeared.

What was this ex-gladiator doing here now?

Boaz reminded himself that five armed men stood behind him. That he had the legal right to evict Amaris. He told himself it didn't matter what Maglorius was doing here. So he took three strides forward and faced Maglorius directly.

The ex-gladiator's silence was ominous. So was the iron bar he held across his waist.

Boaz swallowed hard. This time, however, his mouth was dry from fear, not the lust of the previous afternoon. Boaz hoped his voice would not break when he spoke.

"Out of our way," Boaz said. "This is my house, and I command you to leave the property."

"The house belongs to Simeon Ben-Aryeh," Maglorius said. "You have no authority here."

"It's been granted by a judge," Boaz snapped, losing his fear briefly now that he felt a position of strength. If this was going to be a debate, few could equal him.

"Based upon what?" Maglorius asked.

It seemed to Boaz that Maglorius already knew the answer. Of course he would, if he had talked to Amaris.

"Failure to pay debts according to contracts with various merchants," Boaz answered. Confident. After all, what could an ex-gladiator know about such things?

"Ah, a simple matter then," Maglorius said. "May I see those contracts?"

"Go to the archives," Boaz answered. "The keepers of the records will show them to you."

"No."

What an idiot, Boaz thought. *Muscles but no brains.*

"Of course they will," Boaz sighed. "Let me explain the arrangement here in Jerusalem in a way that any dim-witted foreigner can understand. Nearby on the slope of Acra—I expect you'll need to ask for directions despite the fact that nearly everyone in the city has heard of it—is our Repository of the Archives. The keepers of the records hold all contracts of debt for public display, so that creditors can pursue the obligations of debtors as needed. Creditors like me. Debtors like Ben-Aryeh."

"No."

Dense, Boaz thought. *Very dense.* "Shall I try to explain again?"

"No. If you want to come inside this house, *you* go the archives and bring the contracts here so I can see them first. I'm not leaving."

"Five armed men behind me say otherwise." Boaz quickly shifted his head to confirm that they were still there. What horror, if they'd walked away while he was insulting this ex-gladiator. "They have the legal right to use whatever force necessary to evict Amaris or anyone else who protests."

Maglorius smiled. His hands shifted, and Boaz jumped back. But all he had done was lift the thick iron bar from his waist to the height of his chest.

Still smiling, and with no apparent effort as he kept his eyes on Boaz, Maglorius began to bend the bar into the shape of an upside-down *U*. He did not stop until his hands were almost touching at the center of his chest.

"Strangely enough," Maglorius said, smile in place, "one of my last fights in the arena involved five men. Two armed with nets and tridents, three armed with spears. I faced them barehanded—at least until I took a spear from the first dead man."

With the same apparent lack of effort, Maglorius began to straighten the bar, continuing to speak. "Five of you. I suppose, then, that I can take that as a good omen. Five is a good number for me. As you can see, I am able to tell about it. The five from the arena are not."

Maglorius didn't speak again until he had finished straightening the bar completely. Boaz and his five escorts didn't speak either. They were mesmerized by the exhibition of strength in front of them.

"In the arena," Maglorius said in the same conversational tone as he leaned on the bar as if it were a tall cane, "it was actually a fair fight. You see, there was no way of protecting my back and, all told, I believe those five lasted nearly fifteen minutes. Much longer than the odds they had been given by most bettors. Here, as you can see, I have the wall to ensure that none of your five men can sneak behind me. I suppose since I've aged a little since then and haven't fought in a while, I may need that advantage. But then again, maybe not."

"They are not afraid of you," Boaz said.

"Don't you know who he is?" the nearest man said. The one with a limp. "Maglorius. He fought in Rome. In front of Caesar."

"His request does seem reasonable," another said. An elderly one. "What harm could there be in returning with the contracts?"

"Or with another five of us," a third muttered. He was barely more than a teenager. He directed his next words to Maglorius, and in them was a touch of hero worship. "You've never fought ten at a time, have you?"

"Ten, I think, would be much safer for you," Maglorius said. "But if I only kill five before I'm defeated, how can you be sure you will be among the survivors? Nothing personal, of course."

"This is ridiculous," Boaz said. "Move this man away from the door. I want to take possession of my house."

"We'll escort you to the archives and back," the first said firmly to Boaz. "The city is dangerous right now, and you should be grateful for our help."

"Utterly ridiculous," Boaz said, backing away and keeping his eyes on the iron bar in the hands of Maglorius. "Ridiculous and an outrage."

Still, Boaz thought, it couldn't hurt to return with at least ten. Especially if they were as inept and spineless as these first five.

✛ ✛ ✛

Inside the Court of Israel was the Court of Priests; in essence both formed one large court divided by a low wall. The Court of Israel guarded the Court of Priests, which contained the immense altar and in turn guarded the Holy Place and the entrance to the Holy of Holies, the innermost sanctuary where dwelt the presence of God.

The massive walls of the court supported the various apartments, including the apartment of the high priest, which Ananias by necessity had abandoned when Eleazar organized the rebellion of the priests.

In the walls, too, were various passages that led to tunnels beneath the Temple Mount. Some, like the passage to the well-lit subterranean bath for the use of the priests, were relatively well-known. Others, inside chambers built into the court walls, were kept secret, and the entrances were cleverly hidden by apparently seamless walls with intricate decorations.

Alone, Eleazar stepped into one of these chambers. It would take him into a tunnel that led to secret cisterns beneath the city, always full of water, no matter how much of a drought might strike Judea.

His father, of course, as high priest, knew of the tunnel and the cistern.

It was a risk, Eleazar knew, to go alone. He had no guarantee that Ananias would honor his request for a private meeting. Indeed, if his father decided to have him arrested and executed, the rebellion might be over.

Yet if there was any man Eleazar could trust, no matter the intense differences in their faith and patriotism, it was his own father. Ananias.

So Eleazar moved forward into the cool darkness of the tunnel, armed with only a torch.

✦ ✦ ✦

"You know where he lives, but you don't know his name." Falco's voice had a high-pitched sneer.

"It's obvious by how he's dressed," Joseph said calmly. He would learn nothing from the Roman by replying with the same tone. "Almost in rags. Whatever money he has, he gets by working for a glassblower, but it's the most menial of labor."

"He told you that?"

Joseph shook his head. "Until a few days ago, he was always smudged in charcoal. His fingers blistered from heat. A boy only gets like that from attending the fire for the glassblower. The boy was able to visit only at the end of the day, when his work was finished."

"The end of the day?" Falco sighed, rubbed his face with his cloth again. "If I'm going to have to wait that long, you must send for more water and food and find me a place to sleep while I wait. I'm not enjoying Jerusalem at all."

This statement, to Joseph, was another example of the man's arrogance, so typical of Romans. Falco had been on Joseph's rooftop for fifteen minutes, yet he had barely seemed to notice the amazing view of the Temple Mount across the city. The plated gold of the Temple dome blazed in the sunlight, contrasting magnificently against the gleaming white marble of other buildings nearby. Rightly so, it was known as one of the wonders of the world. Yet Falco was too absorbed in himself to even make a polite visitor's comment about it, more focused instead on devouring pieces of fruit and cheese that servants had brought at Joseph's request.

"You won't have to wait that long," Joseph said.

"I thought you said he usually appeared at the end of the day."

"Since our last Sabbath, he's appeared much earlier in the afternoon. Clean. Not smelling of fire."

"The glassblower," Falco said after a moment's reflection. "No longer blowing glass. No longer employing the boy."

So, Joseph thought, *this man Falco, dispatched like a servant from Rome, does have some intelligence.*

"Yes," Joseph said. "With the city gates closed to most traffic, a glassblower out of charcoal, perhaps. Or deciding that the standoff will continue too long and he doesn't want excess inventory that can be easily destroyed. The lower city market can't be stopped entirely, of course. People still need to eat. But luxuries like glass—"

"I believe I just implied that," Falco said. "Let's not make our wait too tedious."

"Of course." Joseph warned himself to be careful around the Roman.

Silence fell upon the two men until Falco moved to settle on a cushion and sighed with weariness. "Tell me," he said from the cushion. "Why did you become involved in this matter?"

It was an appropriate question. In May, just after riots had nearly torn Jerusalem apart, the boy had appeared one afternoon and insisted upon an audience with Joseph. Negotiated a price for Joseph to arrange for a letter to reach Rome. Returned a week later with half the necessary money and a pledge to pay the remainder in weekly installments. Something about the boy's dignified manner had compelled Joseph to ask far less for his services than he would normally demand. Joseph had been impressed by the boy's utter determination to see the task completed, and he was extremely curious about all of it.

"It's simple," Joseph answered, deciding not to reveal all of those circumstances. "My connections to Rome are well-known within this city. The boy asked me to use those connections and was willing to pay what I asked."

"Obviously you did it for money. I don't care about your motives. What I do care about is why the boy approached you."

"I would hope it is also well-known that I am trustworthy."

"And Romans in this city are not?"

"Perhaps the boy doesn't know any Romans here."

"Don't treat me as if I'm stupid. You've read the letter. You know the boy is simply a messenger, representing two important Roman citizens trapped in the city. So why would they choose you over official channels?"

"At the boy's request, I did not read the letter," Joseph said mildly. "I'm in no position to speculate."

Yet Joseph could not avoid his share of silent speculation. Learning more about the letter from Falco only raised more questions for Joseph. What two important Roman citizens were behind this? The city had been in civil war for only the last five days. Yet the boy had approached Joseph months earlier, when anyone had been free to leave the city. So what had trapped them? And, as Falco had aptly pointed out, why not go through the protection of official Roman channels?

Unless, of course, these citizens felt it was not protection at all.

"The sooner the boy arrives, the sooner I can leave this city," Falco said. He heaved himself up and, like Joseph had done minutes earlier, walked closer to the edge of the roof. He looked past the lush gardens of the upper city and surveyed the valley between these residential quarters and the Temple, as if looking for fighting on the streets of the markets below.

Falco turned back to Joseph, frowning. "Something is wrong about all of this, and I don't like it at all."

THE SEVENTH HOUR

"HERE." Boaz thrust several bound scrolls toward Maglorius. "Contracts. Properly witnessed. Transferred and witnessed again. Penalties agreed upon if payments overdue. It's all legal."

Maglorius had risen as Boaz and the five men approached. Boaz had been unsuccessful raising extra men. He wasn't surprised. Sounds of skirmishes between the royal troops of the upper city and the rebels of the lower city had been reaching him all morning.

"You are too kind," Maglorius said. "If you don't mind, tell me the sum of the debts outstanding and to which merchants they were owed."

"Read them yourself." Boaz had no urge to reveal the insignificant amount compared to the value of the house. He did not want Maglorius to respond with violence. "Everything is legal, as you'll plainly see."

"There's the difficulty," Maglorius said. He made no move to open any of the scrolls. "I don't read."

"You don't read." Boaz was stunned. He'd gone to all this effort. It had been a battle to convince the keepers of the records to let him leave the Repository of the Archives with them. Even the judge who had ruled in favor of Boaz had had no choice but to go to the repository to review the contracts.

"I don't read," Maglorius said. "However, Amaris does. If you'll wait just a moment . . ."

Maglorius smiled and opened the door behind him. Before Boaz could protest, Maglorius took the scrolls inside. And shut the door.

From inside, the sound of a bar coming down to secure the door reached Boaz clearly.

What was he to do? Order these same five inept men to attempt to crash through the door? Hardly. Boaz knew full well that the upper-city residences were well protected. It would take a battering ram to get through.

He began to grind his teeth.

But he could do little else to ease his frustration as he waited. And waited.

✛ ✛ ✛

"It has been weeks since you permitted the last sacrifice on behalf of Caesar," Ananias said to Eleazar. Ananias wore simple peasant's clothing, not the ornate costume of the high priest. Here, he and his son would talk man-to-man. "I am here because I want to plead with you to resume the sacrifices on behalf of Caesar. Rome has not yet acted, but when it does, we are doomed."

They stood in torchlight. Condensation in the cool air trickled down the stone walls and from the ceiling of the tunnel, with an occasional drop landing in the cistern with a plop that was loud in comparison to the natural hush around them.

"If you had the faith of our forefathers," Eleazar said, "you would not declare doom upon our people. God has promised us a Messiah and will not break His covenant with us."

This was the first time that father and son had spoken since Eleazar ended the temple sacrifices for foreigners, and for Ananias, his son's words confirmed the accusation that Annas the Younger had made earlier in the day in front of the Great Sanhedrin.

"My son, my son. You are well intentioned, but if God sends us a Messiah, it will be in His own time. Who among us may force God to act?"

"*If* God sends a Messiah?" Eleazar lost his temper. "I knew you were a puppet of the establishment and a political choice for high priest, but is your faith in God and His promises that little?"

Ananias ignored the insult and ignored an impulse to admonish his son for the lack of respect. "Let me speak truthfully to you. Because if a father cannot trust a son, he can trust no one."

Eleazar crossed his arms. It was a clear-enough signal of resistance to Ananias, yet this might be their only chance to speak freely one to the other.

The cool, damp air in the tunnel far beneath the Temple Mount was unnaturally still, but to Ananias it seemed to become even more still as he dared voice his doubts for the first time.

"There are times," Ananias said, "that I wonder if the Nazarene was who he claimed to be."

He didn't have to explain who he meant. Since the crucifixion of Jesus of Nazareth, his followers, who claimed the Nazarene was Messiah, had become known as Nazarenes.

"Am I hearing you correctly?" Eleazar asked. "You, the high priest, uttering blasphemy?"

"Listen to me," Ananias said gently. "That's all I ask."

Eleazar shifted his weight from foot to foot as if impatient but did not protest.

"You remember James, the brother of the Nazarene."

"I do," Eleazar said. "We stoned Him to death because he proclaimed the same blasphemy as you do now."

"While the Nazarene was on this earth, James rejected Him, ridiculed Him. Yet later, James died rather than deny Him. That has always haunted me. What would it take to believe that your own brother was the Son of God? What would it take to be willing to die for that belief?"

"Insanity," Eleazar muttered.

"Or seeing the Nazarene resurrected, as was claimed by so many witnesses."

"A man does not live after death," Eleazar said. "Not after a whipping and crucifixion. Nor, if taken off the cross still alive, would he have the strength to move a stone that covers a tomb and defeat soldiers sent to guard Him. The witnesses have conspired to spread tales."

"And endured our persecution to maintain that lie? My son, people do not give up their lives for that. Indeed, that's why I've had my doubts. Watching the Jews among us who give up everything because of this faith."

"Our Messiah will not arrive as a lowly carpenter from an obscure town, nor will our Messiah allow himself the humiliation of crucifixion. No, he will lead our people to victory against the oppressors."

Ananias continued as if he had not heard Eleazar's answer. "Many of the Nazarenes in this city have begun to sell their property. They believe the end of the age is upon us."

Eleazar became more agitated as he listened more closely. "Exactly! The end of the age is upon us. The Messiah must come soon, and when he does he will vindicate the Temple of our God and free our people from the tyranny of Rome once and for all. The Nazarenes are right to see the recent events as signs, but they blasphemously misinterpret them, claiming that they are the birth pangs of God's wrath against Israel. Soon they will realize that the riots and wars do not portend God's judgment on Jerusalem but rather the coming of Messiah to free Israel from her enemies. We have worshiped God alone and haven't fallen into idolatry. We've kept the laws. There is no other explanation for what appears to be happening to our people and to Jerusalem than that the coming of Messiah is near."

"I hope that you are right. But if you continue to provoke Rome, you may help prove the Nazarenes correct," Ananias responded. "Surely you know the prophecy that the Nazarene made before he was crucified. Before the end of this generation, he said, those who pierced him would see him coming on clouds. If the Temple is destroyed as he prophesied, *he* will be vindicated, not Israel. God will truly have punished those who pierced the Nazarene."

"The Temple cannot be destroyed. No military power on earth is capable of taking this city, not with Jews ready to die for it, not with God on our side."

"If He isn't?"

"I cannot believe we are having this conversation," Eleazar said. "The upper city wars against the lower city. You lead one side and I lead the other. Who knows when we might again speak alone? Why are you wasting time on this?"

"Because, here, away from the battle, we have time to waste," Ananias said. In his love for Eleazar and his fear that they might not speak again, the voice of Ananias nearly cracked. "And because I, too, am fully aware that only God knows when we will speak again as father and son."

"Then let's speak of ending this standoff."

✦ ✦ ✦

"There has been no letter from Rome."

Valeria shrugged and began to turn away from Joseph Ben-Matthias, toward the stairs that would take her off the roof and down the streets of the upper city that were so familiar to her. Every day—except the Sabbath, for in the strange manner practiced by all Jews, Joseph Ben-Matthias did not engage in anything that suggested commerce—Valeria had stoically prepared herself for this same answer from the man.

There has been no letter from Rome.

Day by day, since sending a letter to Rome begging for help, Valeria had never lost hope because she had never allowed herself any hope. Florus, the most powerful man in Judea, had wanted her family destroyed. Maglorius, a legendary killer of men, wanted to kill her and Quintus to hide the fact that he had murdered their father. Her stepmother, Alypia, had abandoned them during the May riots and fled for Rome, probably intent on securing the family fortune as the Bellator widow and matriarch. The very people Valeria would have turned to for help were the ones who posed the most danger.

Who then had given her and Quintus refuge? Families of Jews. Whom had she been forced to trust with her letter to Rome? Another Jew. The irony. She, the daughter of a noble Roman family, accustomed to Jewish servants, in Jerusalem because her father had overseen the tax collection of this subjugated people, now lived among them in hiding.

What choice did she have?

None, except to find Joseph Ben-Matthias every day but one, even now during the standoff between the upper and lower city. None, except wait until he had a reply for her from Rome. So, unless she was caught crossing the line of demarcation between the upper and lower city, she would return tomorrow to ask the same question.

"Wait," called Joseph from behind her.

Valeria turned back to him. She said nothing. She made it a habit to speak little and, when she did speak, to speak in a near whisper. She had chopped her hair short, and she wore loose men's clothing to disguise her femininity. Her appearance she could hide, but she feared her voice would someday give her away.

"There has been no letter from Rome," Joseph repeated. "But it has been answered. You can go back to Valeria and Quintus to tell them that someone has been sent here to escort them to Rome."

Valeria unconsciously cocked her head. Had she heard correctly?

Joseph was smiling. "Your persistence on their behalf has finally been rewarded."

She had heard correctly. Yet how did he know?

As if understanding her thoughts, he continued. "Falco, the man who arrived today, told me this. As a result, much more about all of this is clear to me."

Valeria relaxed.

"I must caution you," Joseph said. "Falco feared the city was too dangerous for him, and he dared not wait until the rebels are defeated. He went to Florus for help, who sent soldiers with him."

Florus! Valeria began to edge away. *Soldiers!* Were they nearby?

"Please, stop," Joseph said. "Let me explain." He kept his distance from her, showing that he was aware that she was ready to bolt. "Falco and I discussed this at length while we were waiting for you this morning," Joseph said.

This very morning! Were the soldiers nearby? To calm her nerves, Valeria reminded herself that the soldiers did not want a mere messenger boy, as she had represented herself to Joseph.

"Falco and I both concluded that there could be only one reason Valeria sent you to me instead of openly going to Florus with her brother for protection and help to go to Rome. That, of course, would be fear of Florus."

A cry of outrage reached them from somewhere in the lower city. Then screams and wailing. Neither acknowledged it to the other, but both knew. A dart or catapulted stone from the royal troops in the upper city had found a victim in the lower city. It was never the opposite; the rebels did not have military equipment capable of striking the troops from a distance.

Joseph adjusted his tunic and sat on the raised edge of his roof. He looked down across the city and smiled sadly. After a few moments, he spoke to her again. "Falco and I both agreed on one other conclusion. Their fear was justified."

It was, as Valeria was all too aware. Her brother Quintus had told her that Maglorius had murdered their father on the final afternoon of the May riots across the city. But Valeria also knew that the ex-gladiator had taken advantage of the confusion and violence already inflicted on the Bellator household by Roman soldiers sent upon orders from Florus. Bellator had escaped the soldiers, only to be betrayed by Maglorius, who later made it look as though Bellator had died at the soldiers' hands.

But surely neither Joseph nor Falco knew these details. Valeria and Quintus had dared not leave hiding to publicly accuse Maglorius of this.

"You see," Joseph said, once again anticipating the questions that he implicitly raised, "a man like Florus does nothing unless it serves him. All of this city knows he has withheld Roman troops from helping us because he wants civil war to hide his atrocities from Caesar. Yet in the middle of this, he sends soldiers with Falco. Perhaps Florus seeks to curry favor with the senator in Rome helping Valeria and

Quintus, but I argued otherwise with Falco. I believe that Florus wants the Bellator children in his possession."

Valeria had been unaware of how much she'd been hoping her letter to Rome would save them until this moment, with the black despair that filled her when it appeared all was lost.

"Understand this," Joseph said. "Anything that denies Florus is something that helps the Jews. So I've made a proposal to Falco." He gazed steadily at Valeria. "But for it to work, you're going to have to convince the Bellator children to trust me."

What choice did Valeria have? She nodded.

"Good," Joseph said. "Come with me and let me introduce you to Falco. He'll tell you about our plan to escape the soldiers."

✠ ✠ ✠

"I want to end the standoff too," Ananias said to Eleazar. "Yet I cannot shake my questions. If the Nazarene was who he claimed to be, then I foresee that bringing down the wrath of Rome may turn their entire military might against us in fulfillment of his prophecy. Rebels have won battles against Rome in the past, but never wars. Allow the foreigners to sacrifice at the Temple. Help me unite the city."

"No. The Nazarene was not the Messiah. Therefore his prophecy cannot be fulfilled. Jerusalem and the Temple will not fall. God will preserve His people until the Messiah arrives. He did it when He brought us out of Egypt into the Promised Land. When He sent an angel of death to kill the Assyrians. God is faithful to His covenant. He will vindicate His people and His Temple. All through our history, God has saved us and will do so again."

"What if the covenant was fulfilled with the Nazarene? What if he was the Son of God and truly the last sacrifice? Then those in the city now selling their land because they believe his prophecies will be fulfilled in this generation will be the only ones preserved."

"Who has filled your head with these ideas?"

"You and I are not the only father and son divided," Ananias said ruefully. "Your friend Mordecai is a Zealot, but his father . . ."

Eleazar showed astonishment. "Phinehas most surely is not a Nazarene!"

Ananias nodded. "They live in houses side-by-side. At night, Phinehas has secret meetings with Nazarenes on his roof, while next door, Mordecai plots against the Romans, sharing your belief that the cause is holy."

"How do you know this about Phinehas?"

"Before the standoff separated our city, I went to him many times. He's a wise man, and I wanted counsel and solace on how to deal with this division between you and me. He told me about his own problem. Above all, remember that I am your father and you are my son, and my heart breaks because of my love for you."

Silence again fell upon them.

Eleazar lowered himself to his knees and bowed. "Father," he said, without raising his head, "I love you too. And I wish we could be on the same side. But I must do what God has called me to do. Remember Judas Maccabeus and the abomination of desolation in the Temple that Daniel predicted. Remember how God gave him victory."

Ananias thought of how Annas the Younger had used this love against him earlier. It brought tears to his eyes again, and he was glad that Eleazar did not see his face.

Ananias leaned forward and placed a hand on his son's shoulder. "I only pray that you are right. Remember, though, Judas Maccabeus led our people after Antiochus inflicted the abomination upon us. What I fear is that this war will lead to the ultimate abomination that the Nazarene predicted." Ananias helped his son to his feet. "We are here, meeting in secret, because you sent me a message. I doubt you wanted or expected a conversation like this."

"No, Father," Eleazar said. "I have a request."

"A father will always listen to a son's request. Whether I can grant it in this situation . . ."

"Tomorrow is the Festival of Xylophory. We must get enough wood to last until the end of the year."

Eleazar didn't have to explain more. Ananias immediately understood the consequences. And the predicament. "You are asking me to ensure that the royal troops let in those from the countryside."

"It is the festival. You know full well that thousands upon thousands have been traveling for days to bring wood in service to God."

Ananias did. The festival was a popular and joyous occasion, where maidens dressed in white and sang and danced in the vineyards around Jerusalem. As for the wood, the people flooded the Court of the Gentiles, depositing their offerings in an outer temple chamber, where priests disqualified from more important service by skin blemishes were sent to pick out wood that wasn't worm-eaten or otherwise unfit for the altar.

"Many of those thousands upon thousands will be sympathetic to your cause," Ananias said. "I'm not sure I can convince those in the upper city to allow them into the Temple."

"This is not about politics," Eleazar said. "The altar's fire must burn forever in honor of God."

"If it is not about politics," Ananias said, "then allow citizens of the upper city to enter the Temple to honor God as well."

Eleazar shook his head. "I cannot. The upper city has the wealth. Which means you also have the weapons. These peasants are poor, fortunate to own a hoe. They are no danger to anyone."

"You are asking too much and giving too little in return."

"This is not politics."

Ananias sighed. "This is not politics." A moment later he said, "How do I know you won't take advantage of this in some way?"

"All I want is one day of truce to ensure that the altar has sufficient wood and that faithful Jews are not disappointed in their service to God," Eleazar said. He, too, paused briefly. "You have my word, Father. As your son, I promise I will not betray you."

Finally Ananias nodded. "All right then. Because I trust and love you, I will pledge my honor and my position and the Sanhedrin will have no choice but to grant the truce. Service to God is more important than our politics."

✛ ✛ ✛

The door opened in front of Boaz.

Maglorius stepped outside. Without the scrolls. "There's another problem," he said.

"Let me guess," Boaz said. "Amaris doesn't read either. Nice try. Well, let me tell you, the judge was able to read those contracts. Very plainly. That's why the house was provided as a legal settlement for the debts of Ben-Aryeh."

"Amaris can read," Maglorius said. "That's not the problem."

Boaz found himself grinding his teeth again. He spit out each word. "What, then, is the problem?"

"She finds it too hot outside at this time of day."

"I fail to see how—"

"That's exactly it," Maglorius said. He was grave, almost sanctimoniously troubled. "She fails to see in the dimness inside."

"She's not blind."

"No, not at all. But the scrolls have such dense handwriting that it was difficult for her to see the writing very clearly." Maglorius paused. "As you pointed out to her earlier, she's no longer a young woman."

"Once again, I fail to—"

"It was my suggestion, and I'm very sorry for it. I take full blame."

"For what!" Talking to this ex-gladiator was like dealing with a village idiot.

"I brought over an oil lamp. I told her I would hold it steady so that the light would help her vision."

"She could have stood by a window."

"Yes," Maglorius said. "I understand that now. In the moment, I wasn't thinking clearly."

"So you helped her read the contracts with an oil lamp. Good. I'm sure she explained to you that the contracts are valid. Step aside and let us in."

"She didn't get a chance to read the contracts. It really was my fault. I apologize sincerely to you."

"For what!"

"There's no other way to tell you this. I burned the scrolls. Held the lamp too close and just like that, they caught fire." Maglorius held up his hand to forestall any protest from Boaz. "Fortunately, I threw them in an urn so that nothing else could catch on fire. The house is fine. Amaris is upset, but other than that, she's fine too. I know you'd want to know that."

"Put them in an urn," Boaz repeated dully. "And let them burn."

"There wasn't any water nearby."

"You could have dropped them on the floor and stomped the flames out!"

"I understand that now," Maglorius said. "As I mentioned, in the moment, I wasn't thinking clearly. To tell you the truth, I made a choice to let them burn. I know the contracts were upsetting to Amaris and . . ."

"The contracts are gone," Boaz said. Believing, yet not comprehending. "You burned them."

"If it helps," Maglorius said, "I'll apologize again." He looked at the five armed men behind Boaz. "It's embarrassing. I'm much better at fighting than dealing with scrolls."

He received several nods of sympathy from the men. As if they were comrades in the same trade.

"It shouldn't inconvenience you too much, should it?" Maglorius asked Boaz. "It's not too far back to the archives. Right? Amaris and I will wait for you, of course. It's the least we could do."

"You are an idiot," Boaz said. "If the keepers of the records made duplicate contracts of everything, there wouldn't be any room left in there."

"Oh."

"Don't think this means the contracts are void," Boaz said, starting to recover. It wasn't possible, was it, that this man had been smart enough to do all of this deliberately? Because if he was that smart, he would have known he would only accomplish a delay at best, for the final result would be the same. "I'll find the merchants and have them witness new contracts."

"I knew it would only be an inconvenience for you," Maglorius said. "I feel much better."

Was the man trying to hide a smile? Boaz couldn't decide.

Nor was he given much time to examine Maglorius. The ex-gladiator again moved with alarming quickness behind the door and barred it shut. Which, again, left Boaz staring at the door.

It wasn't until Boaz was following his armed guards through the arches of the inner courtyard to the outer courtyard that he realized one important detail.

All of the merchants he needed as witnesses kept their shops in the markets of the lower city. The same lower city that had been held by the rebels for six days already, rebels who allowed no access to anyone from the upper city.

There was no sign of the standoff and siege ending soon. Nor any guarantees that the merchants would survive the battles that the city faced in the near or distant future.

In sudden rage, Boaz kicked a nearby clay pot filled with soil and flowers.

And broke his big toe.

THE TENTH HOUR

"I WANT TO TALK about the boy," came the voice that broke in on Malka's thoughts as a shadow fell upon her.

She sat on a stool in the street in front of the doorway to her shack, where she'd been waiting for Quintus to return. Instead, the footsteps Malka had recognized belonged to the other, the one who looked out for him. The one who claimed to be an older brother, but was not.

"He's not here." Malka tilted her face upward as she spoke.

"I know. That's why I want to talk."

"I told you everything I could yesterday. I don't know where he goes and—"

"Listen to me. Tomorrow, I am going to come to take him away. I want to prepare you for that."

Malka had been preparing for this almost since the first day Quintus had been placed in her care. Still, it felt like a heavy hand squeezing her heart, like the weight of all her years pushing down on her bones.

"He's a fine boy," Malka said. "I will always remember his kindness to me."

"We will remember your kindness too."

Malka smiled, but it was merely a tightening of her lips to hide the pain she felt. This one blocking the sun and standing above Malka as she spoke down, this one had always been formal and distant, emphasizing the employer position.

"There is one thing I need of you," the voice above Malka continued.

Whenever this one spoke, Malka tried to imagine the face that went with the words. From the first day, Malka had known it was a young woman. Malka's vision was gone, but her sense of hearing and smell were heightened. However the one above her disguised herself to the rest of the world, she was unable to fool Malka.

"You must not say good-bye," the voice said. "When I come to get him tomorrow, pretend it is like any other day. He can't know it will be his last day with you."

The hand clenching Malka's heart seemed to squeeze harder. As the days with Quintus had become weeks, and the weeks had become months, the presence of the innocent young boy and his questions and his tears and his laughter had added joy to Malka's life beyond anything she'd expected might ever happen to her again. She'd never had a child of her own.

"Not even good-bye?"

Malka felt air shift around her. Sunlight on her face. The young woman had squatted, Malka guessed.

"Tomorrow Quintus will be able to escape Jerusalem," the voice said, much nearer. Yes, the woman had squatted. Malka felt the young woman's hand on her shoulder. Gentle. "But I'm worried he will want to take you with him."

"I'm blind and I'm old," Malka whispered. "I'm not fit to travel."

As Malka spoke, she realized the implications. If the young woman and Quintus took her, she would be too much of a burden. She would be endangering the boy's freedom. Yet to set him free, she must choose loneliness, made that much more poignant because memories of Quintus would haunt her tiny, impoverished home.

"If there was any other way . . ." The voice trailed off. "So you understand the importance of pretending tomorrow is no different than any other day with Quintus?"

"Yes. Of course." Malka heard the dullness in her own voice.

"You will be rewarded for this," the voice said. "I will make sure that money is sent back to you."

Money would not replace laughter, not in an old woman's miserable shack.

"He is going to a better place?" Malka asked. Then immediately thought how stupid that must have sounded. Any place would be better for the boy than this squalor in the lower city.

"Yes," the voice said. "He is going home."

Malka nodded. Quintus had never spoken about his home, and Malka could only imagine what it might be. But if leaving was going to make the little boy happy, then Malka would set aside her own sorrow and rejoice for him.

She would hide her tears until he was gone.

"One last thing," the voice said. "Don't tell Quintus I was here this afternoon."

✦ ✦ ✦

"Phinehas will lead a meeting of the Nazarenes tonight," Olithar told Annas the Younger. "A sacramental supper, if I understand it correctly."

Olithar was a tall, skinny man with a sparse beard. He had his arms crossed and quietly slapped his right hand against his left forearm. It was a nervous habit that Annas detested as much as the sight of Olithar's straggly beard.

The scrolls that Annas had been studying when Olithar arrived were still open on a table. They were in a chamber in the household of Annas that he had temporarily set up to deal with his business matters. In the stalls at the Court of the Gentiles—controlled by his family for two generations now—it was much more convenient. But the rebel takeover of the Temple had forced him out. The inconvenience was nothing compared to the staggering loss of daily revenue now that Annas could no longer oversee the buying and selling of the animals for sacrifice.

"Does Phinehas suspect you have a spy among them?" This

was an important question for Annas to ask. The city was dangerous now. He did not want to risk a trip into the lower city alone if
there was any chance the Nazarenes would not be gathered.

"No," Olithar answered without hesitation. "Nor does the spy
suspect I report to you."

"What does he look like?" Annas asked and then listened as
Olithar described the man.

"Tell your spy not to be there tonight," Annas said. He most
definitely did not want this spy telling Olithar later about the
meeting. While the spy would eventually hear about it from the
other Nazarenes, Annas wanted at least a day or two to pass before
Olithar found out. Annas trusted no one, least of all Olithar;
Olithar had betrayed Ben-Aryeh to Annas for very little money.
Annas well knew that a man unfaithful to one master would just
as likely be unfaithful to his next.

"Are you having them arrested?"

"What I intend is my business." Annas glared at Olithar and
made a dismissive motion.

Olithar stared at his feet but, surprisingly, did not leave. "I only
ask," he said, "because of the brother of the Nazarene."

Annas was curious as to what had motivated Olithar to this
feeble defiance. Usually Olithar scurried away at the earliest
opportunity. Annas liked his subordinates to be fearful.

"The brother of the Nazarene—James? He doesn't matter
anymore."

"That's why I ask," Olithar said. "You had him stoned to death
when you were . . ."

Olithar looked up, guilty, then down again.

"Yes," Annas said, his voice icy. "When I was high priest."

How he hated any reminder that he'd lost his position. Olithar
was fortunate that he'd helped engineer the downfall of Ben-Aryeh;
otherwise Annas would be in full rage.

"I have a nephew among those Nazarenes tonight," Olithar said.

"If you're going to have them killed too, I would like your permission to warn him away."

"A nephew? You haven't told me this before."

"I . . . I . . . just found out," Olithar answered.

In content and presentation, it was an obvious lie, but Annas decided to let it pass. Once he ruled the city, he'd find a way to make sure Olithar could present no future problems.

"Who is your nephew?" Annas demanded. "Give me his name and description."

Once again, Olithar supplied the information.

"You had better pray he does not take ill or find another reason to be away tonight," Annas told Olithar. "Because if he is missing from the gathering, I will conclude that you warned him away."

If Olithar gave warning to his nephew, then that warning would reach all the other Nazarenes.

Olithar spoke with his head down. "If he is executed, it will break my sister's heart."

"If he is missing from the meeting," Annas said, "you will pay whatever punishment he would have faced. Do you understand? Now go."

Olithar hesitated. "There's one other thing."

"Is it something more you've kept from me about the Nazarenes?" Annas could feel his rage building.

"No," Olithar said quickly. "Ananias has called for another council of the Great Sanhedrin. He wishes to get agreement to allow peasants into the city for the wood-burning festival. I've been requested to see if you will attend."

Annas considered this briefly. More than likely, Ananias was proposing it as an effort to ease hostilities. As such, the Great Sanhedrin would probably agree. Which would put Annas in a position of showing support for Ananias by casting his vote in favor or of alienating his own support in the Great Sanhedrin by voting against Ananias.

"No, I will not," Annas said, making an easy decision. It would

be much better to abstain. The rebels were so entrenched that
offering an olive branch would certainly not end the standoff.
And if his own efforts worked among the Nazarenes this evening,
Annas would be that much closer to removing Ananias from
power anyway.

✝ ✝ ✝

Eleazar was alone on the top of the western temple wall when
Gilad approached him.

"There is something important we need to discuss," Gilad said.
"And I knew I would find you here."

"Am I that predictable?" Eleazar had been leaning on the balus-
trade. He straightened as he spoke to his friend.

"Hardly. But I know how much you love the city. . . ." Gilad
gestured to take in the view. If there was one spot in all of Jerusalem
that encompassed its diversity and glory and squalor, this was it.

The wall guarded the top of the plateau that had been lev-
eled by Herod's workmen for the Temple Mount. It overlooked
the lower city nestled in the Tyropoeon Valley directly below.
Eleazar and Gilad stood halfway between the northwest and the
southwest corners of the mount. To their right, the much-hated
Antonia Fortress rose above the wall, giving the Roman garrison
a clear view down into the Temple area. To their immediate left,
connecting at right angles to the temple wall, was the bridge that
straddled the valley, connecting the temple wall to the tower of
a city wall on the other side of the valley. At least fifty priests
manned the barricaded entrance to the bridge, ensuring that
troops from the tower would not attempt an attack on the
Temple at one of its few vulnerable points.

Beyond, to the north and west, a hill rose, giving sight to the
second wall of the city, and beyond that, higher on the hill and
almost at the horizon, was the third wall, encompassing and protecting Bezetha, the new section of Jerusalem.

To the south and west, flanking the same hill, was Zion, the upper city with its collection of palaces, mansions, and private guards. Herod's palace, an almost impregnable fortress that the hated king had built along the far western wall of the city to protect himself from his own people, dominated the view.

The lower city itself crammed the valley; the roofs of all the tiny houses made it seem like a collection of boxes riddled by a confusing maze. Cutting through it, halfway up toward Zion, was the aqueduct that now served as a line of siege between the upper and lower city.

Gilad joined Eleazar in a pensive moment of gazing across the city.

"'It is beautiful in its loftiness, the joy of the whole earth,'" Gilad said quietly. "'Like the utmost heights of Zaphon is Mount Zion, the city of the Great King. God is in her citadels; he has shown himself to be her fortress.'"

Eleazar smiled sadly and recited more of the psalm of David. "'Walk about Zion, go around her, count her towers, consider well her ramparts, view her citadels, that you may tell of them to the next generation. For this God is our God for ever and ever; he will be our guide even to the end.'"

Eleazar had hoped his time of peace and contemplation would last longer than this, but he knew there was no sense in avoiding whatever Gilad needed to discuss. "Is it good news or bad news?" he asked.

Gilad shook his head. "For me, good. For you?" A pause. "You'll have to decide."

"Anything that isn't clearly good news is not good news."

"Manahem."

"He's decided against joining our battle?"

"Hardly. He and his men are only a few days away."

Eleazar relaxed somewhat.

"We need control of the gates of the city," Gilad said. "You've known this all along."

"No," Eleazar said. "What I've argued is that the mere

knowledge that Manahem is outside the city should be enough to
encourage all the people to join with us."

"That remains to be seen. Besides, I have a better idea on how
to win the hearts of the people."

"I'm listening."

"But first we need to ensure that everyone knows Manahem
will be able to enter the city as soon as he and his army arrive."

"Debatable."

"Which is why I'm here. On one hand, if we can't get control
of the city gates, we have only the possibility that Manahem will be
able to help. With the possibility that his army will eventually stop
waiting outside the city and drift away. Even if they do stay, Florus
might actually send soldiers in this direction to rescue the city.
Time is not on our side."

"On the other hand?" Eleazar said, staring across the city. How
he hated this situation, Jew against Jew. But he hated Roman
oppression even more and believed God would help them prevail
to end it.

"On the other hand, if we do get control of the city gates, it is
certain that Manahem will give us complete victory."

"I can't argue with that. But we've been trying to win control
of the gates for nearly a week. I don't see any way of doing it
before Manahem arrives."

"Tomorrow," Gilad said quietly. "Tomorrow we can storm the
upper city. If you grant the order to go ahead with it, I would like
your permission to have the house of Joseph Ben-Matthias protected. As you know, he saved me from execution in Rome."

Eleazar shook his head impatiently. "We will not storm the
upper city. Not enough men. No weapons for them even if we had
enough. We've been fortunate to hold the line as long as we have.
If we risk it all and lose, we'll never have this chance again."

"Tomorrow," Gilad repeated. "You will have all the men and
weapons you need."

"I don't understand."

"Some of the Zealots from the hills have arrived already for tomorrow's wood-burning festival. Your stand against the upper city has roused a belief that they can finally do something. I'm told thousands will be arriving with their *sicarri* hidden in their tunics. All they need is a signal, and they will rush out of the Temple and attack the upper city."

"We agreed to a truce! The wood-burning festival is holy, not to be used for war!"

"You see it that way," Gilad said. "I don't."

"As governor of the Temple, I made a vow to the high priest that—"

"To the high priest?" Gilad asked. "Or to your father?" Gilad put a hand on Eleazar's shoulder. "My friend, you and I both know that the position of high priest has become the ultimate symbol of corruption to the people. He gets his power only from the king of Judea, who in turn gets his power from Rome. The high priest serves Rome first, the people second."

Gilad pointed at the upper city. "If you have any doubts, look where and how they live. Far above the poor who cry out for justice from them. So is Ananias the high priest to you? Or your father?"

"A vow is a vow, whether I make it to my father or to the high priest. You want me to betray it."

"Eleazar, we are running out of time. Tomorrow, victory is ours if we want it. Eventual defeat is almost as certain if you don't want it. The choice is yours."

✢ ✢ ✢

As she walked away from the old woman, Valeria felt remorse that she hadn't expected.

Earlier in the day, thinking through the problem, it had seemed clear. The old woman could not go with them to Rome. She would be unlikely to survive the journey. Worse, she would slow them down and add difficulty to their escape from Jerusalem.

Tomorrow Valeria intended to pretend she was taking Quintus

to the market. And when she and Quintus were with the body-guards arranged by Joseph and safely on their way out of the city, she would tell Quintus their destination and console him with the same promise she'd made to Malka. When they reached Rome, she would arrange for money to be sent back to the woman to make her last years comfortable.

Wasn't that enough?

Yet seeing the old woman on the stool, with her deep wrinkles and the startling white milkiness of her cataracts, had provoked compassion in Valeria she did not want as a burden.

The woman's quiet acceptance of their departure had also bothered Valeria, and looking past the woman into her shack had given her a sense of what it must be like to live alone in such poverty. Of course the woman would have grown fond of Quintus. Valeria should have foreseen that. But it was too late now.

Their escape was before them, and soon, this cursed Jerusalem would be behind them. Within days or weeks, especially as they approached Rome, Quintus would forget about Malka.

Yes, Valeria told herself with every step down the street, she was definitely doing what was best for all of them.

DUSK

"VALERIUS! Valerius!"

Valeria woke on the rooftop and sat upright on her sleeping mat. Leeba was calling for her, but because Leeba believed Valeria was a boy, she used the masculine version of Valeria's name.

"Valerius!"

Valeria hurried to Leeba. Again the glassblower's house was a disturbing scene. This time, however, Nahum was restraining his wife as she attempted to attack the three priests who were lifting the body of their son, Raanan.

"Stop them," she pleaded to Valeria. "Stop them!"

"This is not your business," Nahum said. "Go back to the rooftop."

"They can't throw him into the valley," Leeba wailed as the three men straightened with the limp body of her son. "Not Gehenna!"

Although she wasn't a Jew, Valeria had witnessed enough death in the previous days to understand. Dead bodies were not permitted to remain in the city overnight and defile the holy mount. Because there were too many killings in a day, the bodies were not given burial, but thrown over the city wall, down the steep incline to the bottom of the Valley of Gehenna.

Valeria remained motionless despite Leeba's pleas. Never had Valeria witnessed such grief.

Leeba kicked futilely at the priests as they passed her. She spit at their backs and cursed them. To no avail.

Her son was gone.

✠ ✠ ✠

On his journey to arrange for the execution of a man he hated but had not met, Annas the Younger stopped halfway up the steps to the flat roof of a small house in the lower city.

Because of Olithar, Annas knew this man would be sitting above, knew who would be surrounding this man at this time, knew why they had gathered. And he intended that he would have each one killed after they had served his purpose.

Dusk had deepened enough that in one direction, the black outlines of the Mount of Olives were almost invisible against the night sky, while from the other direction came the illumination of hundreds of lit torches from the Temple, throwing long, mysterious shadows into the cramped alleys.

Here in the squalor of the lower city, the smells of the cooking spices of a dozen different nationalities assailed his nostrils. It was a calm, hot evening, and the smoke of cooking fires seemed to hang like a shroud.

Annas had paused on the steps because of the voice that carried softly to him from the rooftop. The voice of one of the men that Annas intended for eventual death.

The words were clear to Annas:

"'In the same way, after supper he took the cup, saying, "This cup is the new covenant in my blood; do this, whenever you drink it, in remembrance of me." For whenever you eat this bread and drink this cup, you proclaim the Lord's death until he comes.'"

In the hush that followed—punctuated by the clatter of a clay cooking pot as it shattered in a house farther down the alley and a brief outburst of yelling from a drunken man—Annas found himself surprised by anger. He was a business-man first and a man of religion second, yet he was offended deeply.

Sacrilege!

Annas had his informants in all corners of the city; even without them, he still would have recognized immediately what was happening.

Followers of the Nazarene called it the Lord's Supper. A celebration of their last meal with the man of Nazareth the night before his crucifixion.

Sacrilege!

"In the same way, after supper he took the cup, saying, 'This cup is the new covenant in my blood; do this, whenever you drink it, in remembrance of me.' For whenever you eat this bread and drink this cup, you proclaim the Lord's death until he comes."

In those brief words, the implications were horrendous.

A new covenant between them and God? Did they dare suggest that God's covenant to Abraham and his descendants was broken? Heresy that should be punished by death!

"In my blood"? The Temple and all of its priesthood existed to provide the atonement that came with the sacrifices of animals. Would the followers of the Nazarene then have the arrogance to suggest the Temple no longer necessary? to proclaim that because of one man's death the offering of temple sacrifice was now and forever forbidden? dare to proclaim that the new covenant had been established by the shedding of a man's blood? blood from the false teacher from Nazareth, a common criminal?

Proclaiming the Lord and His death? No one would be Lord but God Himself or the Messiah He had promised. *Heresy!*

"Until he comes"? Dead once and resurrected, followers of the Nazarene claimed. And to believe further the man of Nazareth's promise that within this generation He would arrive on clouds of heaven with power and great glory? that members of all the tribes of God's people would mourn because of it?

Annas, like any educated Jew, understood the symbolism of the words borrowed from the ancient prophets such as Isaiah, who used this apocalyptic language of arriving on clouds to proclaim God's imminent judgment. "See the Lord rides on a swift cloud and is coming to Egypt." So who were these people on the roof to believe and proclaim that God's judgment on Israel was imminent because of what had been done to their supposed Messiah? And to further claim that there would be a final and literal return when all the believers would join in resurrection from death themselves?

Heresy! Heresy! Heresy!

These Nazarenes—Jews, no less, betrayers of the covenant God had made to Israel—now claimed that inheritance of the covenant blessings depended not on one's ancestry, circumcision, or adherence to the Law, but rather on one's belief that Jesus of Nazareth was God's Messiah. These Nazarenes claimed the boundaries were gone—that uncircumcised Gentiles who believed were now included in the covenant, like branches grafted onto a tree. Claimed the covenant was now inclusive, not exclusive. Claimed that there was a new priesthood, that any Jew or Gentile who believed could directly approach God without a sacrifice performed at the Temple by a priest, because Jesus was both intermediary and sacrifice. Claimed Jesus was the living Temple and all that had been true of the Temple was now true of Jesus. Claimed that Jesus would be vindicated when the ruling authorities in Jerusalem had been judged and destroyed along with the old Temple. Claimed that after Jesus, who was sufficient atonement for sin, there was no need for a physical temple or a physical sacrificial system. Claimed that this communion allowed them to participate in the last sacrifice, made by Jesus.

No need for a temple? Or for a land of Israel? A covenant fulfilled and extended to all who wanted to be included apart from the Law? Jesus, the last sacrifice?

Heresy! Heresy! Heresy!

As Annas climbed the remainder of the steps, he smiled with a degree of satisfaction. Perhaps God had arranged it for Annas to hear the sacrilege at precisely this moment. For whatever guilt he'd had about how he intended to kill the men above had vanished in his anger.

With the guilt banished, Annas stepped into the light of the single torch on the flat of the roof.

✠ ✠ ✠

Jachin knocked on the door to the house of Simeon Ben-Aryeh. He would have been more comfortable armed with a torch, but his orders had been total discretion. A lone man with a torch in the upper city in these times was anything but discreet.

He rapped on the door with his knuckles and, when no one came to answer, switched to the hilt of his knife. He pounded the door for at least a minute, with no results.

Although there was no audience, of course, Jachin shrugged. He didn't blame those inside for ignoring him. Especially during these times. Who knew when the lower-city rebels might break through and attack the wealth of the upper city.

Just as Jachin decided to turn away, a sudden and fierce constriction bit into his throat. It took him a moment to realize someone had clamped a forearm around him, and he reacted without hesitating. He was a large, strong man, accustomed to street fighting.

A less-experienced fighter would instinctively pull against the forearm, trying to relieve the pressure. Jachin knew the unexpected would be far more effective. A spin to face his opponent would mean the back of his neck would bear the pressure, and his soft, vulnerable throat would be protected. Then a quick lift of the knee while his opponent was recovering from surprise.

He attempted the spin, but the man behind him clamped his right shoulder and lifted him off the ground.

Jachin would have yelped if he'd been able to expel air from his lungs.

"Drop the knife," came the soft words into his ear. He felt the breath of his opponent, almost like a caress.

Jachin kicked into the air, hating this feeling of helplessness. His size was always an advantage to him, yet now it was useless.

"Drop the knife."

Darkness began to close on the edges of Jachin's consciousness, so he dropped the knife immediately. The pressure on his throat did not ease, however, and seconds later, he lost control of his muscles. He dimly knew he'd fallen, and the impact of his nose against the courtyard tiles was a blinding white light that kept him from blacking out.

His opponent pounced on his back and kept a knee grinding into his spine.

He felt a knife tip press into his neck, in the soft spot behind his jaw, just under his ear.

"Who sent you?"

"Joseph Ben-Matthias," Jachin said, reduced to grunting his words directly into the cool tile pressing his face. "Listen to me. If I meant the household any harm, I would not have knocked loudly on the door. And if you knew anything about me, you'd know if I did mean harm, I could have slit the throat of every person in there and left again. Like a cat."

The knife pressure did not ease.

"Why are you here?" came the soft voice.

"To speak to you," Jachin answered. The man who had disarmed him so easily could only be Maglorius.

"Then speak."

"Let me sit up," Jachin said.

"Make yourself comfortable where you are." The knife tip dug deeper, breaking skin. "What does Ben-Matthias want with me?"

So it was Maglorius. Who had just proven himself the best candidate for what was required.

"Nothing, directly," Jachin answered. Blood trickled down his neck. More blood dripped from his nose onto the tile. "He doesn't even know I'm here, nor does he want to."

"Make sense and make sense soon," Maglorius said.

"Ben-Matthias hired me to escort two Romans out of the city and into Syria. He doesn't care what methods I use, as long as I get it done. Most Jews in the city—at least Jews I would consider for the job—are involved in fighting for the rebels. As you can imagine, not many men qualify for a job like this. So I've come to you, knowing your reputation."

Without warning, Maglorius was off Jachin's back. He yanked him by the neck of his tunic and pulled him to his feet.

Jachin staggered to keep his balance. He faced Maglorius but in the dusk saw only the man's outline, not his features. Such a strong man. So fast. Perhaps after this job, Jachin could convince him to consider more employment. In times of trouble, it wasn't difficult to find ways to make money for men who were strong, fast, and without scruples.

"I'm not interested," Maglorius said. "On your way."

Jachin saw enough of his own knife, in the other man's possession, to see that it was held in a ready fashion. Jachin held his own hands out to make it obvious he would attempt nothing.

"Money won't be a problem," Jachin countered. "Ben-Matthias will be paid well for making sure the two Romans make it safely."

"I'm not interested."

"If it's a matter of conscience," Jachin said, "the two Romans haven't done anything illegal or against the Jews. It's a young boy and his older sister."

"Why are they trying to escape the city?"

Did Jachin imagine a sudden interest in the man's voice? "Apparently Florus wants them for some reason. He sent soldiers to take them back to Caesarea, but how much trouble could soldiers be to someone like you?"

Maglorius moved closer. "Only a boy and a girl? What else did Ben-Matthias tell you?"

"They had sent a letter to Rome, claiming an inheritance. A man named Falco came to get them, but when Florus heard, he sent the soldiers with Falco."

"The names of the brother and sister?"

"That's all I know. Ben-Matthias didn't even want to tell me any of that, but I'd be a fool to accept this type of employment without learning what I did."

"Well then," Maglorius said, "if it's only a boy and a girl trying to get back to Rome, how could I in good conscience not help?"

✛ ✛ ✛

"I am here to speak to Phinehas," Annas announced.

He'd walked boldly to stand beside the single torch, knowing its flickering yellow light would let all the men see his face and recognize him immediately.

He wanted their fear.

There were fewer than ten. All were gathered at a rough wooden table, reclining beside it. They gave Annas silence, their relaxed postures instantly gone as all eyes stared at him.

"I am Phinehas." The man at the head of the table set down a glass of wine and stood. A man taller than Annas. Wearing a simple tunic. He was mainly in shadow, so Annas could not make out the features of the man's face or read his expression.

Phinehas half turned and gestured at the table. "You are welcome to our food."

Grumbles came from some of the men.

Phinehas turned to them. "Our Father loves him too, does he not?"

The men shifted uncomfortably, but none offered more protest.

"Please," Phinehas said. "We would consider your presence at our table an honor."

Annas pointedly moved away from the table, rejecting the other man's offer of hospitality. He felt something unfamiliar. Righteousness.

"Coming up the stairs," Annas said, "I heard the words to your blasphemous rite. All of you, as Jews, could be stoned for your apostasy."

"There is no blasphemy. To be a follower of Messiah does not mean rejecting all we have been taught as God-fearing Jews. If you accept that Messiah has already been among us then—"

Annas shook his head. "That simple statement and all it implies is enough for any lawyer to find your guilt."

"I cannot deny truth."

"I am not here to argue your misguided beliefs."

"Then, brother," Phinehas said softly, "why are you here?"

"First, to emphasize that all of you are open to lawful persecution."

"Your presence alone does that." It wasn't an accusation as much as a sad statement. "You, after all, arranged to kill James, the brother of Jesus, as one of your first acts as high priest."

"Soon I will have that power again. But when I am high priest, perhaps I will instead offer amnesty to the Nazarenes of Jerusalem."

Mutterings of disbelief.

Annas had been prepared for this. "There is enough division among us. I want it ended."

"You've just called our beliefs misguided," Phinehas said. "Yet you offer amnesty."

"You know my reputation. I don't spend hours upon hours in theological debate. I care far less about what you might believe than I do about a peaceful Jerusalem with business that continues without disruptions."

"You had James killed."

"Politics," Annas answered. In the same way that Phinehas had earlier gestured at the table with food, Annas swept his hands wide, taking in the lights that came from torches on the walls of the Temple Mount.

"I could foresee that when the final stone of the Temple was in place," Annas continued, "the Temple would no longer need the eighteen thousand men and the wages they require. With such a glut of workers, too many men would be idle, all of them with bellies tight from hunger. I had hoped that the execution of James would discourage the Nazarenes and defuse any trouble that might happen otherwise."

"You were wrong," Phinehas said.

Annas laughed ruefully. "Wrong about the solution. I lost my position because of it. But I was prophetic about the problem. The Temple was finished and the dissatisfaction erupted as men lost employment.

Jerusalem is divided. I've decided that perhaps the best politics is not in trying to eradicate the Nazarenes but in embracing them."

"How does that help?"

"Many among the poor are grateful for all that you've done. Give me your support, and they in turn will support us against the rebels. When I am high priest, you will be able to worship openly."

This was a lie, but Annas was skilled at lying. What he intended was to let them worship openly long enough to compile a thorough list of all the Nazarenes in Jerusalem, then destroy them.

"Religious politics," Phinehas said. "The same politics crucified our Master. He was rejected because everyone expected the Messiah to overthrow the rule of Rome, but His kingdom was not of this earth."

"But did He not command you to feed the poor? Think of how much more you can do if you don't fear persecution."

"We will talk about it," Phinehas said.

"At this point, that's all I can ask for." Which was true. The talk would spread. Like deceptive poison. And that, too, would serve his purpose.

Annas left them on the rooftop.

Tomorrow he had one last portion of poison to spread. Then he would be well on his way to ridding himself of Ananias and taking control of the city again.

✝ ✝ ✝

"Leeba, Leeba," Nahum said to his weeping wife as he held her, "we had no choice."

She stared at him. With no warning, she pushed away from him and slapped him. "You knew," she said. Cold, almost hateful.

He stared at her.

"You let him join the Zealots."

"Leeba—"

"Royal troops do not attack citizens of the lower city," she said. "They only defend themselves when attacked. If Raanan died to them, it is because he was among a group who led a fight against them."

Leeba's chest heaved as she fought her emotions. The sound of her breathing was loud to Valeria, who dared not move or attract their attention.

"Raanan had reached manhood," Nahum answered. "He made his own choices."

"Year after year, you filled this household with praise for the Zealots. Of course he would join them."

It was obvious they had forgotten the presence of Valeria.

"He made his own choices."

"How long did you know he was with the rebels?"

Nahum looked away.

"How long?"

"He was a courier for them," Nahum said after some hesitation. "He brought messages from post to post along the line." He swallowed hard, stoic yet proud. "I'm told he was one of the bravest among them."

"He's dead, you fool!"

"We all die," Nahum said. "He died fighting for the freedom of our people. He wasn't a coward bound by creditors' notes. But let me tell you, that cowardice has ended."

Leeba stared at him in return. Comprehension filled her eyes. "No. You can't!"

"They killed my son."

"The upper city will win," she said. Her voice was flat. "They have weapons and all the rebels have is determination. They have wealth, and we have the debt to them. If you don't lose your life, you'll lose your livelihood when this rebellion is defeated."

"They killed my son. Do you think I care any longer what my creditors in their mansions above us think?"

"I'm your wife. Do you care if you leave me widowed?"

"You are also a Jew. We serve God first. This battle is for Him, and we will not lose. If you are widowed, at least you will be free of Roman oppression."

"We will lose," she said. "I'm begging you not to join the rebels.

When this is over, we'll leave the city and begin a new life somewhere else."

Nahum was stunned, as if she had slapped him again. "Desert
the city of God? He has never deserted us."

Leeba put her face in her hands for long moments. When she
looked at him again, resolve filled her features. "My husband,
God has never deserted us. But God has always punished us for
rejecting Him."

"We are engaged in a battle for His cause. How can you say we
reject Him when every day we pray for Messiah?"

Her shoulders were square now. "Husband, you are no longer
bound by creditors' notes. I am no longer bound by fear for our
family, for if my son is gone and you are determined to martyr
yourself in a failed cause, then I will speak openly."

"I . . . I . . . don't understand."

"I am a follower of the Nazarene," she said. "Jesus was the Son of
God and predicted God's judgment would fall on those who pierced
Him. 'Behold, you will see me coming on clouds,' He told us."

"You are a Nazarene!"

"Listen to me, Husband. We must flee the city. The end is
upon those who rejected and continue to reject Him. The Messiah
Himself made this prophecy, and we are nearing the end of the
generation that pierced Him on the cross."

"You. A Nazarene."

"And you are one of the best glassblowers in the trade. Surely we
can make a household elsewhere and live in peace. The Temple will
fall, but those who believe in His warnings will be saved."

"Woman, I'll send you away in divorce before I leave the city.
And every holy man in the city would applaud me for it." He
paused. "No, I won't divorce you before I leave the city. I'll do it
immediately. You may no longer consider yourself a wife of mine."

Leeba fell to her knees, sobbing again, but Nahum ignored her.

Nahum pointed at Valeria. "Tonight, I sleep on the roof with you."

⋖ 15 AV ⋗

DAWN

NAHUM WAS AWAKE when the trumpet calls from the Temple began to echo across the city. He'd not slept at all, up on the roof on a pile of blankets he'd made into a temporary bed after declaring his wife divorced.

Nearby, he saw that Valerius shifted on his sleeping mat. A strange, quiet boy. Hardworking to be sure, and willing enough when ordered to do any task, but reclusive to the point of mystery, disappearing and reappearing during the day with no willingness to tell where he'd gone. No matter. With the glassblowing furnaces empty of charcoal until the standoff ended, Nahum had already decided what the boy would do today.

Leaving the boy to tend to his own morning hygiene in privacy, Nahum walked to the edge of the roof and brooded as the brilliant yellow edge of the sun slowly rose above the city walls, casting a beautiful glow across the lower city. No poetic thoughts crossed his mind, however. Dawn would not let him escape the same turmoil that had kept him awake through the night.

He had just declared his wife divorced. To be sure, he would have no trouble finding another wife, but as the slow minutes had formed hours during the dead dark of night, he'd realized how fully he loved her.

How had it happened that he'd made such a rash decision?

It could be nothing else but a lashing out in pain, generated by the death of Raanan, something that he still could not comprehend. Indeed, in this very moment as the city began to stir, he half expected to hear his son's footsteps bounding up toward him. Raanan dead. Killed by royal troops.

Nahum had meant much of what he'd said to Leeba. The boy had died fighting for the Jews' freedom, as had countless other young men all through their history. There was solace in that.

Yet the honor in the boy's death did nothing to remove the heartrending grief that Nahum would not permit the world to see. And now he could not even share this grief with the boy's own mother.

He pondered this, knowing it would stir his anger and rage against the oppressors who lived in the upper city. Anger and rage, right now, were much better for a man than grief and indecision.

Yes, Nahum told himself, *dwell on the injustice of oppression. Savor the rage against those who killed your only son.*

Those who ruled Jerusalem did so by permission of Rome. Short of anything that might defile the holiness of God, the establishment and the royalty always did as Rome directed. They claimed it was for the sake of the people—for war with Rome would lead to destruction—yet it was obvious that obeying Rome and using its power continued to make them rich while the poor continued to suffer.

And, as Eleazar said again and again, wasn't the fear of Rome an indirect blasphemy of their one true God who had promised them a Messiah? And wasn't this the same blasphemy that his own wife was committing by choosing to follow the Nazarene?

With a degree of savage joy, Nahum's resolve returned. He must cast his wife aside for her rejection of God. The rebellion must continue!

Yet most of the lower-city people remained neutral, fearful, like Nahum had been, of the creditors who held so much sway in their lives. How could the tradesmen and the poor side against those who would most certainly defeat them? against those who could sell them into slavery by calling in a note of debt? Nahum had felt no differently, until he'd lost all he cared for when the death of Raanan had

not only robbed him of his first and only born, but driven such a
deep wedge between Nahum and his wife.

If only there were a solution. . . .

Before he could give it much more thought, he heard the shuf-
fling of the apprentice's sandals behind him. Nahum turned to the
boy. "Valerius, you will come with me."

As always, the boy simply regarded him in silence and waited
for whatever else Nahum might say.

"You are young and built with the thinness of a gazelle," Nahum
said. "You will now take Raanan's place and run messages from post
to post along the line of siege."

✠ ✠ ✠

"This man, Joseph Ben-Matthias," Maglorius said to Amaris. "Is he
trustworthy?"

They sat in the inner courtyard where Maglorius had faced Boaz
the day before.

As always when the two of them spent time together in her
household, Amaris had a woman servant nearby. Not because she
was afraid of Maglorius. But because she respected her husband.
Maglorius might be serving her as a bodyguard, but he was still
an unmarried man close to her age. While Romans might not
see anything untoward about such an arrangement, the Jews in
Jerusalem did.

"Very trustworthy," Amaris said without pausing for thought.

"Tell me more about him."

"Tell me why."

"He may be sending you to Rome."

Amaris had been cutting a fig from a plate beside her. She set
it down slowly and stared at Maglorius.

He grinned broadly. "Thought that might get your attention."

"Why should I go to Rome?" Amaris asked, although she knew
the answer.

"Your husband is there with Vitas."

"But this household . . ."

Maglorius snorted. "Will be taken from you. Boaz will return. You know that. He has the law and the establishment on his side. What I did yesterday was more for my satisfaction than anything else."

Amaris closed her eyes and nodded. She opened them again. "Joseph Ben-Matthias. The son of a priest. Descends from the Hasmoneans. Very intelligent. Well respected. A few years ago, he went to Rome."

"Really." Maglorius leaned forward.

"Some priests had been sent there to be tried by Nero, including a chief priest named Gilad, who serves Eleazar directly."

"Sent to Rome. Why?"

"Felix, the former procurator, laid false charges and hoped to cause trouble. Joseph deplored the injustice and decided to defend them, even though he knew it would make an enemy of Felix. Fortunately for him, in Rome, he made friends with Poppaea."

"Caesar's wife?"

"The same."

"I'm impressed."

"You should be," Amaris said. "She secured the release of the priests and sent Joseph back to Jerusalem with gifts. On his return, he shared them widely."

"Generous."

"Perhaps." Amaris smiled. "Or shrewd. He is well admired on both sides of the city."

Maglorius found this interesting. "Why not then appoint him as a mediator?"

"He saw too much of Rome."

"I don't understand," Maglorius said.

"Unlike most in Jerusalem, he understands, or says he understands, the might of the empire. On his return—before all the troubles—he took a very public stand that any rebellion against Rome would end in the destruction of the Jews. Lately, he's avoided public discussions."

"Afraid of the rebels?"

"My husband described him to me once as very practical," Amaris said. "A man who travels to Rome to face Nero is not a coward, Simeon said. I think Joseph believes he can be of the most use if he manages not to take sides in this rebellion."

"In case the rebels win?"

"As I said, practical."

Maglorius pondered this. "His reputation is widespread."

"At least in Jerusalem."

"So it's possible that Valeria would hear of this too?"

"Valeria!" Amaris set her fig down again.

"I don't know how yet, but it seems that Joseph Ben-Matthias has taken responsibility for ensuring safe conduct for Valeria and Quintus from here to Rome."

"Oh, Maglorius," she said, her relief obvious. "I've heard so much about them from you; it's like I know them myself. After all these weeks, they're still alive."

His smile was grave. "It would appear so." He explained the events of the night before.

"You don't seem happy about this," Amaris said.

"They've been in the city since the riots," he answered. "Yet never once came to me for help. Why would they hide from me?"

"You'll see them today. Ask them."

"You could ask them too," he said. "I'm being paid to protect the travelers up to Syria, then to Rome. I'm suggesting you go with us."

✛ ✛ ✛

Two armed temple soldiers escorted Annas through a passageway down to the well-lit subterranean bath, well below the Court of Israel.

Eleazar, who'd already been alerted, was waiting for him. "You can leave now," Eleazar told both temple guards.

They hestitated.

"Did you search him for weapons?" Eleazar asked them.

Both nodded. One said, "He only had a scroll."

"I doubt he'll attempt to assassinate me with it. Leave us in privacy."

As the echo of their footsteps faded, Eleazar kept a steady gaze on Annas. He sat on a stool and gestured for Annas to do the same.

Annas ignored the gesture and walked to one of the baths, a huge basin cut into marble. He dipped his finger into the water.

"Things have changed," Eleazar said dryly. "I decided it was a frivolous luxury to keep it heated. The manpower it takes to replace the cooling water with hot water is much better used elsewhere."

Annas shrugged. "That answers one of my questions then. This conversation won't be between two naked men, stewing like bones in a soup."

"I'm not priggish by any means," Eleazar answered. "But I find nothing appealing about the Roman tradition of bathhouses."

"One must adapt," Annas said.

"Or not." Eleazar's voice hardened. "That sums it up between us, doesn't it? You accommodate Rome. I won't."

"We both want the same thing. Peace for our people."

"No. You want your family to maintain control over the temple markets. You want to be high priest again."

"I won't deny it."

"Remember you are speaking to the son of the high priest."

"You can say that with righteous indignation and keep a straight face?" Annas shook his head. "Or is your grasp of politics so pitiful that you fail to realize your rebellion all but ensures your father's disgrace and fall from power?"

Eleazar stood abruptly. "Why are you here?"

"I'm the one person in Jerusalem who can mediate an effective peace between the upper and lower city."

Eleazar snorted. "That would take someone with honor and integrity, like Joseph Ben-Matthias. Not someone notorious for lack of principles. Someone who was once disgraced and fell from power as high priest and will do anything to get back that position."

Annas smiled. "That's why Ben-Matthias is the wrong man. He wouldn't bear those insults as a means to an end. As for me, you know exactly what I want and that I will do anything to get it. You don't have to question my motives."

"Do you really think I'm prepared to work with you?"

"Either you find someone on our side as an ally or your cause is lost. Your father won't be high priest much longer, and in all likelihood, the position will be mine again. Help me now, and you'll have my support with whatever compromise we can negotiate."

"Or?"

"I don't believe it's necessary to threaten you. Just remember, one way or another, I will be the next high priest. This standoff is only proving that you can't defeat us. Eventually, Florus will send us enough troops, and you'll be destroyed."

"God is mightier than Rome. And if I have to work out a compromise, today's truce is a good start. My father, the high priest, is a man I trust."

"Listen to me," Annas said. "I've already promised amnesty to all the Nazarenes. Irritating as they are to you, many of the poor are grateful to them. If you want support of the people, end the persecution."

"Irritating as they are to me? How about blasphemous! You want me to make an alliance with you when . . . when . . ." Eleazar was at a loss for words.

"I didn't suggest approval. I said amnesty. We'll treat them like Gentiles instead of persecuting them like apostate Jews. It accomplishes two things: gives us political currency and puts distance between them and us. Some foreigners, you know, think there is no difference."

"I've heard enough," Eleazar said. "And I believe I've shown you enough respect. If you stay much longer, however, I can't promise I'll remain so restrained."

"As you wish." Annas took a step, then stopped. "Oh," he said. "The scroll that the guards found on me." He reached inside his clothing and removed it. "It's a copy of the transcript of yesterday's meeting of the Great Sanhedrin. You'll find it of interest."

Annas tossed it at Eleazar's feet.

Eleazar ignored it.

"You really should read it. Remember your father, the high priest? the man you trust?" Annas grinned. "Think about this. There in the transcript, you'll find that he has pledged to throw the first stone at your execution."

✠ ✠ ✠

"Malka, Malka, wake up!"

Malka blinked sightless eyes as Quintus roused her from restless sleep. She shivered beneath a blanket that she clutched to her chest. Although it was summer, her bones never seemed to hold any heat.

"Malka," Quintus said. "Remember what day it is?"

She'd fallen asleep dreading this dawn. Yes, she knew what day it was. Quintus would leave today and not return.

"Feel this," Quintus said.

Before she could reply, he pulled her hands and thrust something into them. Soft fabric.

"New clothes," Quintus said. "So you can look your best today."

"My best?" In the perpetual darkness that surrounded her, Malka was confused. Did Quintus know he was leaving today? If so, why his joy? Unless . . .

Her breath caught. Had the young woman changed her mind and decided Malka would not be such a burden after all? For a moment Malka entertained the notion, allowed herself to feel the joy that she would not be left alone, that she would be allowed to travel with the boy to his home.

"You can look your best!" Quintus answered. "For the wood-burning festival. Today? Remember?"

The Festival of Xylophory.

Evening after evening, she sang songs to Quintus, told him stories about the Jews and their history and their customs. One of his favorite stories had been about Malka meeting her husband, now long dead, during a party on the day of the wood-burning festival.

"This is too much," Malka said. The boy had given her a gift! "We can't afford new clothing. And I have no wood to bring to the Temple."

"Yes, you do," Quintus said. "You told me how important it is for Jews to give wood, so I'm giving you this to take today."

She felt Quintus press coins into her palm.

"Where did you get this?" She was astounded. At the gift. At the boy's thoughtfulness. At his excitement.

"When you're ready," Quintus said, dodging her question, "I'm going to take you to the Temple myself."

Malka reached for his hands, found them, and placed the coins back in his palm. "No. We can't do this."

"It's the wood-burning festival. You're a Jew. You have to go. Remember? You told me how important it was."

The boy would be gone today, Malka told herself. No chance to say good-bye. The boy would escape as long as she said nothing to him about his chance for freedom, and she would be left alone.

What harm could it be for her last memory of him to be of a walk to the Temple, with him leading her by the arm? It would be so lonely without him. At least she could have that to cherish. And the memory of his gift to her to make it possible to partake in the festival.

Malka allowed herself this small piece of selfishness. "We'll go then," she said, thinking of when she was supposed to have the boy ready to be taken from her. "But we must not take long, understand?"

THE SECOND HOUR

VALERIA WAITED AMONG a dozen temple priests, all of them standing on the top of the massive wall that guarded the southwest corner of the Temple Mount.

An hour earlier, Nahum had arrived with her and introduced her to the priest as Valerius, a Greek boy who was his apprentice and who would act as a courier in the place of Raanan.

Nahum had accepted the grave commiseration from the priests at the death of his son. In a guilty way, Valeria had been fascinated to observe. Growing up in a wealthy Roman household had sheltered her from the difficulties of the world and from the ways of men. Here, she was learning about both.

Nahum's son had died less than an entire day before. Nahum had divorced his wife the evening before and had made a decision to join the rebels in a fight to the death. Yet aside from his equally grave acceptance of the priests' sympathy, he'd given little indication that any intense emotions might be tearing him apart.

As for the temple priests, they too said little to show that they were locked in a deadly siege against soldiers who would kill them at the first opportunity. None spoke about other deaths, their families, or their hopes or dreams.

How could this be?

Valeria had listened to conversations with older slave women and had joined in on many herself. Events of this magnitude needed full discussion, a chance for each woman to vent not only opinions but feelings, and then opinions about the feelings. This was the way to deal with tragedy or joy.

In the first half hour after the departure of Nahum, as she'd watched the priests and listened to their trivial banter, it occurred to Valeria that she, too, had been forced into a silence that was placing her in terrible isolation. She rarely spoke because she did not want her voice to betray her gender, but also because the men around her each seemed like self-sufficient islands. Did this explain the malaise that had been settling upon her over the last weeks?

In the second half hour, however, Valeria had begun to fight apprehension. She'd promised Malka that she would be there to get Quintus at the second sounding of the trumpets, and that would be very soon. Yet until the priests sent her away with a message to be delivered to another post, here along the top of the temple wall would be her prison.

The wall was wide enough for five horsemen to ride abreast. On one side, looking down the sheer drop into the Temple courtyard, it was so high that a man below would have difficulty throwing a stone the size of his fist up and onto the top. The other side overlooked the crowded squalor of the lower city, and because the Temple Mount was on a plateau, the drop in that direction plunged straight down at least three times the distance it did on the other side.

The strategic importance of this position was obvious from the armaments nearby. There were catapults, javelins, and stacks of stones the size of a man's head. Pots of oil bubbled over three different fires. In short, attack from below was ridiculously simple to defend against. And because the temple priests controlled the entire perimeter of the temple walls, all of their positions were safe.

Valeria hid her agitation as time passed. She was grateful that she'd decided to take Quintus from Malka a couple of hours ahead of when she was supposed to meet Joseph Ben-Matthias at the Damascus Gate. The old woman would wait for her, she was sure, and as long as she could escape these priests sometime in the next hour, she would have plenty of time to get to the gate.

Yet the temple priests did not give her a message. They chatted quietly, ignoring her, drinking water from leather bags and eating fruits and bread.

Inspiration hit Valeria. She knew how to escape.

✢ ✢ ✢

"Tell me what you see," Malka urged the boy.

They stood on the elevated platform of the colonnades of Solomon's Porch, overlooking the Court of the Gentiles. Quintus held for Malka the wood he had purchased on her behalf, and they were about to join the line of Jews waiting to carry the wood to the entrance of the Court of Israel. To Quintus, the sights of the Temple were a marvel almost beyond his ability to describe.

The outer court of the Temple was capable of holding more than a hundred thousand people. Quintus could not know this nor comprehend a number so large; to him, with three-quarters of the courtyard filled with milling peasants, each holding an armload of wood, it seemed as if the entire world had gathered here.

Nor could he know that the temple priests themselves numbered in the thousands, each with specific daily or weekly tasks, working in rotating shifts through the day and night.

He could see, however, the Levites in a massive choir, singing psalms as was their special privilege, accompanied by other distinguished Israelites who played harps and lutes, as other instruments were only allowed in the Temple for different festivals.

As a backdrop to all of this was the Temple itself, rising on white marble blocks from the center of the courtyard, with a large column of smoke partially obscuring the gold plating of the roof of the Holy of Holies.

He did his best to tell Malka, and it gave him joy to see her smile. He had questions about the Temple, and she answered each one with patience.

As they were about to step off the platform, sharp trumpet blasts came from the western wall, cutting through the noise of the choir and the peasants in the celebrations. Silence fell almost instantly on the entire Temple, so eerie that Quintus stopped.

✝ ✝ ✝

Valeria moved to the nearest priest and waited until he took his attention away from the conversation around him.

"Yes?"

"I need to relieve myself," Valeria said, expecting him to send her to the tower and a staircase that would take her to a public latrine. She'd escape that way. "I won't be long."

"So stand at the edge," he grunted, pointing at the lower city. "Aim at the royal troops at the aqueduct. No one's hit them yet, but it's not for lack of trying."

Some of the other priests laughed.

"It's not my bladder," Valeria said, trying not to squirm with embarrassment.

"Hope you brought your own rags," he said, shrugging. He pointed farther down the wall.

It took her a moment to understand. He was pointing at a bucket.

"When you're finished," he said, pointing again at the lower city, "throw it over the wall into the valley. Send the royal troops a different kind of message."

More laughter. All eyes were on her.

She'd brought this on herself. Now there might be awkward questions if she didn't use the bucket. She was grateful at the looseness of her tunic. If she moved far enough away, it would give her a degree of privacy. But it wouldn't solve her need to escape the top of the tower as soon as possible.

Five trumpet blasts punctuated the air as Valeria began walking toward the bucket. She glanced down into the courtyard.

Among all of the thousands of people, two figures caught her attention, simply because they moved so slowly that all others flowed around them.

It was an old woman. And a young boy, holding an armful of wood. The woman had her hand on the boy's shoulder.

Valeria recognized them immediately.

Malka and Quintus.

✦ ✦ ✦

Malka clutched the shoulder of Quintus.

"What is it?" he asked.

"Did you hear five?" she said, speaking in a near whisper.

"Five?" He, too, was speaking quietly.

"Thekiah. Theruah. Thekiah," she said. "It is always three trumpet blasts. *Thekiah. Theruah. Thekiah.* Proclaiming the kingdom of God, divine providence, and the final judgment. But I heard five. Did you?"

"I wasn't counting," Quintus said. "But something strange is happening."

Forgetting that she was blind, he pointed at the mass of peasants in front of him. Nearly all the men had set down their wood. En masse, they began quietly and purposefully walking to the south entrance of the Temple Mount.

"Tell me," Malka said. "What is it?"

The men began to throw off their cloaks, leaving them behind like leaves scattered from a tree.

"They've got knives," Quintus said. "All of them. They've got short knives."

Malka breathed a single word. "Sicarii."

"Sicarii?"

"Zealot assassins," she said. "Hurry, take us away from here."

✦ ✦ ✦

From the top of the wall, Valeria stared down at the confusion in the Temple courtyard. From her viewpoint, it was obvious that panic had begun—the rear half of the crowd was pushing the front half, unable to see that the gates out of the courtyard were closed.

Quintus! Malka!

Where were they?

He was too small and she was too old. They wouldn't have a chance if the panic grew.

Valeria strained without success to see them.

A hand yanked at her shoulder.

"Boy!" It was the priest who had pointed out the bucket to her. "Didn't you hear me? Have you gone deaf?" He was agitated and angry. "Now's the time to deliver a message for us. Not to be looking for entertainment."

"What's happening down there?"

"You're still not listening," the priest snapped. "You need to run."

"My brother's in the courtyard. He's only a boy."

This, at least, gave the priest some pause. He stopped and drew a breath. "Then he'll be safe," he said, a degree of kindness in his voice, as if he understood why Valeria had not heard him. "The gates to the Temple are closed, and they will remain closed until the fighting in the city is finished."

"Fighting?"

"Sicarii. Thousands of them from the countryside. Armed with short swords. And willing to fight to their deaths to rid us of Rome. That's why you need to run. Get ahead of them to the outposts along the siege line. Let everyone know about it so they can join the fight."

"My brother . . ."

"He's only in danger if we lose today's battle," the priest said. "That's why you need to go. Don't let anything stop you."

✝ ✝ ✝

Quintus and Malka had reached a crowd of people already at the temple gate.

The eerie silence that had fallen on the Temple after the five blasts of the trumpet had long since been replaced by the noise of thousands of men and women and children pushing forward to escape.

Yet the crowd did not move.

Quintus could not see over the people in front of them. Malka kept reassuring herself that she had a grip on his arm by leaning over and calling his name.

"We can't move," he said.

A woman in front of them turned. "The gate is closed. After the men left, someone closed the gate."

"All of the gates!" another said. "I've heard all of the gates are closed."

Pressure began to build behind them as more people crowded forward.

Quintus shoved angrily back. "We can't go anywhere," he shouted. "Stop pushing."

A scream came from the front of the crowd, and a sense of panic moved like a wave among the people.

Quintus kept pushing back at the people behind him. "Leave us alone!"

"Someone is pushing us," a voice answered, desperate.

More screams from near the gates. Then came a voice, clear, ringing above the tumult.

"People! People!"

It frustrated Quintus that he was so trapped. He could not see any farther than the backs and chests of the crowd squeezing him and Malka. He could not identify the voice, but it must have belonged to some kind of authority, because the crowd immediately became silent and expectant.

"People! You've seen the men leave the Temple, armed with sicae. Remember this day! Today is the day we throw off the chains of oppression!"

"Who is it?" Quintus asked Malka.

"Shhh," came a voice from beside him. "It's one of the temple priests."

"We have shut the gates to protect you from the battle that is about to take place in the city!" the voice said with confidence. "No one will be allowed to enter or leave until the Zealots have defeated the soldiers."

"How long?" someone from the crowd shouted.

"Find a place to rest and wait," the temple priest replied. "You will be supplied with food and water."

"How long?" Angry mutters joined in.

"How long?" The priest's voice had lost no confidence. "By nightfall, we will be free!"

The pressure behind Quintus and Malka began to ease, and excited chatter swept through the crowd:

"The Sicarii smuggled in knives with the wood."

"They'll never defeat the soldiers."

"Did you see how many thousands of men went out to fight?"

"Nightfall. What happens if the battle is lost?"

One woman's sharp question to another haunted Quintus the most. "They've shut the gates to protect us. But what if the Zealots are defeated? Then we are trapped in here like sheep for sacrifice."

THE THIRD HOUR

A DOZEN MEMBERS of the royal troops guarded the city gate at the base of the Tower of Hippicus. Their duty was to check the loads of camels and the contents of carts for weapons. The bottleneck resulted in the usual mayhem of a crowd of irritated men standing impatiently in the hot sun, while travelers on foot without merchandise moved past them into the city.

Maglorius had fashioned a makeshift awning from a blanket to shade Amaris as they waited for the arrival of Valeria and Quintus. He stood to the side, alert for anything unusual that would suggest danger, unperturbed by the grunts of camels, the braying of donkeys, and the curses of stock drivers.

Nearby were Falco and Joseph Ben-Matthias, and behind them, standing guard over donkeys loaded with provisions, were Jachin and the thugs Jachin had hired for the journey.

Falco had been complaining constantly at the delay, and again and again Joseph had assured him the boy and girl would arrive.

Then a young man came running through the gates from the city. He scanned the crowd and, at the sight of Joseph, changed direction and dashed toward him.

Although Maglorius doubted the boy was a threat, habit made him move closer.

Joseph put up a hand to stop Maglorius. "My servant."

Falco immediately snapped at Joseph, "After all my efforts to sneak away from the soldiers, you've made it public where we intended to meet the boy and girl?"

Joseph was frowning. "During this time of crisis, I keep my wife informed of where I go. This cannot be good news."

The boy stopped directly in front of Joseph and gasped for breath before speaking. "A message was sent to your house from Eleazar. A warning."

"Warning! Warning!" Falco interrupted shrilly. "What kind of warning?"

"Find your breath and speak calmly," Joseph said to the boy.

The boy took a few more gasps. "The Zealots have begun an assault on the line of siege. Eleazar says he is repaying your efforts to help the priests in Rome. He wants you to have time to make sure your family is gathered in your house. He is sending rebels as guards to keep it safe from attack but cannot promise anyone outside will remain unharmed."

"Attack!" Falco said. "What kind of attack?"

"Keep your voice down," Joseph said sharply. "Do you want to cause panic here?"

The boy looked at Joseph. "Sicarii. Hundreds from the countryside let in for the festival." He gulped in more air. "As I left the house, I heard fighting in the lower city."

Joseph shook his head. "The truce is broken. May God have mercy on us."

"I never should have left the soldiers," Falco said. "Take me somewhere safe."

Joseph turned to Maglorius. "It might be a matter of minutes before the gate is closed and hours or days before it's opened again. Waiting out here won't do the children any good if they are stuck inside."

"We leave now," Falco said. "We've got donkeys and provisions. We'll stay at an inn in a nearby town until the danger has passed, then come back for the boy and girl."

Maglorius reached across and squeezed Falco's shoulder. "The children will not be left behind."

"I think we move inside on foot," Joseph said. "We leave the donkeys out here with one of the men, and we wait inside the wall for the children. If they get here before the gates are closed, you can take the children with Falco as planned."

"If the gates are closed?" asked Maglorius.

"I'm not waiting until the gates are closed," said Falco. "Who knows how close the rebels will be by then? Take me immediately to your house."

"Someone needs to stay at the gate until the children get here," Maglorius said to Joseph. "You go to your wife. Take Amaris with you. If the children get to the gate after it's closed, I bring them to you. If they make it before the gate is closed, I'll take them to the next town and wait with them for Amaris and Falco."

"I wait here," Joseph said. "The boy will be looking for me. He's never seen you before. I should be safe. If rebels get too close, the soldiers will let me into the tower."

Maglorius thought, then nodded. "Leave only one of Jachin's men with the donkeys. Give me the others as protection for Amaris and Falco."

"Yes, yes," Falco said. "Let's go. Now. Quickly."

✦ ✦ ✦

Valeria moved cautiously up a twisting street, stepping over bodies of dead soldiers and rebels.

Her original destination had been the gate north of the Tower of Hippicus, where Joseph had promised to meet after the call of three trumpets marked midday.

Valeria had fallen asleep the night before believing that her plan to get there with Quintus was simple and safe. She'd intended to get her brother a few hours beforehand, leave the city in the southeast corner through the gate near Siloam Pool, traverse the hill outside the city, and get to the gate by coming into the city from the west side.

Turmoil and chaos, of course, had destroyed that plan.

She'd decided the best way to protect Quintus was by helping the rebels, so she had sprinted from post to post, delivering the message from the temple priests. She'd barely stayed ahead of the fighting and, after reaching the most southerly post along the line of the siege, had looked for a way to cross into the upper city. Instead of going around the city, she had no choice but to move through it. Valeria intended to find Joseph Ben-Matthias and arrange for a different time and place to meet. She would look for him at his house first, then at the gate. After that, she'd return to get Quintus from the Temple.

Breaching the upper city had been easy. With the help of the waves of hundreds upon hundreds of fanatical Sicarii, the rebels had been so successful in routing royal troops and Roman soldiers that the entire line had been broken.

What had frustrated Valeria, however, was the time it had taken for the battle to move upward. She'd been unable to proceed until the fighting finished, and the soldiers of the upper city had fought hard before finally succumbing and retreating.

Valeria was frantic with her sense of urgency. For all she knew, Joseph and his promised escort had abandoned the wait for her. Still, even now, with the street ahead of her cleared of battle, she knew that running was too dangerous.

Shrieks and screams of continued battle came from all directions. Around any corner she might run into a pitched fight or get trapped between rebels moving in on soldiers.

She was grateful for her familiarity with the upper city. At least she wouldn't get lost and could take the most direct line toward Herod's Palace, which was just south of the tower.

Shouting and cheering ahead alerted her to possible danger at the next turn. She glanced around, wondering if she should take an alley away from it. She decided against it; the alleys were too narrow.

From behind came the sound of feet pounding the cobblestones.

A group of rebels!

She had no choice now but to race forward, hoping there were more rebels ahead, not soldiers.

When she rounded the corner, she saw that she had no reason

to fear for her own safety. Hundreds of men were massed at the base of a wall, cheering on other men with a battering ram, who were on the point of breaking through the gates.

Valeria recognized the building immediately. It was one of the most famous residences in the upper city and belonged to the high priest of the Jews.

She moved in behind the crowd, intent on passing by without drawing attention to herself.

Again, her fears were needless. Every eye in the crowd was on the gates, which shattered as she neared.

Men poured through, some of them with torches.

"Burn it," they shouted. "Burn it to the ground!"

Valeria began to run again, leaving the riot behind.

First the house of Joseph, she told herself. *Then the gate.* She had to find him if she and Quintus had any chance of escaping with Falco.

✦ ✦ ✦

This can't be happening, Boaz thought.

Unable to visit lower-city merchants, he'd gone to the archives to see if he could find any other contracts of debt placed by Simeon Ben-Aryeh. He'd been inside for hours; when screams and shouts had penetrated his concentration, he'd assumed it was simply part of the ongoing standoff between the upper city and lower city.

Now?

After a fruitless search for anything that would help him take the house of Ben-Aryeh without replicating the contracts that Maglorius had already burned, Boaz had consoled himself by returning to the shelves that held the scrolls of all debts owed to him. He did this once a week anyway, spending an enjoyable hour in the archives as he opened each and scanned the contents with smug satisfaction.

Yet he'd only made it halfway through all his scrolls when his pleasure had been interrupted when peasants armed with swords had flooded the archives, scattering scrolls in all directions.

How had this happened? Where were the soldiers? Surely the

high priest had given orders to protect this building over all others. Without records of debts of contract, the entire economic system of upper city Jerusalem would be destroyed.

"Out! Out!" shouted some of the peasants.

Other men, the keepers of the records, needed no more encouragement. They fled immediately.

Boaz grabbed an armful of the contracts showing debts outstanding to him and held them to his chest like he would cradle a child.

"Out! Out!"

Boaz hobbled forward, trying to make it past several peasants who were trying to push down a shelf. The pain of his throbbing broken toe handicapped him from going faster.

"What's this?" one of the peasants shouted.

Boaz didn't answer and tried to flee. One of his scrolls fell, and he made the mistake of stopping to grab it.

A rough hand pulled him sideways.

Boaz yelped.

Another peasant tried to take the scrolls from him.

Boaz clutched tighter.

The first peasant shrugged, then pulled a knife from his tunic and ran it through the center of the scrolls, plunging the blade into the abdomen of Boaz.

He sank to his knees, again disbelieving the events.

"Leave him," the first peasant barked. "The torches have arrived."

As quickly as the keepers of the records had fled, so too did the rebels.

Boaz tilted and collapsed on his side. Blood soaked his scrolls, but he refused to let go of them.

Moments later, the first tendrils of smoke reached him. He closed his eyes and waited for the fire.

THE FOURTH HOUR

"HERE'S FAR ENOUGH." In the street near the house of Joseph Ben-Matthias, Jachin turned to Maglorius and Amaris and Falco. A long dagger had appeared in his right hand.

His two friends stood on each side, as if braced for attack. They looked formidable; Jachin had picked wisely from men who were accustomed to street crime.

"No, no," Falco said. "Look, the boy is at the gate."

"Your money first, Roman," Jachin said. To the two beside him, he spoke clearly. "Watch the gladiator. He's much faster than he looks."

Both men pulled long daggers and held them steady.

"What is this?" Falco's voice was high.

"Simple robbery," Jachin said. "If the city's gone to war, we want our spoils now."

"But I hired you to—"

"I know you've got a purse full of gold," Jachin said. "Choose between it and your life."

"Impossible. Without gold, I can't get to Rome."

"Shut up." Jachin stared at Maglorius. "Nothing heroic from you. You might get one or two of us, but you'll not be able to protect the woman at the same time."

"Give him the gold," Maglorius told Falco. "Some fights are better won by not starting."

"And leave me destitute in this city of hell? Do what you've been paid to do. Protect me."

"All right," Maglorius said.

He spun Falco around and locked the man's throat in a choke hold with his forearm. He tilted Falco off balance. Falco danced on the tip of his toes to keep balanced, too shocked to sputter even if he'd been able to get breath.

"Take his money," Maglorius said. "Then let us go inside."

Jachin grinned. "That's more like it." Still grinning, he delivered a swift blow to Falco's stomach, driving the breath from his lungs and making him retch.

Maglorius's face darkened, but he said nothing and held Falco fast.

Jachin lifted Falco's tunic, held the money belt with one hand, and with his other placed the edge of his dagger beneath the strap of Falco's money belt and yanked the dagger outward, slashing the leather.

Jachin stepped away with the purse.

"I lied about one thing," Jachin told Falco. "You're a Roman. You had no choice between the gold and your life."

In one swoop, Jachin plunged the dagger forward and ripped upward inside Falco's abdomen. Falco gurgled in agony.

"I'll honor my promise to you," Jachin told Maglorius. "You can take him and the woman inside now."

The other two thugs spread apart, so that Jachin was the center of a dangerous semicircle around Maglorius.

"Remember," Jachin said as Falco sagged in the grip of Maglorius, "you can take one or two of us, but the third will kill the woman."

"Go," Maglorius said, pulling Amaris behind him with his other arm. "And pray we don't meet again."

✢ ✢ ✢

The walls surrounding the palace that Herod the Great had built for himself on the western hill of Jerusalem were almost as high and wide and impregnable as the walls surrounding the Temple. It was here that the religious leaders had fled when it was obvious that the rebels were about to overrun the defenses along the aqueduct.

Men in robes paced back and forth. Some had climbed to the top of the wall to look down on the fires in the upper city. Others were knotted in tiny groups, discussing strategy and allegiances.

One man stood apart. Hunched and very still. Leaning on a cane, hands shaking. The high priest, Ananias. A man who should have been in the center, consulting with other men of high power and offering his opinions in return.

None, however, wanted any association with him now.

He was surprised at how little he cared, for in the last hour, Ananias had discovered something about himself. His position as high priest meant far less than he'd believed possible after a lifetime of maneuvering to get it.

Yet his heart and spirit were broken.

At the height of the tensions, he'd carried a secret admiration and respect for Eleazar. His son had proven to be a man of principle, a man dedicated to serving God in the manner he believed God wanted to be served.

In the aftermath of Eleazar's betrayal of his pledge, this admiration was now shattered. Ananias could hardly believe the events. He was still expecting to hear that Eleazar had been killed and that someone else had been responsible for allowing the Sicarii into the Temple and then sending them out into the city.

He stared at the ground, disconsolate.

He would be high priest no longer. His son had betrayed him. Jerusalem was truly torn, perhaps never to be mended, and he was fully to blame. These thoughts kept running through his mind, and it took great effort not to weep openly.

Footsteps on the courtyard bricks slapped an approach.

Ananias kept his head down.

"Old man," came the voice. It was Annas the Younger.

"Go away," Ananias said.

"I want to ask you something."

"Go away." Ananias refused to lift his head to look at Annas.

"Only after you answer me," Annas the Younger said.

Ananias slowly raised his head. He saw that others were staring at them. "What is it?"

"Tell all of us," Annas the Younger said, "how it feels to be the architect of this disaster. How it feels to know that history will record your actions. How it feels to know that generations from now, children will spit when they hear your name."

Ananias dropped his head again.

"As I thought," Annas the Younger said with undisguised satisfaction. "May you live a long time to remember all of this."

✠ ✠ ✠

Maglorius!

Valeria recoiled in shock as she rounded a street corner.

There, in front of the courtyard entrance to the house of Joseph Ben-Matthias, was the man who she believed had murdered her father. He had stopped near the entrance, flanked by a woman and the man from Rome, Falco. Three other large men stood at the side. At the entrance to the courtyard was a boy, looking back but edging away. One of the three large men seemed to be arguing with Falco, but Valeria was too far away to hear the conversation.

Valeria shrank back into an alley and peered around the corner.

Maglorius!

What was he doing with Falco?

Of course, she told herself. Falco would have immediately searched out Maglorius, for back in Rome, it was known that the famous ex-gladiator was a protector of the Bellators. Neither Falco nor Joseph Ben-Matthias could know about the afternoon in the Bellator household on the final day of the riots, when Maglorius killed Valeria's father.

What to do? she asked herself. *What to do?*

Joseph and Falco were the only way of safety out of Jerusalem for Valeria and Quintus. She'd need to find a way to speak to Joseph privately to ensure that Maglorius did not travel with them.

As the thoughts ran through her head, Valeria watched intently.

Then with horror.

Without warning, Maglorius had grabbed Falco. He wrapped
a powerful forearm around Falco's neck and pulled hard so that the
short fat man was off balance and fighting for breath.

Maglorius kept this grip, allowing one of the other three men
to punch Falco in the abdomen. As Falco slumped, the man ripped
away Falco's tunic and used a knife to cut off Falco's money belt.

Then, with a violent thrust, the man shoved his knife into Falco
and drove it upward.

Falco convulsed.

Valeria didn't see the rest.

She fled.

✛ ✛ ✛

From the top of the western temple wall, Eleazar surveyed the upper
city. He knew it was his imagination, but the echoes of the screams of
those who had died seemed to linger among the haze of columns of
smoke from the smoldering gates and porticoes of the buildings that
he and Gilad had agreed must be destroyed.

Not even the slightest breeze passed through the great city, and
in the aftermath of the battle, it was as hushed as if the hand of
God pressed down upon it. Without a breeze, those columns of
smoke formed straight lines to the heavens, eerily reminiscent
of the smoke from sacrifices that spiraled upward from the temple
altars behind Eleazar.

The symbolism of it was not lost on Eleazar. Many of the rebels
had sacrificed their lives today for the Jewish people.

He consoled himself with the knowledge that it was not in vain.
He and his priests now controlled the city gates. When Manahem
arrived with weapons and men, they would have the strength to
fight any forces that Florus might bring against them.

Furthermore, the power of the upper city had been thoroughly
broken, with each column of smoke marking the location of the
crucial strongholds destroyed by the rebels.

Eleazar took satisfaction to see that the Repository of the Archives had been torched as ordered. With the contracts of debt gone, they would earn the gratitude of the people, and all who had been afraid of reprisals could now support the rebels. Eleazar felt no sympathy for the loss of wealth this represented to the citizens of the upper city; they had grown wealthy because of Roman support for their establishment.

Nor did he feel any pangs at smoke rising from Agrippa's palace. For more than a century the kings of Judea had served Rome far more than they had served the Jews.

Eleazar tried to force himself to be unemotional about the burning of the building most symbolic of the corruption of service to God—the palace of the high priest.

Despite the fact that he'd learned from Annas about his father's public vow to throw the first stone at Eleazar's execution, Eleazar could not escape doubts about his own actions that he knew he'd carry to his grave. As high priest, Ananias would be forced to fulfill his duty. Indeed, among the Jews were fathers who had helped execute sons and daughters for the blasphemy of proclaiming that the Nazarene named Jesus was the Son of God and the promised Messiah.

Could Eleazar convince himself in turn that it had been his duty to betray his father by ordering the silver trumpets to be blown five times? In his mind, he could make an argument that, yes, it had been his duty. But in his heart, he could not. For this was his secret to keep to his grave: Eleazar had not ordered the call of the trumpets after careful consideration of the situation but rather because he'd been stung so badly when he read the words of the transcript.

His father had been prepared to sacrifice him to save the upper city.

So Eleazar in turn had sacrificed his father to the Zealots.

There was no turning back.

23 months after the beginning of the Tribulation

AD 66
ALEXANDRIA
Province of Aegyptus

PATMOS
Province of Asia

✠

I, John, your brother and companion in the suffering and kingdom and patient endurance that are ours in Jesus, was on the island of Patmos because of the word of God and the testimony of Jesus. On the Lord's Day I was in the Spirit, and I heard behind me a loud voice like a trumpet, which said: "Write on a scroll what you see and send it to the seven churches: to Ephesus, Smyrna, Pergamum, Thyatira, Sardis, Philadelphia, and Laodicea."

—REVELATION 1:9-11

❧ MERCURY ❧

HORA SEXTA

"MAKE YOUR MOVE," Nigilius Strabo snarled at the large black goat that glared at him from a distance of less than five paces. "Come on, then. Try me out."

Strabo was almost thirty years old, with a shaved skull and a flat, wide face. He was a dwarf—his full height barely allowed him to stare eyeball-to-eyeball at the goat—and he stood on tiptoe to gain a height advantage.

The black goat snorted and stamped the ground.

Strabo needed to maintain absolute power over the goats in his pen. The moment one of them decided that because of his small stature he was not worthy of respect, he would lose control over the entire herd. New goats like this one had to be taught an early lesson. It might not be pleasant, but it was always effective—if done properly.

"Well, come on!" Strabo said, wobbling as he tried to maintain the extra inch of height. "I'm ready."

He and the goat stood on the hillside of the small island of Patmos, a couple hundred paces down from Strabo's small cottage. The near desolation of the rocks and brown grass and red soil of the hillside were a stark contrast to the cloudless azure sky and the calm blue of the Aegean Sea that stretched eastward, broken only by the distant tips of other islands.

Goat and dwarf were trapped in a small compound marked by rough hemp rope strung between crooked posts made from driftwood. A dozen other goats—all female—were tethered to similar posts farther down the hillside, foraging in dry grass and brush at the end of their ropes, indifferent to the showdown above them.

"Come on," Strabo said. He couldn't maintain the tiptoe stance and settled back on his heels. "Step through the gates of hades."

Strabo held a cudgel with both hands, poised with it over his shoulder, as if he were ready to swing at a passing bird. Any other man on the island would have grasped the cudgel easily, but Strabo's fingers barely managed to encircle the handle.

Dwarf measured goat, blinking against the dust and the heat. Goat measured dwarf with yellow, unblinking eyes.

Strabo shifted from foot to foot. "What's the matter? Afraid?"

The goat lowered his curved horns and charged. As the gap closed, Strabo swung straight down, cracking the goat squarely between the eyes.

The goat collapsed to its front knees and slid forward. Its horns butted Strabo in the belly and flung him backward.

Strabo rolled sideways but lost his grip on the cudgel. The goat was dazed, but within seconds, it found its feet, located its target, and made another charge, this time with less vigor.

Strabo barely sidestepped the goat and, as the animal's momentum carried him past, scrambled to retrieve his cudgel.

The animal spun and charged a third time. Strabo brought the cudgel sideways with a vicious but misjudged swing that glanced off the goat's horns instead of its nose. It diverted the goat only slightly, and Strabo took the brunt of the charge squarely in his stomach. He fell and rolled as the goat skidded over him, hooves thumping his ribs.

Briefly paralyzed, Strabo moaned in a fetal position, clutching his midsection. The goat recovered and whirled and began battering Strabo repeatedly, bleating its rage.

Strabo roared his own anger and grabbed the horns with both hands, pulling the goat in close. He rose and fell, his feet scraping the ground, as the goat tried to swing him loose.

Strabo pulled against the horns and moved his face directly into the goat's face, and it paused briefly. They locked eyes in a brief silence as Strabo grinned maniacally.

Then, with another roar, Strabo clamped his teeth into the soft end of the goat's nose, biting down and clenching as the goat kicked and squirmed. Strabo held on, his roaring reduced to a gurgle. The goat fell to its knees again, still trying to shake Strabo loose.

Finally, with a frantic movement, the goat flung Strabo onto his back and sprang backward, as if it had freed itself from a demon.

Strabo jumped up again, blood from the goat's nose streaming down his chin. He spit out a piece of flesh. "Here's more!" he shouted. He grabbed the cudgel and chased the goat, cracking the retreating animal across the broad bone of the back of its skull. "Think you'll remember this?"

The goat lurched away and ran a frantic circle around the edges of the compound as Strabo ran on stubby legs, jabbing at it with the end of his cudgel and shouting triumphant curses at each successive turn of the beast.

Then movement on the hillside above caught Strabo's attention, and he saw the outlines of two figures screened by bushes.

"You there!" Strabo shouted.

He cocked his head at the sound of scraping sandals. Small rocks clattered from behind the bush, scattering loose pebbles in a miniature avalanche.

Strabo pointed his cudgel at the bush. "Who is it? Come out now or you'll taste the same punishment!"

✠ ✠ ✠

A shout came from one of the crew of Pavo's ship, and all others aboard, including Vitas, looked in the direction the crew members pointed.

Vitas had just been released from his chains. He'd spent the voyage in the shade of an awning set up on the deck for him, grateful that he at least had a fresh breeze. John, who also had been released minutes earlier, had been forced belowdecks and only permitted a half hour a day above.

Although the morning sun had already climbed high, Vitas saw a flash of sunlight on the horizon to the east, so bright it forced him to shut his eyes briefly.

Pharos.

The small island that guarded Alexandria. It was connected to the city by a man-made dike—the Hepstadion—which gave the city two harbors, Eunostos Harbor on the west, and the Great Harbor on the east, with both harbors protected by the island to the north and Alexandria on the mainland to the south.

Yet it was not the island that drew shouts from the crew. The outline of the low-lying island would not be visible for miles yet. The crewmen were filled with wonder at seeing sunlight reflected nearly thirty-five miles from Pharos's lighthouse.

The mirror was mounted on the lighthouse, the tallest man-made structure in existence at nearly four hundred feet tall. A fire reflected off the revolving mirror at night, and sunlight reflected during the day. Legend had it that the light from this mirror could burn enemy ships, and because of this reputed power, crew members of most ships were always nervous on the approach to Alexandria.

Vitas stood at the bow of the ship, thinking about what might be ahead for him in Alexandria. Someone had sent him here for a reason he did not know. All he had were simple instructions: *This injustice inflicted upon you by Nero is an injustice you must endure for a greater cause. Many of us in Rome need you to survive. . . . The pieces are scattered in such a way that only you will be able to put them together.*

What pieces? Why? What battle was he supposed to fight? He wanted to return to Rome, yet if Nero found out he was alive, it would mean the death of his wife. But in staying away from Rome, he could hardly bear the pain of wondering about Sophia's fate. There was an alternative, however, the only one that had given him any hope.

"It's been a long voyage," John said. He stood beside Vitas, still blinking as he tried to adjust his eyes to the sunlight after so much time belowdecks.

"Too long. Too far. It could have been much more enjoyable with your company. I had so many things I wanted to discuss with you."

"I'll be in no hurry once we land," John said. "And I would be happy to spend as much time with you as you want. I had guessed, however, that as soon as we docked, you would want to find a ship to take you back to Rome."

Vitas shook his head, thinking about the one alternative that offered hope. "I've decided to send a letter back to her. Secretly. If Sophia can find a way out of Rome to meet me—" Vitas took a breath—"I'd rather endure exile in poverty with her than live without her."

"I understand," John said.

Vitas studied the horizon, wondering if the smudge was the coastline of Egypt, or his imagination. "And you will find a ship to Ephesus?"

"It's an important place in the empire for a church. I need to continue my work there."

"Ephesus." Vitas snorted. "Right beneath the nose of the beast."

John smiled indulgently. Both knew Vitas was referring to the massive statue of Nero that the emperor had set up for citizens of Ephesus to worship Nero as god. Nero had used the Great Fire of Rome as an excuse to persecute the Christians in part because he detested the fact that they would not acknowledge him as a god. All others in the world were accustomed to worshiping many gods—adding Nero as one more to the household cluster was not a problem for them. The Christians, however, refused to worship any other than the one God of Israel.

"Tell me something," Vitas said. "This is a question I've wanted to ask since the Straits of Messana. My back, after the whipping. You healed it through prayer."

"The God of heaven and earth healed you on the account of the testimony of Jesus, the Christos."

"A miracle. And I should believe, then, all the other miracles that my wife described to me about the Christos?"

"His miracles point to the One who sent him. You have experienced a healing through prayer to the Christos. You know his story already from your wife and the letters of Good News, things written so that you might believe that Jesus is the Christos and so have eternal life. Even while the Christos walked this earth, some rejected Him despite what they saw and heard. Others did not. Now you must make the choice. Who do you say that Jesus is?"

Vitas let out a deep breath. The man's peace and calm were something to covet. Yet . . .

Before Vitas could respond, movement behind John caught his eye.

It was Pavo, the captain, with three armed crew members.

"Start putting together your belongings," Pavo told Vitas, in good cheer now that the voyage was nearly over. "When we dock, I need to take you into Alexandria myself. These three are going to make sure you don't put up a fight."

HORA SEPTINA

SIMEON BEN-ARYEH did not flinch from the cudgel that Strabo pointed at his chin.

In his fifties, Ben-Aryeh was a man with a deceptively strong build. He had short, bowed legs, mismatched to a muscular upper body that belonged on a much taller man. There were peculiar angles to his cheekbones and nose—Ben-Aryeh, like Strabo, would never be seen as handsome. Yet, even tired and filthy from travel, Ben-Aryeh seemed to be cloaked with confidence.

"Put that away," Ben-Aryeh snapped at Strabo, pushing the cudgel to the side. "I'm not a goat."

"An old man with a young woman like her?" Strabo gave a nod and a leer at the woman who had climbed down the hill behind Ben-Aryeh. "If she's not your daughter, I'd say there's good reason to call you a goat."

Ben-Aryeh lifted his right arm and clenched his fist. Strabo jutted his blood-covered chin in response, daring Ben-Aryeh to take a swing.

"Please," Sophia said in a weary voice. "No."

The defeated slump of her body and the exhaustion in her face matched her voice, as if she had not slept well in weeks. Despite this and despite her plain clothing, the beauty of her youth could not be concealed.

"All this travel," Ben-Aryeh sighed, speaking to Sophia. "Who in their right mind would send us this far to someone like him?"

Strabo jabbed Ben-Aryeh in the belly. "You have something against dwarfs?"

Ben-Aryeh, a short man himself, grabbed the cudgel and yanked on it.

Strabo, who refused to let go, stumbled forward, then kicked Ben-Aryeh in the knee.

"I've nothing against dwarfs," Ben-Aryeh said, jaw clenched. He pushed the cudgel away and Strabo with it. "It's rudeness and ignorance I can't stand."

"Then go away. I didn't invite you here."

"Trust me," Ben-Aryeh said. "We wouldn't be here unless we'd been sent."

"Go away. I'm not interested in business with you."

"How have you managed to live this long without encouraging someone to lift you by the throat and strangle you to death?"

Strabo opened his mouth to retort but shut it as he looked past Ben-Aryeh at the woman.

Sophia was weeping soundlessly. "Why do you both have to be so ugly to each other?" she asked in a choked voice.

Ben-Aryeh sighed again and retreated slightly. He put one arm around Sophia's shoulder. With his other hand, he cupped the back of her head and placed her head against his chest, so she was facing away from Strabo.

"Not another word of insult," he said to Strabo. "She's been delicate like this for some weeks."

"I have some water nearby in a jug," Strabo said, instantly subdued by Sophia's tears. "Let me get it."

When he returned, Sophia accepted the jug. She didn't apologize for her tears but walked a few steps away.

Ben-Aryeh spoke to Strabo quietly. "Have you no curiosity about two visitors?"

"Curiosity I can't afford. I tend goats. I make wine. I sell milk and cheese and wine to the soldiers and the exiles. If you were a soldier, you'd have weapons, and if you had the wealth of most of the exiles, you'd be dressed far better and offering me gold. Since you are neither, I have no interest in you."

"'These are they who have come out of the great tribulation,'" Ben-Aryeh said. "'They have washed their robes and made them white in the blood of the Lamb.'"

"What nonsense is this?" Strabo said, beginning to puff with his natural indignation.

"'These are they who have come out of the great tribulation; they—'"

"I'm not deaf," Strabo said in a low hiss, glancing toward Sophia. "Repeating yourself doesn't make it any more clear."

"It has to be clear," Ben-Aryeh said. "You are the one."

✠ ✠ ✠

As the ship entered the Alexandria harbor, John found Vitas belowdecks, gathering his belongings, standing near the base of the mast that rose upward through the deck above.

"Before you ask," Vitas said to John, "no, I don't know where Pavo is going to take me in Alexandria."

"If you sent for me to ask for help," John said, "I will do what I can."

"No," Vitas said. "I doubt I'm in danger. Pavo would have rid himself of me long ago if that were the case. I want to give you something. First, take my cape."

It was already folded. Vitas handed it across to John.

"I've got some money, too," Vitas said, reaching for his money belt. "Half is yours."

John's first impulse was reluctance. He guessed his silence showed that, for Vitas continued.

"It's obvious to me that the same people who put you on the ship put me on the ship," Vitas said. "The money came from them. We should share it."

"You are a gracious man," John said.

"Don't overestimate me. I will probably never see you again. I don't want to feel in debt to you."

"In debt?"

"You cared for me when I was sick. You——"

Vitas paused and looked away for a moment. John wondered if he was reliving the agony of his wounds and the blessed relief of his healing.

Then Vitas continued, "You translated the scroll for me. I owe you. This is my payment."

Many were the moments that John marveled in retrospect at the infinite capacity that his friend Jesus had shown for love, mercy, and sorrow.

It was in the retelling of the events of Jesus' ministry, which John did tirelessly as often as he could find anyone to listen, that John marveled at the emotional capacity of Jesus.

Again and again, John had truly been struck by sorrow for this Roman. Vitas was haunted—that was plain on his face—and by more than the recent events that had forced Vitas from Rome.

While John did not know exactly what burdened the Roman, he knew that Jesus could remove the burden. John's sorrow was great: understanding another human's pain, and being unable to help. Yet this was only an echo of what Jesus had faced. How, John wondered again and again, had Jesus been able to bear all of mankind's sorrow?

There was so much that John wanted to say to Vitas. "You, like all of us, have an awareness of your own sin and a fearful expectation of judgment. The Christos has paid for that sin, Vitas. All you need to do is believe and confess that Jesus is Lord and you will be reconciled to God and forgiven of all of your sin."

"Take the cape and the money," Vitas answered, looking away and making it clear their conversation was over. "You'll need it as you travel to Ephesus."

✝ ✝ ✝

"What one?" Strabo's flat face was crossed with vexation as he stared at Ben-Aryeh. "You say I'm the one, but I know nothing about this."

"We've been sent from Rome to——"

"From Rome! I thought you meant you'd been sent by someone on the island."

"From Rome. We—"

"You just stepped off the supply ship, right? An hour ago? I saw it entering the harbor."

"Yes, we—"

"You asked for directions to find me?"

"Yes, we—"

"I don't need this," Strabo said. "I definitely don't need this. I'm going to have to leave the goat, and who knows how much it's going to take next time to get him where I have him now?"

"Just tell us what we need, and we'll be on our way."

"On your way to trouble," Strabo said. He shook his head. "Much as I'd rather deal with goats, I will not give Lucullus the satisfaction of finding you."

"Lucullus?"

Before Strabo could reply, shouting from above them drew their attention.

It was a small boy, darting along a crooked path down the hillside. "Papa! Papa!" he shouted. "Mama says to tell you that soldiers are coming up the road!"

"Of course," Strabo muttered. "I would have expected nothing less."

It was Ben-Aryeh's turn to frown. "You expected soldiers?"

Strabo shouted at the boy, cupping his hands around his mouth to project his voice. "Hurry back to your mama. Tell her both of you need to hide somewhere in the vineyard until the soldiers tire of looking for you. Understand?"

"Understand," the boy said, immediately turning back.

"My son," Strabo said proudly, letting his eyes linger briefly on the retreating boy. "Only five years old and already taller than me. Smart, too."

"Soldiers?" Ben-Aryeh said. "You expected soldiers?"

"Gossip moves faster than wind on this island. Trust me. If the soldiers find the cottage empty, perhaps they'll believe you found it empty too. Otherwise, I'll pay dearly."

"Soldiers."

"I don't have time to explain," Strabo said, turning and trotting on his short legs. "Both of you, follow me. What cursed luck." He shook his head and his next words were barely audible to Ben-Aryeh. "I hope the goat has a long memory."

✝ ✝ ✝

Wearing the cape that Vitas had given him, John stood alone on the deck as men on the docks tied the ship in place in the Great Harbor. John noted wryly that rats immediately clustered at the top of the ropes. When the ship had stopped moving, it had alerted them to landfall. Depending on their boldness, they would climb down the ropes as soon as men left or wait until darkness.

One of the crew members extended a scroll to John. This man had ragged hair and refused to meet John's eye as he spoke. "I was supposed to give this to you on the first day of the voyage."

John reached for it, but the man pulled it back.

"It was given to me in Rome," the man said quickly. "With instructions that I would be paid by Vitas for making sure you received it. But the crew started talking about omens and sacrificing you and I didn't want to risk anyone thinking I wanted to help you or Vitas."

"Paid how much?" John asked quietly.

The crewman told him. John suspected he was doubling the price, but with the money from Vitas, John was wealthy until he gave the money away as needed. He paid the man, who handed the scroll to John and left immediately, as if still afraid of what other crew members might think of his association with John.

John opened the scroll. The writing was in Hebrew and looked to be from the same hand that had written the previous scroll.

This belongs to Vitas, the instructions began. *It is the second piece of what has been scattered for him to gather. He will be taken to a man with the third and final piece once the ship has reached Alexandria. You know this man, for he is your friend and mine.*

John continued reading silently and translating the Hebrew that followed: *There will be two witnesses, killed yet brought alive. Find them and rejoice with them, then take what is given.*

John thought of the one person in Rome he'd spent the most time with, discussing the Revelation and what it meant. A friend who would understand exactly how John might explain these words to Vitas. John thought of the implications behind this scroll and its important message for Vitas.

And smiled, thinking of how Vitas would be surprised to see him again with the missing piece.

For John now knew exactly where Pavo was taking Vitas.

HORA OCTAVA

NORMALLY BETTO WAS one of the last to get off the ship at harbor. He'd spend at least an hour making notes on his charts, then another half hour making sure they were hidden so well that none of the crew could steal them and sell them to another navigator. Betto had learned to use this time to let his anticipation build after his time at sea—he knew every harbor as well as any navigator alive, and that included which brothels held the women that would please him most.

This journey, however, Betto wasted no time. He wrapped a narrow red cloth around his waist as a belt. He kept his navigational scrolls clutched tightly to his belly as he hurried off the ship.

The scene around him was the usual chaos, with the fish and urine smells mixed with salty air. Workers screamed at each other in assorted languages; slaves scurried along the wharves; rich men of high position, obvious by their togas, walked with heads high and self-important airs.

Betto hoped it wouldn't take too long for the men to find him. He tugged at his belt repeatedly and walked slowly, afraid he would get too far from the ship to be identified.

Finally, three large men stepped out from behind a stack of amphorae. The first one, nose bent almost sideways from an old wound, growled at Betto. "Could you be any more obvious?"

Before Betto could answer, the second one pulled him out of sight of the ship that Betto had just disembarked from. "We're the ones Kaeso found," he said. He was larger than the first and smelled of cheap wine.

"Prove it," Betto said.

"Find a turtle on a post and you'll know it had help," the third said. He glared at Betto. "Could your brother have come up with anything more stupid than that?"

"It can't be that stupid," Betto snapped. "You're here."

"And you're barely here in time," the first snapped back. "We expected you a couple of days after us. Not a week. Our ship leaves for Rome tomorrow to beat the storms."

"What matters is I made sure our trip was delayed enough for you to get here before us."

"And did you find out his name?"

"No," Betto said. "Pavo said nothing. The man said nothing."

"How do you know he's the right one? Your brother said two men were put aboard the ship."

Betto laughed. "I took a guess."

"Guesses aren't worth much to us," the first one snarled. "We've come a long way for this."

"I found a way to confirm my guess," Betto said. "I had one put on a cross to be drowned at sea. When Pavo didn't stop the crew, I knew the one on the cross was worthless. The other jumped overboard to save him, and Pavo made me turn the ship around to rescue him. That proved without a doubt the second one was the man we want."

"You're going to stay and point him out to us as he leaves the ship."

"No," Betto said. He shuddered. If Pavo ever guessed his betrayal, Betto was a dead man. He'd seen Pavo drown a Jew in pig's blood. "I need to get back on the ship immediately. And I don't want to be seen with you."

"Then how will we know the right man?"

"He'll be wearing an expensive cape. And I've marked the back of it with drops of pitch that form a small circle. If you're close enough to attack him, you'll be close enough to see the markings."

"Good enough," the second said.

"When you have him and get back to Rome," Betto said, "my brother will make sure the ransom demand is delivered to the right people."

"We don't know his name," the first thug said.

"No," Betto answered, "but I'm sure three strong and capable men like you will be able to force it from him after enough time alone at sea with him." Betto paused and grinned. "Am I right?"

"Just show us the man we want," the first said. "We'll do our job."

✝ ✝ ✝

"How long has she been like this?" Strabo whispered his question to Ben-Aryeh.

Both of them sat at the mouth of a cave. Deeper inside, Sophia had found a place to huddle, sitting with her arms wrapped around her knees and her head bowed.

"Almost since leaving Rome," Ben-Aryeh answered. Because the hillside dropped sharply below the cave, the vista of the Aegean Sea filled their horizon, and the blue of the water blended with the blue of the sky. "Her husband was sent to the lions by Nero, forcing us to flee."

"Obviously not far enough," Strabo muttered.

"Not far enough?"

"Why are you here?" Strabo said. "Why are you quoting from a letter that could get us killed?"

"See," Ben-Aryeh said, "you did expect us."

"Not for a moment."

"But you refer to our letter."

"*Your* letter? The one they call the last disciple of the Nazarene wrote it. John."

"Then that answers one question for me," Ben-Aryeh said. "Obviously this John sent us here from Rome."

"That doesn't answer anything for me," Strabo said crossly. "My wife and son are in hiding because of soldiers sent to find you. And I have no idea why you and the woman came upon us like a plague."

"The letter gave us instructions on how to find you and said that you had another letter to give us. The soldiers can't possibly know this."

"Give me a bad-tempered goat," Strabo said, imploring the sky. "Not an old man with no sense and a woman who weeps at the drop of a pebble."

"Look here," Ben-Aryeh said.

"'These are they who have come out of the great tribulation; they have washed their robes and made them white in the blood of the Lamb,'" Strabo said. "Of course I know it came from John's letter. Everybody on the island has heard the details of John's vision and how he dictated it to Prochoros. The letter was smuggled off the island and sent to the seven churches and—"

"No." Ben-Aryeh didn't bother to hide his own irritation. "*Our* letter tells us where to find you and that we needed to repeat that phrase for you to trust us."

Strabo stared at the sky in contemplation. A hawk soared into view and soared out of view again. "This makes some sense then," he finally said. "Yet it still makes no sense."

"I'm listening."

"You speak of one letter," Strabo answered, "and I speak of another. The Revelation that has already caused too much trouble."

"Our letter was a short message that needed interpretation to bring us here."

"As I just said. May I see it?"

Ben-Aryeh shook his head. "At a wayside inn, shortly after leaving Rome, it was stolen, along with our gold and all our other possessions. This theft, I believe, is another reason the woman walks in a cloud of darkness."

"You had this letter memorized?"

"I did," Ben-Aryeh said. "But I would not have known it referred to Patmos without the help of Sophia."

"Recite it."

"You doubt me?"

"Recite it."

"'*Go to the island of exile where the last disciple received the vision. Find the household of the man who stands no taller than his goats. There you will be given the rest of the message.*'"

Strabo gave that some thought, nodded, and then asked his next questions. "Robbed? How did you pay for the remainder of travel and your passage here?"

"You want to steal from us what remains?" Ben-Aryeh snapped.

"I want to know if you're telling the truth. Remember, I'm at risk hiding you."

"Without explaining why we need to be hidden."

"If you were robbed shortly after leaving Rome, how did you have enough money to get here?"

Ben-Aryeh looked at the dwarf sourly. "Swallowed coins are in a much safer place than a purse," he said.

"Ah, an experienced traveler." Strabo grinned.

Ben-Aryeh did not respond, and Strabo's grin faded. Both seemed to feel as if it would be much preferable to remain at odds.

"Do you have a message for us?" Ben-Aryeh said. "One from the person in Rome who sent us here?"

"A message from a person you don't know on an island you've never been to. This is a long way to come."

"She lost her husband and household to Rome. What else was there? Do you have a letter or message for us?"

"No."

"I find that difficult to believe."

"If they sent anything of value on your behalf," Strabo snapped, "and if I wanted to keep it from you, wouldn't I have turned you over to the soldiers instead of hiding you in this cave?"

No answer from Ben-Aryeh.

"After all," Strabo continued, "I did accept a bribe to tell the commander of the barracks as soon as you arrived."

"What?" Ben-Aryeh lurched forward. "You said you didn't expect us."

"I have no message for you," Strabo said. "Nor did I really expect you. But last week, when I delivered wine to the barracks, Lucullus forced me to endure a conversation with him."

"The Roman commander."

"The same. He asked if an older man and a woman from Rome had sought me out. When I told him no, he bribed me to turn you over when you arrived."

"This is truth?" Ben-Aryeh said, with a tone that sounded like he didn't want it to be the truth.

"If you asked at the harbor for directions to find me, word reached Lucullus almost immediately. The arrival of the soldiers obviously sent by him speaks clearly of the truth behind my story. That, along with the obvious fact that I am risking myself and my family to keep you away from the soldiers."

"After you accepted the bribe from Lucullus."

"It was such a ludicrous idea. I never expected visitors from Rome. I know no one there. So why not take the money?"

"Yet, despite the bribe, you protect us."

"I have my reasons for hating the soldiers on this island."

With a common enemy to contemplate, their silence became almost companionable.

Ben-Aryeh broke it first. "You speak the truth then."

Strabo nodded.

"That means one thing," Ben-Aryeh said. "Someone else knows of the letter that sent us here."

Another nod from Strabo. "If it isn't Lucullus, then someone with enough authority to command him. I doubt you'll find a way to leave the island now that it is known you are here."

"We came for a message, expecting it would have the answers."

"What you've found is a pitiful future," Strabo said. "Especially if you've been reduced to depending on me for refuge."

✦ ✦ ✦

Pavo rubbed his hands in satisfaction as he led Vitas to the tall wooden gate of a courtyard wall.

"Finally," Pavo said. "I'll be rid of my burden."

An iron circle hung on the gate. Pavo lifted it and let it fall. He did this several times, then turned to Vitas. "You'll tell your friends in Rome that I gave you the best treatment I could."

"I'd almost forgotten the whipping at sea," Vitas said. "Only because you've paraded me like a slave through Alexandria for the last hour."

Vitas had his hands bound behind his back, still guarded by Pavo's silent but ever-vigilant crew members. The guards stood just far enough away to be out of earshot but close enough to react instantly if anything unexpected was to happen.

"I couldn't take the chance that you would run or fight," Pavo said. "Tell them then that I gave you the best treatment under the circumstances. The whipping was necessary to your survival, and delivering you here as ordered is necessary to mine."

"What if I don't stay here?"

"Do what you want when I leave," Pavo said cheerfully. "My instructions were to bring you to the household of the silversmith named Issachar, son of Benjamin. That's all. Once I've done so, I'm going to get thoroughly drunk and forget you ever existed."

Pavo lifted the iron circle and banged it down again.

The eyehole in the gate slid open. The nose and eyes of a man appeared. Even with so little of his face showing, his suspicion was obvious.

Pavo spoke with confidence. "'These are they who have come out of the great tribulation; they have washed their robes and made them white in the blood of the Lamb.'"

"What is this?" The voice came from behind the gate. "A day for lunatics?"

"I'm here to see Issachar," Pavo said. "I have a friend of his from Rome. I've just given you a password that Issachar will recognize. Deliver it to him and he'll command you to let us in."

"Go away."

"How much of your back do you want shredded by the whip?" Pavo asked.

"Go away."

The eyehole slid shut.

Pavo began kicking the door. Methodically, loudly.

The eyehole slid open again. "Stop or I send for soldiers."

"Just let me speak to Issachar."

"He doesn't live here."

"But I was told this was where to find him."

"Not anymore," the voice said firmly. "Now go away."

"Wait. He lived here once?"

"Until a few weeks ago."

Pavo relaxed somewhat. "Where do I find him now?" Pavo dug into a pouch and offered a coin through the eyehole.

Fingers snatched it away. "More," the voice said.

"Sure." Pavo sounded in good humor.

He held out another coin, teasing the man to stick his fingers out to grab it. This time, however, Pavo grabbed the fingers that darted through the eyehole opening.

A howl of pain came from the other side as Pavo bent back the man's fingers.

"Where do I find him?" Pavo had to yell to be heard above the other man.

He eased off enough for the howling to stop.

"Go to the main market of the Jewish Quarter and ask," the man said. "Just like I told the last man who came spouting the same nonsense."

"What man?" Pavo increased the pressure on the man's fingers.

More howling.

Pavo eased the pressure again, and the howl stopped. "Answer quickly before I break every bone."

"Some man. A half hour ago. That's all I know."

"Fine then," Pavo said. "Throw my other coin back over the gate."

"What?"

Pavo bent the man's fingers. The howling resumed. Pavo took the pressure off again. "I told you to throw my first coin back to me."

Seconds later, the coin landed with a clink on the stone of the road.

Pavo let go of the hidden man's fingers. "Thanks," he said cheerfully. He stepped aside and dodged a spray of spit from the eyehole.

It slammed shut.

"Well," Pavo told Vitas, ignoring the curses from the other side of the gate, "it looks like I'm stuck with you for just a while longer."

HORA NONANA

"THIS MUST BE WRONG," Pavo told Vitas. "Absolutely wrong. I've been given the wrong directions."

Five of them stood in an alley—Pavo, Vitas, and the three crew members who had escorted Vitas as if he were a captive slave.

The alley was barely more than a passageway. It was so narrow that the two apartment-building walls seemed to lean into each other above them. No sunlight reached the alley. Vitas had expected the smell of garbage to be especially poignant. Strangely, however, the length of this alley—all the way back to the crowded market behind them— had been cleared of garbage. A few small boxes hung from nails inserted into cracks in the walls of the four-story building; flowers and vines spilled out from the boxes and added welcome color to the bleak scene.

"How could anyone here know anybody in Rome?" Pavo continued, muttering. "This is so wrong."

Vitas remained silent. Pavo had said nothing about their destination, nor the reason he'd taken Vitas off the ship as a captive. They'd walked for nearly an hour already, moving upward and eastward from the Great Harbor to the sprawling Jewish Quarter of Alexandria, walking wide streets past opulent mansions with private oasis gardens behind thick courtyard walls, then seeing smaller but still luxurious homes, then apartment blocks; and as they moved deeper into the Jewish Quarter, a mixture of homes and slums, until reaching a market bazaar with warrens of alleys branching out from it like cracks in parched soil.

"Well," Pavo demanded. "Tell me. Who here would know someone in Rome?"

"I assumed it was a rhetorical question," Vitas said mildly. He wasn't upset. He was certain that Pavo intended no bodily harm and equally certain that he was not being delivered into danger. If someone in Rome had wanted him dead, that person or persons would have left him to face the animals in the arena instead of going to all this complicated and secretive effort to send him out of Nero's reach. Out of curiosity, Vitas had decided to passively go where Pavo led, then at the best opportunity, escape and return to Alexandria's Great Harbor to find a ship going to Rome, where he would give a passenger a letter to deliver to his brother, Damian.

"Rhetorical?" Pavo said. "Don't play Greek logic word games with me."

"My only involvement so far has been to walk where prodded."

"As if you don't know where I'm taking you."

Vitas shrugged.

"Your friends in Rome," Pavo said, "made my task very clear. Deliver you to a man named Issachar in Alexandria. Since they are your friends, why wouldn't you know Issachar?"

Because, Vitas thought, *I have no idea who put me on this ship. Nor why.*

"Look at this," Pavo snapped, gesturing at their surroundings. "Is this where the rich and powerful live?"

His question did not need an answer. That they were at the rear of the Roman-style buildings, facing steps to take them to the top floor, suggested that the only residents ever traveling this path were the poorest of poor, forced to live on the top floor in cramped rooms.

Creaking of the steps above them alerted Vitas and Pavo that someone was climbing down to the alley.

"Good," Pavo said. "Saves me the effort of going up myself to ask for the man."

Moments later, a tall, thin man stepped onto the dirt of the alley. He was stooped and had a gnarled old face. His most distinctive feature was his left hand, where all that remained were his thumb and index finger.

His eyes met Pavo's, and the man flinched as if a cold wind had blown over him.

"By the gods," Pavo roared. "What are you doing here?"

✦ ✦ ✦

"Hello? Hello?"

It was a soft voice calling from the entrance of the cave.

Sophia, curled on her side and staring at nothing, lifted her head from the pillow she had made from her filthy coat. The cave was on the eastern slope of the island hills, already in the shadow of late-afternoon sun. Yet there was enough light in the sky that a bulging outline of a woman was clearly visible at the entrance.

"Hello?" the woman repeated. "Hello? I've brought food and drink."

The woman moved inside slowly. Her right arm seemed pinned in a peculiar manner to her right side. Her left arm was bent at the elbow to hold the handle of a basket.

"Hello?"

For Sophia, finding the strength to sit upright was like pulling herself out of mud. "I'm here," she said in a dull voice.

The woman shuffled slowly deeper into the cave. She was breathing hard. She groaned as she settled heavily beside Sophia.

"Forgive me," she said, her right side facing away from Sophia. She released the basket handle from the crook of her left arm, letting it slide down to her hand. She set the basket down gently. "I'm in my final month, and it feels like I've been pregnant forever."

Pregnant. Sophia was in her third month. Once, the thought had filled her with joy. Now it was merely a burden that made it difficult to keep down food that was tasteless in the first place.

"Strabo and Ben-Aryeh are at the cottage," the woman said. She removed a veil from her head with her left hand. The indirect light from the mouth of the cave was enough to highlight the left side of her face. She was young too, perhaps Sophia's age, with a classic beauty and skin that looked unworn by time or sorrow. "They are discussing goats as if they have been friends for years. They told me you prefer to remain here."

Sophia shrugged. What difference did it make? Strabo and Ben-Aryeh had already decided that she and Ben-Aryeh would spend the night in the cave. Why go through the effort of leaving it? Besides, there was something comforting to Sophia about staying in a cave. Perhaps she would never leave.

"The soldiers didn't stay long," the woman said. "Zeno—he's our son—and I sat in the vineyard and sang songs to each other while we waited for them to tire of looking for us. If it hadn't been for the heat and my pregnancy, it would have been enjoyable. As it was, it wasn't too much of a hardship."

"We're sorry to bring trouble on you," Sophia mumbled. Then, without warning, she found herself weeping.

The woman put her left hand on Sophia's shoulder, but Sophia shook it off. Nothing would help. Nothing mattered.

The woman pretended it had not happened. "My name is Chara," she said. She turned slightly. "I'm Strabo's wife."

Sophia didn't bother to wipe the tears from her face. Perhaps if she refused to talk, the woman would go away.

"You saw Strabo giving a lesson to our new goat," Chara said. "Ben-Aryeh tells me it's the funniest thing he's seen in years."

Sophia didn't care.

"If you're curious," Chara continued, "Strabo does that because whenever he buys a new male goat, he wants to teach the goat to be afraid of him. Out on the hillside, when Strabo is tending to some of the nannies, he doesn't want to worry about the goat attacking him."

Sophia wasn't even a bit curious. She only wanted to lie down again and sleep and never wake.

"A full-sized man doesn't have to worry about such things," Chara said lightly. "But Strabo is a brave man and he accepts his size without complaining." Chara paused. Smiled. "At least, without complaining much." Chara's voice dropped to a whisper. "You lost your husband, I'm told. I am so sorry for you."

Sophia barely shrugged. "Terrible things happen. Everywhere. All the time. Sorrow is so common in this world it is hardly worth a thought."

"Just as love is unique to each of us," Chara said softly, "so is the sorrow that comes when something loved is lost."

"Don't waste pity on me. I don't."

Which was true. Hour by hour, day by day, Sophia felt nothing. Only emptiness, filling a black chasm of apathy. She followed Ben-Aryeh because there was nothing else to be done.

"It's not pity but shared sorrow."

"What do you know about sorrow?" Sophia said. "You have a boy, a baby on the way, a husband, and a home."

"My heart knows that no sorrow is too great for our Father to overcome," Chara answered. "I've been given hope beyond understanding because of this faith."

Sophia didn't bother to answer.

"In Ephesus, there was a man named John," Chara said. "Through his teachings, I heard about this great hope through a Nazarene sent from God."

"Yes, yes," Sophia said, sinking deeper into herself. "The Christos. I'm familiar with the teachings."

"But do you *know* the Christos? No matter how heavy your burden, He will take it from you and—"

"I want to sleep," Sophia said.

"I understand," Chara said.

No, you don't, Sophia thought. *You don't understand the distance between me and God. You don't understand that the teachings of the Christos no longer seem to give solace. You don't understand that sleep has become an escape, yet no amount of sleep removes the exhaustion.*

Chara used her left arm to push herself forward, then, as if a thought hit her, settled back. After long moments, perhaps gathering her words, she spoke. "Lucullus, the commander of the barracks, brings prostitutes to the island from Ephesus on the supply ship. Most women leave on the next ship. Some stay longer, because the money is good and the soldiers have no other place to spend it."

What of it? Sophia thought. *Prostitutes are common.*

"I was one of them," Chara said, as if accurately reading her silence. "And I was one of them who didn't return to Ephesus on the next supply ship."

Chara sighed. "For me, the money was so good that I sent for my son, Zeno. I lived in a small cottage near the sea. My time with Zeno was all that mattered. My time with the soldiers . . ."

Chara stopped, gathering her words again. "My time with soldiers was no different than my time with men in Ephesus. The more money I made, the less value I felt. When John arrived on the island, I felt a hunger to hear more of what he'd been teaching in Ephesus. Day after day, I returned to John to ask about the Christos, until one morning I finally fell on my knees and prayed to the Christos. All my shame and worthlessness was taken away. John baptized me, as he had once seen the Christos baptized. I had worth again. I was healed in a way that no doctor could ever heal me."

"I am familiar with the teachings," Sophia said. "Thank you for your effort to share them with me."

"No matter what tribulation we face, because of the Christos and His sacrifice, Gentile or Jew, through faith in the Christos, we all become part of the true Israel and heirs of God's promises to Abraham."

"I am tired," Sophia said.

Chara did not seem to take insult at Sophia's bluntness. Not that Sophia cared what Chara thought.

"I will leave you in peace," Chara said. Chara kept the left side of her face toward Sophia as she struggled to her feet. "Ben-Aryeh will have blankets to keep you warm while you stay in the cave." She leaned over and pushed the basket toward Sophia. "There is plenty. Strabo is a good man and provides well for his family."

"You are a blessed woman," Sophia said with a trace of bitterness, the only emotion that ever came when she found the strength for any feelings.

Chara must have understood the tone in her voice. "Please forgive me. I did not mean to point out that I have what you don't."

"There is nothing to forgive," Sophia said. "My husband is dead. There is nothing I care about. Truly."

✝ ✝ ✝

Two of Vitas's escorts had the man with the missing fingers pressed against the wall.

Like Pavo, Vitas had recognized the man immediately. One of the crew members on Pavo's ship.

"Grab his left hand," Pavo told the remaining crewman. "Cut off his thumb."

"Not the finger?"

"It will be useless without a thumb. Let him live with that."

"No," the man against the wall wailed.

"How did you find out this is where we were going?"

"I . . . I didn't."

"You're here. Ahead of us. You didn't follow." Pavo's eyes seemed small, cold, like stones. A predator focused on prey. "I want to know how you knew I would be here."

"I didn't know! I swear by the gods."

"Try some fingers from his other hand," Pavo told his men.

"Stop." The quietness of Vitas's command spoke far more forcefully than any other inflection could have.

Pavo whirled on Vitas. "You have answers?"

"Just this. If the man knew this was your destination, don't you think he would have been far more cautious?"

Pavo looked back at the fearful man.

"To me," Vitas continued, "he seemed as surprised to see you as you were to see him."

The tall, thin man nodded frantically.

"Why are you here?" Vitas asked him calmly.

"I was sworn to secrecy."

"Take three fingers on his right hand," Pavo snarled. "Match one hand to the other."

"Bully, maim, kill," Vitas said. "Not much of an original thinker, are you?"

Pavo pushed his face within inches of Vitas's.

Vitas was very aware that his hands were tied behind his back. "Why don't you ask him who swore him to secrecy?" Vitas said. "Ask him when? Give the man a chance to speak."

Without taking his eyes off Vitas, Pavo said, "Who swore you to secrecy? When?"

No answer.

"Now you understand," Pavo told Vitas, "why I prefer to bully and maim and kill when necessary."

Without taking his eyes from Pavo, Vitas spoke to the frightened crewman. "I admire a man who holds to a vow. What can you tell us without breaking that vow?"

"Just before we set sail from Rome, a man approached me while I was standing near the ship. He said if I went to a certain household in Alexandria one day after the ship arrived, I would be paid handsomely to deliver a letter."

"You were to wait a day?"

"I didn't see the harm in coming immediately," the man said. "I wanted money to enjoy women tonight." He spat out bitter words. "Not only was there no money, but now this."

"I suspect," Vitas said mildly, "this is exactly why you were told to wait a day. Were you given a password?"

The crew member's eyes widened in realization. "'These are they who have come out of the great tribulation; they have washed their robes and made them white in the blood of the Lamb.'"

"See?" Vitas said. "You were meant to find me. I assume you also stopped at Issachar's mansion, only to be told he didn't live there anymore."

The man nodded.

"Do you still have the letter?" Vitas asked. "Or did you leave it up there?"

"I wasn't given any money."

"So you still have the letter."

"I was told you would pay me ten thousand sesterces."

"You're a poor liar," Vitas said.

"Two thousand then," the man mumbled.

"I'll see you're paid. You have the letter?"

"Not so fast," Pavo said. "I want to read it."

"You've gone to great effort to obey those who put me on your ship," Vitas said. "Do you really want to cross them now?"

"So who's a bully using the threat of violence?"

"I can't disagree," Vitas said, smiling.

"Give me the letter," Pavo said. To Vitas, he returned the smile, but without sincerity. "If it tells me something about the men behind this, it's worth far more than two thousand sesterces."

With knives jabbed at his throat, the crew member reached into his tunic and pulled out a sealed scroll.

Pavo examined the seal, shrugged, and broke through the wax. He unrolled the letter and, after reading it, frowned.

"You are welcome to this nonsense," Pavo said. He dropped the letter on the dirt in front of Vitas. "The sooner I'm rid of you, the better."

To his three men, Pavo said, "Let him go."

Vitas could not reach to get the letter. He hoped Pavo would untie him soon.

To the crew member, Pavo said, "I don't want a man like you on my ship. Run, and consider your freedom from me as the wages you are owed."

"Shouldn't you ask him who he was supposed to find in the apartment?" Vitas asked.

"Obviously the same person I'm supposed to deliver you to," Pavo snapped.

"Did you give him the same password you gave me?" Vitas asked the crew member.

"I couldn't. He's been sold into slavery."

"No," Pavo groaned. "He's not up there?"

"Only his wife and three young children."

"I hate all of this," Pavo said. "I really, really hate it."

HORA DECIMA

"I DON'T UNDERSTAND THIS. You're going to leave a strange man in my household?"

This question came from Jael. She was a Jewish woman, short and round with long dark hair. She held a sleeping baby to her chest, and her tone of incredulity showed that she was remarkably unafraid, considering that five large men had walked into her tiny apartment without an invitation.

"I want to be rid of him," Pavo said. "I've been instructed by people in Rome to deliver him to your husband."

She asked the obvious question. "Why?"

Pavo shrugged. "I don't know."

"Rome." To her, Rome must have been on the other side of the world. "You have the wrong family. We don't know anybody in Rome. And we certainly don't know *him*."

Aside from the baby she cradled, small twin girls clung to her legs, peeking from behind the woman with obvious fear. Vitas was no expert on children. It seemed to him that they were barely old enough to talk—but they had been mute since he entered.

"Is your husband a silversmith?"

Jael nodded.

"Then this is the right family. That's all I care. If anyone ever comes to you and asks if I delivered a Roman to you in good health, you can answer that I did."

"You can't just leave a man with me and my children. It's beyond comprehension."

"Good-bye," Pavo said. "I'm rid of him."

Pavo nodded at his three crewmen, and the four of them swept out as quickly as they'd barged into the woman's apartment.

Jael looked at Vitas with bewilderment.

"I've been delivered," Vitas said. "Now, if you would be kind enough to untie my hands, I'll leave immediately."

"Just like that." Her voice was now tinged with anger.

"The sooner I am away from you, the sooner you can forget this."

"No," Jael said. "Not until you give me answers. If my family is involved in something, I need to know what to guard against."

"I have no idea why your household was chosen either," Vitas said.

"Your wrists are bound. You are delivered like a captive. Who were those four men? Where are you from?"

The little girls behind her legs had begun to edge out to get a better look at the strange man.

Vitas squatted. He rolled his eyeballs a few times and stuck out his tongue. They retreated and then giggled from the safe vantage point behind their mother.

"I was taken captive in Rome," Vitas told Jael as he rose. "I was put on a ship to Alexandria and, as you can see, taken here."

"Who put you on the ship?"

"Friends, I believe."

"You believe . . ."

"I would have been killed by the emperor had I stayed in Rome. Enemies would have no reason to see that I was spared."

The baby boy in her arms woke and began to cry softly. She rocked him and hummed until he fell asleep again.

"I would say none of this is believable. Yet you are here."

"My hands," Vitas said. "If you could. . ."

"You are a stranger. I must protect my girls."

Vitas understood. They were in an apartment that was little

more than a slum. Crowded as the top floor was with tiny compartments filled with large families, there was an isolation and intimacy here that would frighten any woman with any sense.

"If I go on the street like this," Vitas said gently, "I am prey for any thief."

"I have no reason to trust you or your intentions once you are released."

"Call for a neighbor," Vitas suggested.

She closed her eyes and shook her head. Tears seeped down her cheeks. "I'm forced to accept charity from the people who live around me. How could I explain to them a man alone with me? If they shun me, I will be forced to live on the streets."

"I understand." Vitas meant it. "I'll wait for your husband to return."

Yet to Vitas, that didn't seem like a good alternative, either. What if the husband didn't believe Vitas or his wife? This certainly was a strange situation. Vitas had visions of an angry Jew plunging a knife into his chest while his own hands were helpless behind his back.

The woman began to weep openly. "My husband will not be returning. That's why I am forced to live on the charity of my neighbors."

Her twin daughters began to sob.

"Mama? Mama?" one of the little girls asked. "Will this man take you away too?"

Their terror inspired Jael to force herself to stop weeping. She smiled and knelt to face her daughters, still cradling her son.

"No, no," Jael said. "Mama was sad because she misses your papa too. I will never leave you." Fierceness filled her eyes as she stood and faced Vitas again, her cheeks damp. "What choice do I have but to get you away from us?"

Vitas tried to smile kindly, hoping it would impress the woman.

"Turn around," she said. "I warn you that if you try anything to harm my children, I will fight you to the death."

Vitas did as directed. He felt her fumble awkwardly with the knots of twine that bound his wrists. It was difficult for her to work one-handed, as she had to hold her son with her other arm.

Five minutes later, Vitas was free. His first impulse was to leave as quickly as possible. He truly was free. Pavo had completed the task set upon him by the men in Rome. Vitas wanted to find a ship to get out of Alexandria.

At the doorway, however, he stopped. He stood just outside the cramped apartment, so that any neighbors watching would not be able to accuse him of impropriety.

"Your husband," he asked Jael. "Why was he taken away?"

✝ ✝ ✝

"More wine!" Lucullus roared. "If the dwarf is not in our hands, at least we can enjoy the fruits of his labor!"

A slave scurried from the dinner scene to fetch more wine, leaving behind a dozen guests reclined on couches, all of them drunk except for Lucullus, who had his reasons for pretending to be in the same condition.

"Most excellent pun," an elderly man slurred. He was a former mayor of Smyrna, who had chosen exile on Patmos instead of facing a trial for strangling a young freewoman in the throes of passion. Broken veins on his nose served as evidence that too much alcohol was a frequent state for him. "Wine as the fruits of his labor. Hah!" The elderly man burped. "But I must implore you, Lucullus. If you find Strabo, don't—"

"*If* I find him?" Lucullus said. "On an island this small, it's a matter of *when*. Besides, he needs me. Who else will buy his wine and cheese in the quantities I do?"

"*When* you find him, don't kill him. No one on the island makes better wine." A burp. "But then, no one else on an island this desolate makes wine."

Lucullus smiled indulgently, masking some anger at Strabo. The little man had taken a bribe to turn over the woman and old man as soon as they appeared. "Of course I won't kill him. I like his wine too. A few candle flames applied to the bottom of his feet, I believe, will be sufficient punishment and persuasion to discover where he's hidden his guests."

Lucullus, a big, hairy man missing his two front teeth from a barroom fight long before his enlisted days, gave a nod to the three prostitutes sitting at the feet of the lone Jew in their midst.

"As I've told that handsome young man with you," Lucullus said to the prostitutes, "Strabo lacks for courage. And pride. What other man would return week after week to serve the same soldiers who raped his wife?"

"Really!" one of the girls gasped. "Tell us more."

The young Jew in their midst was as drunk as any of the other guests. "You don't want to hear more," he said, patting the girl's thigh. "Lucullus has described it to me in graphic detail and you won't find it pleasant. Like you, the girl was from Ephesus and occasionally came to Patmos to give well-paid comfort to lonely soldiers."

"Are you calling us whores?" One of the other ones giggled. She leaned over and kissed him on the lips, then pulled away. "Maybe more of that will silence you."

The other guests—three other prostitutes among wealthy exiles bored for entertainment—roared laughter and applauded. All hid well any resentment that Lucullus had ordered three of the six prostitutes who arrived on the supply ship to favor the young Jew.

"Silence?" Lucullus said. He'd been waiting for a reason to turn the conversation to the Jew. "We don't want this young man silent."

The slave returned with a large amphora of wine and began to refill all the goblets.

"Come now, Chayim," Lucullus said as the slave moved from guest to guest. "Tell these beautiful women about your position in Nero's inner court. They need to know how important you are."

"Nero!" The first girl gasped, pushing herself harder against Chayim. "You've met Nero!"

Chayim slurped wine and grinned. "I live in his palace. Share his dinner parties."

"Tell them how you got there," Lucullus said. "I love the story."

Chayim shrugged. "My father is one of the highest placed priests in Jerusalem, where I was raised. Apparently he was ashamed of how much I enjoyed a Roman's life. Bernice, the queen of the Jews, made an arrangement to send me to Nero as a hostage of sorts."

"Hostage?" echoed the second girl.

"As a way to ensure my father did as Bernice requested."

"I don't understand," the second girl said.

"Nobody understands Jewish politics," Chayim said. "But the best answer I can give you is this: Jewish royalty serves Rome, and Jewish religious leaders serve themselves. Bernice thought if Nero had the power of life and death over me, my father would have to obey her wishes."

Lucullus laughed, wanting to encourage the young Jew. "Little did they know you would make such good friends with a god! Far from being a prisoner, here you are, free and serving Nero."

Chayim tried to look modest and failed.

"Tell them," Lucullus said, "why and how you are here. It's fascinating."

Chayim gulped more wine. "There's a woman—"

"Always a woman!" the elderly ex-mayor of Smyrna shouted and the others laughed.

When the laughter died, Lucullus looked at Chayim expectantly. Lucullus hoped this time, Chayim might reveal something that Lucullus hadn't learned before.

"This woman's husband attacked Nero at a dinner party," Chayim said. "She was commanded to commit suicide but fled Rome."

"And you've been sent to find her?" the first girl asked. "How terribly exciting."

"Partly because I can recognize her face from that night at the dinner party," Chayim said. "And partly because there are so few close to Nero that he can trust."

All three girls nodded gravely. They were sitting beside a man who knew Nero!

"This woman's husband actually attacked Nero?" asked the former mayor of Smyrna.

"Tried to kill him." If Chayim was trying to hide his self-importance, he was doing a terrible job. The wine and the close attention of the women were making him careless, something that Lucullus noted with satisfaction. "Actually got his hands around Nero's throat before the guards arrived. Trust me; I was there."

"Attacked Nero at a dinner party?" the third girl asked, gasping. "Tell us more!"

"Does it matter why the man attacked?" Lucullus interrupted. "Chayim, tell them how you managed to get here to Patmos long before the woman you are chasing."

Again, Chayim shrugged with false modesty. "I have a retinue of two dozen soldiers. And a letter from the emperor giving me full credit to spend what I need, when I need, where I need. Trust me; travel has not been an inconvenience."

"Oh, my!" the first girl squeezed his thigh. "I think I'm falling in love."

Laughter again, which irritated Lucullus. He wanted the young Jew as talkative as possible, without distractions. "At a wayside inn a few days' travel outside Rome . . . , " Lucullus coached Chayim.

"They were robbed," Chayim said. "The woman and the old man traveling with her."

"Old man?" the second girl said. "Who is the old man?"

"Doesn't matter," Chayim said. "He'll die when I find the woman. No reason to take two prisoners back to Rome."

"They were robbed . . . , " Lucullus prompted.

"And when we arrived at that town a few days later," Chayim obliged, "inquiring about a woman and an old man traveling together away from Rome, the thieves came forward. They offered to sell me a letter they'd stolen from the two. That letter directed them to Patmos.

Instead of traveling overland like they did, I commandeered a navy ship and cruised here in ease to wait for them."

"Why does Nero want the woman back in Rome?" the first girl asked, innocence in her voice. She glanced at Lucullus for approval. He winked, for he'd slipped her some gold ahead of the meal to ask this. "If Nero wanted her to commit suicide, why not kill her like the old man and save the effort of taking her back to Rome?"

Chayim looked in his near-empty goblet. He took a deep breath, as if he was about to answer.

Lucullus couldn't help but lean forward. Here it was. If he could learn exactly why the woman was so important to Nero, it would be of great value. Enough to get him off this cursed island.

Chayim then grinned like a fox. "Well, if you want the answer to that, ask Helius, the one who sent me here on Nero's behalf."

Lucullus leaned back with a degree of satisfaction. He *had* learned something new. Nero didn't want the woman. Helius did. This, Lucullus thought, was good. Very good.

When he had the woman captured, it would be a simple matter to have Chayim killed. In Chayim's place, Lucullus would take the woman directly to Helius in Rome, not to Nero. It was obvious that the woman would be worth something to Helius. And undoubtedly it would be very profitable, given all the effort spent so far to find her.

It was a good plan indeed. And so close to completion.

"Wine!" Lucullus roared again for the slave. "More wine!"

✠ ✠ ✠

Vitas saw a row of headless men laid neatly side by side by side. Some of the bodies were thin, muscled—obviously those of younger men. Others were fat-bellied, wrinkled, bowlegged. All, however, had the strange inertness and claylike appearance of the dead.

Vitas was in a marble hall, in the middle of the gardens that surrounded Alexandria's library and medical school. The air was strangely cool, but he wondered if that was his imagination, a self-imposed chill that came with such an obvious reminder of mortality.

Vitas had learned to hate death. Most Romans gloried in military might, placed little value on human life except that of a Roman citizen. But for Vitas, memories of warfare only brought nightmares. And haunting questions.

He pushed his thoughts to the present.

At the far end of the hall, a young, dark-haired man was leaning over a table.

Vitas approached him. Closer now, Vitas saw that the man was stuffing the intestinal cavity of a cadaver with a fine salt. The man himself seemed to be about a decade younger than Vitas.

He looked up and nodded politely at Vitas, showing thick eyebrows and eyes that had lively curiosity. "This one is not ready yet," the man said.

"Not ready," Vitas echoed.

The young man must have misunderstood Vitas's lack of comprehension. "I'm assuming you want the entire body, of course," he said, his hands deep in the cadaver. "I suppose if you just need an arm or a leg you could take it. I'll need a few minutes to get the saw."

Vitas finally understood. "I'm not a physician. I'm looking for Issachar."

The young man smiled. "I'm impressed you found me."

Vitas smiled in return. "You were the only one moving in the hall."

"No," Issachar said. He finally removed his hands and wiped them on a nearby cloth. "I'm impressed that you were allowed here. You must be a high-ranking Roman."

Vitas frowned.

"Your accent," Issachar said. "Difficult to disguise. Nothing Greek about it." He explained further. "Romans aren't popular in this city. Especially at this library. It's been over a hundred years, and they still talk about Julius Caesar as if it were yesterday when he burned half of the library's scrolls."

Vitas knew his history, of course. When Julius Caesar pursued

Pompey into Egypt, Caesar found himself outnumbered and trapped in enemy territory because an Egyptian fleet had blockaded him in Alexandria. He ordered the ships in the harbor to be set on fire, destroying the Egyptian fleet, but the fire also spread into the city to the Great Library.

But it was more than that. Romans idealized the ancient Greeks—their art, their methods of learning, the mathematics and science that had changed the world. But Romans held near contempt for the Greek world that had peaked in military might with Alexander the Great, then slowly fragmented until the Romans had, in essence, conquered them.

Here in Alexandria, still the pinnacle of the Greek world despite its location at the mouth of the Nile, the Greeks held themselves in high esteem, still mourning Cleopatra's defeat with Mark Antony. If only the battle at Actium had swung the other way, they believed, Cleopatra's descendants would be ruling the world, instead of Octavian's.

"So who are you?" Issachar asked with another smile.

Vitas had expected a broken man, perhaps bitter that his family and wealth had been taken away from him. Not a cheerful man with no apparent guile.

"As you guessed," Vitas said, "I'm from Rome. What I'd like to know is who sent me from Rome to see you."

Issachar's puzzled expression looked genuine to Vitas. Issachar lifted a hand to rub his face as he thought about Vitas's question, but then pulled it away, as if remembering where he'd just had his hands.

"What a strange question," Issachar said. "Why wouldn't you know who sent you?"

"Truthfully, I'm in no mood to explain. I've already told my story to your wife."

"My wife!" Instantly, the carefree attitude of the young man disappeared. "You spoke to her?"

"She told me I would find you here."

"Tell me everything. How is she? How are my children? Did she seem in good spirits?"

"She sends her love," Vitas said. Vitas understood too well the pain that this man was feeling.

All the vitality seemed to drain from Issachar.

"She didn't tell me anything else, however," Vitas said. "She said if you wanted to explain why you had been taken from the family, you would."

"How I love that woman," Issachar said softly. He raised his hands toward his face again, caught himself again, and sighed.

Vitas was curious about the circumstances that had forced Issachar into such debt he had to sell himself as a slave but would not press the man for it. If he wanted to keep it his business, that was his right.

"'He also forced everyone, small and great, rich and poor, free and slave, to receive a mark on his right hand or on his forehead,'" Issachar said, pressing his lips in frustration as he paused. "'So that no one could buy or sell unless he had the mark, which is the name of the beast or the number of his name.'"

"Six hundred and sixty-six," Vitas said without thinking.

"You?" Issachar's eyes widened. "You, too, are familiar with the Revelation?"

"Only the number of the Beast. That, too, is a long story." This was not the time or place to talk about John.

"The Jewish leaders in Alexandria have boycotted all of the other Jews who follow the Christos," Issachar said. "I am a follower. First I was barred from the guild of silversmiths. Then barred from any dealings with anyone in the Jewish community. I could not buy or sell. It drove my family into poverty and then, finally, total desolation."

Vitas remembered something else John had said to him, on their first night on the boat leaving Rome. *All of us marked by the Lamb are hated by those marked by the Beast.*

"You are marked by the Lamb?" Vitas asked. "Yet I see nothing."

"You're a Roman. Of course you would look for a physical mark.

But one's beliefs and behavior mark whether one serves the Lamb or the Beast. The forehead symbolizes what you believe, and the hand symbolizes what you do. Yes, I have been marked, and my beliefs and actions are plain enough to the guild for them to bar me."

"Tell me," Vitas said. "You endure this slavery. Your family suffers. To prosper, all you have to do is accept Caesar as do many other Jews."

"The Beast will not reign long," Issachar said. "That is one of the hopes given us by the Revelation. And for those who suffer or perish in this battle against the Beast, eternal hope is given."

Vitas was again thinking of what John had explained about the vision and the man who had received it on the island of Patmos. "This Revelation is important then?"

"Copies of it have spread all across the world. In every community, we face persecution from Rome and from Jerusalem. It encourages us to persevere in the midst of tribulation."

"Was it written in Hebrew?" Vitas asked, thinking of the reason he'd come to see Issachar.

"Greek."

"Which you read."

"Of course."

"And what about this?" Vitas handed Issachar the scroll that Pavo's crew member had brought for Jael.

Issachar looked at the handwriting. "It's Hebrew."

"I know," Vitas answered. *The pieces are scattered in such a way that only you will be able to put them together.* There was a reason this had been delivered to Issachar and a reason Vitas had been sent here. Surely Issachar had the answer. "But can you read it?"

"No," Issachar said. "I'm sorry I can't help you."

JUPITER

HORA PRIMA

VITAS WOKE TO THE sensation of furtive rustling against his belly.
He had been sleeping on his back, with his right forearm across his
eyes. He wondered if it was a rat, but he didn't open his eyes.

Instead, he muttered as if still asleep and turned onto his side.
As he turned, he clenched the knife he'd laid beside him on the bed
before going to sleep and tucked it under his body. He was on a
poorly stuffed mattress in a room crowded with snoring men and
women.

Vitas cracked open an eyelid. The dark of night had retreated
to the gray of early dawn. He could see the outlines of the other
customers of the inn on their mattresses, and now that he was fully
awake, he became aware of the stench of unwashed bodies and the
foul air thick with exhaled alcohol. His body itched, and he knew
that bedbugs had engorged themselves on his blood while he slept.

The light touch against his body resumed.

Yes, it was a rat. But a human rat.

In one quick movement, Vitas spun upward, knife in hand.
With his other hand, he reached for and found the wrist that
belonged to the hand that had been searching.

He yanked hard, toppling the person above him. Vitas rolled
with the body of the thief, landing on top and straddling the thief.
He raised his knife hand high, ready to plunge.

In the dim light, he saw that it was a young woman.

"No!" the woman said. There was enough light to see the greasy
long hair and the thin features and the startled openness of her face.

Vitas relaxed. He was far bulkier than the woman, and she wasn't armed. There was no physical danger.

Wordlessly, he rose. He checked the belt around his body, making sure his pouch of coins was secure.

The woman scrambled backward, bumping into an old man who woke and grumbled. When he saw it was a woman, he leered. She spat on the old man.

Vitas ignored her. He still had his money, and it wasn't his place to punish thieves.

Vitas walked away. He wasn't interested in returning to the mattress in an attempt to sleep any longer, especially as the stench and filth of the inn seemed to cling to his skin. He wanted to find a public bath immediately.

"Wait," the woman called after him.

He kept walking.

She caught up to him as he reached the street.

Already it was brighter. He could not see the sun on the horizon. In this section of Alexandria, the buildings pressed too closely on the street for that.

"Wait," she said again. "I have something you want."

"I'm not interested." He spoke without turning to her. He doubted he would ever have desire for another woman again. And if he did, it would be a betrayal of his love for Sophia.

She ran in front of him and stepped into his path. Now he could see the pockmarks on her face. She was younger than he had first guessed and had a feral skinniness that spoke of hard times.

Vitas moved around her without pushing her aside.

She ran in front of him again. This time, she said, "Vitas."

That got his attention. How could she know his name? Or for that matter, where to find him? There was only one person who could have given her the information. The same person who knew he carried a pouch heavy with coins.

"Issachar," Vitas guessed.

"He told me where to find you."

Vitas was vaguely disappointed. Like Issachar, Sophia and John were followers of the Christos. While Vitas did not share their faith, he admired their integrity and the character that seemed to silently set them apart. Issachar, too, had seemed to carry himself the same way, indeed had become a slave rather than give up his faith. Had Issachar lied about the reason for his debt? If so, what did it say about the faith he claimed?

"Remarkable," Vitas said.

"I knew of the inn," she said.

"No. Remarkable that you found me among all the people in that room."

"Issachar told me I would be able to recognize you by your signet ring. He was right. No one else there had any jewelry."

"I'm sure you checked as many as you could. Did you find anything of value on the drunks too far gone to wake?"

Her eyes darted away from him.

"Be sure to share with Issachar," he said. "At least that will make both your efforts worthwhile."

"The others I robbed," she said. "You, I just wanted to make sure you had the coins that Issachar promised."

Vitas snorted. "Because you thought if you woke me up and asked nicely after you found them, that I'd be happy to give them to you."

Instead of answering, she reached into her dirty tunic and pulled out a scroll. "Issachar said you'd pay me for this. It belonged to a Jew. John."

Vitas reached for it. Another scroll. One of the scattered pieces he was meant to put together?

She snatched it back. "Money first," she said.

"Tell me how you got it," he said.

"I'm a slave. John asked me to give it to Issachar. He told me Issachar was a wealthy silversmith and that I would be well paid for my efforts." She made a disparaging gesture. "Only the silversmith did not live where John sent me. Let me tell you, it was a long bit of travel to finally find Issachar. You can't imagine how his wife reacted when I showed up and asked for her husband. She—"

"You're a slave. You visited John."

"I told you that already. He had the scroll and—"

"How did he get it?"

"I'm supposed to know? Look, I just want money. John said I would get it from Issachar. Issachar's a penniless slave. You're the man I need to see, and if you want to see this scroll, I'll need to see money. Understand?"

"John's cape," Vitas said. "Describe it to me."

She did, then paused. "What was it he wanted me to say to you and Issachar to prove the scroll came from him? That's it. 'All of us marked by the Lamb are hated by those marked by the Beast.'"

Vitas stared at her thoughtfully.

"Hah," she said. She smiled, trying to make it coy. But a toothless gap in her bottom teeth ruined the effect. "You know I'm telling the truth now."

Finally, Vitas reached into his tunic. He fumbled with his coin pouch. "Don't ask for more."

She looked at the coin. Bit it hard. Nodded. "Good enough." She gave him the scroll and watched as Vitas unrolled it. "How much are they asking?" she said to Vitas.

The first part was in Hebrew. The second half, however, was in Greek. Vitas recognized John's writing style from the first translation John had done on the ship.

This is the second piece, my friend. "There will be two witnesses, killed yet brought alive. Find them and rejoice with them, then take what is given."

"How much are they asking?" the slave girl repeated, breaking into Vitas's reading of the scroll.

"Asking?"

"It's a ransom note, right? It must be a lot if they were willing to send me in to look after him while he was on the ship."

"They?" Vitas asked. "What are you talking about?"

"Isn't that a ransom note?" she said. "John's on a ship bound for Rome. As a hostage."

✦ ✦ ✦

Strabo was milking a nanny goat near the compound below his cottage when Lucullus arrived with five soldiers. He ignored them, squirting milk into a bucket, until Lucullus yanked the goat by the ears.

The nanny bleated and kicked and pulled against the rope tied to a stake.

Strabo calmly pulled the bucket clear. He moved away from the nanny so Lucullus would have no excuse to harm it. Strabo then placed his hands on his hips and looked upward at Lucullus. The commander was in full armor, as were the soldiers. All of them, of course, towered over Strabo. Lucullus stepped forward from his men.

"The woman and old man arrived on yesterday's supply ship," Lucullus growled. "They inquired at the harbor for the dwarf."

Strabo told himself that Lucullus had worn armor in a deliberate attempt to intimidate him. He enjoyed the sense of anger that came with the thought. It replaced a portion of his fear. "The woman and old man you bribed me to turn over to you?" Strabo asked.

"The same."

"Thank you," Strabo said.

"You thank me?"

"Now that you've warned me they are on the island, I'll watch for them."

Without anger, Lucullus kicked over the bucket of milk, splashing Strabo. "Listen to me, little man," Lucullus said. "They were last seen going up the trail to your cottage."

"When?" Strabo asked. He rubbed his foot across a rivulet of milk in the dust.

"Yesterday afternoon."

Strabo nodded thoughtfully. "That explains it then."

"I'm sure you have an explanation for everything."

"Chara and Zeno were in the vineyard yesterday afternoon. I was looking for a stray goat. It seemed to us that someone had been in the cottage while we were gone. Things had been moved."

It had been the soldiers who had come searching for Ben-Aryeh and Sophia. Strabo knew this, but he was gambling Lucullus could not be certain that Strabo knew it.

This gamble was Strabo's only chance. Patmos was too small, and there were only about a hundred people on it, half of them exiles. There was no place to hide, and Strabo wasn't in a position to be able to move his family, even if he found a sponge diver or a fisherman willing to smuggle them off the island. Not with Chara so far into her pregnancy. Instead of running and hiding, Strabo could only bluff.

"I sent soldiers yesterday afternoon," Lucullus said, watching Strabo closely. "They found no one."

"They looked in our house then." Indignation wouldn't work here, Strabo told himself. But neither would passive acceptance, for Lucullus would wonder why Strabo didn't make even a token protest. Strabo's hands were trembling and he pressed them against his sides. His future and those of Chara, Zeno, and the unborn child depended on how well he handled this.

"If you were the one who sent the soldiers," Strabo said with quiet bitterness, "I suppose complaining won't do any good."

"Where are your wife and son now?" Lucullus said, still intently watching Strabo's eyes.

"I sent them to a vineyard this morning to prune more vines."

"A suspicious man would think you'd sent them out of harm's way. I am such a man."

"If I expected soldiers, of course I would send them away." Strabo spit on the ground. "You, of all people, would know how much Chara fears soldiers."

"To me," Lucullus said, "there are only two possibilities. The first is this: yesterday afternoon, the old man and the woman came up here to look for you. They didn't find you but heard the soldiers

I sent and managed to hide from them and have fled to another part of the island."

Don't agree too eagerly, Strabo told himself. *Don't overplay this.* If Chara had to face Roman soldiers again . . .

"*Managed* to hide?" Strabo said. "Elephants in a latrine would be able to hide from your men."

"Don't push me," Lucullus said.

"Roman law still applies on this island," Strabo said. "I've done nothing wrong and here you are, harassing me. On my property."

"If it's the first possibility," Lucullus said, "that means you haven't lied about any of this. You would have my apologies for this visit. I'm much less concerned about Roman law than I am about a continued supply of wine and fresh milk and cheese."

Strabo told himself to be no different than any other time in conversation with Lucullus. "You know if I could sell to anyone else," Strabo said, "I would."

"The second possibility is that the old man and the woman did find you yesterday afternoon, and that all of you fled at the approach of my soldiers. You're here, expecting me, and you've sent the others away while you hope to convince me of the first possibility."

Lucullus paced, then whirled and paced back. "Did you wonder why I offered you a bribe to turn them over?" Lucullus asked, smiling.

"You're lazy."

"No. I knew I'd hear the moment they stepped off the supply ship. I offered you the bribe to see if you truly were afraid of me. See, if you turned them in, I'd know your fear of me is more than your hatred of me. But if you defied me, then I'd have a better measure of a man who would love to see me dead."

"What does it matter?" Strabo said. "I bring your soldiers wine and cheese and milk. You pay me."

"It matters," Lucullus said, "because if I can't make a little man like you afraid of me, then what respect would I get from my soldiers?"

Lucullus stepped forward and, in a continuous motion, delivered a swift kick into Strabo's ribs, sending him to the ground in a heap.

Before Strabo could recover, Lucullus leaned over and grabbed the collar of Strabo's tunic in one hand and his belt in the other. He carried Strabo back to his soldiers, as if Strabo were a child.

"Here he is," Lucullus told the soldiers. He shook Strabo, who was almost in shock from the impact of the kick. "Such a little, little man. But so much trouble."

Lucullus spit on the back of Strabo's bald skull and smiled as it ran down the side of Strabo's face. "Strabo," he said, "I really need to know which of the two possibilities I should choose. Did you see the old man and woman? Or were you truly away from the cottage when they got here?"

Lucullus clucked his tongue. "To find out, little man, we're going to have some fun with you and candle flames."

HORA SECUNDA

DIRECT SUNSHINE flooded the mouth of the cave but made it difficult for Akakios to see into the darkness beyond.

Akakios was a young man, a sponge diver from a line of men who had earned a living by plunging into the Aegean Sea for as long as their family history could be remembered. He was lithe and well muscled, dark hair cut short to make swimming easier. On this morning, he wore a simple tunic and old sandals.

It was partly because of his youth and physique that Akakios moved forward to the dark shadows so confidently and partly because Strabo had told him where to find the old man and the woman.

He was eager to talk to them. Now, at last, his own curiosity would be satisfied. Who were these two sent all the way from Rome? Where would they be going from Patmos? And why had all of this been cloaked in mystery?

Partway into the cave, as the ceiling dropped and forced Akakios to stoop, he paused. Shouldn't the old man and the woman be awake by now?

"My name is Akakios," he called, expecting a reply.

"What do you want?"

The voice and the question startled Akakios, because they came from behind him.

Akakios whirled. The rising sun in the east was blinding at the mouth of the cave, forcing him to squint. All he saw was a silhouette.

"Answer me," the man's voice said. "What do you want?"

"Strabo sent me here," Akakios said.

"I see." The voice was less antagonistic than before.

"Are you Ben-Aryeh?" Akakios slowly moved forward, shielding his eyes from the sun with a raised hand.

"I am."

Akakios grinned, reaching Ben-Aryeh. He towered over the old man. "Strabo warned me not to expect someone cheerful."

"Humph."

"Where is Sophia?" Akakios asked.

"She'll come to the cave when I tell her it is safe."

"You didn't sleep here through the night?"

No answer.

Akakios grinned again. "I understand. You didn't trust Strabo."

"Humph."

"Well," Akakios said, "I'm not a soldier, am I."

"But you are irritatingly cheerful."

Another grin. "Strabo thinks the same thing."

"Humph."

Sleeping on the hillside had doubtless done nothing to improve this man's mood despite the blankets that Strabo had provided, Akakios thought.

"Did Strabo send you here to irritate me instead of him?" Ben-Aryeh asked.

"No. Chara sent me."

"The woman of mystery," Ben-Aryeh said. "Or of extreme modesty."

"You mean her veil?"

"Cheerful *and* of quick intelligence. Of course I meant her veil."

"She—" Akakios thought better of what he'd been about to say. "She's the one you should have sought. Not Strabo."

Ben-Aryeh cocked his head in puzzlement.

"'Go to the island of exile where the last disciple received the vision.

Find the household of the man who stands no taller than his goats,'"
Akakios said. "Find the *household.* Not the man."

"You're saying . . ."

"It was Chara who's been expecting an old man and a woman.
She's been waiting to direct them as promised. The letter she
received with those instructions warned her of the strictest confidence. She didn't even tell Strabo. And because of what Lucullus
did to her, Strabo didn't tell her that Lucullus had made inquiries
earlier along with the bribe."

"Chara knows about the message waiting for us?" Suddenly,
Ben-Aryeh's expression brightened just the slightest bit.

"She and I were both led to the Christos by John, His last disciple. Whoever sent her the letter from Rome knows this."

"Chara knows about the message."

"That's why I'm here," Akakios answered. "I'm curious, though.
Who in Rome sent you to Patmos?"

"Undoubtedly the same person who sent the letter to Chara."

"Whoever it was," Akakios mused, "is the common point of the
triangle with me at the third corner." Akakios continued, unaware of
how intently Ben-Aryeh was staring at him. "I'm curious too. Why
go to all this trouble? Why give you a letter to go to Chara, who
would send you to me? Why not simply give you what I was sent? It
would have saved you hundreds and hundreds of miles of trouble."

"You? You have whatever it is that is waiting for us on Patmos?"

"That's why I'm here," Akakios answered. "Although it's just
another letter. And one that makes little sense."

Akakios offered a scroll to Ben-Aryeh.

✠ ✠ ✠

"Before you say a word," Pavo told Vitas, "I'm going to tell you
about the night in Cyprus that I got far too drunk and fell asleep in
an alley."

Five minutes earlier, Vitas had stepped onto the ship's gangway.
A crewman guarding the entrance to the ship made Vitas wait while

another went for Pavo. Then Vitas was escorted to the far side of the ship, where Pavo was inspecting a patch on one of the sails.

"You remind me of that night," Pavo said, "because I was so drunk that I didn't even notice I'd lain where a dog had squatted earlier. No matter what I did to remove it, the stench clung to me for days. You, too, are as difficult to be rid of and just as unpleasant."

"Give me money and the help of a few men," Vitas said, "and consider me gone."

"Why in the name of Neptune do you expect me to give you money and help?" Pavo exploded. "You've already caused me more trouble than a crew of drunks."

"You turned your ship around for me."

Pavo grunted. "It's not a fond memory."

"You said it plainly: my survival is your survival."

"You're no longer my responsibility."

"And how will you prove it to my rich and important and powerful friends that you fear so much you turned a ship around to save me?"

"What do you mean, prove it? I delivered you as required."

"If something happens to me," Vitas said, "how will my friends in Rome know this?"

Pavo knelt and pulled at a piece of rope attached to a furled sail. He stood. "I understand now," Pavo said, his face hard, his eyes cold. "And the stench grows. This is blackmail."

"Merely prudence on your part." Vitas held up his right hand. "My friends in Rome recognize my signet. Get me a scroll. I'll write whatever you want me to as proof that I left your ship in good health. I'll seal it in wax with my signet."

"Call it what you want. It's still blackmail."

Vitas shook his head. "Payment for services rendered. I'll also tell you who on your ship has betrayed you."

"Now what nonsense are you spouting?"

"The cape you gave me," Vitas said. "It tells the tale."

"Come closer," Pavo said. "Let me smell your breath for wine."

"You've been betrayed," Vitas said. "I'd expect you would want to know your betrayer before going back out to sea with the man."

"You can prove this to me?"

"I can tell you what I know and what I've concluded. Then you decide if it's proof enough."

Pavo sighed. "All right, I'm listening."

"No," Vitas said. "First the money."

"How much?"

"Enough to buy a slave's freedom."

"Fair enough."

"No," Vitas said, smiling.

"I've just agreed to your terms." Pavo was ominously close to losing his temper again.

"Too quickly. Which tells me that you are happy to let me hold your gold while I speak, then confiscate it before I leave the ship."

"So what do you suggest?"

"Send someone to buy the slave and come back with the papers of freedom so that I know he can return to his family."

Pavo's brow furrowed. "You'll wait on the ship then?"

"Of course," Vitas said. "At this point, it's probably the safest place in Alexandria for me."

✦ ✦ ✦

Ben-Aryeh held the scroll at arm's length, grateful that the bright sun made it easier to see the characters, irritated that with each added year of age, he had more difficulty focusing.

"Can you read it?" Akakios asked.

"If somehow you have enough intelligence to survive to my age," Ben-Aryeh snapped, "you'll understand the shame in mocking an old man's eyes."

"I meant, does the language make sense to you. I only read Latin."

"It's Hebrew," Ben-Aryeh said, unwilling to apologize. "Now keep quiet and let me concentrate."

"*You know the beast you must escape.*" Ben-Aryeh spoke aloud as he began to read from the beginning, more to himself than to Akakios. *"'The one with understanding will solve the number of this beast, for it is the number of a man. His number is 666.'"*

"John!" Akakios exclaimed, startling Ben-Aryeh, who, in his concentration on the scroll and its mysterious message, had almost forgotten the young man beside him.

"John? The Beast we must escape?"

Akakios laughed. "No. That's from the vision John had here on Patmos. 'The one with understanding will solve the number of this beast, for it is the number of a man.' John spoke those very words as he dictated his Revelation."

"I'm holding a copy of his letter of Revelation?"

"It was written in Greek. You said this is Hebrew."

"Yet you recognize the words."

"Read the rest of it to me," Akakios said. "I'll know."

Ben-Aryeh decided there would be no harm in divulging the contents of the scroll to Akakios, as the message was such a mystery. So he read the scroll aloud.

Occasionally Akakios would nod in recognition, but mainly the reading drew frowns of puzzlement. "What you have," Akakios said when Ben-Aryeh finished, "is not the letter of Revelation translated into Hebrew. But it uses language from the Revelation."

"Would you guess I need that letter for this to make sense?"

"Any copies that were on the island have been sent to the mainland for circulation among the believers. It has given great comfort to the followers of the Christos."

The followers of the Christos.

Ben-Aryeh had been traveling for weeks with Sophia, who was a follower of the Christos. Although he was a Jew who found the claims of the Christos and his followers to be blasphemous, although he'd been among those who stoned James, the brother of Jesus, Ben-Aryeh had decided for the sake of peace not to argue with Sophia. Nor, despite his instinctive urge to cry out against the blasphemy of it, would he argue it now with this young Greek.

What he said instead was this: "If you only knew how much it will grieve me to study that letter."

Before Akakios could ask why, the little boy Zeno came running toward them, with Sophia right behind.

"The soldiers," Zeno cried. "They've taken my father!"

HORA TERTIANA

"I'M SURPRISED TO SEE YOU," Chara said as Sophia stepped down the hillside toward her.

Veiled as she had been the day before, Chara was on her knees in the dusty soil, pruning the base of a vine. She straightened after Sophia called to her.

"Zeno told me where to find you," Sophia said. She felt short of breath. Not from exertion. But from a sense of dread, the first emotion she'd felt in weeks.

"And the rascal has already run off," Chara said. She set aside her short hoe and reached upward for Sophia. "He was supposed to spend the morning here with me, but he disappeared as soon as I turned my back. He likes to roam the hills like a little fox."

Sophia took Chara's hand and helped her stand. "Zeno has gone back to Akakios," Sophia said.

"Ah." Chara's face was hidden beneath the veil, but Sophia heard the good cheer in her voice. "I'm glad Akakios found you. He's the one with the letter you need."

"I don't know about the letter," Sophia said. "I wasn't in the cave when he spoke to Ben-Aryeh. But when Zeno showed up, they decided I was the one who needed to speak to you while they got things ready."

Chara tilted her head. "Something is wrong."

"Akakios is getting a boat ready to help you and Zeno leave the island."

"Lucullus has taken Strabo," Chara said.

Sophia was surprised at the certainty and calmness in Chara's voice. She followed as Chara moved slowly across the hillside.

"Zeno saw it," Sophia said. "He ran to the cave to tell us."

"Don't blame yourself," Chara told Sophia. "For a long time now, Lucullus has been looking for an excuse to harm Strabo."

Sophia could hardly believe this. Chara's first thought was for Sophia's feelings.

"I'm supposed to help you down to the water," Sophia said. "Akakios says there's nothing he can do against the soldiers. But he can protect you and Zeno."

"No," Chara said. "Take me to Strabo."

"The soldiers . . ."

"Look at me," Chara said, half turning toward Sophia. Chara lifted her veil.

Sophia couldn't help but bring her hand to her mouth in shock.

The left side of Chara's face was unblemished, perfect, and extraordinarily beautiful. The other side looked like melted wax, hideous and disfigured.

Chara dropped the veil again. "Don't feel sorry for me. I wake every morning and thank the Lord God that He allowed me to live. And I thank Him more that Strabo found me and loved me."

Sophia walked beside Chara, holding her elbow, ashamed at her relief that the veil was back in place again.

"Strabo met me at the barracks when he was delivering cheese," Chara said. "He knew who I was and what I was. But he was always kind to me. After my rebirth in the Christos, he provided a home for Zeno and me, because I'd stopped spending time with the soldiers for money."

They were walking slowly but steadily.

"Lucullus was insane with fury that I refused to be with him anymore," Chara said. "One night, he came out to the hillside with a half dozen other soldiers. They took me into the darkness. I doubt I have to tell you what they did with me."

What made it more horrible to Sophia was the matter-of-fact way Chara told her the story. "Strabo tried to stop them, of course," Chara said. "But he was too small. They hurt him badly and made him watch as Lucullus burned my face. Then they left both of us to die."

Sophia could hardly breathe.

"The next morning, Akakios found us. He sent for John, who nursed us both. I believe I would have died, because the burn became horribly infected. But by the grace and power of Jesus the Christos I was healed. John prayed for me and the pain disappeared."

Chara stopped. Lifted her veil again. Stared Sophia directly in the eyes.

Sophia didn't flinch this time. She met Chara's gaze.

"This is the face that Strabo saw. This is the woman he asked to marry him. He didn't care who I was, or what I looked like. Strabo was in love with me."

Chara took Sophia's hand. Lifted it. Touched it lightly against her own face.

Sophia traced the scars. By looking fully in Chara's face and accepting what was there, she began to see the woman for who she was and no longer felt an instinctive revulsion.

"I believe that had it been our Father's will, even the scars would have been healed with that miracle, that my face would have become unblemished again," Chara said. "But Strabo loves me as I am. And every day I am joyfully reminded that this is how the Christos loves me. Loves us. He sees past our outer appearance and past the ugliness of our sinful desires and angers and hatreds and whatever has happened in our past. I wish you understood that."

Sophia blinked away tears. It felt like her heart was dissolving.

"I will not leave Strabo," Chara said. "Find Ben-Aryeh and go on the boat with Akakios. Protect Zeno until I return."

"I can't!"

"Listen to me. Lucullus won't kill Strabo. He hates him and wants to humiliate him because the two of us refuse to live in fear of him. We will get through this day and continue. When you live with the Christos in your heart, you can face any tribulation. But if Lucullus gets you, he and his soldiers will take you on a hillside and do with you what they did with me."

Chara pushed away. "Go," she said to Sophia. "Go."

✝ ✝ ✝

"Satisfied?" Pavo asked.

Vitas nodded. He was sitting in the shade of an awning set up on the ship's deck.

"Who is my betrayer?" Pavo asked.

"You're familiar with the common practice of kidnapping travelers and holding them for ransom," Vitas answered.

"Wealthy travelers, yes."

"The Jew that was my companion, does he strike you as wealthy?"

"No."

"Yet he was taken hostage."

"Here? In Alexandria?"

Vitas nodded. He explained how he had found out.

"All that proves is the stupidity of the kidnappers," Pavo said. "Certainly not that someone on my ship has betrayed me."

"The cape you gave me," Vitas said. "I gave it to John. He stepped off this ship wearing it."

Pavo was about to utter another caustic remark, but after a brief pause, he snapped his mouth shut.

"Yes," Vitas said. "Someone thought he was me."

"You're trying to tell me that someone was waiting in Alexandria to kidnap you."

"Yes."

"Impossible."

"I know what you're thinking," Vitas said. "Because I wondered too. Ship is the fastest way to get a message to Alexandria from Rome. How could kidnappers in this city know ahead of your ship's arrival that I would be on it?"

"Someone betrayed your friends in Rome."

"No," Vitas said. "I wondered about that too. I was put on your ship on short notice. Remember, you left at night. No time for anyone in Rome to send a letter on another leaving earlier."

Pavo tapped his teeth with his finger. "But with all the bad luck and delays at sea, there was time for someone to send a letter on a ship that left after ours."

"What if it wasn't bad luck?"

Vitas saw comprehension light Pavo's eyes. Pavo snapped his teeth shut with an audible click. His jaw muscles bulged with anger.

"Yes," Vitas said. "If I were you, I would take a closer look at the steering oar that gave your navigator so much trouble. If you want more proof, give me enough men to free John. His kidnappers, I'm sure, will be able to tell you more."

"No. Betto is a weak man. I'll bind his hands and feet and hang him by his heels over the edge of the ship. He'll tell me what I need to know."

"Even so, I need enough men to free John," Vitas said.

"Not my problem anymore."

"Only after John is freed will I write the letter testifying I was delivered safely here in Alexandria."

"Don't need it," Pavo said. "I finally know who you are and who you are fleeing. Nero."

Vitas felt himself flinch. It earned a smile from Pavo.

"Nero," Pavo repeated. "Your friends are rich and powerful and important, but compared to Nero, they are nothing. If any of them threaten me back in Rome, I know where I can find safety."

Pavo's smile widened. "I can afford to indulge your curiosity, as you have earned me a handsome reward. As you pointed out, this was a slow journey. Slow enough that a ship leaving Rome days after we did arrived in this harbor late yesterday."

I was pursued, Vitas thought. *This means my death. And without doubt, the death of Sophia.*

He glanced past Pavo, calculating his chances.

"I can read your eyes," Pavo said. "Now you look for escape. But I've got my men at the gangplank. They're on alert to stop you."

Pavo clucked his tongue. "The only reason I bought that slave for you was because it meant you had to wait aboard the ship until the papers were returned. That also gave me time to send a man out to find those sent by Nero, the same men who came to my ship earlier looking for you, armed with a royal edict with a reward for your arrest."

Sent by Nero. That confirmed the worst of Vitas's fears.

"The price for your slave," Pavo continued, "was a tenth of the price I will earn from Nero for finding a way to keep you on the ship without getting suspicious until my messenger could find them." He shrugged. "I guess your Jew friend is going to remain a hostage until his kidnappers find out he isn't worth any money to them alive."

Then came a sigh of satisfaction. "I must say, in the end, this journey has been worth all the trouble you caused. Even discovering I'll need to find a new pilot."

Vitas wondered if he should throw himself off the ship. He couldn't swim. At least if he drowned, his death would give Sophia a chance of survival.

Vitas shifted his balance, ready to make a dash.

"So tell me, Aedinius Abito," Pavo said, "what exactly did you do to incur the wrath of our emperor?"

Aedinius Abito?

Before Vitas could reply, Pavo's attention turned away from him as two men stepped onto the deck of the ship, one of them a lumbering giant.

"I guess I'll find out when I get back to Rome to claim my reward," Pavo said. "Here come the men from Nero now."

Vitas looked at the approaching men and stifled a gasp of astonishment.

One of them was his brother, Damian.

✠ ✠ ✠

A lit oil lamp had been set well to the side, in the clearing that
Lucullus had chosen, a clearing surrounded by low scrub bushes.
This made it easy for Ben-Aryeh to sneak close enough to watch.
He paid the oil lamp little attention—the rest of the scene was
more compelling.

Lucullus and the soldiers had set up a tall pyramid of four long
poles, set wide at the bottom and leaning together at the top, with
a tight circle of rope at the peak to band the poles solidly together.
Another length of rope hung down from there, and Strabo dangled
head-downward from this rope. They had bound his hands at
his sides, and his head was barely a foot off the ground, hanging
directly in the center of the makeshift pyramid.

Lucullus stood nearby, facing Strabo and looking down on
Strabo's feet and body and holding a large jug of wine. "Here's
a vintage you should enjoy," Lucullus said. The other soldiers,
gathered outside of the triangle, roared with laughter.

Lucullus nodded. One soldier stepped forward and held Strabo's
upside-down body. Another clamped a hand over the dwarf's mouth.

Lucullus began to pour the red liquid into Strabo's nose.

Strabo arched his back and shook his head violently, snorting
and blowing through his nose in an attempt to clear it, which only
made the soldiers laugh harder as the first two tried to contain
Strabo's kicking and bucking. His movement made the pyramid of
poles sway, but true to the engineering tradition of Roman soldiers,
their construction was too solid to collapse.

It was quickly apparent that Strabo was at the point of drowning,
and Ben-Aryeh was profoundly grateful that he'd ordered Zeno to
stay behind with Akakios; no son should ever see his father humiliated in this way.

Ben-Aryeh could not stand to watch it. He was about to stand
and rush forward, even knowing it would be futile against the soldiers, when Lucullus stopped pouring wine.

"I've got plenty left," Lucullus told Strabo, "and this is so much fun. But I don't want to forget that I've promised you the same treatment I gave your whore wife."

Lucullus pointed at one of the soldiers. "Bring the goat," he barked. "The big, black male."

The soldier returned with the black goat at the end of a rope. The rope was tied to its horns, and it strained and bucked to get loose.

"Now you're going to become the butt of our jokes," Lucullus said. "Right, boys?"

More laughter.

"Tie the end of the rope to the little man's waist," Lucullus said. "Let's enjoy the show."

The soldier did as ordered. There was about three feet of slack in the rope—not enough for the goat to leave the circle at the bottom of the poles, but enough to give it some room to maneuver.

The goat faced Strabo. It made a movement as if to charge.

Strabo, upside down and with no place to go, bared his teeth and clicked them together in a biting motion.

The goat stepped backward in fear and respect, pulling Strabo away from center.

"Come on!" Lucullus roared. He took out his sword and jabbed the goat in the hind end, trying to provoke it. It jumped forward but did not attack Strabo.

"Come on!" Another jab.

The goat kicked backward, slamming a hoof into Lucullus's shin. He roared in pain, then slashed the sword across the midsection of the goat, gashing its hide. Blood began to stream onto the ground.

"Attack him!" Lucullus screamed.

The goat darted away, bleating in pain.

There was nothing comical about this to Ben-Aryeh. He saw no way to help Strabo. With the Roman commander going wild, Ben-Aryeh realized it was only going to get far worse.

Another slash of the sword. This time, to sever the rope that held the goat to Strabo. With more bleating, it tried to run, but could only stagger its escape.

"I want the oil lamp," Lucullus yelled. "Now! Remember your wife?" he said to Strabo. "Remember what this did to her?"

Strabo stared back at Lucullus. "Nothing you did or can do will ever destroy our love."

The reply incensed Lucullus. He kicked Strabo, sending the little man's body high into the air like a pendulum.

Lucullus stepped back, gulping for breath and self-control. "Let's try this," he ground out.

He placed the candle on the ground directly below Strabo's bald head. As the heat rose, Strabo arched in pain. He tried to swing himself back and forth, but soldiers held him in place until he screamed in agony.

Lucullus pulled the candle away. "Now," he said, "tell me about the woman. Where is she? Tell me, and I'll spare you and your family."

Strabo blinked but remained silent.

"I'm sure your wife told you how much I like the smell of burning flesh," Lucullus said. "How about this?" He applied the candle flame directly to Strabo's bare feet.

Strabo screamed again.

After five seconds, Lucullus removed it. His face had become dreamy, as if he was losing himself in the torture. "Where's the woman?" The rage in his voice had disappeared. He was speaking almost seductively. "Come on, Strabo; tell me what I need to know."

Tears streamed from Strabo's eyes, down his forehead to drip onto the ground.

"Perhaps a leg," Lucullus said. "I'll get to your face last. Like I did with your wife."

Lucullus pulled Strabo's body sideways so he could get a better angle to Strabo's leg. "How's this?" Lucullus asked gently, applying the flame.

Strabo screamed.

By the looks the soldiers were exchanging, Ben-Aryeh could see that they found their commander's obvious enjoyment of this disturbing.

Lucullus removed the flame.

Strabo drew deep breaths but stopped screaming.

"I've got all day," Lucullus told Strabo in a soothing voice. "And little as you are, there's still plenty I can burn. Unless you'd care to tell me where to find the woman."

Strabo bit his lip and closed his eyes, preparing himself for the worst as Lucullus moved the candle to his midsection.

Ben-Aryeh could not endure it any longer. He burst from the bushes, gambling there would be only one way to ensure Sophia's safety.

"Stop!" he yelled in Aramaic. All the soldiers spun; all of them lifted spears in protection. He continued in Aramaic, striding forward, believing none would be able to understand him. "Leave him alone. You're looking for me."

Lucullus did not appear surprised. "Sounds like a Jew to me," Lucullus said, grinning. "What's he telling us to do? Find him a pig?"

The soldiers laughed.

"See, men," Lucullus said. "I told you this was the perfect place to put out the bait."

He spun and kicked Strabo in the belly.

"Cut him down," Lucullus snarled at his men. "I'll let him wonder for the rest of his life when I'll be coming back to finish this."

HORA QUARTA

HERE HE IS, Jerome thought, *the man whose death will save my children.*

Vitas and Damian were a few paces away from Jerome, in the shade of an inn that overlooked the harbor. The lighthouse of Pharos dominated the horizon. In front, hundreds of ships lined the shoreline. The harbor was full of activity, with ships arriving and leaving it at random.

Jerome couldn't help a glance at Vitas's hands. At the signet ring that Jerome had been commanded to return to Rome.

"How we found you," Damian was saying to Vitas, "is a long but satisfying story."

Damian turned to Jerome. "Am I right?"

Jerome nodded. Satisfying for Damian. To him, all of life was a game. For Jerome, there was nothing lighthearted about this, especially knowing he'd have to find a safe time and place to murder the man in front of him.

"It was clever of me," Damian said, "to deliver Pavo a false name, wouldn't you agree? Aedinius Abito is protecting you, for no one in the palace will know that Gallus Sergius Vitas is alive and well."

Wrong, Jerome thought. *Dead wrong. Someone does and they've sent me after him.*

He could not speak these thoughts, of course. Again, Jerome was overwhelmed by frustration at his inability to communicate.

He had the strength of three men but was able to accomplish less than any child.

"Pavo told me that you had a royal edict with that name on it," Vitas said, remembering the conversation. "Signed by Nero."

"Simple forgery. You have yourself to thank for that."

"Me?" Vitas echoed.

"In my household, there were plenty of official documents involving Nero that came from you." Damian laughed. "I wish I could be there when your captain shows up in Nero's palace, holding the letter and demanding payment."

"And what about your long and satisfying story?" Vitas said, smiling with Damian.

"The pilot's brother," Damian said. "The one that was supposed to be dead. His name is Kaeso. Jerome and I persuaded him to speak freely. That's the short of it. You'll get the long of it after we find the Jew."

"John?" Vitas was clearly surprised. "You know he was with me?"

"Searching for him led me to finding you," Damian said. "In a way, then, you owe him your life."

"More than once. That's why we need to find him." Vitas told Damian about the slave girl who had taken the scroll from John.

"Why do you want to find him?" Damian asked.

"I owe him. Again. He had a short message for me, written in Hebrew. He translated it before making sure it reached me. That tells me he was more concerned about me than his own freedom. And I have the third message for him to translate. Once I have pieced them together—"

"Messages?"

"Later. We need to get him before the ship leaves. The slave girl who brought me the scroll told me which ship."

"On a ship. That means it has a crew, right?"

Vitas nodded. "The slave girl tells me that she counted at least thirty men aboard."

"Thirty?" Damian grinned at Jerome. "What a shame. I was hoping this would be a challenge."

✚ ✚ ✚

Lucullus and Chayim looked through the bars of the prison cell at the old man hunched in the shadows in the corner. It wasn't much of a jail, just a walled-off area a few paces wide and a few paces long.

"Must be an uneducated provincial," Lucullus said. "Doesn't know any Latin or Greek. He just jabbers at us, and we can't understand a word of it."

The old man didn't turn at the voice of Lucullus. He had his cloak over his head and sat hunched in apparent misery.

It had been a few years since Chayim had spoken in Aramaic. He cleared his throat. "You're the Jew who came on the island with the woman, right?"

A shudder seemed to run through the old man. He twisted sideways and peered through his cloak. While he was in shadow, Chayim and Lucullus were easily visible in the light of the torch that Lucullus held.

"Surprised, aren't you?" Chayim said. "Probably didn't expect anyone on the island to speak Aramaic. But trust me, it's to your advantage, because if you help, I can make this easy on you and the woman."

"If it helps loosen his tongue," Lucullus interrupted, "I can order hot irons prepared. Tell him that in your Jew talk."

"The man beside me is a stupid, wine-drinking pig," Chayim said smoothly in Aramaic. "I'd be happy to see him impaled on a post. Let me take you and the woman off the island as soon as possible."

The old man shifted slightly.

"This is what I know," Chayim said to the prisoner. "You and the woman had help leaving Rome. Remember, I found the letter that sent you here. What I want to know is what you found on the island. Tell me, and I can let you and the woman go."

"Why are you here?" The old man spoke in such a quiet whisper that Chayim barely heard the words.

"Did you ask why I am here?" Chayim repeated.

The old man nodded from beneath his cloak.

"I just told you." Perhaps this old Jew *was* a stupid provincial, as Lucullus believed. "I found the letter stolen from you and the woman. I followed the same instructions that sent you here."

"No," came a whispering croak. "Why you instead of anyone else?"

"Me?" Chayim thought this was a ridiculous question, but he was prepared to humor the old man. "I'm a man Helius trusts. And that's how I can promise to help. I have far greater power than this stumbling Roman soldier."

"You don't sound like a Jew from Rome. Your accent suggests Judea."

Chayim was straining to hear the old man's words. He shrugged. "I am from Jerusalem."

"Yet you serve Helius."

Lucullus interrupted. "What's he saying? What's he saying?"

Chayim put up an imperious hand to silence Lucullus. "When he tells me where to find the woman, I'll let you know."

"Words don't work against people like this," Lucullus said. "Flames and pain are much more effective."

"If I don't get the answer when I'm finished with him," Chayim snapped, "bring the flames. Until then, let me speak. Unless you have anyone else on the island who understands this language."

"No," Lucullus said tersely.

"Good then," Chayim said.

To the old man, he spoke in Aramaic again. "Yes, I serve Helius. He sent me looking for you. He wants the woman, but he wants her alive."

"Tell me," the old man whispered from under his cloak. "How did you get from Jerusalem to Rome? You seem young to be an ambassador."

Chayim was fully aware that he was answering questions instead of getting answers, but that didn't matter. It was the old man behind bars, and Chayim had time.

"My father made an arrangement," Chayim said. "I was an embarrassment to him. He was—is—ranked highly in the religious establishment of the Temple."

"Did he love you?"

"He loved the Law."

"But did he love you?"

Chayim blinked. "Yes."

"But he loved the Law and you did not."

"Exactly."

"What if it wasn't the Law he loved, but the one true God he served by protecting those laws?"

What kind of questioning was this?

"Enough," Chayim said. "Where's the woman? I want to spare you torture, and believe me, from everything I've seen and heard, this Roman has a passion for it."

"Think hard," the old man croaked. "Could your father have been zealous for God, for what was right in the eyes of God?"

"Yes," Chayim said. "He was."

"And you were not."

"No."

"Are you ashamed of your father?"

"No," Chayim said, surprised at his answer.

"Was he ashamed of you?"

"It didn't matter. I did not want his ways."

"But he loved you, even though you did not want his ways."

"Yes," Chayim said. "He was tough and unrelenting and self-righteous at times, but I know he loved me."

"Someday," the old man said, "when you have a son of your own, you will understand how difficult it is for a man when his son chooses a path of self-destruction."

"Don't judge me," Chayim said. "You have no right."

The old man did not reply.

"Where is the woman?" Chayim said. "Save yourself. She will be found on this island anyway."

Silence. The old man seemed to settle further into his cloak.

"See?" Lucullus was smug. "Apparently the Roman way might be needed after all."

Chayim felt unsettled. He grabbed the torch from Lucullus. "Open the door," Chayim said. "I'll get the answer you need."

"Last chance," Lucullus said. He fumbled with a key.

Chayim stepped into the cell. He squatted in front of the old man.

"Look at me," he said to the old man. "I want you to see in my face how sincere I am about the danger you face."

When the old man didn't respond, Chayim pulled the cloak off the man's shoulders. He pulled the man's hair and stared him in the face.

And it seemed to Chayim as though all the breath had been pushed from his body.

The old man stared back at him. His father. Tears were trickling down his face.

"At least," Ben-Aryeh said, "you know the truth. Your father does love you, despite the path you have chosen."

Chayim could not find words. He stood. It seemed he had to brace his legs apart to keep his balance. He was spared by the arrival of another soldier, who came running and shouting.

"The woman has been found," the soldier told Lucullus. "She gave herself up."

HORA QUINTA

JEROME HELD A LIT torch as he followed Damian and Vitas, who both carried buckets in each hand. Jerome knew they were drawing stares as they walked along the wharf. He heard men mumble asides as they passed—after all, who would need a lit torch in daylight?—but no one was brave enough to mock their procession openly, undoubtedly because of Jerome's menacing size.

Damian stopped at one ship of dozens moored at this side of the harbor. It was medium sized, about twenty steps long. Blue encaustic paint—melted wax with color added—covered most of the hull. Its sternpost carried a relief, showing men carrying grapes on a pole between them, the grapes obviously exaggerated in size.

Damian set down his buckets and flexed his fingers, groaning with relief to be relieved of his burden. Jerome noticed that, in contrast, Vitas stoically bore his buckets.

"Bountiful Harvest," Damian announced, squinting at the letters engraved below the relief on the sternpost. "This is the one."

This was another reminder to Jerome of what set him apart. He could not speak. He could not read. He could not write. What good were his bulk and strength? Beasts had bulk and strength. Humans could speak to one another.

Damian glanced at the boat again and shook his head. "They must have a different definition of *bountiful* than most."

A gangplank led up to the middle section of the ship. It was guarded by two men about the size of Vitas.

"Let's go then," Vitas said. He didn't hesitate and carried his buckets up the gangway.

The two men on the ship crossed their arms and smirked at Vitas. The one on the left had scars across his bare forearms from rope burns. The one on the right had no obvious scars, but when he spoke, he showed large gaps in his mouth where teeth had been knocked out.

"Any reason you are coming aboard?" the one with the scars asked.

Vitas stared at them, still holding the buckets.

Damian stepped past Vitas with his buckets. "Out of our way," Damian said. "I'm tired of carrying these."

"We've already got all our provisions. We're about ready to sail."

"Sure," Damian said cheerfully. "But first, we want our friend back."

"Your friend?"

"The one in your hold. The hostage you're taking back to Rome."

"The ship is ready to sail."

"Listen to me carefully," Damian said. "You're going to let us past you. We're going to talk to your captain. He's going to give us our friend. We're going to leave. Then you will sail."

"It's early in the day to be drunk," the gap-toothed man said.

"And early for you to die." Damian craned his head. "Jerome?"

Jerome stepped onto the gangway. He was familiar with Damian's methods. Damian loved a good fight but was very bad at fighting. So Damian did what he could to provoke others, and then he let Jerome step in.

"Why don't you tell Jerome here you won't allow us onto the ship," Damian said. "If my good manners aren't enough to persuade you, Jerome will be more than happy to use other methods."

✣ ✣ ✣

"The woman is under guard. In your quarters."

These were the words of Volaginius Auspex, the soldier Lucullus generally put in charge of daily details. Auspex was a decade older than Lucullus, a man with a pitted face and long nose, who had no bravery but a good sense of administration.

Lucullus had been standing in the shade of the wooden walls of the barracks, staring across the Aegean at the jagged tips of other islands, blurred by distance. He had been mentally rehearsing how he would approach Helius, how he would apologetically and modestly tell him about his efforts to save Chayim from the treachery of the old Jew with the woman, rehearsing the details of his lie about a knife the old Jew had hidden in his tunic and how the old Jew had suddenly lashed out with it. He had wondered about the best way to negotiate a handsome reward for bringing the woman all the way back to Rome.

"Good. Was it the threatened torture of the whore?"

"We hardly had her in ropes before she stepped out of hiding."

"Excellent. I hate wasting time."

"What about Strabo?" Auspex asked.

"Release him. And his whore wife."

"He did try to hide them."

"He also makes excellent cheese and supplies us with wine," Lucullus said. "Is this island big enough that he can be replaced easily?"

Auspex shook his head.

"When I leave you in charge of the barracks," Lucullus said, "you need to look beyond day to day. Keep the soldiers happy and you'll be happy. Understand? This is a boring outpost with no difficulties. You'll like it more than I have."

Auspex nodded.

"I've delayed Chayim by telling him I want to speak to the woman alone," Lucullus said. "When he's brought to my quarters, you know what to do." Lucullus stared hard at Auspex. "You aren't going to lose your nerve, are you?"

Auspex gulped.

"Let me repeat. It will not be difficult for you. After Chayim has identified the woman as the one Helius wants, you and I will send the woman with the guards. I'll invite Chayim to stay behind and have a drink in celebration. When he's dead, we'll bring in the old Jew, kill him too, and make it look like they fought."

"Will Chayim be armed?" Auspex asked.

"It doesn't matter," Lucullus said, hiding impatience. "I'll grab him from behind, and I'll have both his arms locked. He's small enough I could hold for an hour in that position. All you need is a sharp knife."

"I've never killed a man before," Auspex admitted.

"You want me to choose someone else to help?" Lucullus needed the leverage of shared murder to keep this secret. He wondered if Auspex was smart enough to realize that refusing at this point would require killing him, too.

"No."

Lucullus patted the man on the shoulder. "Take my advice," he said in a friendly tone. "Turn the knife sideways so the blade is horizontal. It will slide between his ribs instead of bouncing off."

✦ ✦ ✦

The captain of *Bountiful Harvest* had lost his left eye, and a puckered hole in his head remained as evidence of his loss. He tilted his head to peer better with his right eye at Vitas.

"What's he doing?" he demanded of Damian, who stood in the protective shade of Jerome.

Five men were gathered behind the captain.

Damian peered around Jerome at Vitas, who was near the furled sails. "My brother?"

"I don't care who he is. What's he doing with those buckets?"

Vitas had begun to pour a long, thin black line beneath the sails. The line trailed behind Vitas as he backed away.

"Stop that!" the captain shouted.

A few men moved toward Vitas.

Jerome stepped toward them.

The crewmen hesitated, staring at the lit torch in his hand, obviously impressed at his bulk.

Vitas kept backing away from the sails. He'd emptied the contents of one bucket and now had the other. He reached the mast at the center of the ship and poured more black material at the base of it.

"Finished," he said to Damian.

All of this had happened so casually and quickly and brazenly that the captain and his men were still staring, dumbfounded.

"Jerome?" Damian said.

Jerome nodded and handed Damian the torch.

Damian tossed Jerome a sword and moved to the mast.

Jerome walked backward from the captain and his men, guarding Damian with the sword.

"What we have here," Damian said, waving the lit torch, "is a simple exchange. You've got a man below who is a friend of ours. Bring him up and let him go with us, and there will be no trouble."

"Look behind you," the captain snarled. "The only trouble is the trouble you've brought upon yourselves."

"More crew?" Damian asked Vitas without looking.

"Many more," Vitas said.

"Big, mean, and ugly?"

Vitas shook his head at Damian's attempt at humor. "Let's just get John and go."

"Did you hear my brother?" Damian asked the captain. "All we need is the man below."

"All I need to do is say the word, and my men attack."

"Jerome will handle them."

"Not all of them."

"He'll slow them down." Damian tilted the torch and lit the black line between the furled sails and the mast. Flames leaped upward.

The captain screamed in horror.

Damian stamped out the flames. "Tar," Damian said matter-of-factly. "Mixed with oil to thin it some."

He lit it again. Stamped out the new flames.

"Fascinating, isn't it?" Damian said. "How quickly this stuff lights?"

He held the flame of the torch just above the line but didn't dip it.

"You have to ask yourself how fast your men are. Fast enough to stop me from starting a fire in three places? five places? Remember, they're going to have to deal with Jerome over there before they can start to put out the fire."

Damian touched the flame down again. This time, he let the new flame grow.

And grow.

"Stop!" the captain screamed.

Damian had to stamp in several places before he extinguished the new flame.

"You'll give us our friend?" Damian asked.

"With the money he had when they took him," Vitas added.

"With the money he had," Damian said to the captain.

"Bring him up," the captain said between gritted teeth to a nearby crew member.

Damian nodded. "Good. I really don't like violence."

"Send all of your men down below." This came from Vitas.

"I nearly forgot that part, didn't I?" Damian said. "All of your men below."

"What?"

"You'll keep them there until we're safely off the ship," Damian said. "Those directions are simple enough that any idiot can follow. Now get the man we want."

It took several minutes, but John finally emerged from the hold and blinked in the sunlight. When his eyes adjusted to the brightness, he saw Vitas, smiled, and nodded.

When all of the crewmen except for the captain were down in the hold, Damian spoke again. "My friends will be leaving now."

"And you?" the captain snarled.

"I'll wait until they're gone. A person like you would probably, send his crew after them."

Vitas and John stepped off the gangplank onto the dock. Jerome stayed at the top of the gangplank, where ropes tied it in place to the side of the ship. This left Damian poised with the flame of the torch above the line of tar.

"Someday, somehow, I'll find you," the captain said. His right eyeball darted back and forth as he scanned Damian's face. "I'll enjoy feeding your intestines to the fish."

"Even after I made it a point to tell you that I don't like violence?"

"You find this funny. I don't."

"Tut-tut," Damian said, waving the flame. "You're moving closer."

The captain's neck veins bulged with anger, but he restrained himself. Then he glanced over at Jerome, who chopped downward at the ship with his sword.

"What now?" the captain said. His single eyeball appeared to be ready to pop from his skull.

"I expect he's cutting the ropes to the gangway," Damian said. "If you want to feed my intestines to the fish, a good escape is crucial."

With that, Damian dropped the flame of the torch on the tar. A line of fire began to spread.

The captain wailed.

Damian sprinted toward the gangplank.

The captain rushed forward and began stomping the flames.

Damian took advantage of the diversion, sprang down the gangplank, and landed on the dock.

Jerome severed the last rope holding it in place, ran to the dock, grabbed the end, and threw it into the water.

The four of them hurried away from the ship. In a nearby alley, Damian turned to Vitas. "We separate now, but I'll see you in a couple of hours. You know the place."

HORA SEXTA

VITAS AND JOHN sat on a bench in a crowded market square, with the noise and people giving them anonymity and privacy.

Vitas looked up from the scroll from Issachar, which John had spent the previous few minutes transcribing from Hebrew into Greek for him. "All the pieces are together now."

"Caesarea first, then Jerusalem," John said.

"With no idea why."

"Some journeys are like that," John said. "But if you trust whomever has sent you on the journey, you go and see where it leads you."

"Ephesus."

"Yes, for me, Ephesus. But every day of my life since meeting the Christos has been a journey of trust for me."

"You know Damian and Jerome are supposed to be here in the next hour to meet us."

"Yes."

"Here's what I don't understand," Vitas said. "You know he's a bounty hunter. He had you captive once and undoubtedly wants to take you back to Rome."

"Yes."

"You know how badly I wanted the messages translated."

"Yes."

"You translated the second on the ship and made sure I received it."

"Yes."

"Had you sent the slave girl without the translation from Hebrew, I would have been forced to rescue you. Here, you could have bargained with me for your freedom from my brother before translating the final piece of the message. What I don't understand is why you refuse to use what I need for leverage."

"If I can help you, I will."

"It's that simple?" Vitas asked.

"I follow in the footsteps of the Christos."

"Or you're smart enough to guess that I will feel obliged to protect you from my brother."

"Do you really believe that?" John asked. "Or is it something you hope is true so you can feel better about yourself and how you try to control your world?"

Vitas looked away. There was something so compelling about this man's inner peace that he hungered for it himself. He felt like he was on the edge of an abyss, about to step forward.

"Vitas," John said gently. "There is very little we can control. Except our own hearts and our own choices."

"Someone in Rome knows that you know Issachar."

If John was perturbed by the abrupt subject change, he didn't show it. "That looks obvious now, doesn't it?"

"Pavo had been instructed to take me there. You would have shown up later, had you not been taken."

"Issachar and his family provided for me on one of my visits here," John said. "And yes, someone in Rome knew that."

"You won't tell me who?"

That person, Vitas knew, would be linked to the others in Rome who had arranged his freedom from the arena.

"He's gone to great lengths to protect himself," John said. "I would prefer to extend that protection too."

"Fair enough."

A few moments of silence passed between them. Vitas felt as if his heart were trembling. He knew he needed to send John away before Damian arrived, but he couldn't do it yet.

"Will you visit Issachar today? tonight?" This was a way to delay both John's departure and what Vitas needed to do.

"He's a free man now but a man with no future in Alexandria. You've provided me with ample money. I'll ask him if he and his family would like to travel with me to Ephesus." John paused. "Thank you."

Vitas was startled. "Thank you?"

"You wouldn't have asked about Issachar unless you had decided I should leave before Damian arrives."

"John," Vitas said, too distracted by an inner urgency to acknowledge John's simple gratitude, "earlier you told me you could show me the way to remove my burdens, that I could be healed, forgiven."

In his mind, Vitas saw it happening again. The Iceni warriors gathered for a final charge, surrounding the Roman wagons. The women and children behind the wagons, his Iceni wife and young son among them. Then the charge, the warriors upon them, his wife crying in agony as a spear pierced her chest, his son lifted up and—

"I'm ready to listen," Vitas said, his voice hardly more than a croak. "I want the peace that you have."

✛ ✛ ✛

"Here's the kind of travel companion any soldier would want; wouldn't you say, Auspex?"

Sophia had been led through the barracks to the quarters of the commander. He was a shaggy-haired bear of a man, wearing a shiny breastplate and full military regalia that added to the impression of size. He stood close enough that she could feel the heat of his breath as he spoke.

Auspex shifted foot to foot behind the commander, as if he were nervous.

"You have to look past the filthy clothing—" the commander continued speaking to Auspex, circling Sophia as he examined her— "and she smells a bit ripe, but all in all, I'd say this is quite the prize."

Sophia's hands were bound behind her back. She wasn't surprised at her lack of fear. Nor surprised at her sense of calm. Apathy was suitable armor for nearly any danger.

"I'm Lucullus," the commander said, moving around in front of her and lifting her chin with the tip of a forefinger. He leered. "We're going to get to know each other very well over the next weeks; I can promise you that."

"What if she belongs to Helius?" Auspex said. "I doubt he's going to want to hear that another man spoiled his property."

"Good point." Lucullus laughed. "We'll get Chayim to tell us. I can only hope I'll have the freedom to let her amuse me every night on the way to Rome." Lucullus caressed Sophia's cheek.

Sophia closed her eyes. What did she care? Without hope, did it matter if she was alive or dead?

"Does Helius touch you this way?" Lucullus asked.

The faintest heat of anger touched her heart. Not because of the threat to her. But because this was the man who had tortured Chara.

"Or does Helius want you back in Rome for another reason?" Lucullus asked.

Chara. So much had been taken from her, yet the woman faced the world with dignity and joy. She'd refused to let this beast take what was truly important. The heat of new anger began to burn Sophia's shield of apathy.

"If it's for another reason," Lucullus continued, "perhaps you can become my property."

Sophia opened her eyes. Looked directly at the beast. And, without thinking, spit in his face.

His reaction was immediate. He slapped her across the face with an open hand, knocking her to the floor. He began kicking her ribs.

Pain! It broke through what remained of Sophia's apathy.

"I'm going to kill you!" Lucullus shouted. He continued to kick.

With her hands bound behind her back, Sophia could do nothing to protect herself. For the first time in weeks, she thought of the baby she carried. And found herself uttering a prayer.

Christos . . .

With that silent plea, a light seemed to fill her vision, and peace came upon her soul.

"Stop!" This was Auspex. "Stop! What if she belongs to Helius?"

Lucullus gave one last kick and stood over her, breathing hard.

Sophia marveled. The darkness of the previous weeks had fallen away. She clung to her faith in the Christos. Vitas was dead, but she was responsible for his child. That would be her purpose. She uttered a silent prayer of gratitude.

Lucullus walked away, his heavy breathing beginning to abate.

When she opened her eyes, Lucullus was no longer in front of her but at a table, pouring wine from an amphora into three goblets.

He took the first and gulped from it as Auspex helped her to her feet.

Lucullus glanced at Auspex and shrugged, as if nothing had happened.

A knock at the door.

"Enter!" Lucullus called, obviously in a good mood now.

Another man joined them. His eyes flashed in Sophia's direction. She was startled to recognize him, but it took several seconds for her to remember why.

Nero's dinner, she thought. *He was there, among the guests the night that Vitas—*

"Chayim," Lucullus said, pointing at Sophia with the wine goblet in his hand, "my friend. Look what I've found for you."

Chayim glanced at Sophia again and shrugged. "I'm quite happy with the ones from Ephesus. Besides, this one doesn't appear to spend much time on grooming."

"What a sense of humor you have, my friend. Aren't you pleased your wait is over? You can get off this island."

"I'm afraid I don't understand," Chayim answered.

"You're telling me this is not the woman that Helius wants captured," Lucullus said, his voice growing ominous.

"Don't be ridiculous," Chayim snorted. "What kind of game are you playing with me?"

"She's the old man's companion! We captured her at Strabo's cottage."

"I was enjoying my diversions." Chayim, a much smaller man than Lucullus, began to grow angry at the commander. "And you called me away for this?"

"You're denying this is the woman you seek?"

"And you're suggesting I'm too stupid to remember who Helius wants?"

"Listen to me, Jew. An old man and a woman came for the dwarf, just as if they'd once had the letter that sent them here to Patmos. I find it hard to believe—"

"I don't like your tone," Chayim said. "Are you forgetting that on this island I represent Helius and Nero?"

"Are you forgetting that on this island, I command?"

"Nobody," Chayim said softly, "is out of reach of Nero. Is that something you really want to forget?"

"This is not the woman." Lucullus appeared to be holding himself back.

"Hardly."

"Then who is she?"

Chayim shrugged. "Didn't you tell me that more and more visitors come to the island because of some vision reported in a letter? Ask her if she is one of those religious converts."

Lucullus whirled on Sophia. "Are you?"

Sophia could not understand why Chayim had lied to save her. Nor why he'd given her an excuse to explain her presence on the island. But she'd been asked a direct question and could answer it with truth.

"I follow the Christos," she said. "Chara follows him too. She has spoken to you of the Christos, has she not?"

Lucullus flung his goblet across the room. "The Christos! The Christos rose from the dead! The Christos brought Chara back from her deathbed! The Christos spoke in a vision to a man exiled here! Give me the Christos and I'll crucify him myself!"

"I'm not impressed," Chayim said. "You'll understand if I go back to my diversions? Apparently they want to leave on the supply ship today, and if I have to wait on the island for another week or two, I don't want to miss my last few hours with them."

"Go," Lucullus growled at Chayim.

As the door closed, Auspex spoke to Lucullus. "You believe him?"

"What possible reason would he have to lie?" Lucullus said. "We'll just have to wait longer. It's not like he's going to leave the island before the woman arrives."

"And this woman?" Auspex asked. "Have her cleaned up for your pleasure?"

Lucullus examined Sophia.

She waited, her knees trembling. "Bah," he said. "Send her to the old man and get them off this island today with the whores. All this talk about the Christos has spoiled my appetite."

HORA SEPTINA

VITAS HAD REMAINED motionless on the bench in the market square since John's departure. He was so obviously lost in thought that none tried to sell him any wares.

Before listening to John's answer, he'd felt like a man on the edge of an abyss. After, he felt more like a deer, trembling and hidden among the trees, desperate to go down to the clear, cold water of a stream but also afraid.

"'For God so loved the world,'" John had said, "'that he gave his one and only Son, that whoever believes in him shall not perish but have eternal life. For God did not send his Son into the world to condemn the world, but to save the world through Him.'"

For Vitas, with each passing minute, the ache for water was beginning to outweigh the fear of stepping into the open.

Redemption.

It called to Vitas. His soul felt scabbed and weary. All that had given him hope before was the purity of his love for Sophia. But even that wasn't good enough.

Cleansing.

The love between a man and a woman, the love between parents and child was still not a perfect love. It gave a sense of what it felt like to be loved by God, but was still stained by human imperfection, human desires.

Peace.

John was correct. This was not a world that Vitas could control, no matter how smart or strong or resourceful he might be. He was tired of death, tired of the killing that happened as men around him struggled for power. And to what purpose? All would die. Alexander the Great, struck down in his youth by disease after conquering the known world. Caesar, the most powerful man in the empire, betrayed and stabbed to death on the Ides of March. Augustus, dead of old age, but still as dead as any peasant and more forgotten with each passing year.

Hope.

John had explained that there was life beyond death with the one true God who had created mankind, a place for all men and women who believed in the Christos and were redeemed through him.

Forgiveness.

Vitas longed to be forgiven for the death of his son. Longed to be free of the guilt that tormented him in the depths of his soul.

The stream called.

And Vitas trembled.

Could he give away control of his life, surrender to an invisible God? It screamed against everything he'd learned as a Roman but called to his soul with such sweetness. No Roman god could compare to the power of the God John worshiped. There was something miraculous about all of it, and he didn't have to recall any further than the touch that had healed him after the whipping to sense the mysterious beyond his five senses. Yes, the evidence for faith in the Christos was becoming harder and harder to deny.

Vitas sat on the bench, barely aware of any noise around him, of the heat of the sun or the smell of the vegetables and raw chicken and fish of the market.

Could he do it?

A hand touched his shoulder.

✠ ✠ ✠

"You're off on another journey then," Strabo said to Ben-Aryeh. "Ephesus to find a copy of John's letter, then wherever the coded letter takes you."

They stood on the hillside, near the cottage. Several goats were staked nearby.

"Sophia has no home in Rome, and her husband is dead," Ben-Aryeh answered. "Someone in Rome has gone to a lot of effort to make sure Sophia has the letter from Akakios. Where else is there to go but where it leads us?"

The strange letter flashed into Ben-Aryeh's thoughts, for he had memorized it already:

You know the beast you must escape; the one with understanding will solve the number of this beast, for it is the number of a man. His number is 666. You have fled the city of this beast, from the sea it came and on the sea you go. North and west of the city of the second beast, find the first of five kings who have fallen. (The sixth now reigns, and the seventh is yet to come.)

Then go to the woman clothed in finest purple and scarlet linens, decked out with gold and precious stones and pearls. She is the one who slaughtered God's people all over the world. Find the Synagogue of Satan, at the end of the Sabbath, and stand at the gate closest to the den of robbers. Persevere and you will find your reward.

"I want to ask you for something," Strabo said, interrupting Ben-Aryeh's thoughts. "When you find out who has sent you on this journey and why, send me a letter telling me what has happened."

"You can't read."

"Chara can."

"Maybe this letter is one she'll tell you about," Ben-Aryeh said with a smile.

"Yes. If I would have known about Akakios, that would have changed things." Strabo looked at the sea, then back at Ben-Aryeh. "I owe you my life."

"Nonsense." Ben-Aryeh craned his head to look up the hill at the cottage. "How long does it take for two women to say good-bye?"

"Really, Lucullus had a bloodlust in him. If you hadn't stepped out when you did—"

"Doesn't Sophia have any sense of urgency?" Ben-Aryeh said, avoiding Strabo's eyes. "It's a week or two before the next supply ship."

"You had no idea you would be released," Strabo said. "You were sacrificing yourself for me."

Ben-Aryeh sighed and faced Strabo squarely. "Why would I care about a stubborn, opinionated man who constantly smells of goat? I did it for Sophia."

"That explains it," Strabo said. "At least I don't owe you any gratitude."

"Certainly not." Another sigh. "Where is that woman?"

"They were talking about babies when I left them," Strabo answered. He waited a few seconds. "How exactly did you think letting the soldiers capture you would help Sophia?"

"There was no way off the island anyway, and I wanted to force her to make a choice. With me in prison, she could flee the soldiers or join me to protect your family. Either way, it would take her out of the half death she'd been living for weeks. Do you have any idea how miserable a woman in that condition can make a man?"

"No."

"Pray it never happens to you. If you think goats are difficult—"

"I mean, no, I don't believe your excuse. It's turned out that way, and I'll agree Sophia has life in her again. But I think you really did it to rescue me from Lucullus."

"So that we could share a moment like this? Hardly."

"I won't see you again," Strabo said. He paused. "A man like me, well, I don't have many friends."

"Nor do I, my friend." Ben-Aryeh smiled sadly. "Nor do I."

✚ ✚ ✚

"Vitas! Where is John?"

It took Vitas a moment to place himself, to come out of the timelessness that had offered such weightless freedom.

"Damian," Vitas said. Slowly he stood and faced his brother. Jerome was behind Damian, watching with the inscrutability that added to the man's intimidation.

"Where is John? You promised both of you would be here."

"No," Vitas said. "I never made that promise. You simply ordered both of us to meet you."

"Surely you didn't let the man walk away."

"You would hand him over to Helius and certain death."

"I'm a bounty hunter. Am I responsible for the choices he's made to defy Nero?"

"You're aware I've defied Nero."

"You're my brother. Nor have I been paid to capture you."

"And if you were?"

"I owe you my life," Damian said.

"That's no answer. Repay me by letting John go in peace."

"But I've just saved you," Damian protested. "That makes us even."

"Then I'll be in your debt. Let the man go."

"John is worth a lot of money to me. But it's more than that. I'm the best. No one has ever escaped me."

"Nor did John," Vitas said.

"But Jerome and I will be the only ones to know this."

Vitas smiled. "Take pride in that."

"Where is he?" Damian said.

"Brother," Vitas answered, "please don't push me to the point where I have to refuse to answer you."

"So you know where he is?"

"I do."

Vitas could see the conflict cross Damian's face and said nothing. He could not force his brother into any decision.

"All right then," Damian said. "I'll return to Rome and search for him there. Fruitlessly."

"Thank you."

"What will you do?" Damian asked.

Again, Vitas was aware of the concentrated stare of Jerome. The man had intelligence; that much was obvious in his eyes. He would be a terrifying enemy.

"It's certain death to return to Rome," Vitas answered. He thought of his decision and the prayer he would make at the first private moment ahead. "I'm tired of the empire. Of the politics. Of the battles. The revolts and intrigue."

In saying it, he realized how true it was. He had three pieces of scroll with instructions from men in Rome with power, men who wanted Vitas to survive. Unlike Piso. The implication was very strong. But like Piso's coconspirators, those unseen, unknown men wanted Vitas to help them against Nero.

He was done with that.

"I want a simple, peaceful life," Vitas said. "With my wife."

Damian frowned at Vitas, but Vitas was so sure of his decision that he didn't take note of it.

"When you return to Rome," Vitas said, "please find a way to smuggle a letter to Sophia. Let her know I'm alive and waiting in Alexandria."

"Sophia," Damian repeated. Again, Vitas did not take notice of his brother's frown.

"If you could arrange for her to secretly board a grain ship coming here, we would be in your debt for all our lives."

"I thought you knew," Damian said. He looked at the ground.

To Vitas, a cold wind suddenly sucked all the air from inside him. Without asking, he knew what Damian would say next. "I did not know."

"Brother . . ."

With the coldness that filled Vitas came a hardness of soul. He straightened. He was a Roman.

"Don't pretend I'm weak," Vitas said. "Tell me."

"Nero invited her to open her veins."

The peace and calm that had warmed the soul of Vitas became an icy hatred. "Helius betrayed me. He promised . . ."

Vitas closed his eyes. With the hatred, he was growing stronger, more resolved. He let the hatred push aside images of Sophia, his love for her.

"I will destroy that man," Vitas said. "And the man he serves." With both hands, Vitas grabbed his brother by the shoulders. "Help me. Don't return to Rome. Join me."

"Are you talking sedition?"

"There are powerful men in Rome willing to help," Vitas said. "How much power do you think you could grab if you joined us now?"

Damian grinned.

"Listen. I have all three pieces of my message here." Vitas withdrew the scroll from his tunic. "Let me read it to you. It's from the men in Rome who saved me from the arena to conspire against Nero."

Damian cocked his head.

Vitas read aloud from the beginning:

"You know the beast you must escape; the one with understanding will solve the number of this beast, for it is the number of a man. His number is 666. You have fled the city of this beast, from the sea it came and on the sea you go. North and west of the city of the second beast, find the first of five kings who have fallen. (The sixth now reigns, and the seventh is yet to come.) There will be two witnesses, killed yet brought alive. Find them and rejoice with them, then take what is given.

Then go to the woman clothed in finest purple and scarlet linens, decked out with gold and precious stones and pearls. She is the one who slaughtered God's people all over the world. Find the Synagogue of Satan, at the end of the Sabbath, and stand at the gate closest to the den of robbers. Persevere and—"

"Stop!" Damian said. "What is this?"

"When we decipher it—all of it—we'll have our answer. And, I suspect, the key to ending Nero's reign."

"You suspect? That's all you have. A guess. Not certainty? Remember, I've sworn off gambling."

"An elaborate conspiracy brought me this far," Vitas said. "The end of the journey must have, as promised, a great reward." He grinned back at his brother. Coldly, feeling his hatred for Helius, but still a grin. "Aren't you the one always looking for adventure?"

"And women," Damian said. "Don't forget women."

"Then come with me." The hunger for revenge felt good to Vitas. Later he would mourn Sophia. But for now, he had a purpose that could set aside the weakness of grief. He would not be that trembling deer, thirsty for a clear pool of water in a quiet forest. But a stalking lion determined to drink the hot blood of an enemy torn in pieces. "And bring Jerome. We'll need a man like him."

"Come with you," Damian said, appearing to warm to the idea. "Any guesses where next?"

"Caesarea." Later he would tell Damian how John had interpreted the symbols for him. "Then Jerusalem."

"Jerusalem! We'll rejoin Maglorius."

"Jerusalem," Vitas repeated. The icy fire in him would sustain him until he could wrap his fingers around the neck of Helius and choke the life from him.

"Why not?" Damian said. "We've got Jerome to protect us. We're Romans. We rule the world. What kind of danger could be ahead of us there?"

AFTERWORD

MUCH HAS BEEN MADE of the differences in the interpretation of Scripture applied by the Last Disciple series and the Left Behind series. One of the key distinctions between the end-times theologies (called "eschatologies") employed by these two series has to do with when the writing of the New Testament was completed.

The Last Disciple series is based on an interpretation of Scripture that holds that the entire New Testament was completed prior to the destruction of the Temple in AD 70. In contrast, the Left Behind series is based on the assumption that Revelation was written in AD 95, long after Jerusalem's destruction. It asserts that Revelation describes events that will likely take place in the twenty-first century rather than the first century. In author Tim LaHaye's words, "Revelation was written by John in AD 95, which means the book of Revelation describes yet future events of the last days just before Jesus comes back to this earth."[1] LaHaye has even gone so far as to dismiss the notion that Revelation was written before AD 70 as "historically ridiculous."[2] A closer look at the evidence, however, reveals not only that such dismissive language is unwarranted but that the late-date position is untenable.

First, it is instructive to note that the late dating for Revelation is largely dependent on a single—and markedly ambiguous—sentence in the writings of Irenaeus, Bishop of Lyons. This sentence can be taken to mean either that *John* or that John's *apocalyptic*

390 THE LAST SACRIFICE

vision was seen toward the end of Domitian's reign. Moreover, the credibility of Irenaeus as a source is called into question by his contention in the same volume that Jesus was crucified when He was about fifty years old.

Furthermore, if the apostle John were indeed writing in AD 95, it seems incredible that he would make no mention whatsoever of the most apocalyptic event in Jewish history—the demolition of Jerusalem and the destruction of the Temple at the hands of Titus. This would be tantamount to writing a history of New York City today and making no mention of the destruction of the World Trade Center at the hands of terrorists on September 11, 2001. More directly, imagine writing a thesis on the future of terrorism in America and failing to mention the Manhattan Massacre.

Consider another parallel. Imagine that you are reading a history concerning Jewish struggles in Nazi Germany and find no mention whatsoever of the Holocaust. Would it be historically ridiculous or historically reasonable to suppose this history had been written prior to the outbreak of World War II? The answer is self-evident. Just as it stretches credulity to suggest that a history on the Jews in Germany written in the aftermath of World War II would make no mention of the Holocaust, so too it is quite unlikely that Revelation could have been written twenty-five years after the destruction of Jerusalem and yet make no mention of the most apocalyptic event in Jewish history.

Finally, those who hold that the book of Revelation was written in AD 95 face an even more formidable obstacle! Consider one of the most amazing prophecies in all of Scripture. Jesus was leaving the Temple one day when His disciples called His attention to its buildings. As they gazed upon its massive stones and magnificent structures, Jesus uttered the unthinkable: "I tell you the truth, not one stone here will be left on another; every one will be thrown down. . . . This generation will certainly not pass away until all these things have happened." (Matthew 24:2, 34; Mark 13:2, 30; Luke 21:6, 32). Less than forty years later, this prophecy, no doubt still emblazoned upon the tablet of their collective consciousness,

became a vivid and horrifying reality. Flavius Josephus described
the utter devastation as the altar was surrounded by "heaps of
corpses, while blood flowed down the steps of the sanctuary." Wrote
Josephus, "While the temple was in flames, the victors stole everything they could lay their hands on, and slaughtered all who were
caught. No pity was shown to age or rank, old men or children, the
laity or priests—all were massacred." He also noted that the Temple
was doomed August 30 AD 70, "the very day on which the former
temple had been destroyed by the king of Babylon."[3]

As incredible as Christ's prophecy and its fulfillment one generation later are, it is equally incredible to suppose that the apostle
John would make no mention of it. As the student of Scripture
well knows, New Testament writers were quick to highlight fulfilled
prophecy. The phrase "This was to fulfill what was spoken of by the
prophet" permeates the pages of Scripture and demonstrates con-
clusively that the Bible is divine rather than human in origin. Thus,
it is inconceivable that Jesus would make an apocalyptic prophecy
concerning the destruction of Jerusalem and the Temple and that
John would fail to mention that the prophecy was fulfilled one
generation later just as Jesus had predicted.

Before closing, allow us to highlight just one more piece of internal evidence that should give pause to those who are dogmatic about
the late dating of Revelation. In the eleventh chapter of Revelation,
John says, "I was given a reed like a measuring rod and was told, 'Go
and measure the temple of God and the altar, and count the worshipers there. But exclude the outer court; do not measure it, because it
has been given to the Gentiles. They will trample on the holy city for
42 months'" (Revelation 11:1-2). Revelation, in keeping with the rest
of the New Testament, speaks of the Temple and Jerusalem as if the
Temple were still standing at the time of its writing. Note also that
Jesus had sent his angel "to show his servants what must soon take
place" (Revelation 1:1). Thus, the prophecy of the trampling of the
holy city concerns a future event—not one that took place twenty-
five years earlier.

In summary, from all the reasons we are well justified in believing that the book of Revelation was not written twenty-five years after the destruction of Jerusalem, three tower above the rest. First, just as it is unreasonable to suppose that someone writing a history of New York City in the aftermath of September 11, 2001, would fail to mention the destruction of the twin towers, so too it stretches credulity to suggest that Revelation could have been written in the aftermath of the devastation of Jerusalem and the Temple and yet make no mention of this apocalypse. Additionally, if John wrote in AD 95, it is incredible to suppose he would not mention the fulfillment of Christ's most improbable and apocalyptic vision. Finally, New Testament documents—including the book of Revelation—speak of Jerusalem and the Jewish Temple as intact at the time they were written.

The point of all this is that if Revelation was written *before* AD 70, then it is reasonable to assume that the vision given to John was meant to reveal the apocalyptic events surrounding the destruction of Jerusalem—events that were still in John's future but that are in our past. This is not to say, however, that *all* of the prophecies in Revelation have already been fulfilled. Some reviewers have suggested that the Last Disciple series espouses a hyper-preterist theology, which is essentially the belief that every prophecy in Scripture—including the second coming of Christ—was fulfilled long ago. But that clearly is not the position of the Last Disciple series. Thoughtful readers of Revelation should be quick to distance themselves from either a purely preterist or a fully futurist label. Revelation not only predicted forefuture events, such as the coming apocalypse in John's lifetime, but also chronicles events that will take place in the far and final future. For one day the Lord himself will come down from heaven and the dwelling of God will forever be with men (Revelation 21:3); each person will be resurrected and "judged according to what he had done" (Revelation 20:13); and the problem of sin will be fully and finally resolved (Revelation 21:27).

DISCUSSION QUESTIONS

What was your understanding of Revelation before beginning this series? How has that changed?

Why do you think John never reveals his identity or his connection to the letter (and the vision) to Vitas?

Why does Helius take such delight in other people's pain and discomfort?

How is Valeria different in The Last Sacrifice than she was in The Last Disciple? How well is she handling her situation?

What motivates Chayim's actions? Do you find him likable? Pitiable? Despicable?

Zealous Jews in Jerusalem fully believe that God will never allow the city or the Temple to be destroyed. Is there anything in our society that we are tempted to think of this way? In your life?

How would you characterize the relationship between Strabo the goatherd and his wife, Chara?

Jerome is one of many characters placed in mortal fear for his family's safety. What do you think Jerome will choose to do?

When Vitas comes very close to following Christ, what holds him back? Consider what Jesus says in Luke 9:61-62. Does this apply to Vitas?

Other Books by Hank Hanegraaff

Has God Spoken? Memorable Proofs of the Bible's Divine Inspiration
The Apocalypse Code: Find Out What the Bible Really Says
    About the End Times and Why It Matters Today
The Creation Answer Book
The Complete Bible Answer Book—Collector's Edition
The Bible Answer Book, Volume 1
The Bible Answer Book, Volume 2
The Bible Answer Book for Students
Christianity in Crisis
Christianity in Crisis: 21st Century
Counterfeit Revival
The Legacy Study Bible
The Heart of Christmas
The Da Vinci Code: Fact or Fiction (coauthored with Paul L. Maier)
The Face that Demonstrates the Farce of Evolution
Fatal Flaws: What Evolutionists Don't Want You to Know
The Millennium Bug Debugged
The Prayer of Jesus: Secrets to Real Intimacy with God
The Covering: God's Plan to Protect You from Evil
The Covering—Student Edition (coauthored with Jay Strack)
Resurrection
The Third Day

Other Books by Sigmund Brouwer

Novels

The Weeping Chamber
Out of the Shadows
Crown of Thorns

The Lies of Saints
Degrees of Guilt—Tyrone's Story
Fuse of Armageddon (coauthored with Hank Hanegraaff)
The Leper
Pony Express Christmas
Wings of Dawn
Double Helix
Blood Ties
Evening Star
Silver Moon
Sun Dance
Thunder Voice
Broken Angel
Flight of Shadows
The Canary List
The Orphan King

Nonfiction

Rock & Roll Literacy
Who Made the Moon

Kids' Books

Bug's Eye View series
The Little Spider, a Christmas picture book
Watch Out for Joel series
CyberQuest
Accidental Detective series
Sports Mystery series
Lightning on Ice series
Short Cuts
Robot Wars series
The Winds of Light

CHRISTIAN RESEARCH INSTITUTE

THE CHRISTIAN RESEARCH INSTITUTE (CRI) exists to provide Christians worldwide with carefully researched information and well-reasoned answers that encourage them in their faith and equip them to intelligently represent it to people influenced by ideas and teachings that assault or undermine orthodox, biblical Christianity. In carrying out this mission, CRI's strategy is expressed in the acronym EQUIP.

The *E* in EQUIP represents the word *essentials*. CRI is committed to the maxim "In essentials unity, in nonessentials liberty, and in all things charity."

The *Q* in EQUIP represents the word *questions*. In addition to focusing on essentials, CRI answers people's questions regarding cults, culture, and Christianity.

The *U* in EQUIP represents the word *user-friendly*. As much as possible, CRI is committed to taking complex issues and making them understandable and accessible to the lay Christian.

The *I* in EQUIP represents the word *integrity*. Recall Paul's admonition: "Watch your life and doctrine closely. Persevere in them, because if you do, you will save both yourself and your hearers" (1 Timothy 4:16).

The *P* in EQUIP represents the word *para-church*. CRI is deeply committed to the local church as the God-ordained vehicle for equipping, evangelism, and education.

Contact Christian Research Institute:

By Mail:

Christian Research Institute
P.O. Box 8500
Charlotte, NC 28271-8500

In Canada:
CRI Canada
56051 Airways P.O.
Calgary, Alberta T2E 8K5

By Phone:
U.S.: 888-7000-CRI (700-0274)
Canada: 800-665-5851

On the Internet:
www.equip.org

On the Broadcast:
To contact the *Bible Answer Man* broadcast with your questions,
call toll free in the U.S. and Canada, 888-ASK HANK (275-4265).

For a list of stations airing the *Bible Answer Man* or to listen to the
broadcast via the Internet, log on to our Web site at www.equip.org.